ABOUT THE AUTHOR

Elena Schwolsky is a retired nurse, activist, and writer, living in Brooklyn, NY. In addition to her award-winning memoir, Waking in Havana: A Memoir of AIDS and Healing in Cuba (She Writes Press, 2019), her work has appeared in several anthologies, the American Journal of Nursing and Intima: A Journal of Narrative Medicine. Writing activist fiction has allowed her to explore the universal issues that she has faced as a woman and a mother dedicated to the movement for social change for more than 60 years.

THE ACTIVIST FICTION WRITERS' CIRCLE

The Activist Fiction Writers' Circle is a collective of activists creating works of fiction featuring activist characters and social movement settings. Our work depicts activists' adventures, struggles, romances, conflicts, and humor in ordinary life and in the extraordinary times during movements for a just and compassionate world.

ABOUT THURSDAY'S CHILD

Thursday's Child is my first work of fiction. The impetus to try my hand at fiction grew out of my desire to write about an issue that I barely touched on in my memoir, Waking in Havana: A Memoir of AIDS and Healing in Cuba. Like Ruthie, the protagonist of Thursday's Child, I had traveled to Cuba with the Venceremos Brigade in the 1970's. And like her I had left my young son behind in the care of his father, my ex-husband on a communal ranch in California. You must have missed him terribly. How did you feel? How could you do that? were comments I heard frequently from readers of my memoir. I wanted to explore my feelings about this more deeply, but I was finished with memoir for a while. Never having written even a short story, let alone a novel, I looked for some guidance and googled some suggestions for complete beginners. The one that stuck went something like this: *Pick an important event in your life and begin telling the story. Pick a moment in the story that was a turning point, leave the "true" story behind and invent a path in whole new direction. Follow that path till you capture the story you want to tell.* And that is how Thursday's Child came to be. Later I would learn that it fits into a genre called autobiographical or auto-fiction.

I leave the reader to guess where Ruthie's path diverged from my own. Many of the characters are drawn from my own experience, but some just showed up unexpectedly and I followed their lead (yes, that really can happen in writing fiction, and it is very exciting).

THURSDAY'S CHILD

A novel of lost and Found

Elena Schwolsky

Life in the Liberated Zone Books
In Collaboration with Entre Mundos Productions
Thursday's Child, a novel of lost and found by Elena Schwolsky
Published by Life in the Liberated Zone (LLZ) Books in collaboration with Entre Mundos Productions, Brooklyn, NY, USA

ISBN 978-1-877850-10-3
Library of Congress Control Number Copyright 2026 by Elena Schwolsky
This edition of @ Life in the Liberated Zone Books in collaboration with Entre Mundos Productions

Cover Design: Elena Schwolsky In Association with Chat GPT

LLZ Books is an imprint of the *Activist Fiction Writer's Circle, creators and publishers of fiction featuring activists in ordinary life and in extraordinary times during movements for a jost and compassionate world. This edition is in collaboration with Entre Mundos Publications, Brooklyn, NY, USA.*

Life in the Liberated Zone.org
Published in the U.S.A.

*For Jonah and Angelica
and all the beloved children in my life
who taught me to be a mama and are
teaching me still…*

Monday's child is fair of face
Tuesday's child is full of grace
Wednesday's child is full of woe
Thursday's child has far to go
Friday's child is loving and giving
Saturday's child works hard for a living
And the child that is born on the Sabbath Day
Is bonny and blithe and good and gay
English Nursery Rhyme

Prologue

May 1973

"Welcome to the R & R" Ruthie said, swinging open the heavy oak door to greet the small group gathered on the porch. "We're still waiting for a couple of people to arrive—so come in, grab a snack and find a place to sit."

"Cuba, Cuba, Cuba…my mama's going to Cuba. Going on a venture. Da-da-da-da-da." The group parted to make way for a one-person sing-song marching band—Ruthie's 4-year-old daughter–who was waving a small Cuban flag in one hand and trumpeting loudly through her closed fist with the other. Ruthie laughed and shooed her inside.

"Hola, I'm Sasha. I know how to say hello in Spanish. Are you going to Cuba with my Mama? Do you wanna chocolate chip cookie? Me and Brother Big made some for you."

Sasha continued her march around the room as the group took their seats on the assorted couches and cushions scattered on the worn wooden floor, joined by Loki, the big mutt that served as the R & R's mascot.

"Sash, you can go bring in the cookies now, pumpkin—carry them very carefully. Hey everyone—coffee will be ready in a few minutes. This is the R & R GI coffeehouse and we're really happy to be hosting the first meeting of the Colorado Venceremos Brigade. I'm Ruthie and I'm part of the civilian staff. My daughter and I have been living here for 2 years."

"R & R like in 'rest and relaxation'?" A young woman piped up from the green corduroy couch in the corner. "Is this like a commune or something?"
"R & R stands for Rise and Resist. We do live and work communally here—supporting GIs from Ft. Carson when they get back from Vietnam…oh, but more about that later. Here are Peter and Sarah from the national Brigade, and I think they're ready to get started. Sasha, come sit by Mama."

Ruthie took a seat on the floor with Sasha curled up on her lap and

looked around at the folks with whom she'd soon be traveling to Cuba. Larry, a black Vietnam vet who had stayed on to work at the R & R after discharge, was the only familiar face. He was already deep in conversation with a young Chicana woman who was braiding and unbraiding the same strand of long, dark hair as she spoke. Anxious, Ruthie thought. Yeah, me too.

"We'll be meeting every week for the next month," Peter was saying, "and talking about the articles in this reading packet and a lot of logistics, expectations and stuff. So, get ready to work hard even before we get to Cuba." Nervous laughter circled the room. Cutting sugar cane all day long with a machete under a hot tropical sun was no joke, but before they could get to that, there was a lot to learn. Starting with who they were and why they had chosen to join the brigade.

Ruthie went first, describing her early political experience—joining the civil rights movement in her hometown of Hartford, Connecticut when she was 15 and helping to organize a rent strike. The bumpy ride to the March on Washington on a yellow school bus and the thrill of being a part of history. From there it was a short stint in college and then dropping out to work with the anti-Vietnam war movement, which had led her to Colorado and the R & R.

"I'm tired of going from group to group and always being 'against' something," Ruthie responded to Sarah's question about what she hoped to learn in Cuba. "I guess I want to know what it's like when a movement grows into a revolution that changes a whole country. Like here there are so many things we are fighting---the war, all the racism our black sisters and brothers face every day, as women struggling to control our own choices-- how do we change such a powerful system."

Ruthie was glad to see some heads nodding as she spoke. She didn't yet consider herself a "serious" revolutionary, but she wanted to move in that direction. Hard to do when your 4-year-old was tickling you under your chin while you spoke. "Sasha, stop. Go see if Brother Big has any more snacks to bring out, sweetie. Thanks."

The conversation continued around the circle and Ruthie was struck by the range of experiences shared. The brigade had made it a priority to recruit a diverse group, and they had succeeded. Ruthie had snagged the only slot for a white woman and Larry was one of two vets, joined by a couple of Chicano students from the university, an ex-Black Panther and a farmworker organizer from the eastern plains.

The meeting broke up just in time for Ruthie to get Sasha ready for bed in the big room on the 2nd floor that they shared. Teeth brushed, bedtime story and their customary "nite, nite, sleep tight, don't let the bedbugs bite and Sasha was all tucked in and fell right asleep after an exciting afternoon. Ruthie would miss this routine. It would be hard to be away from her little girl for the first time. And in Cuba, the forbidden island, where she would not be able to write or call. Not for the first time, Ruthie wondered if she was doing the right thing. But the meeting had been so inspiring. And when would she have another opportunity like this? A month later, Ruthie stood in a long line of brigadistas in the Mexico City airport, waiting to transfer for the plane that would carry them to Cuba.

"Here we go." Angie, the young woman standing next to her, turned to Ruthie and let her thick braid swing over her shoulder. They had become good friends during the month of preparation, and Ruthie knew how anxious she was—her first time out of Colorado.

"Too late to turn back now," Ruthie laughed, making light of her own nerves that were mounting as they moved slowly toward the gate.

Suddenly cameras were flashing in all directions and they were forced into a single file march through a phalanx of dark-suited men.

"FBI," Sarah said. "Just keep walking. They can't keep us from boarding the plane. We are on our way."

Ruthie kept walking, watching Angie's braid swinging back and forth in front of her.

From one of the many pockets of her travel jacket she drew a Polaroid. Sasha, on the steps of the trailer in the country where she would be spending the next 3 months with her dad, holding her Cuban flag and looking off into the distance. It had been Ruthie's last glimpse of her daughter, captured in a photo that she would tuck under her pillow to keep her company.

"We're off, Sash. Mama's venture is about to begin. See you soon."

And with that, Ruthie squeezed her duffel through the narrow door, took a deep breath, and slipped the photo back in her pocket.

"Ready or not," she whispered to herself as she took her seat on the small prop plane that would carry her to Cuba. "Here I come."

PART ONE
Mother & Child Reunion

Stormy Weather

Mid-July 1973

Ruthie braced herself against the strong gusts and salty mist that whipped over the deck rail and held the photo of Sasha tight in her hand. The sun was high in the sky and a hot wind blew her long wavy hair back from her face. It was a relief to breathe fresh air after days below deck on this converted cattle boat that was carrying her home to her daughter.

The Luis Miguel had run into a storm off the coast of the Carolinas and the rolling waves and slippery planks had made the deck off limits. A chorus of shouts erupted as the shoreline came into view and Ruthie scanned the faces of her travel weary new friends lining the rail.

"Look! Mira! Land! Right there!" And there it was —the rocky coast of Nova Scotia, sailboats bobbing in the small harbor, red-roofed cottages dotting the hills.

Sasha had called this trip her "venture." It had been an adventure all right. Three months as part of an international solidarity brigade building houses for workers in Cuba. A phalanx of FBI agents snapping their pictures as they boarded a Russian made prop plane in Mexico at the start of their journey to that revolutionary island. And now the long trip back, having to detour all the way to Canada because the U.S. government banned travel to Cuba.

Like Ruthie, her fellow brigadistas were young and idealistic and recruited from all over the country. She had joined from Colorado where she and Sasha were living in a big old Victorian wreck on the outskirts of Ft. Carson that served as a coffee house and informal gathering place for anti-war GIs and vets—the R & R. In army lingo the name of their project meant rest and relaxation—short breaks from the war—but this R & R stood for Rise Up and Resist. Ruthie was part of the civilian staff—she did outreach at the base, ran the Friday night discussion groups and edited the monthly newspaper. The war was winding down, but young soldiers were coming home from Vietnam disillusioned and looking for connection. The R & R gave them a safe space to process what they'd been through and figure out what came next. And it gave Ruthie and Sasha a home and a family to be part of.

"The first thing I'm gonna do is call my little girl," Ruthie said to her friend Manny who had come up beside her.

"I know you're ready to hear her voice." Manny was a bear of a man who spoke in a deep rumble. He had listened to her stories about Sasha on many a long night under the tropical moon and invited her to cry on his shoulder more than once.

"You can say that again. I can't wait for you to meet her, Manny. I keep having these worried thoughts though—like what if she would rather stay with her dad in the country. What if he doesn't want her to live with me in Boston? He has all these strong opinions about how we should raise her. What if he decides to fight me for custody?" Ruthie swayed as the ship moved across a current and gripped the rail tighter.

Ruthie's thoughts of Sasha had sometimes kept her awake long after the squeals of the metal bunk beds and settling in sounds of her bunkmates had ceased. As she tossed and turned on the thin foam mattress, she wondered how much Sasha had grown, what new feats she had mastered and how she had spent these months with her dad Carl. But Manny was the only person she had really confided in—her yearning to be with Sasha and her worry about having left her behind.

"Yeah, well—that sounds hard," Manny said, throwing an arm over her shoulder, "but no use worrying about it now. Just focus on how happy she will be to see her Mama. And what great stories you'll have to tell her about our adventure."

For three months, Ruthie had bounced along rutted dirt roads in the back of a truck, trundled wheelbarrows full of cement over narrow planks, watched cinder block houses take shape, yawned through planning meetings after long days at work, sang, and danced and debated with her compañeros., as she had learned to call her friends in the brigade. She had been exhausted, exhilarated, dirty, hot, and sore—and she had felt free and more herself than she had in a very long time. After the painful disentangling from her marriage to Carl, after four years as a single parent trying to balance caring for Sasha with her work at the GI anti-war organizing project, scraping by on a waitress's salary—this time away was just what she needed. So often she felt so much older than her 24 years, but in Cuba, she was young again.

"Hey Ruthie, I didn't desert you." Manny was back at her side as they drew closer to shore. "Just making a plan to get together with the Jersey comrades when we get back. I'm ready to get serious about this revolution stuff–take it to the next level."

"Oh, me too, Manny. I just have to figure out a way to be an organizer and a good Mama at the same time." "You will, amiga. I know you will."

Ruthie took one more look at the photo and tucked it back into the pocket of her windbreaker. The Polaroid camera had caught Sasha in a pensive mood, her auburn curls fanned out behind her. Her chubby legs were planted firmly on the steps of her father's trailer at the Rainbow Ranch, and she was holding the small Cuban flag she carried everywhere, getting ready for her Mama's trip. The edges of the photo were wrinkled and discolored from being in Ruthie's pocket. In the women's dormitory, Ruthie had kept Sasha's picture under the flat, hard pillow on her upper bunk in the women's dormitory and said good night to her every night. Every night, she heard Sasha's sleepy voice in her head saying, "Good night, Mama," and kept her promise to repeat their bedtime ritual, whispering, "Night, Night, sleep tight. Don't let the bed bugs bite."

This experience had been amazing, challenging— life-changing, really. But she was ready to plant her feet on solid ground in her own country. She was almost home. And home for Ruthie meant Sasha.

Only A Heartbeat Away

As soon as they docked, collected their things, and cleared customs— easy and fast in the small harbor station, Ruthie headed for the row of pay phones in the waiting area. The storm had added a couple of days to their journey. Carl and Sasha should definitely be waiting for her in her cousin Claudia's apartment near Harvard, where Claudia was in grad school. She had invited Ruthie and Sasha to "housesit" her apartment for a year while she was in England doing research for her thesis. That was the plan. They were really looking forward to it.

Ruthie dialed Claudia's number in Cambridge with shaking fingers. The phone rang for a long time, and she almost hung up. Finally, she heard her cousin's voice.

"Hi Claudie, it's me, Ruthie. I'm back. Can you put Sasha on the phone?" Ruthie rocked on her heels, anticipation building. It was all she could do to hold the receiver in her trembling hand.

"Oh, hey, Ruthie, welcome back. Hey, listen, Carl and Sasha aren't here," Claudia said. "He called a couple of weeks ago to say he had made a different plan, but I had no way to reach you."

"What do you mean a different plan? There was only one plan. He was supposed to drive across country and meet me at your place. They should be there by now. Oh, why does he always have to be so annoying?"

"Calm down, cuz, okay? He didn't say where they were, just that they were taking a detour. Can't you call that ranch he's been living at?

"Yeah, yeah. Let me do that," Ruthie said, letting her cousin know she would arrive the next day with a friend, if that was okay. They would probably stay a couple of days. Ruthie fidgeted with the phone cord as Claudia gave her directions from the bus station, then abruptly ended the call, digging in her change purse for more quarters. Her fingers dragged as she dialed the number at the ranch.

"Ye-a-h?" Finally, she heard the long-drawn-out twang of Ken's voice that matched his lanky, weather-beaten body. He owned the land Carl had moved to—still ranched part of it but had invited his hippie friends from the city to move up and settle on the rest.

"What can I do you for?" he said now.

"Hey, Ken. It's Ruthie. Sasha's mom. Is Carl there? Can you get him please? I'm back—well, I'm in Canada, and I need to talk to him." The words came out fast, all jammed together.

There was a long pause.

Ruthie fished for more quarters in her pocket. She'd keep it short. She just had to hear Carl's voice, to know that Sasha was okay.

She held the receiver close to her ear as Ken explained that Carl and Sasha weren't there, had in fact "taken off " a few weeks earlier. No, he didn't know where they were or when they would be back. Oh, and Cindy was with them.

Ruthie twisted the phone cord in sweaty fingers and tried to remember who Cindy was among all the women Carl had introduced her to when she had brought Sasha to the ranch. Was she Carl's girlfriend? They all looked alike to her–blonde, ironed-straight hair hanging down their backs, long Indian skirts, flowy blouses, whiffs of patchouli and grass coming off their bodies. Her own dark brown hair hadn't been washed in days and curled over the neck of the grimy yellow brigade T-shirt she'd worn the whole time on the ship.

Ken was saying something about not thinking Carl was headed for Boston. Why? They were supposed to be coming to Boston to bring Sasha to her. Where the hell were they?

Ruthie hung up the phone, her sweaty hands leaving it damp and slippery. She sat on the nearest bench, piling her bags at her feet, trying to make sense of the call and pushing away the anxious thoughts spinning through her mind. Ken had sounded so casual. That was good, wasn't it? No big deal—just a little trip, probably, a getaway. But Ken was casual about everything. And why hadn't Carl told him where they were going? Or left a message for her with Claudia? She was ready to see her daughter now.

"Hey Ruthie, the buses are getting ready to leave. Get your stuff and c'mon." It was Manny, looking out for her like he always did. They would be traveling to Boston on a chartered bus with other brigadistas from the area.

Manny lifted Ruthie's backpack onto one of his broad shoulders and grabbed her duffel. He took her hand, then noticed her frown and downcast eyes.

"Hey girl—what's wrong?"

"I'll tell you on the bus," Ruthie said, trudging behind him, trying to hold herself together.

They found empty seats near the back of the bus. Manny stashed her duffel on the rack above the seats and Ruthie shoved the backpack under her feet. She leaned her head on Manny's shoulder, feeling the stubble of his beard against her forehead and nuzzling into the soft cushion of his cotton shirt as the bus pulled away from the station. Somewhere in the front, someone started a song in a high, thin soprano. Cuba que linda es Cuba. Ruthie closed her eyes.

"C'mon, Ruthie. Tell me now. What's got you so upset?"

Ruthie had met Manny soon after they arrived in Cuba, and he had quickly become a good friend. He had a boyish grin that lifted his eyebrows in two question marks above his dark brown eyes. Born in Puerto Rico but raised in New York—a Nuyorican, he called himself. He was always joking, fooling around—but underneath all that, he was kind, tender-hearted.

"Ruthie, c'mon now. It can't be that bad. Did you talk to Sasha?"

"She's not at my cousin's place," Ruthie said in a flat voice that sounded like a recording to her ears. "And they're not at the ranch. Carl took her somewhere."

"What do you mean, took her?" Manny said, turning to look at her, jostling her head off his shoulder.

"Like he left the ranch with her a couple of weeks ago. With his new girlfriend, Cindy." She winced to hear the jealousy in her voice when she said that name. "No one seems to know where they went."

Manny shook his head in disbelief. He started to ask a question, but Ruthie shrank into her seat.

"I don't know what to do, Manny. Oh God, I miss her so much. I just want to see her now!" Ruthie said, and then silent tears began to roll down her sun-chapped cheeks. A girl across the aisle looked over with concern, but Manny waved her away. "Thanks," he said. "I got this."

"You said he can be kind of a clueless jerk sometimes. That's probably all this is, right?" Manny spoke quietly and turned to look at her in the dim light of the bus. Ruthie took a deep breath and blew her nose with the wrinkled tissue Manny had pulled from his pocket. She lay her head back down on his shoulder.

Her thoughts were doing a tug of war in her head—pulling her back and forth between the end of the world and probably no big deal.

Was it wrong to leave her little girl? It had just seemed like such a great opportunity to put her politics into action. The Vietnam War was still raging, black activists were being arrested and even killed, her project in Colorado was torn apart by infighting and wouldn't last much longer. She had been unsure about what was next for her and Sasha. And then this trip had come along. And Carl had offered to take care of Sasha while she was gone. And her cousin Claudia had offered her a free apartment in Cambridge to stay in for a year when she got back. Everything had fallen into place.

Ruthie felt sure Carl would never harm Sasha, but it was still hard not to worry. He had such strong opinions about how to raise their daughter—hadn't wanted Sasha to move around so much, hadn't wanted her to grow up in a house full of "GIs and radicals," as he had put it during one heated discussion, hadn't liked Ruthie's plan to move to Cambridge when she returned from Cuba. And every move he had made since they divorced had taken him farther off the grid. "Kids should grow up in nature," he had said. "They should run free, learn from everything around them—not sit in rows like automatons being fed useless knowledge." Ruthie had waved it off. Carl could never get it together to follow through on any of his pronouncements, let alone take on full-time care of a 5-year-old child.

She had imagined Sasha enjoying a few months of a "Born Free" life on the ranch, nothing more. She had imagined her basking in her dad's attention. Safe. Now she didn't know what to think.

Manny snored lightly in the seat beside her, his chest rising and falling, the quiet murmur of his heart filling her ear, which rested against it. In Cuba, everyone had assumed they were a couple—but a short fling on a tropical island wasn't what Ruthie wanted. At first, Manny had wanted something different, but he had accepted her terms. She had needed a friend, and she had found one.

Manny stirred beside her, sat up and yawned.

"How you doin', girl?" he asked, rubbing his eyes and looking at Ruthie. "Man, que mucho hambre. Are they gonna feed us or what?"

Ruthie grinned despite her anxious mood. Food was never far from Manny's thoughts. At the camp in Cuba, he had flirted shamelessly with the kitchen staff to ensure that second helpings of the simple but hearty meals would come his way. Ruthie wondered what her mother would make of Manny—big man, big smile, big appetite, not caring what anyone thought of his Spanglish or what he said. She wished for a little of his confidence.

It was late afternoon the next day when the bus finally pulled into Boston. Ruthie clung to Manny's arm as they said their good-byes to the forty or so young Americans they had lived and worked with for the past three months. There were tears, promises to keep in touch, and addresses scribbled on scraps of paper. A crowd formed around Manny. Ruthie couldn't handle it.

"I'm gonna make a phone call. I'll be right back," she told Manny, who was lost in the middle of a group of hugging girls. She spied the pay phones on a dingy wall near the restrooms—why did they always seem to be near the restrooms? —and pulled a small plastic change purse filled with quarters, nickels, and dimes from her jacket pocket.

Ken first, she thought, dialing the number. Maybe they're back. It was mid-afternoon in California.

"This better be important." It was Ken's voice, sleepy, annoyed. "Ken, it's Ruthie again? Are they back? I'm in Boston?"

She held her breath as Ken explained that there was no sign of them yet, but he was sure they'd be back. After all, he still had most of their stuff and couldn't keep it forever.

"Okay." Ruthie breathed out her disappointment. "Well, I'll check in with you again soon."

Ruthie placed the phone back on the hook and headed for the bathroom, shaking out a cramp in her leg as she walked. She caught a glimpse of herself in the mirror over the sink—eyes red-rimmed, skin pale beneath her Cuba tan, sun-bleached wavy hair a tangled mess—and quickly turned away.

"Hey girl, where you been? I been lookin' for you." Manny took her hand. He was happy to be home, Ruthie realized with a tinge of envy. Happy and carefree, that's Manny, she thought. But she knew better. Manny had had a rough life. He deserved whatever happiness he could find.

"So, what's up. They back yet? Everything cool?" Her frown answered his question.

"Oh, that bad, huh? Well, they'll turn up soon, Ruthie. I know they will. Probly just a misunderstanding." And with that, Manny grabbed her duffel, and they walked together in the direction of the train that would carry them to Cambridge.

And for the moment, despite her growing worry, Ruthie chose to believe him.

Harvard Yard

"I never thought I would pahk my cah in Hahvahd Yahd," Manny teased as they climbed up out of the darkness of the subway at the Harvard Square stop. "I'm comin' up in the world."

They were greeted by the light from dozens of flickering candles held aloft by a group gathered in one corner of the Square. The candles illuminated a large, colorful banner.

"Divest Now. Harvard Says No to Apartheid in South Africa." Manny read aloud. "How do you like that?" he said. "C'mon. Let's go join them and find out what's been going on while we were away. Looks like Vietnam is no longer on the front burner."

"Quit it, Manny," Ruthie said, pulling her arm free from his gentle tug.

"I don't want to join them. I can't think about anything but Sasha right now." "O.k. O.k. I get it," Manny shrugged in surrender. "But aren't you just a little bit excited that the struggle at home has been heating up while we've been busting our asses building houses and studying revolution in Cuba, que linda es Cuba?" He sang the last few words—the song about beautiful Cuba they had sung every morning, bouncing along in open trucks on the way to the work site. Ruthie stopped walking and wheeled on him.

"Manny, I don't care. Right now, I can't think about any of this." And then, under her breath, "It's probably what's gotten me into this mess." She could no longer ignore the voice of blame growing louder in her head: why had she left her little girl, why had she trusted Carl to keep her safe, why had she assumed everything would be the same when she got back? What a selfish fool she was.

Manny was still talking. She could feel his warm breath on her face. "What got you into this mess, if it is a mess, which we don't really know yet, my dear amiga, is your sorry-assed, clueless, irresponsible ex-husband. It is NOT, I repeat NOT, your commitment to a better world. So, stop blaming yourself for this, compañera. Manny is here to tell you it ain't your fault."

They walked the few short blocks from the T station at Harvard Square to Claudia's apartment in silence. Claudia and Ruthie had spent a lot of time together growing up. They would head straight to Ruthie's bedroom whenever their families gathered for the holidays—sharing secrets and giggling until Claudia's mom, who was the older sister of Ruthie's, came to gather her up. "Time to go, Claudie. Tell your cousin goodbye."

Aunt Helen worked as a secretary, and Uncle Norm was a quiet man with a big belly who had worked his way up from salesman to manager of a small chain of Big and Tall Men's Shops. Ruthie's mom had been the first and only one in her family to go to college, helped by her older siblings. A bit ironic, Ruthie thought, as they got closer to Claudia's building, that she's the Harvard student and I'm the college dropout.

Claudia opened the door with a shout of delight. "Look at you," she said. "My long-lost cousin." She drew Ruthie into the small foyer and extended a hand to Manny.

"I'm Ruthie's brilliant cousin. I'm not being snooty; I'm just practicing for my year abroad in London. They say 'brilliant' for everything." Manny laughed with her.

"Oh, sorry, let me help you with your stuff." Manny had ended up with Ruthie's duffel and his bag, and his hands were full.

They piled their things in a corner of Claudia's small bedroom and settled on the futon couch in the living room. Manny sat across from them in an upholstered chair that Ruthie remembered from their grandparents' living room. Sliding glass doors to a small balcony let in a weak, gray light that matched Ruthie's mood.

"So cuz, Harvard, huh?"

"Yup. Do you believe it? I always thought you'd be the one here. You were the smart one."

Manny gave her a sideways look like this was news to him.

Ruthie strained to listen as Claudia chattered on about how lively Harvard Square was on weekends–even though the anti-war demos were dying down now that the Peace Accords were finally signed, there was always somebody protesting something–Watergate, South Africa. She'd love to show them around.

"Oh my god, I almost forgot. How was Cuba? Tell me!"

Claudia bounced on the edge of the futon like she had on Ruthie's bed when they were kids.

"It was amazing," Manny piped up from his chair.

"Yeah, really amazing, Claud," Ruthie agreed, but already she could feel some of the strength and passion she had felt on the island slipping away. She wasn't sure how Claudia would handle the news about Carl's disappearance with Sasha. Ruthie didn't want stories about her latest fuck-up to spread through their large network of cousins before she had a chance to tell her parents. Ruthie had distanced herself from her family when she left home, but Claudia always knew who had married a jerk, who was smoking pot, who got a great job but didn't deserve it—and she didn't always keep that info to herself.

"I'm pretty tired, so no sightseeing for me today, Claudia," Ruthie said, shifting her weight on the lumpy futon and pulling a cushion behind her back. "But maybe Manny would like to see some sights. It's his first time here. Okay if we stick around for a day or two? I'm hoping Carl will show up by then. I'll bring Sasha down to visit my family when they get here."

"Sure, Ruthie. I'll be busy doing last-minute stuff for my trip, but you guys can hang out as long as you need to," Claudia said, including Manny in her invitation.

"Oh wow! Thanks," Manny said. "I have a week before I'm due back at work so maybe I can see a bit of Boston before I go. Wouldn't mind checking out Harvard Square right now if you're up for it, Claudia," he said, winking at Ruthie. She and Manny were so in synch sometimes. Like right now, he probably sensed she needed to be alone to think some things through. It was one of the things she loved about him.

When Manny and Claudia left, promising to bring her back something from the diner on the Square, Ruthie settled into the calm and silence of the small apartment. She had been here once before during Claudia's first year at Harvard, but then she had moved west—first to California and then to Colorado—and trips back East were few and far between. But now she wished she had found a way to visit more often. She liked Claudia, and it was nice to have at least one family member she felt close to.

She looked around the living room. It was not much different from a dorm room—scuffed wooden floors, beige cinder block walls, a bookshelf crammed with thick textbooks, a typing table with a green Selectric typewriter on it, papers scattered left and right on the floor. The lumpy futon and their grandmother's chair—that was about it. But it was homey and comfortable, with a kitchenette, a small bedroom, and a private bathroom—unheard-of luxuries for college living. Again, Ruthie felt a pang of envy and then heard her mother's voice in her head.

"You made your bed, Ruthie. Now I guess you'll just have to lie in it."

She went to the bedroom, kicked off her shoes, and lay down on the narrow bed—as if obeying her mother's command—then laughed aloud— "I'm lying in Claudia's bed, Mom. How do you like that?"

An atlas lay open on the nightstand next to the bed—open to a map of England, where Claudia would be studying next semester. Ruthie sat up, marked Claudia's place with a bobby pin she found in the nightstand, and leafed through the atlas until she found a U.S. map—and then California. It was a big state, stretching from the Pacific Northwest down to Mexico. Carl and Sasha could be anywhere. Carl liked to travel and camp along the coast. She traced the line where water met land with her finger. Where would they have gone? Where could they be?

She paged through the atlas until she came to a map of the Caribbean— the Greater Antilles, a chain of islands. The biggest, shaped a bit like a crocodile, was Cuba. It had beckoned to her, lured her with the promise of adventure, meaningful work, revolutionary ideals—a step away from single motherhood, from her routine. She had assumed—wouldn't anyone—that it would all be waiting for her when she returned. That she could pick up her life where she had left it. But now…

She closed the atlas with a snap, pulled off her soiled T-shirt, and headed for the shower. She wrapped a towel around her clean hair when she heard Manny and Claudia's voices in the hall.

"Hey girl, we have milkshakes and French fries. C'mon, Ruthie. I know you're hungry."

Ruthie pulled on a clean white T-shirt and some cutoff shorts, then sat on the bed, rubbing her hair dry with the towel. Through the rustle of paper bags, the clink of glasses and silverware being set on the card table, and the murmur of voices, she heard Sasha's high-pitched cry.

"Mama, Mama. Hide-and-seek. Come and find me. I'm hiding. Come find me, Mama."

"Ruthie, get your ass in here before I scarf up all these fries," Manny called from the living room.

She stood, smoothed the bedcovers, and walked slowly out of the dark bedroom to join them.

Claudia and Manny had pulled a card table over to the couch and spread a flowered tablecloth that looked like another grandma donation over it. Hamburgers and fries were laid out on greasy paper dotted with ketchup, and Manny was slurping chocolate milkshake from a straw.

"I hope that's not mine," Ruthie said, trying for a light-hearted tone. Even she was getting tired of her heavy, somber mood. Claudia produced another milkshake, untouched, from a large brown paper bag.

"You will never, ever have a more delicious milkshake than Cookie's," she said. "It's my favorite place in Cambridge."

"Hey, those are mine," Manny cried out as Claudia playfully stole a few fries from his plate. Ruthie pushed back from the table, almost knocking over her milkshake. How could they be so oblivious? Didn't they realize how anxious she was? She wasn't hungry and she had more serious things on her mind.

Manny and Claudia exchanged a puzzled glance and began clearing their dinner plates.

"Okay if I use the phone in your bedroom, Claud?" "Sure," Claudia said. "Help yourself."

Ruthie sat with the phone receiver in her hand for what felt like a long time, but she couldn't think of a single person to call. It was too soon to call Ken again. He would be pissed off if she kept harassing him. Carl's parents? Her own parents? No, she couldn't face talking to them right now. She shook out the tension in her shoulders and neck and put the phone back on the hook. She thought about Claudia's question—how was Cuba? —and a scene popped into her head—a moment from her first week there. It turned out they were not destined to cut sugarcane after all but were assigned to a brigade building cement-block houses—a town for Cuban workers. And along with several other women in her work group, Ruthie's job was to straighten the nails they pulled from the framing boards so they could be used again—an important job in Cuba, where everything that could be recycled was. Towards the end of a long workday, she and Yolanda, the other woman assigned to this task, took a break and leaned back against the large trunk of a mango tree, which provided welcome shade from the late afternoon sun. Orange globes dotted the branches above them, and occasionally one would fall to the ground below. Ruthie had learned to peel the dusty fruit and eat around the pit, letting the sticky juice dribble down her chin.

"What made you decide to come, Ruthie?" Yolanda asked, pausing her hammering for a minute. Yolanda was the head of her work brigade—a young Afro-Cuban woman, just out of university, small and wiry, yet she had no problem wheeling the heavy bags of cement to the cinder-block house they were building. She had majored in political science and was constantly peppering them with questions.

"To join the brigade?" Ruthie let her hammer drop and thought for a minute. She should be used to the question by now. Everyone asked—starting with her announcement to friends and family that she would be joining the Venceremos Brigade and spending three months in Cuba. Why Cuba? Isn't it illegal to go there? Aren't you afraid? Are you a communist? What will you be doing there? So many questions. But she still had to think about it. There were no easy answers.

"I wanted to see for myself, I guess," she said, "You know, what it's like here. And contribute." She pulled off the red plaid bandana that held her wavy auburn hair back and wiped her sweaty face. "And learn what it means to be part of a real revolution." She shrugged. Not much of an answer, but the sun was bearing down, and she was tired.

"And what have you learned?" Yolanda was so young…and serious. "How hard it is to straighten nails," Ruthie said, and they both laughed and took up their hammers again.

"What's so funny?" Angie asked, plopping down on the ground at Ruthie's feet and pouring water from her thermos over her head. "I could use a good laugh. This sun is so God-damned hot today."

"Yoli wants to know why we came to Cuba."

"Rev-o-lu-tion, baby," Angie said, squinting into the sun. "And all the useful new skills I'm learning," she added, grabbing Ruthie's hammer and pounding a nail. "What do you miss the most about home?" Yolanda continued, not to be deterred from her interview.

"That's easy," Angie shot back. "My mama's tamales. Remember Ruthie how good they are. People bought dozens when we sold them at the college to raise money for this trip. Tell Yoli."

But Ruthie was staring at a photo she had pulled from her pocket. She passed it to Yoli.

"¿Quién es esta niñita linda?" Yoli asked. Who is this beautiful little girl?

"That's Sasha, my daughter. She is what I miss most. It's the first time we've been apart."

"Ay mi amiga," Yoli's eyes were full of unspoken questions.

"¿Pero cómo? How could you leave her? It must have been so hard. I don't have children, but I could never imagine…." Her voice trailed off.

"Me neither," Angie chimed in. "But didn't revolutionary women have to leave their kids when they joined the guerilleros in the mountains?"

Ruthie stayed quiet, waiting to see what Yoli would say. She had been told there would be other women with kids on the brigade, but so far, she had not met anyone in her situation.

"Si, algunas…yes, some, but it was duro, muy duro, so hard. There was a saying from Ho Chi Minh, the leader of the Vietnam revolution, that they used to quote. If you want to be a revolutionary, postpone falling in love. If you fall in love, postpone getting married. And if you get married, postpone having children. Because the revolution needs you and it will demand everything." Yoli shook her head and resumed her hammering.

Maybe Ho Chi Minh was right, Ruthie thought. Maybe he had a point. "Hey, Ruthie. What's goin' on in there?" Manny called out from the living room. "Come play with us. Claudia has Monopoly, and I'm about to get rich." From revolution to capitalism in one day, Ruthie thought.

"Coming," she called out from the bedroom. "But I suck at Monopoly."

Gone

Ruthie woke the next morning to the sound of a siren and the bright sun streaming through a window. Wait, where was she? She looked around in confusion, and then it registered. Claudia's apartment. Cambridge. Manny sleeping beside her on the futon couch in the living room.

And Sasha?

Manny stirred and sat up, and Ruthie couldn't help but giggle. His thick, kinky hair stood on end in all directions, and he looked like a giant baby bird that had fallen from the nest and didn't know what to do next.

"Hey, what's up?" he croaked. "And where's the coffee? Did you talk to Sasha? Are they headed this way?"

"She's gone," Ruthie said in a flat voice that sounded like a recording in her ears. "Gone."

"You don't know where she and Carl are right now, Ruthie. I get it. But what do you mean by gone?" Manny said, turning to look at her as he pulled on his pants.

"Gone, like not there. I can just feel it. Carl took her somewhere, and he's not bringing her back." As soon as she said the words out loud, Ruthie felt their truth. This wasn't just Carl losing track of time or taking a detour on his way to Boston. This was Carl deciding that Sasha was better off living with him.

Manny shook his head in disbelief. He started to ask a question, but Ruthie held out a hand to stop him. Her thoughts kept circling the word "gone," as if it were a drain that would suck her in.

"I've got to get out there, Manny, and talk to people, figure out what's happening. I'll go crazy if I have to just sit around here waiting," Ruthie said.

"Okay, okay, Ruthie, that makes sense. We'll go and find them. They gotta be somewhere, right?"

Ruthie fumbled with Claudia's coffee maker, and as the aroma of rich, dark coffee filled the small apartment, she began making a mental list. She had to get to California fast. She would need a plane ticket and some money. That meant a trip to her parents. That meant telling them what had happened and hearing her mother's voice dripping with "I told you so." But they would help her. They had to.

Otherwise, Ruthie didn't know what she would do.

Claudia stumbled into the kitchenette and filled a mug with coffee. She and Manny had stayed up late, playing game after game of Monopoly while Ruthie tossed and turned on the uncomfortable futon.

"Morning, cuz. Did Carl and Sasha get in touch? I didn't hear the phone, but I can sleep through a hurricane."

"Nope. Not a word. I've decided to go to San Francisco and see what I can find out. But I've got to pass through Hartford first and see if my dad will help with a plane ticket. I'll take the bus there tomorrow."

"Oh, Uncle Max will help you, Ruthie. I know he will. And it'll all turn out fine in the end. You'll see."

Ruthie shrugged. She didn't feel her cousin's optimism.

"Hey, why don't I go with you to Hartford? I think you could use some moral support. And it's on the way to Jersey," Manny said, slurping the last of his coffee and folding the futon.

"So… you'll go with Ruthie?" Claudia asked. "To meet Aunt Rose? That should be interesting. What has Ruthie told you about her?"

"Not a whole lot," Manny said, settling onto the couch. "She kinda hints at some stuff, but I know she doesn't really want to talk about it. And I get that. I do."

Yeah, you do, Ruthie thought. For all his teasing, Manny respected her boundaries. From the few stories he had shared about his own childhood, Ruthie knew he understood her need for self-protection. His mother had left him and his older sister, Mimi, with his abusive father when he was only 9 years old. Running for her life, he said. And he hadn't seen her for years, until she had faded to a wisp of memory—a cloud of black hair framing a pensive face, the ashes of the fragrant incense she burned in front of a little statue of the Virgen.

When he was old enough to make his own choices, he drew close to her and forgave her. What a big heart he had.

"Seriously, though," Claudia said. "My Aunt Rose is a real ball-buster. Ruthie, do you remember that time she pinched me so hard it left a mark on my arm? What did I do? Probably reached for a second cookie or something. God, what is her thing about food?"

Ruthie winced, not at a specific memory because she had no clear recollections of her childhood—as if it were a picture drawn in pale pastel chalk and then smudged and blurred. Her mind snagged on the thought of her mother hurting her sweet cousin—just reaching out and hurting her.

Claudia pulled her legs up underneath her and sat facing Manny, who was snapping his fingers in front of Ruthie's face.

"Earth to Ruthie. Come in, please. Wow, girl. You went somewhere far, far away in another galaxy. O.K., so prep me now for my meeting with the scary Rose. I want to make a good impression."

Claudia and Ruthie looked at Manny and then at each other. They burst into giggles—like when they were kids at the table and laughed till milk came out of their noses, then got sent to their room to "compose themselves."

"What, What? Let me in on the secret. What's so damned funny?" Manny demanded, irritation creeping into his voice.

"It's just, it's just," Claudia began, stammering through her laughter.

She shrugged, then took a deep breath.

"You just can't make a good first impression, Manny. She'll hate you and let you know it in a million little oh so polite ways."

"Claudia." Ruthie stopped her cousin with a sharp look. She didn't want to have to explain her mother to Manny right now.

"C'mon, Ruthie. You know it's true. What boyfriend—what friend of yours has she ever liked? She couldn't stand Carl, even though his parents are rich. And Manny—well…"

Manny got up and went to the glass door to the little balcony. He turned his back on them. Ruthie came up behind him and tentatively reached out a hand, afraid he might really be angry.

"Manny," she said, placing her hand softly on his broad back. He wheeled around, eyes blazing. Ruthie drew back.

"I am Manny. The dragon slayer from the Bronx," he shouted, "and I will vanquish this fearsome Rose. Take me to her, fair lady Ruth."

"But first," this was directed at Claudia, "let's see some more of this college town of yours. I just might pick up some class along the way."

Just Passing Through

"I don't see my dad," Ruthie said the next day as their bus pulled up to the familiar station.

"Let's just get a cab."

Being there reminded her of all the trips she had made with Sasha to visit her parents— the mix of excitement and dread that always accompanied a trip home. Now it was only dread—of what her parents might say— whether they would help or judge. Probably a combination of the two.

They were quiet as the cab passed through the streets of the Blue Hills Avenue neighborhood, where Ruthie had grown up and gone to school before their move to the suburbs. A World War II GI Bill housing development of small, boxlike houses, it had fallen on hard times.

"Wow, purple door," Manny said, as the cab pulled up in front of her parents' house. "Now I see where you got your style, girl. But I thought you were rich."

Ruthie looked at the house, the block, trying to see it as Manny might. Smallish houses, some with colonial pretensions, others Cape Cod, a mix of wood and brick, none more than a driveway's width apart, postage-stamp front yards, mowed and trimmed.

"Well…relatively speaking," Ruthie said. For all the years since she had joined the civil rights movement at sixteen, she had been equivocating or apologizing for her background—father a lawyer (but he's a public defender), educated professional Mom (first in her family to go to college), comfortable home in a lily-white suburb (I couldn't get out of there fast enough).

"Did you grow up here?" Manny asked as they approached the purple door.

Ruthie slowed her steps, wanting to prolong the moment, postpone the inevitable.

"Not really—just junior high and high school."

Ruthie still remembered her first glimpse of this house—the steep stairway, the narrow rooms, her small bedroom on the second floor in the front, the fenced in yard.

"You'll finally have your own bedroom, Ruth Ann," her mother had said, but when she saw it, with its frilly wallpaper covered in little bows and its window high above the street, Ruthie hated it.

"Why did we have to move anyway?" She had pouted all the way through their first meal in the formal dining room—in the old house, they ate in the kitchen at an old wooden table. "I liked our old neighborhood. I had friends. This is so—so quiet."

On Pembroke St. in their old neighborhood, the houses were smaller, and the yards were bigger—one big, unfenced space where Ruthie's gang of friends—she was often the only girl—roamed freely till they were called in for dinner. Bikes, skates thrown every which way, hopscotch grids chalked on broken front sidewalks, flat pads for marble games scratched out in dirt patches.

That had been home. The new house was all about better schools, your own bedroom, and making new friends. And of course, with time, she had—but it had never felt like home.

The sunroom at the back of the house was the site of happy hour, where three or four of her mother's friends gathered for cocktails most afternoons. Ruthie went to her friends' houses after school, where their mothers waited with milk and cookies—yes, really—and asked about their day.

"Earth to Ruthie. Aren't we going in?" Manny was waiting on the slight stoop, a duffel in each hand. Just then, the door swung open. Ruthie looked at her father through the spotless glass of the storm door. Her mother lurked just behind him.

"Ruthie," he said with a grin. "And you must be Manny. C'mon in."

The door creaked on rusty hinges, and her father reached for one of the bags.

"Welcome home, dear," her mother said.

Ruthie sighed—time to face the music.

Ruthie followed her father through the door, shooting Manny a look over her shoulder meant to say BEHAVE. She stood at the bottom of the stairs, now carpeted in thick gold, once bare wood that had amplified her steps throughout her teen years as she stormed up to her room, slamming the door to shut out her mother's muttering complaints.

"Can I get you both something to drink?" her father said. "Water, coffee?"

"Just water would be great," Manny said.

"Sit, sit down, make yourselves at home." Her father walked them into the sunroom and pointed to the couch that filled one wall. It had been a nubbly green tweed, but Ruthie noticed it had been reupholstered in a blue faux-leather material—smooth and slippery. The couch was an original Castro Convertible sofa bed, upon which, it was rumored, her brother had been conceived.

"Where's Marty?" Ruthie asked. "I can't wait to see him."

"Oh, he's probably out riding around with one of his buddies. That's all they do these days." Ruthie's father called from the kitchen. Ruthie's brother was still living at home and taking a few classes at the local community college. They couldn't be more different, yet they were united by the sibling solidarity they had needed to survive in this family.

Ruthie's mother had not said a word. She was studying Manny over her drink of choice—a diet Coke, probably already spiked with vodka, though it was not yet happy hour.

"So, Manny," her mother said. "Tell me a little about yourself. What is it that you do when you're not making the revolution?" These last words were delivered with air quotes around them.

Here we go, Ruthie thought. This is it—that hidden black ice you don't see coming—that you're sure to slip on. She telegraphed a look to Manny. BE CAREFUL. He raised an eyebrow as if to say, "Don't worry, girl. I got this."

"Well, Mrs. M."

"Oh, please, call me Rose. After all, you are a close friend of my daughter's, aren't you?"

"Oh yeah---well, Ruthie and I got real close on the trip. We have a lot in common." It was Ruthie's mother's turn to raise an eyebrow.

Manny went on.

"Well, I live in New Jersey, and I work with a Puerto Rican organization there and…"

"Oh, I mean, what do you do as in "profession? Where did you go to school, by the way?"

Oh-oh, he's stepping in the quicksand now, Ruthie thought.

Manny looked confused at first, then explained that he had graduated

from high school and now worked as a shipping clerk at a Venetian blind factory.

Her mother swished her glass and raised it, ice clinking, to her lips. She turned her body away from Manny as if to say this conversation is over.

She hasn't even asked me about Sasha, Ruthie thought. How is she? Where is she? Typical. But for once, Ruthie was grateful for her mother's lack of interest. She didn't want to have to explain.

"Hey, you two. Are you hungry?" Her father poked his head into the room, breaking the uncomfortable silence. "I can rustle up some sandwiches. And I made pickles last week. Ruthie loves my homemade pickles," he said, grinning at Manny.

"Thanks, Dad. That would be great. Let me help you." Ruthie jumped up before her father could say no and followed him into the kitchen. Manny would have to navigate the slippery slope of her mother's interrogation on his own. She needed to talk to her father.

Ruthie found her father in the kitchen, with sandwich fixings already spread out on the Formica countertop—Levy's rye bread, soft and fragrant, roast beef slices, pink and moist, a jar of Gulden's mustard, and a plate of his homemade half-sours, cold and crisp. He had donned one of her mother's flowered aprons and looked slightly ridiculous. Ruthie came up behind him and hugged him.

"Hey, Ruthie-bear. What was that for?" "Just cause I love you, Dad."

"And I love you too, Ruthie. Now tell me—how are you? How's it going with you?"

Her father glanced through the open doorway to the sunroom, where her mother and Manny were sitting, as if he, too, expected her mom to be listening to their conversation.

Ruthie lowered her voice. "I'm fine, Dad. It's just… well, something's happened, and I need your help."

Her father put down the knife he had been using to spread the mustard and opened his arms to her. Ruthie let him hold her, let the sharp smell of mustard and pickles that he carried waft over her. He stroked her hair. She closed her eyes.

She let her father lead her to the small breakfast nook, the formica table where she had hurried through her school-day breakfasts and wriggled through her after-school homework.

"Tell me, Ruthie. Tell your dad what's happened."

The tears started before she could do anything to stop them. Her father's hand rested lightly on her shoulder, then withdrew as they both heard her mother's voice from the other room.

"Hey, you two. What's going on in there? Manny and I are waiting for our sandwiches." It was that sixth sense her mother had—she always knew somehow when she was being left out.

"We're fine, dear. Sandwiches will be out in a minute."

Stay here—her father mouthed the words silently, put the sandwiches on a plate, grabbed a few napkins and headed for the sunroom. "Where's Ruthie? What's going on? I know you two are up to something, Max?"

"We're just having a little father-daughter chat, dear—nothing to worry about. Enjoy your sandwich, Manny—and let me know how you like those pickles. You can take a jar home if you want."

Ruthie lay her head down on the cool table and breathed into her tears.

She just had to tell him. There was no way around it. She felt her father's hand on her shoulder again and mumbled into her arms, crossed under her head on the table.

"Sasha's gone. With Carl. I don't know where they are."

Her father sat on the bench beside her. He waited. She went on.

"I called as soon as we got back," Ruthie said, then told her father that Carl had taken Sasha away weeks earlier, and nobody knew where they had gone. She could hear her father breathing quietly beside her. Say something, please say something, she thought. She braced herself for his words. Would he understand? "Don't say anything to your mother," he said. "Let me handle her. What do you need, Ruthie? How can I help?"

The back door slammed before Ruthie could answer, and Marty strode into the room, slung his black leather jacket on a chair, and enveloped Ruthie in a bone-crunching hug.

"Hey sis," he said. "What brings you to the castle?" He pulled back and looked at her. "And where's my favorite niece?"

Her little brother Marty was already 5 inches taller than she was and seemed to have grown another couple of inches since the last time she'd seen him. His sandy-colored hair was slicked back in a ridiculous pompadour, and he wore his customary outfit: a white T-shirt and jeans, with well-worn construction boots. Ruthie called it his 'James Dean' look—all he was missing was the motorcycle.

"I'm heading out to California to pick her up from Carl," Ruthie said. "Tomorrow."

"Road trip," Marty crowed. "Cool—I can help drive. I can be ready in an hour."

"You planning to take some time away from the job you don't have, Marty?

Is that what you have in mind?" Her father's voice had gone cold and hard. Ruthie broke in before this familiar argument could pick up steam.

"No road trip this time, Marty," she said. "I need to get there fast. I have to fly."

She looked in her father's direction—hoping he would get the message. He nodded in response. Ruthie breathed. There. That was done.

Her mother appeared in the doorway. "Oh, Marty," she said. "You're home. Hang up your jacket, then come meet Ruthie's new friend, Manny. He's such an interesting young man."

Ruthie winced at the familiar judgmental tone in her mother's voice. Poor Manny. She had left him alone with her too long.

"Let's all sit in the living room and continue our chat," her mother said.

"Max, will you fix the drinks, dear. And Marty, wash that ridiculous grease out of your hair."

Ruthie followed her mother to the long, narrow room that had seen very little living during her years in this house. Thick gold carpet, off-white walls with paintings carefully arranged, two stiff upholstered armchairs, and a long, low gold silk sofa that Ruthie was afraid to sit on lest she spill something. A colonial white brick fireplace where they'd never lit a fire and a baby grand piano under the windows where she had taken piano lessons when she was too young to refuse. The only use it got now, besides being a prop in the formal setting her mother had so carefully created, was when her father sat down to play the first few bars of Fur Elise—the only part he could still remember of a piano piece learned long ago.

Ruthie pointed Manny to one of the armchairs and sat in the other. He flashed her mother a big grin as she sat across from him on the sofa.

"So, Mrs. M, Rose. Please tell me more about your work at the hospital. The patients must love you."

Leave it to Manny, Ruthie thought, to find a way to her mother's heart.

"Oh, the drinks. Ruthie, help your father, please."

Ruthie jumped up, glad to have a reason to leave her mother's gaze, and found her father in the kitchen loading a tray with pickles, olives, cheese, and crackers.

"Don't worry, dear. I know what you need. We'll talk more later and call to reserve your flight. Will Manny be going with you?"

"Max, where are those drinks? What's taking so long in there?" her mother called.

It was dark by the time Ruthie freed herself from the chat her mother always insisted on whenever she came home—the chat that, for Ruthie, felt like the Inquisition and kept her on her toes, trying to invent new ways to avoid revealing any real information or feelings.

Manny followed her up the stairs to what had been her bedroom—now converted to a guest room. The pastel bows on the wallpaper she had begged to change were finally painted over in a robin's egg blue—the color she had picked out but never been allowed to paint.

She sat on the white eyelet bedspread and patted the place next to her for Manny to sit. Her father had deposited her bag in this room but had put Manny's next door in Marty's room. Manny looked at her. "Did they like him? Carl, I mean?"

"Not really," Ruthie said. "Even though his parents were rich, and he was Jewish. He was too quiet for my mother, and my dad didn't understand why he would waste his education being an auto mechanic. I think they like you better, actually."

Manny grinned, slid off the bed, and onto one knee in front of Ruthie. "Oh, Ruthie. Will you marry me? Can I ask your mother for your hand in marriage?" Ruthie pushed him away, and he tumbled onto the carpet. She fell next to him, giggling uncontrollably until tears ran down her cheeks.

"What's going on in here?" It was Marty, looking more like the little brother she remembered, his hair grease-free and tousled. His ears stuck out from his head, giving him the look of a clown. Ruthie remembered when he had tied a bandana around his head while he slept, hoping it would make his ears lie flat. She had been so relieved when the military draft ended at the beginning of the month. And she didn't have to worry about Marty being forced to fight in Vietnam.

She pulled him down to the floor next to her—all 6 feet of him—and snuggled her head against his chest—no longer that of a little boy.

"Oh, Marty," she sighed. "I'm so glad to see you."

"What's up with you, Ruthie? I know something's wrong. You're hiding something from Mom. I can tell."

Ruthie sat up and then hoisted herself back on the bed. Marty and Manny stretched out before her like knights awaiting orders from their Queen. She was lucky to have them both in her life.

"Sasha's gone, Mart," she said. "Carl's taken her somewhere, and I don't know why or where. I have to go find them." Then she added quickly, "Don't tell Mom."

"Don't tell Mom what, may I ask. Are you two keeping things from me again?" Her mother stood in the doorway, a drink in one hand, a book in the other.

"You know the rules. No secrets. Well, I'm going to lie down before dinner. We'll talk later." She moved off to the large main bedroom she shared with Ruthie's Dad—the bedroom she and Marty were not allowed to enter unless invited.

"Shit," Ruthie said after her mother had gone. "Shit."

"Don't worry, Ru," Marty said. "She'll forget all about it after a couple more drinks."

"I dunno. She's got those x-ray eyes that bore right into you and read your thoughts."

Manny raised himself from the carpet and bugged his eyes out, making gurgling monster noises.

"I see you, Ruth Ann. You can't hide from me. I can see into your brain." Manny stalked Ruthie around the small room.

"Hey, I like this guy," Marty said. "You should marry him."

Ruthie kicked Marty and Manny out of the room so she could change for dinner. She pulled a brightly embroidered peasant blouse she had bought in Mexico from her backpack. She and Carl and his brother had driven down the coast into Baja and camped on whatever beach struck their fancy for a couple of weeks. She had bought the blouse from a young girl with shiny black hair in ribboned braids who spread her wares on a woven blanket under the shade of a royal palm.

This blouse had caught her eye because—rather than flowers—it was adorned with yellow-and-black monarch butterflies. She had not seen one like it since. A long black rayon skirt and a multicolored woven belt completed the look. She left her hair down and wavy.

Ruthie swirled around in front of the mirror on the back of the closet door. She liked the way she looked. Her mother would hate it.

Whoeee! Manny let out a long wolf whistle at the door. "Compañera Ruthie. Qué bella."

He had changed into a Cuban guayabera shirt and khaki slacks, taming his wild Afro with a brush.

"Hey, what's this? Who's into needlework? It looks like something my Abuelita would make." Manny was standing in front of the only artifact of Ruthie's occupation of this room—a framed nursery rhyme she had embroidered at summer camp when she was 10, the stitches clumsy and thick. She remembered how hard it had been to push the fat needle through the dense fabric. Why had her mother left it up? Manny began to read aloud in a sing-song voice.

"Monday's child is fair of face, Tuesday's child is full of grace, Wednesday's child is full of woe

Thursday's child has far to go…

"Stop, Manny, c'mon…" And with those few words, the tears began again. Ruthie tried to muffle the sound with her arm.

"Hey—what? Tell me…" Manny said. "I didn't know this would upset you."

"It's just, it was something private between Sasha and me. We were… are… both Thursday girls—born on Thursdays — and we used to tease each other about how tired we were because we always had so far to go. Just silly." Ruthie wiped her nose and flicked her hair back over her shoulder.

"C'mon, let's go down and get this over with," Ruthie said, taking his arm. "Let the games begin."

"Ok, Thursday's child. I've got cha."

The table was set with her mother's best china—a delicate blue and white patterned set that her father had brought back from England after the war. A blue ceramic casserole dish sat on a trivet in the middle of her grandmother's lace tablecloth, and the delicious fragrance of her mother's brisket made Ruthie realize how hungry she was.

They took their seats around the table on the straight-backed Hitchcock chairs that Ruthie remembered well from childhood family dinners at this table. Marty thundered down the stairs and flopped into a chair opposite Ruthie.

"Martin," her mother hissed. "Watch your manners."

"Sorry, my liege," Marty said, bowing to her mother. Ruthie envied him his ability to let their mother's prying, controlling ways just roll off his back. But he was the boy, the pride of a Jewish family—and if not exactly a golden boy now, he had that potential. Since he came into his own as an irresistible, tow-headed toddler, Ruthie had always felt like the afterthought. In the photo albums her father put together, complete with labels and balloons with funny comments—she was struck by how she was often captured looking off to the side, not at the camera, with a sad, pensive look on her face.

"What kind of an outfit is that, Ruth Ann?" her mother said. "Are you going through a Mexican phase now? Are we done with torn jeans and tie-dyed shirts?"

Her mother had donned a flowing purple blouse and black slacks, which accentuated her olive complexion and steel-gray hair.

Ruthie's mother dressed like a sophisticated artistic type, never a suburban Mom—but she had always tried to get Ruthie into Fair Isle sweaters, white blouses with Peter Pan collars, and pleated wool skirts. What was that about?

Ruthie ignored her comment and responded to her father's invitation to "dig in before it gets cold" by serving herself a large spoonful of brisket, roast potatoes, and carrots, and then passing the spoon to Manny.

"It's not my best," Ruthie's mother said, with a slightly flirtatious smile in Manny's direction.

"Looks pretty good to me," he said, taking up his fork. "It's delicious."

"That's a family code," Ruthie said, "for the women in my family. My grandmother always said it whenever she served us anything, even her chocolate babka, which was to die for. It seems we are never doing our best—or maybe we're saving it for someone else. I've always wondered about that."

"Ruth Ann." Her mother's sharp gaze traveled down the table, and Ruthie shut her mouth.

Flight

They left at the crack of dawn. Marty was still asleep, his long limbs dangling off the end of his childhood bed. Ruthie tousled his hair and followed Manny down the stairs. Her mother was waiting at the bottom, wearing an elegant red-and-purple-painted Japanese silk kimono, her hair brushed, and a touch of lipstick adding color to her face. Her arms were folded across her chest, and she was frowning.

"I don't see why you can't stay another day," her mother said.

"I'll be back for a longer visit after I see Sasha, Mom. She's waiting for me. I gotta go pick her up."

Her mother sighed, disappointed in her again. "You know, Ruth Ann, I…" "All righty-everyone ready. Let's get going. We've got a plane to catch," her

father said, and then caught himself. "I mean a bus; we've got a bus to catch." Manny bent over her mother's hand in a mock kiss.

"It's been a pleasure, Mrs. M. So glad to finally meet you after hearing so much about you."

Ruthie grabbed his arm and pulled him toward their Ford Country Squire station wagon, idling in the driveway with the back open, waiting for their bags.

"Bye, Ma. Gotta go. Talk soon."

Her father drove down Albany Avenue to the bus station. The streets were empty as they passed the stately buildings that housed the insurance companies that gave Hartford its name as Insurance Capital of the World.

"Chickin in the Basket," Ruthie cried, pointing out the small restaurant with a red plastic basket overflowing with fried chicken on its roof. "I can't believe it's still here. Every Friday night when we were kids, right, Dad?"

Ruthie's father maneuvered the car into a parking spot in front of the bus station. The sun was coming up, turning the grimy façade of the old building pink and warming their backs.

"You take care now, Ruthie girl. And call me if you need me, you hear." Manny said, singing a few bars of a song they both loved

You just call out my name

And you know, wherever I am, I'll come running You've got a friend

He crushed Ruthie in a bear hug, then pushed her back to look at her full-on. "You're gonna be O.K., girl. You'll find Sasha waiting for you there. I got a good feeling about this."

"Oh, Manny, I love you so much," Ruthie said, pulling back from his gaze and turning toward the car. "I'll call you when I get there. You go take New Jersey by storm and show them what a real revolutionary looks like."

Manny picked up his duffel and walked into the station, throwing a kiss as he went.

Ruthie slid in next to her father on the slippery plastic-covered seats of the wagon.

"Remember when Marty and me used to sit in the way back and shoot our cap pistols at all the cars behind us?" she said, looking at her dad as he pulled the car carefully out of the parking spot and pointed it in the direction of the highway.

"How could I forget?" he said. "No matter how much I yelled at you to put those guns away..." His voice trailed off.

"You know, Ruthie, your mother and I had our worries about this trip of yours."

"I know, Dad, I know. But not now, please..."

How could Ruthie not have been aware of their disapproval? It was written in invisible ink between the lines and in the margins of every letter they wrote to her, and it weighed down the unspoken words at the end of every phone call.

She looked out the window at the sun coming up over the river that snaked its way alongside the highway and remembered when they had visited the small farms in this area to buy fresh corn and giant watermelons in the summer. Now, a network of intersecting roadways connected Hartford with

Bradley Airport just over the Massachusetts line.

She had thought about whether it was a good idea to be so long away from Sasha. It's not like she hadn't thought about it at all. But Carl had seemed so happy

---

to have her with him—she had thought it would be good for all of them, she really had. Sasha would have time with her dad. Carl would get to be a real Dad again for a while, and Ruthie, well Ruthie would get to be somebody new, doing something exciting for a change. Was it so wrong to have wanted that?

On the sidewalk in front of the terminal, her father put his hand on Ruthie's arm.

"One thing I have to say, Ruthie…" her father began.

Ruthie's father got that look on his face—what she and Marty called his "lawyer look" and looked at his watch.

"Yeah, not now, Dad. I don't have time for a serious conversation. Gotta catch a plane."

"Let me just say this, Ruthie. I know you always give Carl the benefit of the doubt, but if he has, in fact, taken Sasha away and not told anyone where they went, that could be serious."

"I know it could be serious," Ruthie said, eyeing the crowd moving toward the airport lobby and wanting to join them. "Why do you think I'm going to San Francisco?"

"What I mean is," her father's voice took on the deep gravel they called his "courtroom voice. "You may have to go to the authorities—and I know that is something you don't want to do, Ruthie, but you may have to report this to the police."

Ruthie sighed. Sometimes she felt as if she lived in a completely different world from her parents. Well, really, she did.

"And say what, Dad? 'Hi, I just got back from an illegal trip to Cuba with a bunch of Black Panthers—helping the revolution there—and, oh by the way, can you please find my daughter who I left for 3 months.'" All the fear that had been building in her since she learned that Carl had left the ranch with Sasha came tumbling out in those words, and behind them, the tears.

"I can't do that, Dad. I can't trust them to help me. They'll probably put me in jail and throw away the key." She glanced again at the revolving door and the line forming just inside it.

"And right now, I've got to get on that plane."

"Okay, Ruthie. You go and get your plane. But this is not the end of this conversation. We'll talk about it again after you see what's going on in San Francisco." And the lawyer look left her father's face, replaced by a tender smile and a big hug.

"Love you, Ruthie-bear. Go find my granddaughter—and call when you get there. And remember, your mother and I love you." Ruthie lifted an eyebrow.

"Look, I know she can be difficult, but we both love you. Don't try to do this alone."

"Thanks, Dad. For everything. I mean it. I love you too."

She picked up her duffel and walked quickly through the revolving doors, throwing a wave over her shoulder. She didn't wait to watch her father pull away from the curb. From this point on, she needed to keep moving forward.

Ruthie arrived at the gate just as the plane was boarding. She found her window seat (thank you, Dad), stashed her duffel in the overhead compartment, and settled in, drawing her multi-colored woven shawl around her against the chilly air of the plane. Window seat, non-stop flight—and so far, no one in the seat next to her. She had hit the jackpot.

Ruthie closed her eyes as the plane took off. She could count on one hand the number of times she had flown—starting at 18 with her first trip home from college—and she still felt butterflies in her stomach on take-offs and landings. The plane evened out, and she opened her eyes to cotton-candy clouds floating by in a deep blue sky. Below the tobacco fields of the Connecticut valley, white gauzy tents faded to green and brown squares as the plane gained altitude.

The flight to Cuba had been Ruthie's first experience on a propjet. They had piled into a fleet of small Russian-made planes in Mexico City, walking proudly up the rickety stairs, and Ruthie had left her fear behind. Had she thought of Sasha in that moment—as the engines roared and the propellers spun? Probably not, she thought with a twinge of guilt—a reaction of her body that was becoming as familiar as blinking. They had all been chattering away like excited school kids on a field trip—which in a way they were.

She hadn't noticed Manny at first—probably wouldn't have paid him much attention if she had. She had her eye on David—thin, wiry, dapper in a tweed cap, a former Young Lord from Chicago—a bit of the bad boy look she had always been attracted to. Way out of her league, probably, but you never knew.

"Something to drink?" the stewardess interrupted her memories.

"A Coke, please," Ruthie said, eyeing her crisp uniform. She had once thought being a stewardess would be cool—flying all around the world. She had let go of that dream, along with many others that had disappeared as her real life unfolded.

Ruthie felt the pop in her ears before she heard the announcement that they were preparing for landing—seats in the upright position, trays up and locked in place. She pushed her backpack under the seat in front of her.

How different she felt from her last landing—just three months earlier. Then she had been excited. The plane was filled with happy chatter. The announcement welcomed them to the Primer Territorio Libre de America Latina—the first free territory of Latin America. The wheels touched down on a small runway ringed by palm trees. The propellers slowed, then stopped, and they were in Cuba.

Now she felt only uncertainty mixed with dread. She hadn't made more than a vague plan—stay somewhere, maybe Annie and Will's, —contact Carl's parents and brother for any possible news—then head for the ranch to see what she could find out.

Maybe this had all been a misunderstanding. Maybe they had told Ken they were going away for a few weeks, and he had forgotten. Maybe they were back.

Ruthie grabbed her bags and headed into the chilly terminal. She needed a bathroom first, then a phone.

The last time she had been in an airport was in Havana, where the old terminal, named for Jose Marti, the father of Cuban independence, was as hot and sticky as the tarmac. A crowd waited beyond the luggage carousels, holding flowers and signs; tearful reunions were happening all around them.

"Need help with that?" A broad-shouldered, soft-bellied guy in a safari vest and a broad-brimmed canvas hat had pulled up beside her. "I'm Manny," he said. "From Puerto Rico by way of Hoboken, N.J.—and he stuck out a large, callused hand in her direction.

"Really?" Ruthie said. "Hoboken is real? I thought it was a place my father invented. He always used to say—tell me the story, but don't go by way of Hoboken."

They had shared their first laugh and walked together in the hot afternoon sun to the yellow school bus that would take them to their camp.

Now Ruthie was alone, and for a moment she wished she had accepted Manny's offer to come with her. No, this was better, come what may. She searched her pockets for change and made her way to one of the payphone kiosks scattered across the polished floors. All around her, luggage was being collected, reunions were happening, and people were walking off together, in couples, in family groups, tourists following their guide, who walked ahead with a fluorescent orange flag held high on a stick. Only a few business types, armored in suits, briefcases swinging at their sides, hurried alone to waiting cabs "Annie?" Ruthie said, so happy to hear the warm, deep tones of her friend's voice.

"Ruthie, is that you? You're back? Where are you?"

"I'm at the airport, Annie. I'm in San Francisco. I'm wondering if I can stay with you guys for a few days, if there's room. Something's happened. I'll tell you about it when I see you. I just need a place to stay for a few days."

"Of course, you can," Annie said. "Do you need Will to come pick you up? He's at the school. I can call him."

"No. No. Don't bother him. I have money for a cab." She fingered the $50 her father had slipped into her pocket as they said good-bye. "See you soon," she said.

"Can't wait," Annie said. "And Ruthie—don't worry. Whatever it is, we'll handle it."

This is what Ruthie remembered and loved about Annie, the matriarch of their small commune. She took a deep breath, gathered her things, and made her way through the airport to find a cab.

Homecoming

As Ruthie's cab moved through the landscape of little houses lined up like dominos over the brown rolling hills of South San Francisco, she hummed a tune to herself—the song about little boxes made of ticky-tacky that all look the same. Well, no one could accuse me of living in a little box, Ruthie thought. I left that behind long ago.

The cab dropped her off her off right in front of Mission Dolores Park. A large green space in this hilly neighborhood of small, colorful wooden houses, the park itself was built around a hill. It had been several years since Ruthie had climbed to the top, and she decided to do so now. The fresh air would do her good after the long flight. She braced her body against the stiff crosswinds that always blew strongly in this spot. It was great for flying kites, and Frisbees flew far beyond their intended target.

The last time she had climbed this hill, she had been pulling a reluctant Sasha behind her—her toddler's legs no match for the hill and the wind.

"Uppa, Mama, uppa," Sasha had whined, holding her arms up to be carried. Ruthie had insisted that she walk all the way up herself, 'like a big girl, and when they got to the top, they both threw their arms wide in triumph and then fell to the ground, giggling and wheezing with the effort of the climb.

Ruthie's heavy backpack slowed her down, but it felt good to climb. She savored the wind in her hair, the scent of eucalyptus from a small grove near the top, and the bright, colorful squares on the street below. Sasha was still pulling at her, if only in her mind, but together they would reach the top. That long-ago day, with little Sasha, they had straightened their bodies like logs and rolled all the way back down the hill—wobble-walking and dizzy at the bottom.

Now Ruthie wove her way down on two legs—between picnicking families spread out on patterned Indian bedspreads and teenagers huddling together, trying to look cool and light their cigarettes in the wind. This park, and the tall Victorian house across the street, felt like home—or as much like home as any place these days.

Ruthie sat on a bench at the bottom of the park to catch her breath, looking straight across at the Family Place. It anchored the corner in this changing neighborhood, weathered but strong, bright colors of red and yellow highlighting its gingerbread moldings and the crown at the top. Ruthie's eyes were drawn upward to the small dormer windows just under the eaves that had sheltered her and brought light into her life when she lived there with Carl and Sasha.

A streetcar lumbered by, rattling the bench she sat on, and she remembered how the passing of the streetcars on Dolores Street had gently rocked the Chinese laundry basket hung from the attic beams that had served as Sasha's first bed, soothing her back to sleep.

She noticed that the front door had been freshly painted, and it looked like Annie had made some changes in the narrow garden that surrounded the house. She remembered the first time she had eaten a salad tossed from that garden and bit into a bright orange nasturtium—a flower—in the salad. So many new discoveries and delights in that first year of Sasha's life.

"Ruthie. Ruthie, is that you?"

A tall, slender woman with short, cropped pale blonde hair, skin tan and as weathered as the house, stood on the small front porch waving to her—a garden trowel in her hand.

"Ruthie. What are you doing? C'mon over."

Ruthie shook herself out of her daydream. The high school across from the park on Mission Street was letting out for lunch, and the street was crowded with clumps of teenagers laughing, shouting to one another, and heading for the park.

Ruthie suddenly felt nervous and shy to see Annie after all that had happened. Annie was so strong, so unwavering in her convictions, so rooted in her family—her husband Will, a musician and teacher, and her kids, always at the center of a bright, noisy gang at school. She knew how to make things grow in the ground, how to mix flowers into a salad. Annie stood on the porch, a welcoming smile, and Ruthie could see it all the way across the street.

Ruthie wove her way through the traffic on Dolores St., stepping up her pace as a big green streetcar followed the track down the hill. She opened the small wrought iron gate of the low fence that surrounded the house and stepped inside.

Annie hurtled down the stairs and wrapped her arms around her—the trowel sending showers of loose dirt down Ruthie's back. She smelled of warm, moist earth, she smelled of the savory stew that was probably right now bubbling on the stove, she smelled of sunlight and sweat—and all of it felt like love.

Annie pulled back and looked at her—her blue eyes twinkling and full of gentle questions.

"Oh, Annie," Ruthie said, and the tears came tumbling. "I'm so glad to see you. I don't know what to do next. What can I do?"

"Well, for starters, you can come in, have a bowl of stew, and tell me all about it," Annie said, putting one arm around her shoulders and guiding her through the narrow doorway.

"Watch the shoes," Annie said. "You remember." And Ruthie did remember. She remembered it all—the shoes tumbled together in the small foyer, the mishmash of coats hanging on pegs in the hallway, the colorful finger paintings Scotch-taped to the faded wallpaper, the fragrant smells wafting from whatever was cooking in the kitchen (and always, it seemed, something was cooking), the worn wooden staircase lined with books and piles of clean clothes waiting to be carried up. She glanced up the stairs, wondering who now occupied the top bedroom.

"Sit down. Get comfortable. You're home now," Annie said, guiding Ruthie to the overstuffed armchair by the large bay window and gently pushing her down.

"Home?" Ruthie said, looking up at her—and the tears started again.

The Family Place

After devouring a bowl of Annie's hearty stew, Ruthie pushed back from the table. "Can we talk a bit later?" she said as Annie piled their dishes into the big farmhouse sink in the well-worn kitchen. "I'd like to take a look at our old room."

"Sure, go ahead. I'll fix us some tea, and we can talk whenever you want. The kids won't be home for a while yet.

Ruthie climbed the narrow stairs to the top of the house and stepped into the wood-paneled room. When it had been her room, the room she and Carl and then Sasha lived in, it had felt like a nest, snug and warm, high above the clatter of the street below. She had felt safe here—to be herself, to live her life and nourish Sasha's.

Now the room was full of old furniture and boxes—mattresses leaning against one sloping wall, discarded toys scattered across the floor.

"We're using it as storage now," Annie said, coming up behind her. "No one moved in after you and Carl left."

Ruthie moved to an old chair pushed under the small window in one corner and sat on the edge of the seat.

"It must be hard for you, huh?" Annie said from the doorway. "So many memories here."

"Oh yeah, it's hard. Sasha's life began here," Ruthie said. "And so did the lies."

"Well, I'll leave you for a bit. Call if you need anything." Annie's steps echoed on the creaking stairs as Ruthie fought against the memories that came bubbling up when she thought about her time in this room. She didn't want to soften toward Carl—she would need a kind of firm resolve that was not natural for her if he was trying to take Sasha away from her. But soon she was lost in images of that summer—the summer before Sasha—the Summer of Love.

They had moved into this house with several other families from the Children's Place, the alternative school where Ruthie had found a job teaching reading and drama. They christened it the Family Place, and though it was worn and weary looking on the outside—it had survived the earthquake and fire of 1906—inside it was a riot of primary colors—from the oranges, reds and yellows of the walls to the multi-colored carpet formed of discarded samples they had pieced together themselves. Kids everywhere—they formed an intentional family. Annie, the matriarch, taught Ruthie to make hearty soups and rustic breads, parenting her own two kids with a steady, gentle hand.

No wonder the desire had grown in Ruthie to bring a child of her own into this loving family, into this wood-beamed room she and Carl shared at the tippy-top of the house, with its small windows looking out at the tops of the trees in the park.

Ruthie had ignored the growing distance between them, the petty arguments, and the long silences. A baby would bring them together. A baby would strengthen their love.

At first, it seemed she was right. She remembered Sasha's birth, attened to by a midwife with Annie gently massaging her shoulders and whispering in her ear.

"Ruthie, Ruthie, that's my girl. Focus on your breath. You're doing great. Okay, now push."

And Carl looking jumpy at the end of the bed until finally she saw the dark crown of her baby's head and he shouted "It's a girl, Ruthie. We have a baby girl."

They had planned the home birth for months—determined to avoid the sterile hospital environment—and Ruthie had never felt closer to him than at that moment in their attic nest—the water bed lined with colorful towels ready to catch their baby, Annie's quiet presence like a warm blanket over her laboring body, the straw laundry basket they had found in Chinatown swaying gently on its hook, suspended, waiting for Sasha.

Carl was often passive and withdrawn, which drove Ruthie crazy, but when he was engaged, he was the kind of man who held nothing back—and that's how he had been with Sasha in those first months—lying with one elbow crooked under his head, gazing at them as Ruthie nursed in the middle of the night, walking the floors with her when she fussed, bundling her into her baby carrier and walking through the park, proudly showing off his baby girl.

Ruthie had been tired all the time—maybe depressed, she realized years later—and had welcomed his involvement, his attention, and enthusiasm.

But then there had been a shift. It came on slowly, so slowly she didn't notice at first—little barbed remarks lobbed in her direction, faults uncovered, flaws exposed, until she had felt raw, on edge around him.

And then they began to argue—a whispered back-and-forth in the night, a voice raised, then hushed as the baby stirred. And the barbs became sharper—like heat-seeking missiles zeroing in on her most vulnerable, tender spots, going in for the kill.

Ruthie still didn't fully understand what had happened to them or why things had spiraled so fast. Maybe they were just too young and inexperienced to get past the stress parenting brought to their relationship—or too cavalier about the consequences to really work at it.

Ruthie drew in her breath at the memory of the weekend when it all finally fell apart. Sasha, a toddler—round-faced, chubby-cheeked, curly-haired. Carl spending longer hours at the garage, barely talking to her when he was home. And Ruthie trying to figure a way out.

The long, steady destruction of the love between Carl and Ruthie had started with one lie spoken aloud in this room, with their baby asleep beside them. A lie whispered in the night to excuse an absence. Ruthie had not known it was a lie at first. She had accepted it as an explanation. It was not until the lies piled up like the crumpled tissues next to their bed of tears that she thought back to that first lie and understood when it had all started.

"How could I have trusted him with Sasha? What was I thinking?" Ruthie shook her head, and Annie appeared out of nowhere, pulled her close, and stroked her hair.

"You couldn't have known, Ruthie. No way you could have known. He cheated on you, but he loved Sasha. Everyone knew that."

They stayed like that for a while, still and close in the late afternoon light, with glimmering specks of dust floating around their heads. Annie drew away first, looking at her watch and untying the apron from her waist.

"Sorry, kiddo. Gotta go wait on the corner for the kids. Our friend Al's dropping them off on his way home. C'mon down, and you can help get dinner started."

Halfway down the stairs, Ruthie heard the creak of the loose stair—the one that had announced Carl's arrival in the early morning hours when the lies began. "Ruthie, Ruthie…it's Ruthie." Two human cannonballs ricocheted across the dining room and almost knocked Ruthie off her feet. They wrapped skinny arms around her knees and held on tight.

"Sage, Oliver. Let Ruthie breathe," Annie gently scolded, gently removing their arms and nudging them over to the large purple velvet sofa facing the mantel in the front parlor. "Now, tell Ruthie all about your day at school while I fix a snack."

"We went to Muir Beach, and I found…" Oliver pulled a sand-encrusted starfish from one pocket and plunked it down on the rainbow-striped wire cable spool that served as a coffee table.

"No, me, me…I get to go first," Sage insisted in the way only younger sisters can, wedging her scrawny body under Ruthie's arm and opening her grimy fist to reveal a perfectly smooth piece of aqua colored sea glass.

"Wow, what treasures you have. And how big you both are." Ruthie said, shaking sand from her skirt.

"But where is Shasha?" Sage peeked around the sofa, as if she might find Sasha hiding there. She had been only three years old when Ruthie and Sasha left for Colorado, and "Shasha" was her approximation of Sasha's name. Soon, everyone started calling her that, and it became her Children's Place nickname.

"Sagie, Ollie…come sit in the kitchen and have your snack," Annie said, rescuing Ruthie from the need to answer that question. "Ruthie, would you like a cup of peppermint tea or something. I have some great oatmeal cookies."

"You know what," Ruthie said, stretching and yawning. "I think I'll take a short nap and maybe make a few calls before dinner if that's okay."

"Of course," Annie said. "You must be tired after all that travel. The blue box is still connected to the phone upstairs if you need to make a long- distance call." Ruthie gave her a quizzical look. "You remember the blue box, don't you? There are instructions by the phone. Just dial the number on the box using the phone, wait for the ring tone, and then dial the number you are calling with the buttons on the box. You'll remember it when you see it, I think. Didn't you have one in Colorado?"

"Nah," Ruthie said. "We had to be careful there about anything illegal. The military police and the CID were keeping a close eye on us. We couldn't even smoke weed in the house—had to go out into the woods."

"Wow, I want to hear all about it when we have a chance," Annie said. "And Cuba.. Now go and get some rest. Holler if you have any trouble with the phone."

Ruthie climbed the stairs to the second floor, where she had been installed in the small den that doubled as a guest room. A twin bed with a cheerful patchwork quilt laid across it invited her to lie down, but first she wanted to call the Ranch again. And maybe she would screw up her courage and get in touch with Carl's parents.

Ruthie examined the contraption attached to the squat black phone that sat on a small wooden desk next to the bed, and the memory of being taught how to use it emerged from where it had been hiding in some recess of her brain. It was Carl who had introduced this device to the House. It would save them so much money, he had said, as they gathered to practice punching in the tones that allowed them to bypass the dialing process. And besides, we don't want to give our money to Pacific Bell.

So much of their lives in those years had been about creating alternatives—an alternative school for their kids, this communal house as an alternative to living in their own family units, and the People's Garage that Carl had started to help people fix their own cars. Ruthie had loved it at first— feeling like she was part of building something of value—but after a while she grew impatient, restless. There was a war going on, and young men Carl's age were being drafted, sent to Vietnam, and dying. There was poverty, and young mothers like her could barely feed their kids. And the kids at the high school across the street were just being prepared to be cannon fodder. She wanted to change things, not just escape them.

Ruthie settled into the wooden chair next to the phone and studied the Blue Box. She had to admit it was pretty ingenious—and she didn't really want to spend what little money she had on phone calls. She got out her address book, punched in the code, and then the number at the Ranch. Probably wouldn't be too long before she had it memorized.

She had only visited the Ranch once, to drop Sasha off before leaving for Cuba. It hadn't looked like anybody worked very hard there. But that's what Carl liked—a "laid back" lifestyle, living in the country off the land. The rest of the world could do whatever it wanted as far as he was concerned.

"Hel-lo, Rainbow Ranch. Hope you're having a great day." It was one of the hippie chicks Ruthie remembered from her visit–her breath all wispy and her voice curling up at the end of each sentence.

"Oh, hi, this is Ruthie, Sasha's mom. Is Ken around?"

"Oh, sorry, he took off for town about an hour ago. Won't be back for a while. This is Sylvie. Can I help you with somethin'?"

"Well, can you tell him I called, and I'm in San Francisco. I'll probably be heading up that way in a couple of days, but I'll call first before I do. Has anyone heard from Carl?"

"Not that I know of, Ruthie. I'll tell Ken you called, though."

Ruthie hung up the phone, trying to picture Sylvie in her mind, wondering if she had been keeping something from her.

"Ruthie," Annie hollered her name up the stairs and then rang the dinner bell—the same brass gong that Ruthie remembered from her time in the house.

"Dinner's ready."

"Be right down."

Ruthie splashed some cold water on her face in the little bathroom at the top of the stairs and raked her fingers through her unruly hair. She drew in a breath in anticipation of having to share her story with Will. He was a practical, down to earth kind of guy. Maybe he could make some sense out of it.

"Hey Ruthie. C'mere, girl." Will rose from his seat on the bench in the dining room and held his arms open wide. He tightened them around her as Ruthie stepped into his embrace. It felt good to be held. Safe. Will pushed her away gently and gave her what they had come to call one of his "Will looks" at

---

Family Place— loving, no-nonsense "you need to tell me something" looks that few could wriggle around. His deep brown eyes were like pools of wisdom in his nut-brown face, and Ruthie longed to just let it all pour out. But she was silent.

"Annie tells me you've got a big problem with Sash…" Will cut off his sentence abruptly as Annie flashed him a look across the table, and Oliver and Sage looked at her with questions in their eyes. "We'll talk after dinner," Will said quickly. "Now, dig in, everybody, while the food is still hot."

For a while, they were too occupied with passing heavy serving dishes around the long rectangular table to talk, and all that could be heard was the clinking of forks on ceramic plates as they devoured Annie's hearty beef stew, sopping up the sauce with big chunks of homemade sourdough.

"What's for dessert?" Oliver said.

"And why is Shasha a big problem?" piped up Sage.

After dinner, with the kids happily ensconced in the kitchen, bowls of Annie's apple crisp, crayons, and paper for drawing at hand, Ruthie told Will everything. They sat quietly together in the bay window's curve, sipping chamomile tea while Annie shuttled between them and the kids.

"Wow, Ruthie, who woulda thought," Will said. "I know Carl was a creep when you were splitting up, but I never would have thought he'd just up and leave like this without a word to you. Chances are, he'll be back soon, though. I don't figure him for the kind of guy to just disappear."

"Yeah," Ruthie said, "I guess," though with each day she was beginning to question her trust in Carl.

"Well, you know me and Annie are here for you, girl. Whatever you need. Always."

They sat in a comfortable silence for a while, listening to the squeals of laughter from the kitchen, and then Will unfolded his lanky body from the soft armchair in the window. He squeezed Ruthie's shoulder.

"Gotta do some prep for tomorrow," he said, yawning and stretching his long limbs and rubbing his hand over his close-cropped Afro. "It's Friday—you remember—talent show day. Why don't you come along. The kids would love to see you."

Will was the "headmaster" at Children's Place, which was patterned after Summerhill School in England–a school where the kids get to decide what and how they will learn, and the teachers are there to support their learning. The school was housed in a small warehouse in the Tenderloin District, San Francisco's Skid Row, and they often had to dodge down and out men sleeping it off on the sidewalk. It was a coop, so parents took turns teaching. Will was the only one to draw a modest salary and he and Annie and the kids managed to live on that and his disability pension from the U.S. Army—he had been wounded in Vietnam, purple heart and all.

Ruthie had worked at Children's Place pretty much full-time during her pregnancy–teaching reading with index cards from stories the kids made up themselves. After Sasha was born, they had rigged up a cozy corner for her bassinet, and the kids had taken turns rocking her to sleep and letting Ruthie know when she was awake and crying. Ruthie had imagined Sasha growing up in the school with her, and Carl just a few blocks away at the People's Garage. A secure and happy childhood. Even when she wasn't very happy with Carl, she tried hard for Sasha's sake.

But then…

"So, how about it? Will you help me out with the Talent Show?" Will's questions broke into her memory.

"Well, um, I-I guess so," she stammered. Will and Annie were being so kind. She should at least make an effort. "Sure. What time do I need to be ready?"

After they had planned for the morning, Ruthie said goodnight to Annie and Will and headed up to her room. Sage and Oliver were already tucked into their beds, their doors cracked open to let in a little light. Ruthie paused outside Sage's door and peeked inside. Sagie was curled up in a ball with her thumb in her mouth, clutching a worn pink bunny in one hand.

"Nite Nite. Sleep Tight. Don't Let the Bedbugs Bite," she whispered, and in her head, she heard Sasha's voice, "Nite nite, Mama."

House of Lies

Ruthie had been too tired to call Carl's parents and had gone to bed lulled by the sound of Sasha's voice in her head. She awoke with a headache, disoriented and anxious. Around 7 AM., Will poked his head in.

"Mornin', Ruthie. Hope you slept well. Breakfast is on the table. We should be leaving in about half an hour."

"Will, I think I better stick around here today. I'm not feeling so well, and I've got to make some phone calls. Hope that's OK?"

"Of course, sweetheart. Of course, it's okay. You can come another day next week. Any day you want," Will said. She heard his heavy footsteps moving quickly down the stairs, then lay her head back on the pillow.

She had to call Carl's parents, but what would she say?

The conversation with Carl's mother, Lottie, had been short and sweet. No, they hadn't heard from Carl for a couple of months now, but that wasn't unusual. No, they had no idea where he might be. They had a lovely visit with Sasha in May, when she first arrived in California. What a big girl! Why didn't Ruthie take the train down, have dinner with them, and spend the night? Then they could talk more, and Douglas would be home. He was off to a golf tournament for the day. The last thing Ruthie wanted to do was spend the night at Carl's parents' house, but she needed all the help she could get—and maybe they would offer some. She called to check the train schedule and decided to leave around 1 PM. She would get a cab at the station.

Annie was in the kitchen chopping vegetables when Ruthie finally got herself together to come downstairs.

"Hey, Ruthie. Will told me you are not feeling great today. Can I get you some tea?"

"Don't bother, Annie. I'll just fix myself a sandwich, and then I'm gonna head out. I called Carl's parents and Lottie insisted I come down for dinner and spend the night. I don't really want to spend that much time with them, but maybe they can help in some way."

"OK, hon. Just remember we'll be here no matter what."

"I know, Annie, and I'm so grateful." Ruthie moved to the counter and wrapped her arms around Annie's waist. "I don't know what I would do without you and Will right now."

The cab traversed the curvy roads from the train station in San Mateo to Carl's parents' home, slung low on the hills above the city, an unassuming silhouette that belied the elegance within and the wealth of its owners. The first time she visited, Lottie had shown her around proudly, pointing out all the Japanese-inspired furnishings and artwork. Her hobby was flower arranging and bonsai, and examples of her handiwork were scattered throughout the two wings (shit, this house has wings, Ruthie remembered thinking. You're not in Kansas anymore, Dorothy). Stunted trees shaped to the gardener's will. Now there's a metaphor. Carl had been lucky to get out alive.

After that first dinner, served by the maid and prepared by an unseen chef, Douglas and Lottie had disappeared. "Where'd they go?" Ruthie had asked.

"Oh, they're having an argument," Carl replied. "Their usual—about me, I suppose. They're not happy with my choices."

An argument? Their usual? Ruthie's mouth had fallen open, but she had no words. Arguments in her house had been loud and messy, moving from room to room, shouting, banging of doors, heard on the street even.

Ruthie had imagined Douglas and Lottie sitting erect on a Japanese couch in their vast bedroom, the embroidered fabric scratching the backs of their legs, whispering their disappointment with Carl through clenched teeth.

She had been seized by the sudden desire to shout at Carl—to show them what a real argument was like—like Jason Robards in one of her all-time favorite movies, A Thousand Clowns, when he stands alone on Park Avenue at dawn and shouts up to the silent windows above—All right, all you rich people. I want everyone out on the shuffleboard court in 5 minutes. She had wanted to do something outrageous, but she hadn't had the nerve back then, and she and

Carl had crept away like thieves in the morning.

Lottie and Douglas were in a corner of the large, airy living room, talking quietly, when Ruthie arrived. The room hadn't changed much since she had last visited with Carl—an open space with subtle lighting and Japanese accents that opened onto a beautifully manicured garden. Ruthie had been afraid to touch anything in the perfectly decorated house, and she still was.

Lottie and Douglas hadn't changed much either. Lottie was small and sprightly with ginger hair brushed back from a freckled face. Her eyes turned into almonds, and her forehead crinkled when she smiled, which was often. Ruthie had the feeling they could have been close if it wasn't for the cold distance between Carl and his father. Douglas was looking at her sternly over Lottie's shoulder, wearing his cashmere cardigan and striped shirt and tie even on this warm California Sunday afternoon.

What would they say? Would they help her?

They hadn't liked her from the first—sure that she was leading their son astray. Carl had been a straightlaced engineering student when they met. His parents were convinced that Ruthie had enticed him to drop out of college, seduced him into her wild, hippy ways. When she and Carl married and Sasha was born, they had softened a bit, charmed by their first grandchild. But when they separated after just a few years together, Carl went off the deep end— joined a cultish commune and refused to see his father. That they couldn't blame on her. Ruthie had shouldered the responsibility of raising Sasha on her own and had done a good job. By the time Carl came to his senses and quit the commune, his parents wanted nothing to do with him.

But Ruthie was desperate. She needed their help to find Carl and Sasha.

Did they know where he was?

"Would you like something to drink, dear?" Lottie asked, sitting on the chair opposite Ruthie.

"No, no thanks." Ruthie was afraid her hands would shake, spilling tea on the precious cream-colored Oriental carpet. "I'm good."

Douglas cleared his throat.

"Well, Ruthie," he began, getting up from the couch and moving to stand by the fireplace. Ruthie held her breath.

"We'd like to help you, really, we would, but we have no idea where Carl may have gone. You know, dear, he hasn't visited us at all for over a year. We met him in San Francisco for an afternoon to see Sasha when she first got here, but we haven't heard from him since. Carl has been a great disappointment to us."

Why had she come all the way down here, Ruthie thought. They would never help her. They didn't care about her, or even about their granddaughter, Sasha. She had been just another adornment to them—something pretty to show their friends—as long as she didn't run through the house or make too much noise in her play.

Douglas was speaking again. "I do hope we can keep this in the family, dear. No need to get the authorities involved. I'm sure it is all just a misunderstanding and will be resolved amicably."

Ruthie restrained an impulse to get up and shake him. Of course, that's what they would worry about. Appearances. A stain on their family's reputation. Didn't they know her at least well enough to know that she would never go to the police? She hadn't contested the divorce even though all she got was

$100 a month in child support despite Carl's trust fund. She had just returned from Cuba for Pete's sake—a communist island, off limits to Americans. She had broken the law by going there. She had been living with Sasha in a radical collective in a military town. She hadn't had what anyone would consider a "real job" in years—had even resorted to welfare for a while.

What would the police make of her leaving her daughter and going off to Cuba in the first place? Who would look like the "bad guy" here up against all Carl's family's wealth and status.

"No," Ruthie said in the tight voice that seemed to take over whenever she was in their presence. "No authorities. But I can't just do nothing." She counted in her mind. "It's been a month since anyone has heard from Carl. And we had a whole plan, an agreement. He was supposed to meet me in Cambridge, at my cousin Claudia's. Sasha and I are going to live there for a year."

Lottie put a hand over Ruthie's which was clenched in her lap. "They'll turn up soon, dear. I'm sure they will."

And with that, it seemed, the discussion was over. No offer of help, money, moral support—nothing but platitudes and worthless assurances. Ruthie was furious but it was too late to catch a train back to San Francisco. She would have to get through the night somehow.

Ruthie looked at the ornate gilded clock on the wall beside her bed. She felt like she had been tossing and turning all night, but it was only 3 AM. She would have to wait till at least 7 to catch a commuter train back for San Francisco but she couldn't stay here. It was a lie—this cushioned wannabee Japanese house, the fake polite smiles, the hushed conversations—all of it was a lie. She didn't belong here. She never had.

Ruthie opened the sliding door to her room and crept in her stockinged feet over the shiny bamboo floors to the kitchen. No creaking of loose boards in this house—everything was polished and in its place. She would make a cup of tea and read until dawn—then go to the train station and leave this cold house behind. There was nothing for her here.

Ruthie opened the cupboard doors in the gleaming kitchen, searching for a cup, a teabag, the sugar. Nothing was in a box or a bag—everything was repackaged in porcelain canisters with Japanese flower designs, and it took her a while to find everything she needed. Now where would a teapot be hiding? She jumped when she heard a voice behind her.

"Ruthie?"

She turned to find Lottie—an old, pale, tired-looking version of her bright day time self, standing at the grey stone island in the middle of the vast kitchen.

"What are you doing dear? It's the middle of the night?"

Lottie's voice was strained. Maybe she and Douglas had been having one of their usual arguments. It can't be easy being estranged from your oldest son who has disappeared with your only granddaughter. Even if you don't really care about them—or anything but this beautiful façade of a life you show to the world.

"Ruthie? Are you all right?"

"How can I be all right, Lottie? No, I'm not all right."

Ruthie felt a flush rising along the back of her neck, and she could hear her voice rising with each word. Calm down, the voice of reason in her head told her. But it was too late for that.

"My daughter, your granddaughter, has disappeared and your son has taken her. Do you think that makes me feel fucking all right?" Ruthie threw her hand out and swept the porcelain sugar container off the spotless countertop. It hit the hard tiles of the kitchen floor with a crack and then splintered into a thousand pieces. Sugar mixed with fragments of white china, jigsaw pieces of red and orange flowers spread across the floor at their feet. Lottie stood rooted in place, short, leaning, her bushy fading red hair standing up around the collar of her green silk robe.

She looks like one of her goddamned bonsai trees, Ruthie thought, and suppressed a giggle. There was a belly laugh waiting behind the giggle and it burbled up and out before she could stop it. She sank to the floor, sugar clinging to her socks, glass shards pricking through the legs of her thick jeans. She laughed and laughed until the laughter turned to hiccups, until water flowed from her eyes, until her shoulders shook with sobs.

She looked at Lottie, who was frozen in the midst of all this chaos. See this, Lottie, Ruthie thought. This is not a lie. This is the truth.

Sitting in the middle of Lottie's pristine kitchen, with sugar on her socks and bits of porcelain scattered around her, Ruthie felt something give way inside her. Her sobs slowly quieted to sniffles, then sighs. Her shoulders relaxed, and her back slumped against the cabinets behind her. It felt as if she had been locked in a closet, surrounded by dark woolen coats smelling of mothballs, and the door had opened a crack to let in light and air.

She didn't have to hide her pain anymore; she wouldn't. Lottie cleared her throat and began to speak in a nervous rush of words.

"Ruthie, I'm sorry. I had no idea. You poor darling. How you must be suffering."

Ruthie stood up, slowly shaking sugar and slivers of glass onto the floor.

Lottie's words landed in a hollow space in her chest, offering no real comfort. "I'll sweep up this mess if you show me where you keep the broom," she said, not meeting Lottie's eyes.

"Oh no, don't worry about that. Teresa will clean up when she gets here. Would you like a cup of tea, dear?"

"No, no. I'm getting ready to leave. I'll take the first train back to San Francisco. I need to see some friends there before I head out."

"Well, at least let me take you to the train. I'll get dressed," Lottie said, and slid from the kitchen, stepping carefully over the mess on the floor.

Ruthie found a glass and filled it with cool water, drinking it down in long, noisy gulps. She took slow, deep breaths to calm her racing heart, then went to the guest room to collect her backpack.

She would let Lottie drive her to the station and that would be the end of it. They probably didn't know anything about where Carl had gone with Sasha. They were clueless.

Lottie emerged from her bedroom dressed, her hair brushed down with its customary crisp waves, a buttery tan leather jacket slung over one shoulder. She had even stopped to blush her cheeks and put on a bit of lipstick. Everything back in place, Ruthie thought.

They walked together out the door and into the slightly chilly air of a northern California morning. Sunlight glinted off the pines and eucalyptus trees surrounding the house and birds called loudly between the branches.

"It's beautiful here," Ruthie said, not meaning to have said it aloud. "Yes, dear, it is," Lottie said, opening the door to her silver BMW sedan.

Ruthie settled into the gray leather seat. What would it be like to live like this every day, surrounded by beauty and comfort, shutting out all the pain and ugliness of the world? And what would it do to your soul, she wondered, as the car glided down the driveway and began to descend through the twisting hills to the town below.

"You know dear, we would help you if we could," Lottie began. "It's just…" "I know," Ruthie said. "Don't worry about it. I'll let you know if I find out anything new."

They had reached the station entrance. Lottie slipped a hundred-dollar bill into the pocket of Ruthie's jeans jacket. Ruthie pretended not to notice. A herd of men in identical looking suits carrying briefcases ran to catch the first morning train. Ruthie remembered Sasha's question the first time they took such a train together and chuckled a bit at the memory.

"Mama, they all have on the exact same shoes," she had said, excited by this discovery from her vantage point amid all the gray flannelled legs.

"But why, Mama? Why are they all the same?"

Why indeed, Ruthie thought, taking her leave of Lottie and rushing into the herd to catch her train.

It was a relief to be back "home" and Ruthie would have liked nothing more than to relax in the warmth of comfort of Family Place, but after a few days of rest she felt ready to tackle the trip to the Ranch. Annie and Will helped her map out a route—a bus to Stockton would get her most of the way there. When she called Ken to let him know she would be coming, he suggested hitching a ride was the best way to get to the ranch from the bus station.

"It's only about twelve miles," he said, "and everyone round these parts knows the Rainbow Ranch. Just stick out your thumb—all friendly folks in these parts."

Annie packed her a lunch and Will dropped her at the bus terminal, and she was off. What she would find at Rainbow Ranch was a mystery, but she had to go and see for herself.

Rainbow Ranch

Ruthie did what Ken had suggested. She took a bus to Stockton, a trip of about two hours, then started hitchhiking the rest of the way to the ranch through strawberry fields and dry brown hills. Ken was right. One older woman in a meticulously maintained ancient Chevy pulled over without hesitation when she saw Ruthie with her thumb out, made friendly conversation, and let her out about three miles from her destination. The last stretch was sparse, and she waited a long time for a ride, sweating under the hot sun. Finally, just when she thought she might have to walk the last two or three miles to the ranch, a motorcycle slowed, then pulled to a stop beside her, churning up the gravel on the shoulder. Ruthie brushed the dirt off her face and eyed the driver—handlebar mustache, red bandanna tied around salt-and-pepper hair that curled down to his shoulders, black leather vest over a white T. He looked the part, mounted on his Harley, that Ruthie could almost imagine him pawing the ground with impatience, like a racehorse ready to run.

"Need a lift, hon?" the driver asked.

"No, well, um, sort of," Ruthie said, flustered, unsure if she should accept a ride from this guy who called her hon.

"Well, I can sort of give you one. Say the word."

Ruthie glanced at the wide leather seat. Plenty of room for two. She'd have to hold on somehow, around his waist probably, but it wasn't far. She looked at the road, waves of heat almost visible rising from the asphalt. No cars were coming. It would be a long walk.

"Sure, thanks. I'm just going a few miles. To Ken's ranch. Do you know it?"

"You mean the hippie place? Rainbow something or other? Yeah, I've been there a few times when they had parties. You going to join up? Name's Bob, by the way. And you are…?"

"Oh, Ruthie...pleased to meet you," she said, then blushed to hear how ridiculous that sounded.

"No, I have friends there. Well, my ex and my daughter are supposed to be there. It's a long story," Ruthie said.

"Well, I'd say you can tell me all about it on the ride, but this baby..." He patted the Harley, and again Ruthie imagined a thoroughbred under his muscular legs. "...doesn't allow for much conversation," Bob said, taking Ruthie's backpack and stashing it in a storage compartment on the side of the bike.

"Hop on," he said. "Let's get you to your ranch, Ruthie."

Ruthie swung her leg over the seat and settled into a comfortable position, her arms lightly around Bob's waist. The bike roared off the shoulder and onto the empty highway. Ruthie chuckled. What a surprise it would have been for Sasha to see her Mama arriving on the back of a Harley.

When they came to the turnoff for the ranch, Bob insisted on taking her all the way there. The bike kicked up clods of dirt and rocks as he gunned it up the hard clay road that led to Ken's place. Ruthie closed her eyes, partly to protect them from flying pebbles, partly because she wanted to open them to find Sasha, curls flying behind her, running toward the bike crying "Mama, Mama!"

It was Ken who greeted them, flanked by two mongrel ranch dogs, felt cowboy hat tilted back on his head, the lazy grin Ruthie remembered.

"Well, hullo darling. Didn't know you were comin' today." He stuck out a big, knuckled hand to Bob. "Bob, is it?" he said. "Nice to see you again, brother."

Ruthie moved her leg up and over the seat. Her thighs ached from holding on so tight. Her voice trembled.

"I called, but no answer. Are they back, Ken? Have you heard from them?"

"Not a word," Ken said. "But like I said on the phone—they just went off for a while. They'll be back. No need to come all the way up here." He sounded annoyed. "I told you I'd call you if I heard anything."

"Well, she's here now, friend. And she worked pretty hard to get here," Bob said, getting off the bike and standing to his full height—a bit taller than

Ken even with the cowboy hat.

Oh no, Ruthie thought. Not a cockfight, please.

"You gonna be OK?" Bob said, keeping his eyes on Ken.

"Uh sure. I'll be fine. Can I spend the night, Ken? I'll head back in the morning."

Back where, she thought, to do what? What next?

"Sure, darlin'. You can stay in Carl's trailer. It's empty. Might need a little straightenin' up. I can get you a sleeping bag from the dorm."

"Thanks, Bob, for the ride. My first time on a Harley. It was fun."

Bob handed Ruthie her backpack and gave Ken a mock salute. Then he was off with a roar in a cloud of dust.

"Let me show you the trailer. Oh, well, I almost forgot. You've been here before, when you left Sasha."

Is that what I did, Ruthie thought. I guess so. Her mother's voice chimed in with her thoughts. "You made your bed, Ruth Ann. Now you'll just have to lie in it."

They passed a couple of young women on the way to the trailer, who gave Ruthie curious looks.

"Howdy, ladies. How ya doin'? This here is Ruthie, Sasha's mom. She's gonna be stayin' the night with us."

The girls looked like sisters—long flowing sandy colored hair, blue eyes, freckled cheeks, clear sun-tanned skin. They both wore embroidered white peasant blouses and long skirts with uneven hems that looked hand sewn. Dusty cowboy boots completed their outfits.

"Hi Ruthie, I'm Sarah and this is Emily. Sasha is so adorable. We just love her," the taller of the two said in a squeaky voice.

"Yeah, we can't wait for her to come back," the other, Emily, said. "Me too," Ruthie said. "Yeah, me too."

In a meadow of tall grasses and wildflowers, Ruthie spied Carl's trailer. One of the dogs raced off to sniff at the door. Ken pulled a ring of keys on a long, braided leather thong from his pocket and fingered them until he found the right one.

"We don't normally lock up around here, but I figured since they've been gone awhile…" his voice trailed off as he turned the key. The door creaked open on rusty hinges. Ruthie half-expected to see Sasha curled up asleep on the bunk, thumb in her mouth, her favorite stuffed toy, Lambie, hugged to her chest.

The trailer looked like they had left in a hurry. But no Sasha.

"I'm gonna leave you now, Ruthie. Got some chores that need doin'. You'll be okay, won't ya?" Ken said, halfway out the door of the small trailer. "I'll bring that sleeping bag by in a bit. And if you get hungry, feel free to wander down to the kitchen. Doubt you'll find anything edible in here."

Ruthie sat on the small bed in the alcove—Sasha's bed—and looked around the trailer. It was small but well-designed—Carl had probably fitted it out—he liked to do that. He had once built them a cozy home in an old VW camper that they'd driven across Canada the summer he thought he'd be drafted and sent to Vietnam. Their "Draft Dodger Mobile" they had called it as they crossed from Vancouver to Montreal, stopping in small towns along the way for a day or two, thinking about staying. In the middle of the vast empty plains of Saskatchewan, they got the news that Carl's draft board had mysteriously burned to the ground taking his Selective Service records with it. They'd been relieved, and finished the trip with lighter hearts, lingering in Montreal, then heading down the east coast to visit Ruthie's family.

So many memories. Ruthie fingered the soft fabric of the patchwork quilt on Sasha's bed. It looked handmade. Maybe, why could she never remember her name—Cindy, maybe Cindy had made it. Ruthie couldn't sew—had almost flunked home economics when she had to produce a straight skirt with a kick pleat. The ruffled curtains over the small window above the sink in the kitchenette were made of the same fabric.

Rainbow Ranch—that's what Carl had called it. He needed to get out of the city, he had told her. He wanted a healthier life. By that time, he was on some special diet—eating only foods that "hummed" to him and avoiding those that "beckoned," so Ruthie was not surprised.

Ruthie pulled herself off the bed and rummaged through the cabinets over the sink. She was starting to get hungry. She heard thunder in the distance and a minute later rain was beating against the flimsy windows, pounding out a rhythm on the metal roof of the trailer.

She opened the door and looked out the torn screen. Small streams were forming in the clay. The dogs that had been with Ken earlier had taken shelter under a shed next to a covered woodpile. They stood up and wagged their tails when they noticed Ruthie at the door.

"Oh, no boys. You're not coming in here." Ruthie said, and closed the door against the rain, falling like slanted spears now, wetting the floor. Raining like cats and dogs, she thought, and remembered how the Cubans at the building site in Los Naranjos had laughed when they heard her use that expression. "Como gatos y perros," Manny had tried to explain and then they had all laughed at the ridiculous idea of cats and dogs falling like rain.

Ruthie sighed. She missed Manny. He always knew how to cheer her up—even hold her up—when she needed it. She pushed aside a red velvet curtain at the end of the kitchen area. A double bed, neatly made with an Indian spread --they must have enriched a lot of Indian street vendors to create the Rainbow Ranch, she thought. A metal milk crate painted blue served as a nightstand, and on it a framed photo—Sasha propped up on their bed at the R & R in Colorado Springs, reading a book. Sasha was clutching Lambie, her tattered but much-loved stuffed lamb made of real Persian lamb wool. And the book with a cover made from flowery paper glued onto cardboard is the one Ruthie made her to read while she was gone—all about Ruthie's trip on a plane and a boat and the island of Cuba—ending with a picture of Ruthie and Sasha in a great big hug. Ruthie wasn't an artist, and the pictures were simple, but Sasha loved it and made Ruthie read it to her over and over.

She rummaged around in the nightstand by the bed but didn't find any of Sasha's books or Lambie. She must have taken them with her. But she did find a worn black leather address. book. She thumbed through it and found addresses and phone numbers for some of their college friends and San Francisco contacts. Her name was there—with several addresses crossed out. Why had Carl left his address book behind? Another mystery. Ruthie slipped it into her backpack. Maybe it would be useful.

Ruthie took the photo out of its tarnished silver frame and put it in her pocket, joining the one that had already made its home there—her girl. Somewhere out there waiting for Ruthie to find her.

After the rain had stopped, Ruthie took a walk around the Ranch, trailed by the dogs who seemed to have adopted her for the moment. A little way down a path from the trailer she discovered a small play area—a tire swing hanging from the gnarly branch of a cottonwood tree, a small playhouse with a door that swung open, and a wooden box filled with sand and dotted with small plastic trucks and shovels. No wonder Carl liked it here. Sasha must have been thrilled to have so much space to explore and play in. Ruthie wondered if there were other kids—she hadn't seen any on the way in.

Why would Carl want to take her away from this peaceful place? To keep her from you, a voice in her head answered. The answers she got to her questions from these voices were starting to be more judgmental, but she didn't know how to stop them.

A bell rang in the distance—much louder and more insistent than the gong at the Family Place—and Ruthie realized she hadn't eaten since early morning. Maybe it was time for supper.

She wandered in the direction she thought the mess hall was in. Ken had pointed it out to her as they passed. Maybe she could get something to eat and talk to a few more people—see what they might know about where Carl had gone.

Ruthie pushed open the screen door of the long, low wooden building that housed the mess hall and was greeted by the clatter of metal trays, the clinking of forks and spoons, and the chattering voices of the 30 or so people gathered at long picnic-style tables, sharing a meal. She had that "out-of-place" feeling familiar from her junior high school days, when where to sit in the cafeteria had seemed like the biggest problem in the world. One of the flowy flower girls noticed her hesitation and rescued her.

"Good to see you again. Why don't you get something to eat and then come sit down with us?" She pointed out a small group gathered at one end of a table. Ruthie wished she could remember her name.

"Sure, I'd love to. Let me just grab some food and I'll be with you in a minute."

She found a ceramic plate and some silverware, then pushed her metal tray down a smooth wooden ledge in front of several large metal pots. A deeply tanned woman with curly light brown hair framing a serious face stood ready with a ladle in hand.

"Black beans and rice?" she asked, ready to scoop some onto Ruthie's plate.

"Sure, that sounds good," Ruthie said. "Thanks."

"Hey, are you Sasha's Mom?" the woman said, filling Ruthie's plate and adding a piece of cornbread on the side. "You've got the same hair and smile." Ruthie blushed, happy to be recognized as Sasha's Mom.

"Yes, I am. Ruthie," she said.

"I'm Lizzie," the woman said, lifting some salad into a small bowl and placing it on Ruthie's tray next to her heaping plate of rice and beans. "We sure do miss Sasha around here."

"Oh, me too," Ruthie said. "I'm so anxious to see her."

"Mebbe you shouldn't a left her then." A deep voice behind her stopped Ruthie in her tracks. She turned to the voice and was surprised to see a short, pudgy teenager with a face full of acne staring her down.

"Go on, Shorty. Leave Sasha's Mom alone. No one asked for your opinion," Lizzie said, coming out from behind the pots and putting an arm around Ruthie's shoulder. Ruthie had begun to cry. Is that what everyone thought? That she had deliberately left her child? Didn't want her?

"Some folks around here don't understand how a mother could be away from her child for such a long time, but I've raised three girls, and I get it. I do. Sometimes you just need something of your own." Lizzie pulled Ruthie over to the table where the flowery girls were sitting. "Here are two of them right here," she said, pointing to the girls Ruthie had met on her way into the Ranch. "They look like twins, don't they? But they are a year apart. And the third one, Cindy, took off with Carl, and I haven't heard a thing from her. So, I know how you feel. I do."

"Oh," Ruthie said, wiping at her eyes with a napkin she found on the table. "Carl's not a bad guy," Lizzie went on. "Just a little confused sometimes about what he wants. And Cindy loves Sasha like her own, so don't you worry about her. But they should've let us know where they were going. I need to know where my girl is."

Ruthie settled herself on the bench and began scooping forkfuls of rice and beans into her mouth, mechanically. She said nothing because there was nothing to be said. This was Carl's home. She didn't belong here and there was nothing more to be learned from hanging around. She would leave in the morning.

"Oh, Ruthie," Lizzie said, turning back to her pots. "If you leave me a number where I can reach you, I will let you know if I hear from Cindy. I promise you that."

"Thanks, Lizzie," Ruthie said between spoons full of beans. "I really appreciate that."

Ken caught up with her after dinner on the path back to the trailer.

"Hey, Ruthie. Hope you're enjoying your time at the Rainbow. Listen, Lizzie has to go to Frisco tomorrow, it turns out, to pick up a couple of things, so she can drive you down. She's leaving first thing in the morning, so you can meet her at the mess hall at around 7:30 if that's okay."

"Yeah. Fine. Great. Thanks, Ken. I'll do that."

Ruthie was awakened by the crowing conversation of a couple of roosters and for a minute she thought she was in Cuba. She had tossed and turned in the double bed most of the night, imagining Sasha climbing in bed with Carl and Cindy for a snuggle, or waking them up in the night when she'd had a bad dream. The thought that she could be replaced frightened her. Of all the worries she had had before she left—that Sasha would get hurt, that she would start wetting the bed again, that she would miss Ruthie too much—having another woman take her place had never occurred to her. Now she wondered why Carl had never mentioned Cindy to her.

She threw on the same clothes she had worn the day before, washed up and ran a brush through her hair. Ruthie started out the door and then returned to the bedroom and scooped up Carl's address book from the nightstand and nestled it into her purse. It might come in handy.

Then she stepped out into the chilly morning air to meet Lizzie.

Lizzie was wearing a black knit pantsuit and had pulled her hair back into a sort of bun.

"I know, you can hardly believe it's me," she said, laughing at the look on Ruthie's face. "But I gotta see a man about a loan, so I figure I better look respectable."

"You look great," Ruthie said, climbing into the passenger seat of a VW bus painted all the colors of the rainbow and bearing the words "Rainbow Ranch" in big black letters on the side. "Just don't let him see your van."

There was no traffic on the road so early and they breezed down the highway to the city. They were mostly quiet, each lost in their own thoughts, but from time to time they would chat for a few minutes. Lizzie told Ruthie some funny stories about Sasha on the ranch—how scared she had been when she found out that what she thought were birds swooping over the big campfire at night had been bats—and then how she'd wanted to catch one and keep it in the trailer as a pet.

"I can't tell you that Carl and Cindy are really serious," she said at one point, "but they do seem to get along pretty well." Ruthie didn't know what to say to that. She didn't want to hear any more about how well Sasha and Cindy got along at that moment. How selfish I have been, she thought, to think that I could go off for a few months and Sasha wouldn't need a mother's kind of love, wouldn't look for it. She shook off the feeling. Regret wasn't going to help her be strong enough to do what she had to do to find her girl.

Lizzie dropped her right at the Family Place, refusing Ruthie's invitation to come in for a cup of tea. Ruthie watched the Rainbow bus disappear down Mission St. and then climbed the steep steps to the house, imagining that each step would somehow bring her closer to Sasha.

The Children's Place

End of July 1973

The next few days went by in a blur. It was uncomfortable to be back in the place where she, Carl, and Sasha had been a family. Ruthie helped Annie plant in the garden, bought herself a datebook to keep track of the days, and sometimes just sat and thought for what felt like hours on end. Finally, she was ready for that visit to Children's Place school and told Will she would accompany him the next day.

"That's great, Ruthie. The kids will be glad to see you, and a lot of parents will be there too because they are putting on a play." Ruthie remembered the days when she had been the drama teacher—Sasha peacefully dozing on a mat in a corner, then big enough to toddle out to find her Mama when she woke up, trying to insert herself into whatever play-acting they were up to. "Me, Mama, me, me," she had demanded. And Ruthie had found a way for her to take part. It would be hard to be there, where they had made so many happy memories, but she needed to do it.

Ruthie was shocked by how the neighborhood around the school was deteriorating. More homeless guys than ever slept under soiled Army blankets on the sidewalk, and it looked like a lot of the small shops and warehouses were empty.

"Yep, going downhill fast," Will said, anticipating her reaction. "We might have to find another home soon."

But Children's Place…well, Children's Place was, as always, warm and inviting. Multicolored patches, samples they had begged from a carpet store in the neighborhood, made the concrete floor safe for even the most boisterous rough-housing, and the walls seemed to have sprouted murals in every direction. Her reading corner was still there—piled with cozy quilts and books everywhere to be plucked off shelves or out of boxes. She followed Will back to the meeting room where the morning circle had already begun and took her place on the floor, cross-legged, as quietly as she could.

The morning circle was a time for kids to talk and adults to listen, unlike the assemblies in traditional schools. The kids always had plenty to say–ideas for new activities, grievances about one thing or another, and always the whys– why couldn't they walk to the corner store by themselves, why did they have to learn math, why couldn't they go to the beach more. The kids knew the adults took their thoughts and questions seriously, and plenty of things got shifted around and changed after morning circle.

A tall, slim girl of about twelve approached Ruthie tentatively as the circle was breaking up and kids were rushing off to their next activity.

"Ruthie?" she said in a voice that sounded familiar.

"Tania? Oh my god, you are so grown. I can't believe it's you." Ruthie was astounded to see her star drama student standing in front of her, or an older version of her. Tania—with her beautiful, golden-brown skin, tight cornrows, and shining eyes. Her mother was a feminist poet who had hung out with the Beats and, Tania had told Ruthie once with great solemnity, her father was "away in the war." Ruthie had thought she meant Vietnam until Tania's mother told her that this was her daughter's way of understanding that her father, a Black Panther militant, was fighting for black liberation and no longer living with them.

It had been three years—of course she had grown up. She pulled the girl to her and gave her a big hug.

"Where is Shasha? Did she come with?" Tania asked now, looking around for a glimpse of Sasha who she had loved to pull around in the shiny red wagon they had fitted out with a seat and railings for her.

"No, she's with Carl, her dad, right now," Ruthie said, hoping that would be enough.

But the questions echoed throughout the day at Children's Place, and Ruthie grew weary of finding a new way to say the same thing. It was natural, of course, that everyone would ask about Sasha and want to see her. She had been like a mascot at the school, beloved by everyone. But Ruthie could feel herself sinking into sadness.

After the play, Ruthie grabbed a much-needed coffee and stood in the sunny reading corner watching a tableau of parents chatting and kids racing around.

"Ruthie, is that you? I can't believe it."

Ruthie flashed a brief smile at Carol, Maddie's mother, who was not one of her favorite parents. She was a stay-at-home mom, married to a professor at San Francisco State, and always seemed to look down her nose at the hippie parents who were the majority. Ruthie often wondered why she sent Maddie to the Children's Place.

"I heard you were in Cuba for 3 months," she said now, leaning toward Ruthie as if it was a secret. "I don't know how you could bear being away from Sasha for all that time. When Maddie has a sleepover, I'm up all night with worry. Is she okay? Sasha, I mean. Poor dear. She must have been traumatized." "She's fine, Carol. Thanks for asking," she said, her jaw tightening with the effort of keeping her cool. She did not want to let this woman see how vulnerable she was feeling. Ruthie drifted away from Carol and headed off to find Will.

When she caught up with him, it was clear Will was nowhere near ready to leave, and she had had all she could take. Ruthie tugged his sleeve to let him know she was going to take the streetcar home.

It was a relief to board the car, crowded with strangers who would not ask any questions. "I might be better off in Cambridge, where no one knows me," Ruthie thought, imagining for the first time that she could return to Claudia's apartment and make a life there while she figured out what to do next.

The People's Lawyer

Ruthie was clearing the small desk in the guest room to make a to do list when she came across the address book she had taken from Carl's trailer. She leafed through pages of addresses written in his familiar neat script, marking names she recognized as mutual friends: his brother Stan, Priscilla who they folk-danced with, Phil, a guy who sometimes hung out in the garage with Carl–– and a few others whose names she recognized. She glanced at the clock—10 AM. She could try to call them, leave messages at least. Maybe somebody had heard from Carl, knew where he might be. It was worth a try.

Ruthie curled up on the bed with the phone on her lap and started with Stan, the brother. He and Carl weren't really close but they might be in touch. The number you have called is not in service at this time. Not a total surprise. She had always thought Stan was a bit flaky. Priscilla had an answering machine at least so Ruthie left a brief message. The next two numbers she tried just rang and rang. She hung up the phone with a sigh. People moved around so much, and Carl wasn't the type to keep in touch, so…it was just so frustrating. How was she going to find him if he didn't want to be found?

Ruthie put the address book back on the desk and picked up a scrap of paper Will had passed to her a few nights earlier. The name and phone number of a lawyer was scrawled across it.

"He calls himself a "people's lawyer," and he's a pretty good guy, Ruthie," Will had said about Paul Amado, the lawyer. "He'll be honest with you, and he won't charge you an arm and a leg. Some cases he doesn't even charge for."

Why not, Ruthie thought now, moving the note to the top of the pile of papers she was making. Everyone keeps bugging me to talk to the police. This feels safer. And maybe he'll have some ideas about what to do.

The next morning, before breakfast, she dialed the number, and the lawyer himself answered. Paul, as he had told her to call him, had a deep, warm voice that calmed her nerves, and Ruthie made an appointment for later that afternoon.

His office was above a thrift store on Mission St., just a few blocks away.

Ruthie paused on the corner of Mission and Dolores and took a deep breath. Her nerves had returned, and her thoughts were racing. She hadn't told her story to anyone in a position of authority before and she was worried about how it would be received, even by this lawyer who should be more sympathetic than most. Would he understand why she left Sasha and help her get her back? Or would he just become just one more voice in her head reminding her of what a fool she had been?

Ruthie climbed the worn wooden stairs to the office. A musty smell wafted up from the store below, and a single dim fixture lit the narrow hallway. FREE ANGELA DAVIS AND ALL POLITICAL PRISONERS proclaimed a yellow poster with bold red letters on a door at the end of the hall. Looks like I'm in the right place, Ruthie thought as she opened the door to find Paul the lawyer sitting behind a gray metal desk. The room's single window let in a trickle of light, filtered through what looked like years of caked-on grime. A torn, yellowed shade was pulled halfway down.

"Ruthie?" The deep voice Ruthie remembered from the phone greeted her as Paul came around the corner of the desk and held out his hand. "Good to meet you. Please—have a seat."

Ruthie lowered herself carefully onto the only seat in the room—a brown metal folding chair that scraped the floor as she settled herself on it.

"Sorry," she said, folding her hands in her lap.

"No need," Paul said, drawing a long yellow pad and sharpened pencil from a drawer.

"Why don't you start at the beginning and tell me what brought you here today."

Ruthie sighed and fidgeted with the moonstone ring on her right hand.

She began in a soft, quavery voice she hated, with her divorce and ended with her efforts to find Sasha after her return from Cuba. Paul listened thoughtfully, interrupting with a couple of questions and jotting notes on his pad, then sat forward with his arms folded across the desk when she had finished.

"I admire you, Ruthie," Paul said. "You must be going through a terrible time, but you're keeping it together. I'm glad you came to me for advice. Let me start by saying that we'll have a conversation today, I'll make a few suggestions, and then we can decide together whether there's a reason to retain me as your lawyer. There won't be a charge for our conversation."

Ruthie leaned back in her chair so hard she almost fell over, and they both laughed. Then the tears started.

"So much for keeping it together," she said, taking the tissue Paul handed her across the desk and lowering her shoulders.

"So, for starters, let me just say that you have done nothing wrong. I understand your concern about the trip to Cuba. Technically, you broke the U.S. travel ban, along with everyone else in the brigade, but as far as I know, no one has been prosecuted for these trips in the past few years. That said, the FBI does keep track of the participants."

"So, you don't think I need to worry too much about that?"

Paul looked down at his notes and continued. "Not in terms of any immediate legal action, no, but you're right to be concerned about how it might be used against you in a custody case in court. And the other thing you should know is that California recently amended the custody laws to be much more favorable to the father—or rather, to give both parents equal rights to custody of the child. I believe you and Carl were awarded joint custody, is that right?"

Ruthie nodded. This was not sounding good.

"So technically, you should have had Carl's permission to move with Sasha to Colorado. Is that something you guys agreed on?"

"More like, he was unhappy about it but went along with it," Ruthie said. Paul paused for a minute, doodling on the pad as he thought.

"So, here's what I think, Ruthie. You're probably right that getting the cops involved won't be much help at this point, and you certainly don't want the FBI involved. Hiring a private investigator is going to cost you a lot of money, and there isn't much to go on yet about where they might be."

Ruthie shifted in her chair. Paul was just confirming what she had already suspected. She was on her own.

"You mentioned having a place to live in Cambridge. If and when you do decide to go the authorities for help, it's going to be important for you to be able to show that you can provide a stable home for Sasha, so maybe heading back there, getting a job, letting a bit more time pass in the hopes that Carl gets in touch might be your best bet."

Ruthie stood up and moved to the window that looked out on the lively street below.

"I hear what you're saying, but how can I just do nothing to find my little girl?' She turned to face Paul who had swiveled in his chair. "I can't just do nothing." "I know how hard this must be—but you won't be doing nothing. You'll be making a home for you and Sasha, putting some money aside for when you do find her, and from what you've told me there's no reason to think that Carl will hurt her or run away with her—sounds like he's just being incredibly selfish and kind of a dick."

Ruthie laughed despite her bleak mood. "That hits the nail on the head."

"Let's stay in touch," Paul said, rising to join her at the window. "If I think of anything else, I'll let you know. In the meantime, reach out to his friends and family, keep calling the Ranch, keep trying to figure out where he might have gone, and keep a list of everything you are doing." He paused again. "Can I give you a hug?"

Ruthie nodded and Paul pulled her in for a strong bear hug, then walked her to the door.

He really is not like any other lawyer I've ever seen, Ruthie thought, glad she had confided in him, even though his advice was hard to swallow.

"And please remember," Paul said, ushering her into the hallway. "You have done nothing wrong. I represent one Mom who is in jail for her political beliefs and has to watch other people raise her daughter. I tell her the same thing. You have done nothing wrong. You are a good mother. It's just our society that's all fucked up." He shrugged and gently closed the door behind her.

Angela Davis's determined face followed her down the hall. Her fist was raised in a salute, her eyes stared into the distance, perhaps envisioning a better world. She was a fighter, and Ruthie knew that she could be too…in her own way.

An Old Friend

Ruthie arrived home to a strangely quiet house. "Annie," Ruthie called out. "Anyone home?"

"She had to go out for a few minutes. She invited me to wait for you here. Hope it's okay." A short, slight man who belonged to the voice appeared in the hallway. Three years, maybe more, since she had seen him, but Ruthie could never forget those freckles across his nose, those blue twinkling eyes.

"Scottie? But…how did you know I was here?" It was Scottie McBride, a dear longtime friend. "You look good. You look…"

"Clean," Scottie said in that soft voice Ruthie had loved to listen to as they told each other stories long into the night. When they had all lived in that squatters' flat in the Haight-Ashbury, before Children's Place, before Sasha. 1967, the Summer of Love—and what a summer it had been. Carl had hated it there—hated the smell of weed and hash that permeated the thick draperies and cushions that served as seating in the large common room, hated the beggars sitting on flattened cardboard boxes on Haight Street, and hated her friendship with Scottie. It's true he had taken a long, slow dive into speed, the first of their friends to succumb, and become unrecognizable—thin, gaunt, with dark circles under his sleepless eyes, alternately talking a mile a minute and then staring off into nothing. But he was Scottie, their friend, and Ruthie loved him.

After they moved into the Family Place, Carl gave her a hard time about seeing Scottie, and they grew apart. She should have known then. You don't do that to a friend. But she had gone along with it, not wanting to make waves that would disturb the fragile peace between them. For Sasha. Everything for Sasha. "Come let's sit," Ruthie said, leading him to the living room, to the purple velvet couch, to a seat beside her. "I'm so sorry, Scottie, about…"

"Say no more," Scottie said, in that lilting voice of his, taking her hand and squeezing it hard. "We all went through a lot back then. But here we are."

They talked for an hour, alone in the house, revisiting the past through a filter that softened it, almost romantic. About carrying still-warm, crusty loaves of wheat bread back from the Digger's Free Bakery in the morning. Spreading a blanket on the lawn in Golden Gate Park to listen to Grace Slick and the Jefferson Airplane rock it out—glowing joints passing from hand to hand, then later fruit punch laced with LSD. It had been magical, until it wasn't.

"Remember Altamont," Scottie said, "how cool it was at first—Santana, the Airplane, the fucking Rolling Stones in a free concert." Ruthie remembered. How could she forget? December of '69—Sasha had been 18 months old, and it was one of the first times Ruthie had left her for more than a couple of hours. She ignored Carl's negativity and joined Scottie and a few old friends at the concert. She remembered the excitement of walking the long dirt path to the speedway, the throb of the music, dancing in a circle of strangers with so much joy, the anticipation. And then the fear—thousands of people jammed up against each other, some freaking out on bad drugs, fights and scuffles breaking out all over, and the Hell's Angels pummeling their way through the crowd. It wasn't until they got home that they learned that four people had died.

"That was the bottom for me, Ruthie. That's when I knew I had to get out," Scottie said. He had left the city for a year—gone to live with friends on a rural commune in Oregon—and kicked his habit. He had come back to San Francisco a couple of years ago and was managing an Army-Navy Store on Market St.

"I remember that place, Scottie. That's been there forever. I used to buy used overalls there when I was pregnant with Sasha." Ruthie said—and then she told him about everything he had missed—about her split with Carl and the R & R in Colorado and Cuba and...

"Ruthie, you back? Is Scottie still here?" They heard the rustle of bags in the kitchen, and suddenly Annie was beside them. "Oh, good. Stay for dinner," Annie said in that matter-of-fact way she had that made you say yes.

They laughed through dinner and a bottle of wine. Scottie wanted to hear all about Cuba and, for the first time since her return, Ruthie tried to explain to her friends what that experience had been like, what it had taught her.

"It was so amazing to be in a whole country where the intention is to work for the common good, not just for your own individual self or family. I mean, we try to create that in our little communes but imagine a whole country! And like a mechanic and a doctor could live in the same apartment building and just be considered equals because the work they did was equally important. And May Day—we were standing in Revolution Square listening to Fidel for hours with hundreds of thousands of Cuban workers—it was amazing. I don't know, I just see things differently now. Like Cuba just changed me."

Ruthie stole a glance at Scottie, embarrassed that she was going on about Cuba for so long and not quite believing he was back in her life. She noticed he turned down the wine, yet he was just as jovial and relaxed as he had ever been. How good it was to have her dear old friend by her side, especially in this moment.

After dinner, Scottie came upstairs with her, and they sat facing each other on her bed. She told him the hardest story, about Sasha being gone, missing. When she finished, Scottie was quiet for a bit, then took her hands in his—she remembered the touch of his small, warm hands—and looked straight into her eyes. His blue eyes seemed to grow darker as he struggled with his thoughts.

"I can tell you are blaming yourself, Ruthie, but please don't. You have done nothing but be a good friend and a good mother. Carl wants to control things; you know that about him. This is about him taking control—not you leaving, or not caring, or being a bad mother. No!" He said the last word, the NO, with such emphasis that the bed shook, but it was the phrase before that—the two words, bad mother—that Ruthie realized she had been thinking all along, that she had been waiting for someone to say out loud. She felt such gratitude that Scottie could bring it out in the open like that and then chase it away. She leaned over and gave him a peck on the cheek, and he drew her into an embrace. He had the old familiar scent of the Scottie she remembered— not the grungy speed freak, but the sweet, cuddly guy from Ohio who always smelled like Irish Spring.

Will came to the door and chuckled.

"Looks like you two are having a great reunion. Scottie, would you like to spend the night?"

"Oh, hey, that's a nice offer, but my gal is waiting for me at home." He blushed under his freckles and ducked his head—dear bashful Scottie.

"Tell me," Ruthie demanded, bouncing on the bed.

"Her name's Lisa. I met her up in Oregon. She saw me through a lot, and she worries, so I gotta get home." Scottie said, rising to go.

"Oh, Scottie, I'm so glad," Ruthie said, following him down the stairs. "Just one more word of advice from an old friend?" Scottie said, wrapping

a blue wool scarf around his neck against the chilly San Francisco evening air. "Go back to Cambridge. Wait there for Sasha. Isn't that where Carl thinks you will be? Doesn't he have that phone number? Make a life there and wait. There's nothing you can do here except beat yourself up. Take it from someone who knows. Okay, my dear?" He tipped her chin up and gave her a light kiss on the lips, and then closed the door behind him.

He's right, Ruthie thought—Scottie's right. There's nothing more I can do here right now. I need to get back to Cambridge.

A Decision

It was three hours later in New Jersey but there was someone Ruthie needed to connect with, and he stayed up late. She listened to the phone go through its routine clicks and clacks and then heard it ringing and ringing, willing Manny to be home, to be up, to answer the phone. She really needed to hear his voice.

"Hola, nunca es tarde para la lucha." The phone vibrated in Ruthie's hand at the sound of Manny's deep voice, and she almost dropped it. She let out a sigh of relief, stretching the phone cord into her room and closing the door.

"It's never too late for the struggle? Hey Manny, you could get in trouble answering the phone that way you know. What if I was an FBI agent?"

"Wow, compañera, what timing. I was just sitting here thinking about you and wondering how things are going out there in Hippielandia. Catch me up on what's been happening. Any news from Carl?"

"Nope, not a word. I visited his parents, and it was just as awful as I had imagined. Then I headed up to the Ranch, but— nothing. Looks like he has a young girlfriend with him wherever he is." Ruthie sat on the bed and heard a thump as the phone base hit the floor in the hallway.

"So…what's next?" Manny said in a quiet voice.

"I'm thinking about going back to Cambridge for a while. Annie and Will have been wonderful, but I need to figure out what's next, and I don't think San Francisco is the place to do that. Besides, Carl thinks I'm in Cambridge, and Claudia's leaving in a few days, so there won't be anyone there to answer the phone if he tries to get in touch with me …" Her voice trailed off into thoughts about how she would survive the waiting.

"Makes sense to me," Manny said. "I can come up for a weekend when you get back and boost your spirits. I'm only a bus ride away."

"That would be wonderful, Manny. I think the first thing I'll do is look for some kind of a temporary job to replenish my savings, so I'll be ready to get to Sasha when the time comes."

"Ruthie, take care, hermanita, and give me a call when you get to Claudia's." The phone clicked off, and Ruthie opened her door and placed it back in the receiver.

She looked at the clock on her bedside table. It was 11:30 PM and she was exhausted. She'd sleep on her decision and tell Annie and Will in the morning.

The next morning, after they finished their breakfast of Annie's delicious cinnamon oatmeal, Will took the kids to the park while Annie and Ruthie tackled the dishes. After her talk with Scottie and a good night's sleep, Ruthie had made up her mind. It wasn't doing her any good to hang out in all the places that had belonged to her and Sasha together. It just brought back memories that piled up in her mind until she couldn't think straight. And there was nothing she could do right now that required her to be in San Francisco. She would keep on writing and calling people who knew Carl, keep in touch with the Ranch, and keep trying to figure out where they might have gone—but she could do all that from Cambridge, plus she had a free apartment to live in and had promised Claudia to look after it. Plus, she could find a job and make some money. And there wouldn't be people who knew Sasha constantly asking her where she was, or worse, how she could have gone away and left her.

Maybe she was trying to talk herself into it, but it felt right. It was going to be hard to tell Annie, but she needed to have that conversation so she could move on with her plans.

"I've made a decision," Ruthie said, drying one of the rustic, misshapen clay bowls they used for oatmeal and placing it carefully on the shelf.

Annie slid the soapy plate she was washing carefully back into the sink. "Sounds serious," she said. "Let's hear it."

"I'm going to go back to Cambridge to stay at Claudia's place for a while. I need to think things through, and I just can't do that here where everything reminds me of Sasha. And people are judging me all the time."

"I'm not judging you, Ruthie, if that's what you're thinking. I just think maybe there are some things you could be doing…"

"Like what?" Ruthie dropped the plate she was holding, and it shattered into a million pieces.

Annie put her arm around her shoulder and led her to the table. "We'll clean that up later," she said. "We need to talk."

Ruthie rested her head in her hands like a child waiting to be punished and mumbled her response.

"Talk then, Annie. I know you've been holding back."

There was a long pause, and then Annie spoke in a soft, gentle voice.

"Ruthie, I know how hard this is for you. Believe me, I do. I know you don't want to think that Carl would do anything to hurt you, but it's been – how long has it been since he was supposed to meet you?"

Ruthie counted in her head. "About a month, I guess."

"And he hasn't been in touch in all that time," Annie went on. "He's gotta know that you would be worried. He's gotta know that you would be trying to figure out what to do. Whatever is going on, it's seriously wrong with what Carl is doing. I know you don't want to go to the police, and I get it. We haven't had many reasons to trust the cops. But maybe in this situation…or…maybe the FBI…or have you thought about hiring a private investigator to look for them? Something more than just sitting around and waiting?"

Ruthie lifted her head and looked at her friend. She was judging her no matter what she said. And if Annie was judging her and thinking it was her fault, everyone must think that. That's why she had to get out of this place—she felt like a swimmer caught in a rip tide, frantic but making no progress. She couldn't think or plan…or anything.

"Everyone keeps suggesting that—go to the cops, hire an investigator. But the lawyer didn't think that would be much help. And when I try to imagine what I'll say and how they'll react—like, "So, lady, you just left your daughter with your ex and went where? To do what? And doesn't he have visitation rights?" I'm scared they'll blame this all on me. I have, really. I have thought about it, but imagine the headline, Annie. Radical commie hippie chick just back from an illegal trip to Cuba calls the FBI, who has been snapping her picture and recording her activities for years, to find the daughter she left behind, granddaughter of a wealthy and important Peninsula family. I hope I won't ever have to go down that path, but definitely not yet. Besides, I don't want Carl to get in that kind of trouble. He's clueless, but he's not a criminal."

"You've always cut him more slack than he deserves, my dear, but I get it, I do." Annie squeezed Ruthie's shoulder and pushed back from the table.

"You do what you have to, Ruthie, she said as she pulled the broom from the pantry and began sweeping up the broken crockery. "Just know I'll always be here if you need me."

Ruthie sighed. "I do know, Annie. You are the best friend in the world."

PART TWO
Ruthie in Exile

Making a Life

Early August 1973

Ruthie turned the key and unlocked the door to the four walls that would shelter her until she figured out what to do next—how to find her daughter. Claudia was a year younger than Ruthie and already building a career—and with a family so supportive of their only child that they had offered to pay for this apartment even while Claudia was spending a year in England. The apartment was in a rectangular, two-story 1950s-era cement building with external stairways that made it look like a motel. But it would be Ruthie's for as long as she needed it. That was all that mattered.

Ruthie dumped her backpack and duffel bag on the twin bed in Claudia's bedroom. "Don't go there," she admonished the voice that had appeared in her head since Sasha's disappearance. Blame, guilt, and a storm of "what ifs" had been her constant companions in the weeks she had spent in California. She needed a time out, space to breathe, think, and plan. She needed to earn some money, and Claudia had offered this space. Ruthie should be grateful, yet she resented her cousin's carefree student life and easy choices.

She sat on the couch, loosened her hair from the braid that trailed down her back and shook it out over her shoulders, kicked off her sneakers and curled her legs under her. She opened the Cambridge Times, bought from a newsstand in the Square and put her finger on Help Wanted, Female. Now to find a job.

Did she want to work as a waitress again? Most of the jobs Ruthie saw were either waitressing or clerical. She couldn't imagine herself working in an office from 9 to 5. She had so much restless energy—a waitressing job might be the way to go. She had worked at Friendly's after school in high school and at the Woolworth's lunch counter in Colorado Springs during her time there.

Ruthie found a red crayon in Claudia's junk drawer and circled a couple of possibilities. Cookie's Diner – wasn't that the place Claudia had said had the best milkshakes in Cambridge, where she and Manny had bought takeout when they first got to Cambridge? Well, anyway, it had a nice ring to it, and the address was only a few blocks from the apartment, so she decided to start there.

Ruthie took a deep breath and pulled the pink Princess phone from the coffee table into her lap. Just like Claudia to have a pastel Princess phone and make everyone wonder whether she was being ironic or for real. She tapped in the numbers slowly and listened as the phone rang and rang on the other end. She imagined a busy diner—short-order cooks moving fast to get the food out and waitresses carrying dishes stacked up their arms, gliding across the floor. She was clumsy—the absentminded professor her father had called her—maybe she wasn't cut out to be a waitress, maybe she should hang up the phone.

"Hello"—a voice, female, breathy, in a hurry.

"Oh, hi," Ruthie said. "I'm calling about the waitress position. Is it still open?"

"Yup—yeah—it's open all right. When can you come in?" "You mean for an interview?"

"I'm Cookie. I run this joint. Do you have any experience? I need someone to start ASAP, honey. We can talk for a minute, but if everything works out, I'll put you to work. What's your name?" The voice slowed down and let some warmth creep in.

"So, I'm Ruthie, and well, I've worked at a few different places. I worked at a Woolworth's Lunch Counter for a couple of years. I think I can do it. I really need a job."

"Great, that's great. Why don't you come in this afternoon, and we can get you started?"

This afternoon? Ruthie thought, but she didn't dare let her surprise show. She was tired from the long flight, but she didn't want to say no and miss an opportunity. Maybe this was how you got a waitressing job in this part of the world.

"Uh, yeah sure—I can be there. What time should I come? What should I wear—I mean, should I bring anything?"

"Just wear some really comfortable shoes, sweetheart. We'll get you a uniform and show you the ropes. See you at 4—after lunch and before dinner. I should have some time to get you going."

And with that, Cookie hung up the phone.

Ruthie placed the slim pink phone back in the receiver and returned it to the coffee table. She had a couple of hours to get ready, but what did that mean? Get ready? She had never landed a job in a 10-minute phone conversation before.

OK, Sasha, this is it. Your mama's gonna be a waitress and start saving to find you. Wish me luck, pumpkin.

Ruthie's imagined conversations with Sasha were growing more freqent now that she was alone so much. It brought her comfort to hear her own voice, to speak her intentions into the air, like a plane writing in the sky. She imagined a clear blue sky with white puffy writing trailing from the underbelly of a small black plane—Search for Sasha Part II, the writing said. But now it was time to stop imagining and get ready for work at Cookie's Diner.

Cookie's Diner

Cookie's Diner looked just as she had imagined it when she saw the name in the Cambridge Times ad. The name was written in big loopy blue letters across the large window, through which she could see a lunch counter with stools and several large booths. A bell tinkled on the door when she pulled it open. A red-haired woman with a pencil tucked behind her ear sat at a large black cash register that dwarfed her petite frame.

"Cookie?" Ruthie said. "Hi, are you Cookie?'

"Who wants to know?" the woman said in a husky, smoker's voice, and then she laughed, a cross between a cough and a laugh, deep in her chest, and smiled a big, welcoming smile.

"Oh, hi," Ruthie said again. Why was she so nervous? "I'm Ruthie. I called about the waitress job."

A big guy sitting on one of the small metal stools at the counter looked her over.

"Finish your pie, Irv, and leave my new waitress alone," Cookie said.

Then, "C'mon, honey. Let's go to the back where we can talk in peace."

Cookie stood up from her seat behind the register, and Ruthie realized she was even smaller than she appeared—maybe 5 feet, just. But everything else about her was big and full of attitude. Her bottle-red hair was shellacked into a tall beehive, from which another pencil peeked out. Her large, full mouth was painted a bright berry red that clashed with her hair. Her hips swayed with authority as she led Ruthie to the back, winding between the Formica lunch counter, at which Irv sat alone, a few scattered red metal tables, and the large, comfy-looking booths that lined the side windows of the Diner.

"Welcome to Cookie's," she said in that raspy voice, pulling a pack of Pall Mall's from a pocket in the white flouncy apron tied at her waist. "Serving the Harvard intelligentsia since 1954," she said, jerking a thumb in Irv's direction and laughing.

"Sit, sit," she said, pulling out a metal folding chair at a small table and gesturing to Ruthie to do the same. "Ruthie, is it?"

"Yes, yes," Ruthie said, struggling not to cough from the smoke that Cookie was blowing across the table into her face.

"So, what brings you to Cambridge?" Cookie asked. Was it so obvious then that Ruthie didn't belong here—or anywhere now?

"Well, I'm just here for a while, actually." Oh shit, why had she said that?

Maybe Cookie was looking for someone to settle in and stay for a long time.

"Oh, everybody says that at the beginning," Cookie said, flicking a long ash from the end of her cigarette into a coffee cup that sat on the table in a sticky beige ring. "But the place kind of pulls you in."

"So, tell me a little about yourself," Cookie said, putting her elbows up on the table, resting her chin on her hands, and gazing at Ruthie with big blue eyes she hadn't noticed before under the thick mascara and eye shadow. It was a look that held no nonsense honesty, and Ruthie hesitated. There was a lot about herself she didn't want anyone here to know.

"Don't worry about any deep, dark secrets," Cookie said, as if she'd read Ruthie's mind. "We've all got 'em, and we don't meddle in the personal stuff. Just tell me about that waitressing experience you mentioned and what kind of shifts you're looking for."

"Oh, okay," Ruthie said, hoping her relief wasn't totally apparent in her voice.

"Well, I worked at a lunch counter at Woolworth's in the little town where I went to college. And in high school…"

"A college girl huh? Well, you'll fit right in here." There was something in the way Cookie said "college girl" that made Ruthie want to take it back.

"Well, I didn't graduate. Just a couple of years. But this is such a comfortable place. I'd love to work here. And I'm looking for as many hours as I can get." Ruthie said.

"Saving up for something big, huh?" Cookie said, and Ruthie had that feeling again, that she could see right through her. It was something big, all right.

She had made a list the night before of all the things she would need money for: a flight back to California, travel to wherever Carl had taken Sasha, maybe eventually hiring a private detective or paying Paul to be her lawyer.

"Well, we're like family here, and I do need a full-time waitress, so you are in luck. Vi, come over here and meet Ruthie," Cookie hollered at a short, plump, brown-skinned woman with shiny black hair braided and coiled around her head, who was walking carefully with dishes stacked up her arm from wrist to shoulder.

"Un minuto, in a minute," the woman, Vi, called back over her shoulder as she delivered a plate of fries, a thick hamburger, and a side of slaw to a man eating alone in one of the large booths.

"That's Vi," Cookie said, "she's my other full-timer. The rest are college girls. They come and go."

The woman approached their table, wiped her hands on the white apron that covered her blue uniform, and reached one out to Ruthie. "Violeta," she said, pronouncing it Vee-oh-let-a, the Spanish way. "They call me Vi." She had an accent Ruthie didn't recognize—a lilting, musical lift to her words that was very different from the guttural hard sounds she had become accustomed to in Cuba.

"Ruthie," she said, shaking Violeta's hand. "Mucho gusto."

"All right, that's enough of that Spanish," Cookie broke into their greeting. "Take a load off for a minute, Vi, and tell our new waitress all about Cookie's. Leave out the bad parts. I've got to go check the orders. And can you get Ruthie her uniform and show her where to change? Oh, and introduce her to Sal while you're at it—she might as well …well, maybe she can get a smile out of him."

Vi shrugged and led Ruthie to a small room that served as both a customer bathroom and a changing room, calling out to a tall, broad-shouldered man with a food-stained apron stretched across his big belly who was cracking eggs over a hot grill. "Sal, meet Ruthie, our new waitress," she said.

"Hope she's better at it than you," Sal said in a deep voice that held a hint of laughter, even as he scowled at Violeta.

"Don't let him scare you," Violeta said, pushing Ruthie gently into the bathroom and handing her a folded uniform. "How do you say it? He barks more than he bites."

Ruthie stumbled through her first shift, relieved that the worst mishaps were a couple of mixed-up orders. Her calves ached and her feet were sore, so she was happy to see Cookie turn the door sign to "CLOSED" at 9 PM, after a group of students who had occupied the corner booth for a couple of hours finally finished their coffee and left. She sank into a chair at the little table in the back, where Violeta soon joined her.

"¿Cansada?" Violeta asked. "I was so tired at first. Every night I just fell asleep on the couch without even taking a bath. But you'll get used to it."

They spent twenty minutes refilling ketchup and mustard containers and salt and pepper shakers, till Cookie called out "All right everybody. That's it. Another day, another dollar. Let's go home."

Violeta headed for the bus stop—she lived far from the Square, on the outskirts of Cambridge, she told Ruthie. Ruthie walked back alone through the darkened streets, enjoying the cool night air and the gentle breeze after the hustle and bustle at Cookie's. She was due back at noon the next day to work the lunch and dinner shifts.

And just like that, Ruthie had a job. She was a waitress at Cookie's Diner in Harvard Square. She could check off one important item on her to-do list.

Any News?

Hello? What can I do you for?

Hi Ken. It's Ruthie. Sasha's mom. Is Lizzie there? Hold on. Let me give her a holler.

Hello, who's this?

Hi Lizzie. It's Ruthie, Sasha's mom. Just checking in with you to see if you've heard from Cindy or heard anything about where they might be?

Oh God, Ruthie. I wish I had some news. I'm gonna give that girl a piece of my mind when she finally turns up. I'm going crazy with worry from not hearing anything from her. I have no idea where she is or when she's coming back and it's been, what, like almost 3 months now? I didn't raise her to do something like this. And you must be tearing your hair out.

Yeah, kind of. I got a job, and I have a place to stay, so as soon as I get some money saved or hear something I'll be back out that way again to go looking for my daughter.

Well, like I said, I will get in touch if I hear anything at all. Gotta go get dinner started for the Rainbow gang.

You take care now, Ruthie.

Violeta

The college girls came and went as Cookie had described, but Ruthie and Violeta almost always worked the same shifts and, over the course of the hectic weeks that followed Ruthie's first day on the job, they began to get to know one another. Violeta was older than Ruthie, in her thirties, and had been in the U.S. for 12 years, leaving her small town in Chile at the urging of a cousin who had migrated to Boston and was doing well. She lived in a rooming house with that cousin and had not been home to Chile since.

"¿Habla usted español?" Violeta asked, with a glance at the register where Cookie was sorting through a stack of papers. The lunch rush was over, and they were sitting together at the back table for a well-earned break.

"Sí, un poco." Ruthie answered. "Entiendo más que hablo," she added. Violeta's Spanish was slower and easier to understand than the fast-moving exchanges she had tried to keep up with in Cuba.

"Yo soy de Chile," Violeta offered. "From the mountains near Valparaíso. ¿La conoces?"

"No, ¿pero es linda, no?" Ruthie's Spanish ran out at that point, and she said in English "You must miss it." Violeta's deep brown eyes clouded with an emotion Ruthie read as sadness, and she sighed deeply.

"Ay, sí, cómo no. Mi familia—they are all there. It is not possible to travel when you don't have papers, but I speak to my mother and my tía—once every month. And my son writes me letters, when he remembers." Violeta said that with a little wink. This was the first Ruthie had heard about a son.

"Wow, I didn't know you had a son. ¿Qué edad tiene?" she said, more curious than ever about Violeta who had left a son behind in Chile.

"Tiene diecinueve ahora. He's 19 now," Violeta said. "But he was just seven years old when I left Chile. It was so hard, but I had no choice."

Ruthie wanted to know more, so much more, but Cookie shooed them away from the back table when the booths started filling up with the afternoon college crowd. It was her least favorite time of the day. The students acted like she was invisible and left just a few measly coins on the table for her tip.

At the end of the day, in the changing room, Ruthie had an idea.

"Why don't you come over to my apartment for dinner tomorrow night, Violeta?" she said, pulling her jeans up and stashing her uniform in her backpack. "Tomorrow's my day off and you work the morning shift. You could come over around five when you get off work. How about it?"

Violeta's face lit up like a little kid who has just received an invitation to a birthday party.

"Si, Si, me gusta la idea," she said, clapping her hands with excitement.

"I'd love to see your apartment. And we can talk like hermanas, like sisters."

Ruthie took her order pad out of her uniform pocket, tore off a page, and scribbled her address and phone number.

"Here you go. Call if you get lost, but it's just a few blocks from here and you know the neighborhood. Do you like lasagna? That's my one and only specialty." Ruthie said, laughing.

"La-sag-na," Violeta sounded out the clearly unfamiliar word. "I've never tasted it, but I can't wait."

"Good," Ruthie said. "See you at around 6 PM then?" And they went their separate ways.

Ruthie awoke the next morning with a mission. Her first visitor, her first dinner party, her first new friend, since Manny, in a long, lonely time.

She spent the morning tidying up the apartment, sweeping the scuffed floors, scrubbing and mopping the tiny kitchen and the bathroom. Then she made a shopping list: lasagna noodles, tomato sauce, ground beef, ricotta, mozzarella, and ingredients for a nice green salad. At the last minute, she added a crusty loaf of Italian bread and some garlic. Why not splurge? It wasn't like she was throwing dinner parties every week.

Ruthie wheeled her small cart around the market, checking off the items on her list. When she got to the garlic, she laughed out loud at a memory, drawing a sharp glance from a silver-haired, matronly fellow shopper. It was her first turn to cook in the communal house where she and Carl had lived. Spaghetti was on the menu, and she made a list of the ingredients from the recipe she had found in the well-worn Betty Crocker cookbook they kept on a shelf above the stove. Ruthie had never cooked until she left home. Her mother didn't like anyone else in "her" kitchen and didn't have the patience to teach Ruthie how to cook. When Ruthie tried to help by vacuuming or dusting, her mother would usually grab the vacuum cleaner with an exasperated click of her tongue and tell her to go read a book. It seemed she never did anything right. She did all right in her first venture into cooking spaghetti until she got to the instruction to "mince one clove of garlic and add it to the pan." She looked at the round bulb of garlic, turned it around in her hand, and then chopped the entire bulb and browned it with the onions. The spaghetti Ruthie cooked was memorable and took its place in the accumulation of funny stories about life in the commune.

Later, at the R & R, she had been famous for her lasagna—the recipe passed on from her father who was allowed in the kitchen but made only a few things—lasagna, homemade dill pickles and great cold cut sandwiches.

Claudia's kitchen was small but efficiently laid out, and before long, Ruthie had a large pot boiling on the stove for the lasagna noodles and a pot of sauce simmering on another burner. The garlic bread was ready to go in the oven and the salad was waiting in a large wooden bowl to be dressed.

Ruthie had fun finishing the lasagna—placing the alternating layers of noodles, cheese, meat, and sauce just so in the Pyrex pan—popped it in the oven, then moved to the bedroom to change her clothes. She was really looking forward to this visit and to deepening her friendship with Violeta.

The intercom buzzed at exactly 6 PM. Ruthie buzzed back and went to the door.

"¡Ay, qué chulo!" Violeta said as Ruthie opened the door. "What a nice apartment." Already, Ruthie felt better, seeing her life through someone else's admiring eyes.

"¿Quieres tomar algo? ¿Una copa de vino? ¿Un refresco?" Ruthie settled Violeta in the floral upholstered armchair, the most comfortable seat in the apartment, and went to pour them both a glass of wine.

"Gracias, Ruthie. ¿Y este chamanto, de dónde es? It looks like the ones my grandmother makes in the mountains," Violeta said, moving to sit next to her on the futon couch and examine the colorful shawl she had draped over the back.

"I brought it back from Mexico on a trip Carl and I took there. In Mexico, they call it a manta." Ruthie slipped the shawl over Violeta's shoulders. "Would you like to have it, to remind you of your grandmother?" Violeta smiled and flushed.

"¿De verdad? Gracias, Ruthie. ¡Qué simpática! You are a true amiga. Oh, I almost forgot, I brought you something too." From the large woven bag Violeta had placed at her feet, she drew a handful of green pebbled globes and placed them one by one in Ruthie's open palms. "Palto—avocados, you say. They grow near my home in the mountains when it is the season. But here you can get them anytime."

"Wonderful," Ruthie said, standing and carrying the avocados to the kitchen. "I'll put them in the salad. My Puerto Rican friends call them aguacate. Are you ready to eat?"

Ruthie set the table with colorful placemats and napkins she had found in a drawer in Claudia's dresser, then laid out their sumptuous feast. After they had each finished two helpings and cleared the table, they stood side by side at the small kitchen sink, washing and drying the dishes.

"How I have missed such simple things—a good meal and washing the dishes together," Violeta said.

When the last plate had been dried and placed on the shelf, Ruthie poured them each a cup of the deep, rich espresso coffee she had snuck back from Cuba, and they sat together on the couch.

"Tell me something about yourself, Ruthie. You mentioned someone named Carl. ¿Es tu esposo?" Violeta sipped the hot coffee and waited for a response.

"Well," Ruthie paused, unsure of how much she wanted to open up. But how could she make a friend if everything about her was a secret? "Yes, well, that is—he was. We've been divorced for a few years now."

"Ay, qué triste. Tell me about him. Si no te molesta."

"Well, we met at college. We were both going to college. After we met," she went on, putting her purple ceramic mug on the scuffed wooden coffee table marked with rings of years of other mugs that had been set down upon it. "It took a long time to become friends. And then an even longer time to become lovers."

Violeta giggled. She was getting used to Ruthie's frankness, so different from the reserve of her few girlfriends back home, but still it made her uncomfortable to hear the word "lover" so casually slip off Ruthie's tongue.

"Tell me about the first time, your very first time," Violeta said quietly.

It was clear from her hesitation that she had never asked anyone that before.

Now it was Ruthie's turn to giggle. "Really? You want to know? It's not that exciting. Kinda funny though," Ruthie said, turning to face her friend. "Okay, but then you have to tell me. About your first, I mean."

A shadow crossed Violeta's face. "No quiero hablar de eso," she said. "I really don't want to talk about that."

Their light-hearted conversation had moved into new territory.

"Tell me whatever you want to, amiga," Ruthie said. "I'll go first." She moved around on the lumpy couch, trying to get comfortable, turning to face Violeta.

"We were in college," she began. "I was eighteen. He was two years older. Every Friday night there was a folk dance, un baile folklorico," she explained, standing and twirling around, her long tie-dyed skirt held out in a circle.

Violeta laughed.

"Well, Carl liked to dance," Ruthie plopped back on the couch, arranging a pillow behind her back, "and I liked to watch," she said.

"¿Y así se conocieron?" Violeta asked. "¿Amor a primera vista, no?"
"No," Ruthie replied. "Not love but friendship. We began to spend

time together—in the study hall, in my dorm, in the caf, at the Saturday night flicks—movies," she said, noticing Violeta's puzzled look.

"And then one night, late, after studying together, we walked to the bakery in the village center to buy bread right out of the oven, hot and crusty.

We were walking back through the dark streets, and he stopped me and tucked the bread under his arm and kissed me."

"¿Y?" Violeta was sitting on the edge of the couch, leaning into Ruthie. "¿Qué pasó?"

"Nothing," Ruthie said. "Just one kiss. Oh, and the bread got crushed."

They both dissolved into a fit of giggles, leaning back, legs in the air, until they had to stop to breathe. "¿Y?" Violeta said.

"And we ate it anyway." They shook the flimsy couch with their laughter.

When Ruthie had caught her breath she said, "It's a long story. I'll finish another time. Now tell me yours. Your turn."

A cloud passed over Violeta's face, chasing the twinkle of laughter from her eyes. "No es tan graciosa como la tuya, amiga. No hay mucho que decir. There's not a lot to tell. Soy una persona sencilla. ¿Está bien si hablo en español? My English is not good enough for this story."

Ruthie nodded. Violeta drew in her breath and went on, her brown eyes squinting with the effort to force the words out. Her thick black braid had fallen over her shoulder.

"Soy una persona humilde. I'm a humble person. I was born in Chile near Valparaíso in a small village on the coast. We had a hard life. My father was a fisherman, and my mother sold what we were able to grow on our small plot of land in the market. There were five of us and I was the youngest. I was good in school and got the chance to go to the university. And then, when I was 19, the same age my Javi is now, I had my first boyfriend. I met him at the university, but he dropped out to go to work on the docks. I became a teacher and got a job at a school close to my home. Things were going good. Then I found out I was pregnant. My parents were very religious and strict. They didn't really like my boyfriend—he was rough in his ways—but they said if I was going to be with him and have his baby, I had to marry him. He was nice before we got married—he took me to the top of Cerro Alegre on the ascensores where we could see all of Valpo and the ships in the harbor. But then he changed. He resented my educated friends at the school. Sometimes he followed me and watched me. If I talked to a man, a friend, he dragged me away and when we got home, he beat me. He got drunk every night and after he lost his job on the ships, he drank in the day too. The beatings got worse. He accused me of everything. He called me puta. But I was a good girl, a good wife—I cooked and cleaned. We lived in a two-room shack, but I kept it clean. Even after I got my belly, he beat me, kicked me, threw me out of the house and made me sleep in the street."

Violeta paused. Ruthie reached out for her hand and held it gently in hers.

"You can stop if you want, Violeta. I know this has to be hard to talk about."

"No, I am glad to have someone to share this secret with. In all my time here in this cold, cold country I have told no one. Only my cousin knows what I have been through. Why I had to come here. Why I had to leave my son." Violeta began to cry softly and withdrew her hand from Ruthie's.

"I feel so ashamed. Tengo tanta pena."

"No, no mi amiga. No hay que tener pena. You only did what you could to save yourself. And you are taking care of your son still from here. But how did you get away?"

"I ran for my life. I left my job at the school and ran to my parents. They found me a place to live high in the hills until my son was born. I had no job. I had my baby, and I couldn't work. My parents brought me food. They took care of me. I couldn't go anywhere because I was afraid he would find me. After some months, I heard he had another woman. I found a job in the market and took care of my son by myself. It was a hard life for those years. We had so little money, often not enough to eat, but we were surviving. Javi was smart and funny, and we were happy. But I knew it wouldn't last. Things were getting harder in my country. No one had work. The army was looking for guerrilleros in the mountains." Violeta paused. "Ay, Ruthie, tú no puedes imaginar. You can't imagine. They were rounding up the students, and even teachers like me were not safe. I had no future there—no future with my son. Then my cousin Gloria wrote to me. She had left for El Norte to make a better life for her family. I should do the same she said. She would give me a bed in her home and help me find a job. So I left. It was a sad day."

Violeta had left Javi, who was then seven years old, with her parents and had made a dangerous journey across the entire continent of South America— from Chile, through Argentina and Uruguay, crossing rushing rivers and hiding during the cold, desert nights. At first, she had only her cousin, but that and the job at Cookie's Diner, where her warm smile and valiant attempts to communicate in English had soon won her many friends, had been enough for a start.

The sky was dark through the sliding glass windows that looked out on a parking lot. They sat quietly for a while watching the shadows creep across the floor. Then Ruthie squeezed Violeta's hand and rose from the couch. She drew the curtains and made two cups of chamomile tea. Violeta rummaged in her purse and drew out a wallet, opening it to several small photos.

Ruthie placed the cups on the coffee table with a couple of Stella Doro cookies she had found in the cupboard and took the wallet.

"Oh, is this Javi? He is so handsome, Oh, and he was such an adorable baby," she said., holding up a photo of a chubby smiling toddler with black hair and dark round eyes. "You must miss him so much."

"It is hard, so hard. I can't visit because I have no papers and he can't come here. But I call every week and we write to each other...well, now that he's at university and so busy with his studies he forgets sometimes," Violeta said, taking the wallet from Ruthie and putting it back in her purse.

"It's late, Vi. You should stay here tonight. I can fix you a bed on this couch and we can go to work together in the morning. I have breakfast and lunch tomorrow. How about you?"

Violeta's eyes were red from crying, but she looked like a tremendous weight had been lifted off her shoulders. Her voice was firm and steady when she spoke.

"Sí, también. Me too. Breakfast and lunch. Is it really okay to stay? I have a long bus ride home."

"Claro que sí. Absolutely fine. We can have a pajama party." Violeta threw her a puzzled look. "¿Fiesta de pijamas?"

Ruthie laughed. "When we were kids, our girlfriends would sleep over, and we would put sleeping bags on the floor and watch movies and eat popcorn. That's what's called a fiesta de pijamas "

Pajama Party

Ruthie brought Violeta a nightgown and together they pulled out the futon and made up the bed with clean sheets and a light summer blanket. Violeta changed in the bathroom and came out looking like a little girl—her long dark hair soft and loose around her shoulders, her face shiny, her eyes bright with expectation. She lay down on the bed and motioned Ruthie to do the same.

"Como una pijamada," Violeta said. "That's what we call it in Chile. We have to stay up all night and you have to tell me a secret. I told you mine, now it's your turn."

Ruthie settled her body next to Violeta's on the bed and turned away from her.

"No one else here knows what I'm about to tell you, and you have to promise not to tell. ¿Me prometes? Do you promise?" Violeta made the sign of the cross and folded her arms across her chest. "Sí, amiga, te prometo en la vida de mi hijo, te prometo."

"Well," Ruthie began. "I did marry Carl just after I turned twenty years old, and we ended up living in California. It's a big state out west, have you heard of it?"

"Sí, California, Hollywood, sí…"

"And soon after we got there, I got pregnant with my daughter Sasha…"

Ruthie disappeared into her bedroom and emerged with the photo of Sasha she had taken from Carl's trailer, still in its tarnished silver frame, that she kept on the nightstand by her bed.

"She's bigger now. She'll be six soon."

Violeta's eyes grew wide, and a big smile lit her face.

"Una hija, qué linda, pero ¿dónde…?"

"Sí, voy a contar lo que pasó. We were living in a big house called the Family Place with three other families—a commune, it's called, una casa comunal. We all shared the housekeeping, cooking, and childcare. Carl and I were happy at first, and it was so exciting after Sasha, mi hija se llama Sasha, was born. I took her everywhere I went, even to my job at a school."

Violeta clapped her hands. "You were una maestra también. You were a teacher too. I knew we were truly hermanas."

"Well, it wasn't an official school, una escuela alternativa. Some of us were teachers, and some were just volunteers like me. Sasha slept in a basket, una canasta, in the corner while I worked with the kids. We were happy… al principio."

"Did Carl…did he beat you, hermana?"

"No, nothing like that, Vi. But we slowly grew apart… and he… well he found another woman."

"Ay, los hombres. Siempre nos maltratan. They always mistreat us," Violeta said, reaching out for Ruthie's hand.

"Pero ¿dónde está Sasha? And why is she not here, with you?"

Ruthie took a deep breath. This part of the story was hard to convey. Why did she go to Cuba? Why did she leave Sasha with Carl? That he had taken her away? Why was she here now? She rushed through it a bit, just to get it over with—leaving out that she had gone to Cuba, turning it into a "trip she needed to take"—not sure how Violeta would react to the choice she had made. When she finished, she looked over at her new friend. Violeta had tears in her eyes. Her features, touched by her indigenous roots—full lips, a wide nose, and skin the color of deeply aged copper—were sorrowful and somber.

"Lo siento tanto, mi amiga. I am so, so sorry that you are going through this. Just like me, missing your child, but worse even because you don't know where she is. Si hay algo, anything I can do, I am here for you." And with those words, Violeta moved closer on the couch and took Ruthie into her arms. Ruthie felt something give way inside her, and for the first time since leaving the warmth of the Family Place she felt seen and understood. She let herself melt into Violeta's embrace and they just breathed together for a long while.

Ruthie shook herself free of Violeta's arms and stood.

"Well, now you know. I have to find her. I will find her. But I don't know exactly where or how yet. So, for now, I am working at Cookie's, saving my money, and waiting…"

They were both quiet, and a comfortable silence grew between them.

Ruthie busied herself getting ready for bed. She changed into a long cotton nightgown with embroidered flowers at the neck, one she had brought back from a trip to Mexico with Carl. A big smile broke across Violeta's face when she saw Ruthie.

"Now you really look like my sister," she said—making room for Ruthie on the bed.

Why not, Ruthie thought. It's been a long time since I felt the warmth of another body next to mine while I slept. They settled foot to head on the lumpy mattress and Ruthie pulled the soft cotton patchwork quilt over them both.

"Buenas noches, hermana." Violeta's quiet voice broke the stillness of their breathing. "Que duermas bien."

"Nitey night. Sleep tight. Don't let the bedbugs bite." Violeta's soft giggle was the only response and soon they were asleep…each in their own world… their shared secrets binding them together.

Lonely

In the weeks that followed their pajama party, Ruthie and Violeta drew even closer. They shared a secret now, and the bond of mothers missing their children. Ruthie felt the burden of that secret lift a bit from her shoulders.

On her one day off from work, a day that varied and was posted on a bulletin board in the dingy back hallway of the diner, Ruthie often wandered through Harvard Square. She had forgotten how hot and humid a northeastern city could be in the summer and sought an empty bench in the shade, leaving her boxy, overheated apartment behind. Sometimes she brought a book, sometimes her knitting—she was making a sweater for Sasha out of purple and pink yarn, her favorite colors. But often, she just sat and watched the people in the Square. It was free.

When she had first landed in Cambridge, she had avoided the Square—hating the students who hung out there smoking pot and plucking chords on their guitars without a care in the world. She was only a few years older than they were and felt like she was dragging around a whole other body's weight of burdens—a failed marriage, divorce, interrupted education and now—she didn't want to say the words out loud, hadn't told anyone but Violeta in this cold, unfriendly city—a missing child.

Now, as she looked around for a place to sit, Ruthie imagined herself standing on a bench and shouting out her secret like a crazy woman—long wavy hair flowing over her shoulders, tie-dyed skirt billowing in the wind.

"I left my little girl and now she is gone," she would shout, and the students would glance at her and then return to their glowing joints and guitars.

She had abandoned her child. In the hours before dawn, when she woke early in the still unfamiliar bedroom of her cousin's apartment, she knew it to be true. She had abandoned Sasha, her curly-haired imp — left her, deserted her, disappeared from her life.

She had been selfish, self-centered, clueless, and oblivious. And now she was paying the price. She tasted the consequences like the dregs of bitter coffee left to turn dark at the bottom of the pot at the diner. What must it feel like to Sasha? How did she process Ruthie's absence in her mind, so young and tender, protected—until this?

For all her life, Mama was there every night tucking her into bed, softly singing

her favorite lullaby—a Spanish one Ruthie had learned from an album of Will's-- Duerme, duerme negrita. Their only separation–the every other weekend time spent with Carl. When they moved to Colorado, even that separation ended, and they were together every night, sleeping in the same soft bed, enveloped by the creaks of the big old house settling in for the night.

Then, Mama was gone. It must have felt sudden to Sasha despite all the bedtime stories about Mama's trip. Despite the days and nights Ruthie spent at the ranch making sure Sasha was comfortable—with Carl, with this new temporary home. Despite Ruthie's patient answers to Sasha's endless questions:

When will you be back, Mama? Why can't I go with you, Mama? How long is soon? Will you be able to see me while you're gone? Will I see you? Who will braid my hair, Mama? Daddy doesn't know how to do it.

Ruthie shook her head to clear Sasha's voice from her mind. She set her gaze on two elderly black men who were playing chess on a board laid out on an overturned wire milk crate. They stared at the board for a long time between each move—but when they were ready, their bony hands would dart to move a piece, and one or another would shout Hah! or slap a knee, or just stroke a chin. Ruthie was lost in this scene and didn't notice the bearded white guy in khaki shorts, Birkenstocks, and a plaid shirt open at the collar until he was standing right in front of her.

"Is this seat taken?" he asked.

Ruthie recognized him as one of the regulars at Cookie's, often sitting by himself at the counter, accepting endless refills for his stained beige coffee mug and scribbling notes in red in the margins of a manuscript. He was sometimes greeted by raucous groups of back-slapping, laughing students at the tables, but he never joined them. He could be a professor or maybe a grad student, some kind of writer perhaps. Ruthie didn't really care. And she really didn't want him to sit down on her bench, to have to make small talk, or worse, to have her tender wounds probed by his curiosity. "You look so familiar," he said now. "Do you go to Harvard? I'm Michael."

He stuck out his hand.

"Ruthie," she said, giving his hand a quick shake and then withdrawing her own to the book open on her lap. She hoped he would get the message and leave her alone. Instead, he sat down next to her on the bench, crossed one bare leg over the other and smiled at her with 100 questions in his eyes.

Michael took a pack of Pall Mall cigarettes from a pocket of his cargo shorts, tapped it against his leg and drew one out. He extended the pack to Ruthie.

"No thanks," she said. "I don't smoke." She almost added, "I stopped when I got pregnant," but left it unsaid. Watching Michael light his cigarette, draw a deep breath, and blow a cloud of smoke that curled around his fingers, she thought of her mother.

She thought of her mother sitting in a plastic lounge chair in their small backyard with a cigarette in one hand and a drink in the other.

"Penny for your thoughts," Michael said. "Where did you go?"

Ruthie shook her head, chasing away the memories, and smiled. Her jaw hurt with the effort, and she realized how infrequently she smiled these days. A little smile couldn't hurt, could it? She couldn't be sad all the time.

"That's better," Michael said. "Such a pretty smile—it's a shame to hide it."

Ruthie pulled her lips back into a straight, neutral line and looked down at her book.

"What are you reading?" Michael asked. "Anything interesting?"

She flipped to the cover and pushed the book toward him. "I loved that book, but it's not exactly light reading in Spanish. I'm impressed." Tears welled in her eyes, blurring the title— "Cien Años de Soledad" 100 Years of Solitude. She would sentence herself to all those years if that's what it took to get Sasha back.

Michael didn't notice. She could see the first question forming on his lips. He stubbed the cigarette out on the edge of the bench and wrapped the butt in a napkin. A careful man.

"So, where do you call home?" Michael asked, tucking the wrapped-up cigarette butt into a pocket of his shorts. "Not from here, I would guess. I'm from Indiana myself. Midwestern boy makes good at Harvard." He laughed, a deep belly laugh that crinkled his face and made Ruthie want to laugh with him. She suppressed the urge.

Home? She knew for sure that this city of brick sidewalks and meandering cobblestone streets, of ivy-covered buildings that announced their serious intentions—this city of youth and privilege—would never be home to her. Ruthie had known that as soon as she arrived. But where was her home? Not the city where she grew up, barely visible in her rearview mirror—or any of the places she had briefly touched down after fleeing the stifling sameness of her childhood home. She had always been good at nesting, at creating a home on whatever swaying branch she found herself—paintings on the walls, colorful cushions strewn around, family photos marking any four walls that happened to shelter her for however long they were hers.

But not this time. She had left the paintings and colorful cushions packed away in a friend's basement and couldn't bear to look at the family photos— Sasha in her naked, baby-plump self on a quilt in Dolores Park, Sasha laughing in the jolly jumper she and Carl had fashioned from canvas and leather and hung from a beam in their cozy attic bedroom, Sasha's wobbly first steps across a square of sunlight, Sasha waving goodbye from the door of Carl's trailer, her bedraggled Lambie clutched to her small chest.

She had placed the photos face down in the bottom drawer of her cousin's old wooden dresser in the small room where she tossed and turned at night. The walls were mostly bare—Claudia was all about her studies, not about creating a cozy nest. Like Ruthie's life these days, they held no color, no hint of home. The walls contained her, sheltered her, but they were not home. Home was a place she would create again with Sasha when she found her. Until then, this would have to do.

"Hey, it wasn't meant to be a trick question," Michael's voice cut into her thoughts.

"Oh yeah," Ruthie laughed, a scratchy tight sound in her throat. "Just I've lived a lot of places in the last few years. Won't be here long either I don't think." Maybe now he would get the hint that he was wasting his time trying to strike up a friendship with her. Or was he interested in more? Ruthie had forgotten what it felt like to be the object of a man's attention.

"Well, I've got to go now," she said, gathering her long skirt around her and rising from the bench. She slipped her paperback into the colorful woven bag Violeta had given her and stuck out her hand. "Nice talking to you," she said, shaking the hand Michael offered. "Maybe I'll see you around the campus." Michael smiled. "I hope so," he said. "I'll be looking for you."

Ruthie walked away slowly. Why had she said that—about seeing him around the campus? As lonely as she got sometimes, she didn't want anyone looking for her. And she didn't plan to see him again—anywhere.

Happy Birthday, Sasha

August 17th—Sasha's birthday. Ruthie studied the calendar taped to the fridge and wondered if Carl would remember how, as soon as Sasha could walk and understand her instructions, Ruthie had filled the house with surprises for her to find on her birthday.

The first year—was it her 2nd birthday, no probably her 3rd—Ruthie had made a trail of glitter for Sasha to follow into corners, to the hall closet, to the reading nook by the big bay window, to the space under her bed. Her squeals of delight echoed through the house as she pulled out whatever surprise was waiting there for her—finger paints and a special smock with her name on it, a storybook full of magical pop-up forests and castles, a stuffed puppy she had admired in the toy store and had immediately named Spot, though it was brown and tan with no spots in sight.

Who would be keeping Sasha company on this first birthday without her Mama? Last year, when Sasha turned five, everyone in the house in Colorado had participated in her surprises. Brother Big had cooked her favorite meal and bought her a chef 's hat and apron so she could be his official helper in the kitchen. Andy, the artist, had sketched a beautiful charcoal portrait of Sasha in her favorite pose, curled up in the big armchair by the window with her thumb in her mouth and her nose in a book. Loki, the R & R's rescue mutt, who followed Sasha everywhere, had been decked out with a big red bow around his neck, and dangling from it a small box from which she drew numbered clues for all her gifts. How they had laughed together that day.

For this birthday, Sasha's sixth, there would be no hidden clues. Ruthie had bought a small chocolate cupcake at the bakery next to the diner yesterday.

She put it on a plate, placed one candle at the center, closed her eyes, wished Sasha all the wonderful surprises the world could hold, and blew it out.

Dear Priscilla

You may not remember me, but we met at college, and I married your good friend Carl. We moved to the Bay Area and had a daughter, Sasha, who is now 5 years old. Oh actually, yesterday was her 6th birthday! A couple of years ago we divorced. The thing is that I traveled to Cuba for a few months with a solidarity brigade and Sasha was staying with Carl at this ranch-commune in Sonoma–the Rainbow Ranch. Well, to make a long story short, when I got back to the States and the place we were supposed to meet, Carl didn't show up with Sasha. Have you heard from him recently by any chance? I know you two were good friends and may have kept in touch. As you can imagine, I'm pretty desperate to make contact with Carl and know where Sasha is. If you have heard anything at all, or hear from him in the future can you please call me or drop me a note to:

Ruthie Moreinis
64 Harvard St.
Cambridge, Mass
1-617-417-7528
Thanks! Hope things are going well for you.

A Night at the Movies

A week later, on a night when the late summer heat had become unbearable, Ruthie fled her apartment, heading for the Cinema in the Square, hoping it would be air-conditioned.

Ruthie walked fast, passing the front gardens of the stately homes on Harvard St. Even the lavender that grew like weeds and perfumed the night air looked parched and longing for coolness. The Cinema was having a Fellini festival, one of the benefits Ruthie enjoyed about living near a university, and she would see La Strada, her favorite, and let herself cry as she always did with the heartbreak of the ending.

"One, please," she said, pushing her $1.50 through the glass enclosure of the ticket booth.

"Make that two." A deep voice behind her. She turned to find the Birkenstock guy from the Square (Michael, was it?) with a $5 bill in his hand and that big grin of his plastered on his face.

"Fancy meeting you here," he said with a chuckle. "You don't have air conditioning either I guess."

Ruthie knew La Strada by heart. She had first seen it in the mid-60's at the art cinema in the small Ohio town where she went to college, and then again at the Thalia in New York City where she sat alone in the darkened theater and let Gelsomina, a lonely waif who is bought by a brutish strongman in the circus to take on the road, capture her heart. He teaches her to play the trumpet, and the haunting melody had stayed with Ruthie all these years later.

As they found seats together toward the back of the small theater, Ruthie wondered if Michael, like her, had seen the film before. She let the cool air waft over her, conscious of the warmth of Michael's shoulder brushing hers and the soft hairs on his bare arm on their shared armrest.

"I don't like to talk about films right after I've seen them," she whispered as the lights dimmed. "Especially not this one."

"Got it," Michael said, flashing her a thumbs-up sign, and they both settled into the opening strains of music that always made Ruthie's heart leap. The theater was not crowded and mercifully quiet as the story on the screen unfolded. Even though she had seen it twice before, Ruthie gasped when the strongman Zampano, played by Anthony Quinn, beat Gelsomina's only circus friend to death. And her tears flowed freely at the end, when the trumpet's notes underscored the tragedy of Gelsomina's abandonment and Zampano's belated realization that he had loved her. Ruthie stole a glance at Michael and noticed he was dabbing at his eyes with a handkerchief.

"So," Michael said as they strolled up Harvard St. away from the Square. It turned out Michael lived just a couple of blocks from Ruthie in one of the stately brick buildings closer to the university. "Would you like to come up for a glass of wine?" Michael asked. "I can walk you back home later."

"Um…" No was the response on the tip of Ruthie's tongue, but she was tired of saying no to life. Michael was nice, and she was flattered that a Harvard graduate student who taught there would be interested in her. "Sure," she heard herself say. "A glass of wine would be nice."

Michael's apartment was even smaller than Claudia's—just one big room with a kitchenette against one wall and a bathroom at the end of a short hallway. It was neater and more orderly than Ruthie expected—his bed separated from the sitting area by a bamboo folding screen, soft lighting, and neatly framed art posters on the wall. One small bookcase sagged against the wall, weighed down with serious-looking volumes with titles embossed in gold that Ruthie couldn't read from where she sat on a low platform pushed against the wall between two windows, mounded with colorful woven cushions. It was comfortable, pleasant even, and Ruthie began to relax.

"Red, or white wine, Ruthie?" Michael asked, opening the fridge.

"You wouldn't by any chance have a cold beer, would you?" Ruthie sat back against the cushions. "I love a cold beer on a hot night like this."

"As a matter of fact, I do. Nothing fancy. Schaefer OK? Want a glass?"

"Nope, can is fine."

Michael carried two frosty cans of beer and a bowl of pretzels on a tray and set it down on a small wooden crate, which he pulled in front of the cushioned platform. Ruthie moved over to give him some room, but he plunked himself down right next to her.

Ruthie took a swig of her beer and sighed. "This is nice," she said. "Have you lived here long?"

"Moved in at the beginning of this year—when I got hired as a TA." "And what is it that you teach?" Ruthie asked.

"Oh, it's a Russian literature class— you know, Dostoevsky, Tolstoy, Chekhov, Gorky, etc., etc. But a survey course really—we don't have time in one semester to go too deep."

"Wow, that's amazing. For the little bit of time I was in college, I was a Russian Lit major. Fell in love with Alyosha in the Brothers K and never looked back." Ruthie took another long swig of beer.

"Ah, the mystery woman reveals a secret," Michael said. "So, I guess you aren't here as a student. How'd you end up in Cambridge, then?"

"So many questions," Ruthie said, trying to figure out how to answer. She sipped on her beer, swallowed, and then impulsively drew closer to Michael and kissed him gently but firmly, holding her lips to his until she felt him respond. "Ok, no more questions," Michael whispered into her hair. "This feels good."

Yes, it does. Ruthie thought. It sure does.

The alarm was insistent—a sharp beep tapping at the edges of her dream. Ruthie groped for the clock in the still-dark room but felt only empty space where the nightstand should have been. She rolled over, searching the covers for the clock. Maybe it had fallen into the bed with her. Her shoulder brushed against something soft and warm beside her.

"Sasha," she gasped, opening her eyes. "Sasha…wait, what…" "Ruthie, you're having a bad dream. Who is Sasha?"

It was Michael beside her in the bed. Michael's bed in Michael's room.

Michael's clock waking him up for class.

Ruthie jumped from the bed and stepped across the unfamiliar carpeted floor to a door with a faint light behind it. It must be the bathroom. She moved quickly inside, shut and locked the door behind her, and lowered herself to the floor. She leaned her back against the cold, hard side of the porcelain tub, and the voice in her head, increasingly familiar, began to scold her.

How could you have let this happen? You're supposed to be focused on finding Sasha. You promised not to let anyone get too close.

But this time she pushed back. Michael likes me, and I like him. I'm lonely.

There's no mystery in that, no crime.

Ruthie grabbed the edge of the sink and pulled herself up from the floor. She looked at her reflection in the mirror over the sink—between rust stains and flecks of white paint. Her hair was massed in wavy tangles, blocking her eyes. She pushed it aside. Her brown eyes stared back at her. Small almond-shaped eyes like her father's, fringed with short, light brown lashes. She had grown accustomed to staring at her own reflection, searching for answers there. Usually she found none—only anguish and torment, or, on some days, a flat, dull acceptance.

But today there was something new, something different in her eyes. A spark of life. And she liked it.

Michael insisted on walking her home. In the cool morning air, they passed a small courtyard where a group of inline roller skaters were practicing a routine—twirling, skating figure 8's, and executing dance moves with great precision.

"Wow. I was a skating champ on my block in Hartford but all we had were four-wheel metal skates we tightened on our sneakers with a key that we hung around our necks. This is really something," Ruthie said.

"I was something of a whiz myself," Michael said, "but I graduated to big-boy skates. There's a disco skating rink in Dorchester that's a lot of fun. Maybe we could try it sometime."

"Maybe…" Ruthie said, feeling herself tighten up again as Michael talked about the future.

"Well, this is where I get off. See you around the campus."

She reached up and gave Michael a peck on the cheek, then moved quickly toward the entrance to her building before he could say anything else, waving as she inserted her key into the lock.

Protest

Ruthie worried all through her shift at the diner. A few days earlier, Michael had stopped by and left a flyer for her—announcing a protest on campus—and invited her to come. Students were rallying to protest the continued bombing of Cambodia that Nixon ordered, even after the Peace Accords had been signed to end the Vietnam War, and his role in the Watergate scandal. She was torn about going to the rally. She'd promised herself to stay away from all those activities that had drawn her in and away from Sasha—the seduction of politics that now she thought had ruined her life.

But there was something else that was making Ruthie feel uneasy. In the few weeks since she and Michael had met at the movies, she had let down the walls she had built around herself a bit. Dinner at Michael's place one night, a moonlit walk by the river, a new Truffaut film at the Cinema—and after each occasion, they had ended up in Michael's bed. Ruthie hadn't realized how lonely she had been, how much she had missed having someone's arms around her, until she let herself melt into Michael's embrace. Carl had been her first lover, followed by a few short-lived romances at the R & R with GIs who carried a lot of emotional baggage from the war. It was exciting to explore another man's body and to feel herself come alive to another man's touch.

They had settled into a comfortable pattern for Ruthie when one morning, as they washed the breakfast dishes together, Michael turned to her with soapy hands and a serious look on his face.

"Can we talk?" he said, drying his hands and guiding her to the couch. Ruthie braced herself. In her experience, those words usually meant trouble. "I really like you, Ruthie. I'm so glad we're spending time together and getting to know each other. I hope you are too. But sometimes I feel like you're—I don't know—holding back or something. Almost like you're hiding something. I just want you to know that you don't have to be that way with me. I'm a good guy." He laughed and threw an arm around her.

"Really."

"Yes, you are," Ruthie said, buying a little time while she figured out what to say that would not be hurtful and not give him the wrong idea about what might happen between them.

"I'm just cautious, I guess. Relationships haven't always been easy for me—and there have been some not-so-good guys. But I like how we are together. Can that be enough for now?"

"I guess so," Michael sighed, "but I hope you'll give me a chance. Ruthie let his words hang in the air without a response.

This isn't going to work, she thought. He wants more and I can't let that happen.

That morning, before she left for work, Michael called to ask whether she would come to the rally. He explained its purpose to her as if she were a new recruit, uninitiated and unaccustomed to protests—and Ruthie let him believe that was who she was. It was not that she didn't trust Michael, the specific person. She didn't trust him as a representative of a world that had hurt her and could still hurt her.

But she had finally said—yeah, sure, I'll meet you there at 7.

After all, Nixon was still causing the deaths of innocent civilians in Cambodia and lying about the Watergate break-in. Besides, the activist still living inside her was insisting that she do something.

"Hey, sweetie. Watch it," Leo, one of her regular after-work customers for a cup of coffee and a slice of pie, called out. "You're spilling my coffee."

"Oh sorry, Leo. Did I splash any on you? I'll get you another cup." "No, don't bother. Gotta get home anyway. You take care."

Take care, Ruthie thought. Sure—but just how do I do that?

Ruthie walked slowly toward the group gathering in one corner of the Square. She could see their banner from where she stood. Get the Liar out of the White House. Impeach Nixon Now! Michael was holding up one end of it. Despite her misgivings, she felt a familiar anticipation kick in—her heart beating faster, her steps carrying her quickly to the group It.

It was as if her body was reminding her of all the years she had proudly walked on picket lines and in marches.

Was she really going to do this? She could turn and run, leave a message for Michael when she got home. But Michael had seen her, passed his banner pole to someone else and was walking toward her across the ancient red bricks. Too late to run. Ruthie took a breath, pasted a smile on her face and walked to meet him.

"You came!" he said.

"I came," she repeated. "Can't stay long though. I have the early shift tomorrow."

"Come meet the group," Michael said, tugging her gently toward the banner and the crowd.

His warmth, his enthusiasm, the glow that shone in his eyes when he looked at her—it was sweet, but it made Ruthie anxious. She wanted to hide herself in a windowless room—where no one could see in, and she didn't have to look out. She wanted to stay there until, magically, her daughter appeared beside her to take her hand and bring her out into the world. But it was not going to happen that way.

Ruthie let Michael lead her into the crowd. Names floated by her as he introduced her to one, then another.

"This is Ruthie. She works at Cookie's. This is her first protest."

His words gave Ruthie pause. Was she some kind of working-class trophy recruit for Michael? Was that what this was really about?

Ruthie took her place in the line, holding a sign that someone had thrust into her hands, and stood awkwardly, mouthing the chant along with the others. Then something inside her that had been waiting to get out kicked in, and soon she was chanting loudly and shaking her fist, her anger at Carl and Nixon and everything that was so fucked up about the war and the bombing and this whole unjust world merging until she was shaking with emotion, and she needed to get out of there fast.

"I've got to go, Michael. I'm not feeling well. Some kind of stomach thing, off and on. Maybe I'll see you tomorrow."

She turned and walked quickly across the Square without looking back. She couldn't do this today. Maybe not ever.

Ruthie heard the chants start up again as she left the Square.

Liar Liar Pants on Fire. Impeach Nixon Now.

She was fuming all the way home.

How dare Michael assume she knew nothing about protests! Maybe she should tell him about the time her gang of college dropouts infiltrated the Ohio State Fair while LBJ was giving a speech, unfurled a banner that read Hey, Hey LBJ How Many Kids Did You Kill Today, and held it in the middle of his speech. Their chants that day were loud and fearless, and the crowd would have torn their limbs off if it hadn't been for the National Guard, who formed a wall around them and led them off the field.

Yes, Michael. I too went to college, but I didn't stay locked away in an ivory tower. I went out into the real world. Maybe she should tell him about her friend Emma (not her real name), part of the underground movement that blew up recruiting stations and defense research labs, about their meetings in out-of-the-way places—how Emma called her comrade and relied on Ruthie to tell her the truth about how "the people," as she described the rest of the world, felt about their actions. Ruthie never knew how they used the feedback she provided. It was not illegal exactly what she was doing, but it was risky. Maybe she should tell him that Emma wanted to meet with her again, right here in the ivied bubble of Cambridge.

Maybe she should tell him about the R & R coffeehouse—years spent organizing GIs at Fort Carson against the war, her fingers always stained with blue mimeograph ink from the basement machine that produced newsletters and flyers—being chased off the base by MPs, opening the door to find the FBI on the doorstep.

Maybe she should tell him about Cuba—how she was recruited to support a real revolution, not just words, and how she answered the call, traveled there illegally on a converted cattle boat, and learned from real revolutionaries.

Maybe she should tell him what she sacrificed for politics, what she lost.

Maybe she should tell him about Sasha.

By the time she reached her front door, Ruthie's hands were shaking so badly she could barely fit the key into the lock. As soon as the door closed behind her, Ruthie began sobbing. She slipped to the floor, her back against the gray metal door, rocking and crying.

How could she go on seeing Michael if it made her feel like this? The phone was ringing. She ignored it. It rang again.

Ruthie walked slowly to pick it up. She would try to explain. She didn't want to break things off with Michael yet. When she had to, she would.

Happy First Day of School, Sasha

September 1973

Ruthie dragged her feet over the dry leaves that were beginning to form small piles on the uneven bricks. Fall came earlier in Boston than she was used to, and she had already begun wearing a sweater over her uniform. She looked down at her feet and saw that her white shoes were badly scuffed and in need of polish. Oh well.

On the corner, in front of the old brick school building that had sat empty all summer, there were now lines of children. Ruthie had to step into the street to get by and was surprised to find them there. They formed ragged lines in front of cardboard signs taped to the wrought-iron fence—Mrs. Murphy, Room 201; Mrs. Reilly, Room 202; Miss Schwartz, Room 203. Of course. It was the first day of school.

Ruthie stole a furtive glance at the lines—fresh-faced kids sporting brand-new bookbags, new haircuts, and new back-to-school outfits. Some clung to their mothers, while others raced off to find old friends. The sound of their chatter and laughter followed her down the street.

This would be Sasha's first day of school, too, and Ruthie wondered whether Carl would find a school for her wherever they were. Probably not— he hadn't wanted Ruthie to send her to public school in Colorado last year, where, he said, they would brainwash her and turn her into a robot.

But Ruthie had insisted and won out—braiding Sasha's hair and tying it with purple ribbons at the ends, letting her pick out her own lunchbox and proudly print her name in big letters on her composition book. Her clothes had been hand-me-downs from a friend's daughter, but they were new and special to Sasha—a white blouse with ladybugs dancing all over it, tucked into a navy-blue pleated skirt—and her lace-topped socks and Mary Janes were brand new.

She had been so excited—racing ahead of Ruthie on the sidewalk, finding her teacher's name and taking her place in line—just like these kids in Cambridge, whose sounds faded into the distance as Ruthie turned the corner and opened the smudged glass door of the diner.

"Hola, chica. You okay?" Violeta greeted her from the back, where she was filling the ketchup and mustard containers.

"Oh, just a little sad today, Vi. First day of school."

"Ah, sí, yo entiendo," Vi said, and she did understand.

It was comforting to have a friend, and especially one who knew what it felt like to be missing her child.

Hi Lottie

Hello. '

Hi Lottie. It's Ruthie. Ruthie dear. How are you?

I've been better. Yesterday would have been Sasha's first day of school and still no word from Carl. Have you heard anything?

No, dear, I'm afraid we haven't. It's not like Carl to go this long without being in touch, but well, what can we do?

Yeah. Well. I'm not gonna stop looking.

Why don't you talk to Stan? He and Carl aren't that close these days, but he may have some ideas about where they may have gone. He lives in the middle of nowhere and doesn't have a phone, but I can give you his address, and you can drop him a line. I'm sure he'd be glad to hear from you.

Yeah. O.K. Let me get a pen.

And Ruthie, take care of yourself, dear.

.

A Coup in Chile

September 11, 1973

Ruthie was sipping her first cup of coffee of the morning when the phone rang. Probably Claudia. They spoke once a week. Claudia was enthusiastic, bubbly even—loving everything about London, unabashedly mimicking a British accent as she chattered on about her wonderful life. Ruthie did not look forward to their phone conversations. She stumbled out of bed across the chilly cork tiles, glancing at the clock radio on her way—10 AM. Not Claudia. Maybe it was Michael. Ruthie had gotten over her anger at him after the rally, and he hadn't even noticed. Really, he was so patient and understanding with her. She wished things could be different.

"Hola, Ruthie." It was Violeta. Ruthie wondered why she was calling. She hardly ever called here, and they would see each other tomorrow at the Diner. "Can I come over to talk to you? Something really bad is happening in my country. Mi tía me llamó anoche. My aunt called last night, but we could only talk for a couple of minutes before the call dropped. I'm scared, Ruthie, really scared." "Sí, sí, ven ahora mismo. Come over. I'll walk over to Out-of-Town News and see if I can find anything in the newspaper. They might even have a copy of a newspaper from Chile. What is it called, the main newspaper?"

"El Mercurio," Violeta said, with venom in her voice that surprised Ruthie. "Pero nunca dicen la verdad. Han estado en contra de Allende desde el principio. Publican mentiras, solo mentiras."

"Okay, why don't you catch the bus as soon as you're ready. It will take me about half an hour to hit the newsstand."

"Hit the newsstand?" Violeta asked with a giggle. She was getting used to Ruthie's slang way of talking in English and couldn't help but laugh, even through her fear.

Ruthie grabbed her purse, then picked up the phone to call Michael. Maybe he would have some ideas. But the phone kept ringing. He was probably in class or in the library. She would check in with him later.

This is good, Ruthie thought as her feet crunched over the red and yellow leaves already clustering on the sidewalk. Not good that something bad was happening in Chile, but good that she had something to think about. She was getting tired of spending her days spinning around and around in her own pain. Maybe she could help someone else for a change. She used to be able to do that—feel the pain of the world, of a friend, feel moved to tears or action. Lately all she had been able to think about was Sasha.

She walked quickly to the Square. The Out-of-Town News was a cluttered collection of newspapers and magazines from around the world, housed in a wooden shed next to the entrance to the MTA. Sheldon, the owner, was the "unofficial mayor of Cambridge," according to Cookie, who had been there since he first opened in 1955, hawking newspapers out of boxes. Ruthie often stopped by on a Sunday to pick up a copy of her hometown newspaper, the Hartford Courant, and browse the international papers for any news about Cuba. Maybe she could find a copy of El Mercurio that would help Violeta better understand what was happening in her homeland.

Ruthie headed for the rack where Sheldon kept the Hartford Courant and took in the headline. "Junta Grabs Chile. Allende Dead." The article went on to report that the socialist President's death was a suicide—yeah, sure, Ruthie thought—and that the Junta had imposed martial law, banned all press but El Mercurio, and imposed a curfew. What would happen to Chile? To Violeta's family?

"Is Sheldon here today," Ruthie asked the freckle faced teenager who was at the register. Sheldon would know which papers had the best news stories and if a copy of El Mercurio was among all of the papers piled high on rickety shelves.

"Nah, he took the day off," the kid replied, snapping a big wad of chewing gum in his mouth.

"Do you know if you have any newspapers from Chile?" she asked next.

"Chili papers? Nah, I don't think so," he said then, his grin revealing that he thought he had made a good joke. "Get it, Chili papers?"

Ruthie sighed and headed for the foreign newspaper section to see for herself. And there, tucked between El Pais from Spain and Le Monde from France she spied the bold black letters of the Mercurio headline:

JUNTA MILITAR CONTROLA EL PAIS MURIO ALLENDE

Ruthie bought El Mercurio and the Courant and a couple of other papers from Europe and rolled them up under her arm. Before heading home, she stopped in at the deli to pick up a crusty loaf of bread and some ham and cheese. Violeta would need sustenance for what was to come.

Ruthie was opening the newspapers and laying them out on the card table she used as a dining table when the doorbell rang.

Violeta arrived at her door breathing heavily, with red and swollen eyes. "¿Podemos prender la tele? I heard a sentence on the radio before I left my house—fighting in the capital, soldiers in the streets. El presidente muerto, dead. I am so worried about my boy. I've tried to call. I can't get through. Ay, Dios, ¿qué va a pasar con mi hijo?"

Violeta sat on the edge of her seat on the futon couch while Ruthie fiddled with the rabbit ears on the TV and twirled the dial trying to find some news.

There it was—a grainy shot of a throng of young people marching up a wide avenue, tattered banners, handkerchiefs held over their mouths. They were approaching a phalanx of heavily armored soldiers—bayonets thrust forward, helmeted, menacing.

It appears that Salvador Allende, the Marxist President of Chile is dead, and a military junta now controls the country. Martial law with a strict curfew has been imposed and it is said that supporters of the late President Allende are being detained in a soccer stadium in the capital. The U.S. denies any involvement in the coup. We will bring you more news when we have it.

The screen went black and then the canned laughter of an afternoon soap opera assaulted their ears. Violeta was crying softly beside her.

"This is what I am afraid of for so long," she said. "And my boy he will go to the capital. He will put his body there."

She leaned forward and rested her head on her knees. Ruthie laid one hand lightly on her back—to say I'm here. I know how much it hurts. I'm here.

On the 4th or 5th day after Violeta had first learned of the catastrophe in her country, Ruthie laid the Boston Globe on the back table at the dinerand opened to a black and white picture on the second page.

"El estadio en la capital…¿por qué?" Violeta said, stumbling into Spanish. The grainy photo that looked like it had been captured in a hurry showed a section of the large soccer stadium in the center of Santiago.

Violeta read the text through eyes blurring with tears. This was where they were bringing them then—the youth of her country who only wanted to breathe free. Was her Javi among them? There was no way to know.

Violeta traced the words down the page till she came to a name she knew—Victor, Victor Jara, a popular troubadour, a people's singer who had been rounded up with the rest. She heard his strong pure tenor voice in her head, singing of the right to live in peace—el derecho de vivir en paz. And then she read what they had done to him. It was almost too much to bear, she doubled over in pain but forced herself to go on. First, they had thrown him in the arena with everyone else-- no food, no water, hot sun beating down on their heads. He took up his guitar and began singing so they smashed it. Victor kept on singing, driving out fear, building a chorus of voices around him. They broke his fingers one by one—his long callused, brown fingers that could coax such pain and beauty from his guitar strings. They broke the bones, separated the knuckles from the flesh, bringing their rifle butts down and down again. Victor kept on singing as they dragged him away.

Who were these soldiers who could do these acts? Were they not also mother's sons? Violeta closed the paper and collapsed into the metal chair. She felt Ruthie's gentle touch on her shoulder. Out of the corner of her eye she saw Cookie waiting on one of her tables. She lay her head down on the cool formica surface, sticky with maple syrup and ketchup, and closed her eyes.

Violeta accepted Ruthie's invitation to come back to her place for dinner after their shift at the diner. She didn't want to be alone with her thoughts any longer than she had to. She would not spend the night as Ruthie had suggested because she needed to be home in case her mother or one of her tías managed to get through with some news.

Ruthie heated up some leftovers—a beef stew and some brown rice—but Violeta only picked around the edges of her bowl. She had not been eating much. At 6 o'clock, Ruthie switched on the TV, and they looked for news of

Chile, of the coup. It had been a week and already the scant coverage at the beginning had just about disappeared, but ABC news had a special seven-minute report. Grainy images of the soccer stadium flashed across the small screen of Ruthie's TV and Violeta moved closer, squinting her eyes and peering intently as if she might see Javi among the now clearly dispirited students who had been held there for days. Allende, the beloved president whose election 3 years earlier had brought the workers and students in her neighborhood in Valparaiso into the streets, banging pots and pans in hope and elation, was being described as a Marxist who brought the country to chaos and ruin.

"Asesinas" Ruthie muttered under her breath, placing a cup of strong coffee for Violeta on the table next to the futon couch. Violeta suspected that her friend was what Chileans called una izquierdista, a leftist, from the comments she made about the news, but they had never really talked deeply about their political beliefs. Violeta could feel Ruthie hanging back when certain issues came up in conversations in the diner—with customers and among the staff—always on the verge of saying something, but not letting go. She must have her reasons, Violeta thought, understanding why some things must not be spoken of. But Violeta's crisis seemed to have opened a door for Ruthie and with her next question she walked through it.

"Did you know that I went to Cuba?" Ruthie asked, sitting down next to Violeta on the couch. "Last year. I made a good friend there from Chile. His name is Andres. I'm worried about him now."

Violeta was astonished at this revelation. How could she not have known? Why had Ruthie held this back from her? She thought they had talked about everything, shared all of their secrets. Violeta knew that Ruthie had gone on a trip leaving her daughter behind. But to Cuba?

"Tell me about him," she said, wanting to know more but unsure what to ask.

"He is a student in Santiago. He gave me this record—she drew an album from a small stack by the record player on a shelf in the corner and handed it to Violeta.

"Los Angeles Negros," the music everyone in Chile was listening to—romantic, lush. Ruthie slid the disc from the sleeve and onto the turntable. A few scratchy turns and the yearning of violins filled the small room. They both closed their eyes and lost themselves in the music.

Desaparacido

Mid-September 1973

During the first dark days of waiting for news from Chile, news of Javi, Violeta wore the scarf her abuela had wrapped around her neck when she left her homeland all the time. Even at night when she slept, she folded it beneath her head as if its multi-colored strands could protect her and those she loved from the terrible events unfolding each day.

Her abuela had woven the scarf on a hand loom that was a vestige of her early life in the countryside on a finca where the wool from the sheep that grazed the green hills would be sheared and spun into yarn. The strands were dyed with colors extracted from the plants that grew there and from the earth itself. Indigo blue, deep terracotta red, the green of the firs that dotted the hills. For Violeta's scarf, her abuela had purchased the yarn in the market, selected from deep woven baskets that had been carried by burros from the hills to the city. She set up her loom in the kitchen by the back door, propped open to let in sunlight, air and the small insects that flitted around her hands as they moved---back and forth, back and forth—weaving the strands into one beautiful cloth. When she was a little girl, Violeta had played on the tiled floor of the kitchen, creating families with the small figurines her abuelo fashioned out of red clay brought from the mountains. She had watched her abuela's fingers move across the loom—pulling, tightening, weaving. Despite the knobby knuckles of her hands, swollen and stiff even then from years of hard work, they moved like lightning.

Violeta brought the fabric to her lips, across her nose. She imagined the smell of the smoky fires of the countryside, the sharp tangy scent of the pines, the faint perfume of her abuela. How she longed to feel wrapped in those strong arms again—to be home and safe.

Violeta walked up the stairs—a grand sweep of polished marble flanked by two fierce looking brass lions—to the main floor of the Boston Public

Library. She clutched the instructions Ruthie had written out about where she should go to look for news of the coup in Chile, but now that she was here, she was overwhelmed. There had been only a one-room library in her small neighborhood in Valparaiso and it was always crowded with students, but this library was huge with enormous rooms and shelves and shelves of books everywhere she looked. And so quiet. She was embarrassed by the squeak of her sneakers on the spotless floors, but no one looked up as she entered a room that was called the Main Reading Room.

Around long wooden tables, so polished that she could see her reflection in them, sat solitary people, absorbed by the books or newspapers spread before them. Violeta chose a seat at the end of one table, next to a ruddy faced older man with a Boston Red Sox cap tipped back on his head who was reading the sports page of the paper. She chuckled to think that people came to this castle of art and knowledge to read about sports. He looked up briefly and tipped his hat in her direction with a smile that revealed a set of nicotine-stained teeth.

"Top o' the mornin'" he whispered. A young woman across the table with stringy, unwashed brown hair hanging down around her face and a pile of books in front of her gave them a dirty look.

Violeta pulled out her chair and the sound it made as the legs scraped the floor caused the whole table to look up. She shrugged and mouthed 'I'm sorry' as she sat. From her Harvard Coop tote bag, she took a notebook— crimson with the word Harvard emblazoned in white on the cover, unused. No one would mistake her, a foreigner, a waitress on her one day off a week, for a Harvard student. She opened the notebook to the first blank page, took out the BIC ballpoint pen she had bought at the bookstore with the notebook, and wrote a heading on the top of the page.

COSAS PARA SABER
Things to know

Her attention wandered to the shaft of sunlight pouring from the large stained-glass skylight in the center of the soaring painted ceiling of the reading room. Plump nymphs and cherubs in muted tones cavorted around the circle of light. A touch of reflected blue lit up the head of a studious girl as she bent over her books.

Violeta returned her attention to her notebook and wrote a column of numbers under the heading: uno, dos, tres, cuatro, cinco. What was it she wanted to know?

Violeta went in search of the section Ruthie had told her about where papers from all over the world were available, clamped onto a series of wooden rods like laundry laid on a drying rack. She lifted a copy of El Mercurio carefully from the rod and carried it back to her table.

The newspaper was larger than the Globe and had a pinkish tinge. A bold headline proclaimed the dawn of a new age in Chile above a photo of Los Generales—the generals who had plotted and succeeded in removing the democratically elected government. She scanned for news of the soccer stadium, where thousands were rumored to be detained and where Javi might be. Nothing. The generals had a tight grip on the newspapers and radio. A photo of a group of middle-aged women in housedresses, banging on pots and pans in support of the new military government, took up half the front page. Violeta clenched her jaw. She wanted to rip the newspaper to shreds.

She looked for news from Valparaíso, the port city that was home to her family. It had been the first to fall, surrounded by navy ships. That much she had learned from the U.S. papers.

These papers were useless. Violeta folded the large pink sheets and laid them across the rod, smoothing and arranging so that the headline was front and center.

There must be a way to get more news, to read the truth. But Violeta didn't know what it was. She had run out of ideas. She left the library at dusk—the page in her notebook still blank. She was no closer to finding out what had happened to Javi. But she wouldn't give up.

Violeta shivered in her thick wool sweater, wrapping her scarf more tightly around her neck and hugging her arms around her. She could never seem to get warm enough during the cold Boston winters. The old cast iron radiator in her small room hissed and clanked alive every morning but the heat it provided was weak. And when she went out to the street there was always ice or snow or slush underfoot—the cold seeping into her body from the soles of her feet and the exposed thin skin of her wrists. It was only September, but already chilly and soon it would be winter.

In Valparaiso, it was the beginning of summer—the air warming day by day, the sun shining brightly through the fog that came down from the mountains that surrounded her town on three sides.

The sea formed the fourth boundary of Valparaíso, and she imagined the fishing boats getting ready for their early morning forays into the crashing waves. The funicular cars would be climbing up from the sea to the small barrios in the hills—and it was in one of those that her abuela and her tías would be getting ready for bed just as she, Violeta, was rising and preparing to go to work.

Or maybe they would be sitting together at the small table in the doorway on straw-backed chairs, drinking their mate tea, passing the metal cup from hand to hand and sharing the same metal straw, in a ritual that drew them together twice a day.

Javi, her son, was the missing piece in the jigsaw puzzle of home she had put together in her mind. Javi, surely in the streets, running with the other students, shouting "¡Abajo los generales!"—down with the generals—or perhaps already captured, waiting with thousands in the soccer stadium.

She had not found any more news in the papers or on TV, but the picture Ruthie had shown her in the Boston Globe was etched in her mind.

Violeta shook the sweater off her shoulders and pulled on her quilted coat and the well-worn leather boots she had found in a thrift store. She grabbed the canvas bag that held her white waitress shoes and apron, clicked off the light, and locked the door behind her.

Vámonos, she said to herself. She noticed she was talking to herself a lot in these anxious days. A ver lo que trae ese día. Let's see what the day brings. Maybe Ruthie will have an idea. Putting one foot in front of the other, as she had done since she first came to this land, she walked to the bus stop.

Take Care of your own Damn Kid

On the way home from work, Ruthie stopped at the small market in her neighborhood. She pushed the shopping cart through the aisles in a daze, pausing for a moment by the grapes, green and red, mounded high in their bin, droplets of water gleaming on the colorful globes. It had been years since she had bitten into a juicy grape—the farmworkers on the West Coast had started a boycott to win their demand for a union, and she wasn't sure it was over yet. Ruthie bypassed the grapes and pulled a cantaloupe from a pile in the next bin just as a crash and a scream woke her from her dreamy state.

"What have you done now, you stupid girl?" A pale young woman with orange-dyed hair, a halter top, and cutoff jeans was pulling a child away from the melons, which were careening around the produce section.

"It's really not her fault." The words slipped out before Ruthie could stop them and were met by a cold stare.

"Mind your own god-damned business. Take care of your own damn kid, why don'tcha?" The woman threw these words over her shoulder as she marched away, dragging the girl toward the checkout line.

Take care of your own damn kid…the words circled in her mind as Ruthie finished her shopping–no cantaloupes in her basket–and walked the few blocks toward home. I will, she vowed. I will take such good care of my kid. I will be so patient. I will not get angry. I will not yell. I will take good care of Sasha.

But a tape of "what if 's" had begun to play in her mind.

What if she had fought harder when they divorced for sole custody and child support?

What if she had left Sasha with her friend Terry instead of Carl? What if she hadn't gone to Cuba?

These thoughts followed her through the darkening streets, and right on their heels came the voices of blame. How could you be so stupid? What were you thinking—leaving a 5-year-old girl for months? Leaving her with someone so unpredictable? What did you expect?

She paused at the lobby mailbox and withdrew a stack of junk mail. She never got anything personal, never the news she longed for. Something fluttered out from between two ad flyers and landed on the dirty tile floor of the vestibule. Ruthie picked it up with gloved fingers. It was a postcard addressed to her c/o Claudia. Could it be a message from Carl? She drew in a breath and looked at the back. No return address, just 6 words in block printing, squeezed into the space. NEED TO MEET. URGENT. CALL ME.

Ruthie turned over the card—a picture of Pike's Peak, tall, rugged, snowcapped, with the words in red cursive—Hello from Colorado. She had an idea of who it was from, but how had Emma known she was here, in Cambridge, at Claudia's address?

Ruthie trudged up the three flights of stairs to her apartment, clutching the mail under her arm and dangling the bag of groceries from her hand.

Autumn was here. She could feel it in the air and see it in the changing colors on the tree-lined streets of her neighborhood. She was close to her goal. She was almost ready to take her next step, even if she wasn't sure what or where. She didn't need any complications. And this, the arrival of this message, was definitely a complication.

She draped her peacoat over the overstuffed armchair and set the groceries on the counter in the tiny kitchenette. She placed the mail on the card table—she would sort it later—and took the postcard with her to the futon couch, where she sat, drawing her feet under her and turning it over in her hand.

Colorado. It was Emma, all right. Had to be. It had been almost a year since Ruthie had seen her. What did she want from her now?

She still remembered the phone number, though she hadn't used it in years—803-775-3975. She dialed it in her mind and imagined Emma's husky voice on the line. She wanted to set up a meeting and would insist on it. That meant something had happened—or they were considering an action and wanted Ruthie's feedback again. But she couldn't, she wouldn't meet with Emma.

She was through with all that. She had to be. She had to stay focused. She had to find Sasha. Meeting with Emma was too risky.

Not that she had ever done anything illegal–or that they had asked her to. Emma would just show up out of the blue and ask her to meet at a designated place on the outskirts of town near the R & R GI organizing project. Emma was from Philly, younger than Ruthie but much more sophisticated and sure of herself. They had been roommates for one semester in college, though they never became close friends. They were both involved in the growing campus chapter of Students for a Democratic Society (SDS). When Ruthie married, left school, and moved to California, she lost track of Emma. A few weeks after the Days of Rage protests in Chicago in 1969, Emma called, wanting to get together and catch up. She was in San Francisco, she said. Could Ruthie meet her at the Presidio at 2 PM on Tuesday afternoon?

"I've joined the Weather Underground," Emma had said when they met on the windy slope of the national park overlooking the rocky coastline. "Don't worry. I'm not making bombs and blowing things up–we're just trying to shift the conversation, expose the real enemy…" Her words trailed off in the wind. "I'm building relationships with individuals and organizations to get feedback and stay in touch with the above-ground movement." Ruthie had been honest with her friend–the group's rhetoric was stiff and didactic, they were turning people off, and people didn't understand why they had suddenly turned to violence.

When they parted that day, they agreed to stay in touch, but that wasn't illegal, was it? Once Ruthie became a member of the R & R Collective, which made her a more "serious" revolutionary in Emma's eyes, their meetings became more frequent. They would walk along the path through the woods near the R & R house, and Emma would pepper her with questions—were people starting to see that only armed struggle would bring down imperialism? Did they see that the WU was serious and committed to the struggle? What were the issues on their minds now that the war was winding down? Ruthie was flattered, in a way, that Emma saw her opinions as important and useful. She didn't think she was doing anything dangerous or wrong. But would the authorities see it the same way? That was one of the reasons she still couldn't bring herself to go to the police about Sasha's disappearance. She didn't trust them to help her, and she didn't want their eyes and their laws on her family.

She wished she could call Michael. He cared about her, and he was smart. But she couldn't. She hadn't told him about Cuba or about Sasha. She had kept so much from him—trying to keep her past life tucked away in a secret compartment. Or Manny. Manny would know what to do. But Ruthie didn't want to lean on Manny too much. This was a burden she needed to carry alone.

Ruthie tore the postcard into little pieces and threw them into the garbage can under the sink. But she knew that was probably not the last she would hear from her old comrade. Emma probably knew that she had traveled with the brigade to Cuba. She would be eager to hear what people were saying about the Weather Underground.

Ruthie would not meet with her again. She would continue helping Violeta and find her own way back into the struggle when she had Sasha with her and was ready.

It was growing late, and Ruthie's stomach was grumbling. She set out one plate, one fork, one knife, and one napkin on the rickety card table that passed for a dining table, then ate her dinner, a plate of leftovers from the Diner, warmed in the oven. Her life was about absence, about missing, yearning, and longing for.

She was surrounded by people at work. She smiled, took orders, bantered with the cooks, even flirted occasionally. She was surrounded by people on the T, in the streets, in her building. Millions of people. She was a shadow moving among them. Except for the time she spent with Michael, Ruthie had never felt more alone in her life. Only asleep and dreaming, holding her little girl in her arms again, did she really come alive.

She thought of Violeta, and wondered what she was doing tonight, wondered what it would be like not to be able to go home, maybe not ever.

Ruthie woke the next morning early on the narrow bed in her windowless room where it was impossible to tell when morning had come except by looking at the clock. The sheets were damp with her perspiration. Thoughts mixed with dream fragments were tumbling through her mind. One in particular kept repeating until finally she opened her eyes and sat up on the bed.

You need to make a move. Nothing will change until you do.

She had fled to this place in shame and confusion. She had created a sort of a life—job, apartment, a good friend—and pushed everything and everyone from her past away.

But now it was time to act—she knew that in her heart, but she was terrified.

Ruthie shuffled across the floor to the small card table where she ate her lonely meals. On the faux-wood vinyl surface of the table sat a box—a wooden box inlaid with a shiny geometric pattern she had found at a thrift store. She drew her bank passbook from the box—Cambridge Savings in gold letters on the pebbled green cover. She looked at the only page that was marked, with only deposits, one each week, in a column of black numbers. She was proud of herself, at least for this—she had saved some money for the first time in her life. Her gaze swept the page to the total—$837.00. What could she do with that? Another trip across the country to search for Sasha? It wasn't enough to hire a private detective—she had finally agreed that might be a good idea, but Carl's parents had refused to help—afraid of what dirt he might dig up. And her father thought it would be a waste of time and money and was still mad at her for not going to the police. The lawyer had said she needed to show that she could create a stable life for Sasha when she found her. She wasn't there yet.

Ruthie sighed and crawled back under the covers.

She would have to wait just a little bit longer.

A Step into Action

Ruthie was heading to another campus rally. This time, it was to demand that Harvard divest from the apartheid system in South Africa. Students planned to erect a symbolic shantytown as part of the protest. Students, young kids really, were being thrown in jail and tortured.

Michael would be there. They had gotten past her angry exit from the anti-war rally, but they weren't seeing each other as often. His teaching and political activities kept him busy, and Ruthie spent much of her spare time with Violeta. She still felt the push and pull between them—Michael wanting more, Ruthie holding back—but he seemed to be accepting the boundaries she set. She wanted to give him an update on what was going on in Chile, tell him about Violeta's missing son, and see if his group could help her in any way. Violeta had agreed to speak to the group about the coup, on the condition that Ruthie translate.

A candlelight vigil was already underway by the time Ruthie reached the grassy expanse of Harvard Yard. A large spotlight illuminated groups of students who were busy erecting makeshift shanties and putting up signs and banners right in front of the President's office. Freshmen hung out of the windows of the dorms that surrounded the Yard, and students kept arriving through the many iron gates. There were a lot more people here than Ruthie had expected.

Banners and signs were scattered on the ground and hung from trees——"Harvard Must Divest," "Free Student Protestors in South Africa," and one large banner that read "Harvard Makes Money from Apartheid" in bold red and black letters, with red paint spatters that looked like blood across the white canvas. In the center of the Yard, a group of students was busy building a large, tower-like structure out of boards and plywood painted white. A sign next to the structure identified it as THE IVORY TOWER. Clever, Ruthie thought, admiring their creativity. Michael had told her that a rotating group of students planned to occupy the shantytown until graduation. Ruthie wondered if they would last that long, but they seemed serious about their action, and she was impressed. She felt some of her fear and resentment melting away as she wandered through the encampment.

"This is amazing. How can I help?" she asked Michael when she found him at the center of a group of placard-holding students.

"Hey Ruthie," Michael said with a big grin. "So glad you could make it. We're getting ready to build one of the shanties–these are students from my class," he said, waving an arm at the students, who looked ready to go. "Hey gang, let's get some plywood and get started."

Ruthie followed him to a square in a corner of the Yard, taped off and marked with the number "12" in red chalk at the center.

"This is us–number 12. Let's build this thing," Michael shouted, brandishing a hammer and holding a slab of plywood up with his shoulder.

Ruthie grabbed a hammer and some nails. The feel of the tools in her hands reminded her of Cuba–and her job on the brigade, straightening nails taken from the framing boards on a rock in the shade of a mango tree. The ringing of hammers resounded throughout the Yard as ramshackle structures rose in every corner. And the deep bass notes and driving rhythms of the South African miners' work song echoed against the century-old red bricks of the administration building as students sang in harmony.

Shosholoza

Ku lezantaba

Stimela sipu'me South Africa

Ruthie added her shaky alto to the mix and felt her voice swell with each passionate note of defiance. Close to 100,000 workers had gone on strike in Durban earlier in the year, and this song had become their anthem. Now the Harvard students made it their own.

Ruthie pounded nails into the boards they were using to frame the shanty. With each blow of her hammer, she felt her strength and resolve grow, until she fell into a rhythm and a mantra she repeated silently as she worked: one blow for freedom in South Africa, one step closer to Sasha…one blow for freedom in South Africa, one step closer to…

"Ruthie? I had a feeling you might be here?"

The voice was familiar, but it wasn't until Ruthie paused mid-blow and looked up that her breath caught in her chest.

"Emma? How did you find me?"

"Would you believe me if I said I just happened to be in the neighborhood and am dying to hear about your trip to Cuba?" Emma laughed; the throaty laugh Ruthie remembered so well.

Ruthie scowled. "It's not funny, Emma. I really can't do this anymore." "But we need you more than ever, Ruthie. We've gotten much more serious— we're doing real organizing. Women are playing an important role. I brought you a draft of the manifesto we're working on." She took the hammer from Ruthie's hands and handed her a thick stapled bundle of paper. Ruthie shuffled through the pages, then skimmed the introduction, which ended with "We have only begun. At this time, the unity and consolidation of anti- imperialist forces around a revolutionary program is an urgent and pressing strategic necessity. PRAIRIE FIRE is offered as a contribution to this unity of action and purpose. Now it is in your hands."

It felt like fire in her hands. She tried to hand it back to Emma, but Emma refused to take it.

"It's yours now, sister. Read it and you'll see that we've changed. And like I said–we need your feedback more than ever. By the way, I'm really sorry about your little girl. Maybe we can help you find her. We're pretty good at that."

Ruthie sighed, then caught sight of Michael approaching them. She did not want to have to explain Emma to him.

"You need to leave now," she said. "I'll read this and think about it, but I can't get involved right now. Please try to understand, Emma. I'm really scared." "Okay, Ruthie, okay. I don't want to make things harder for you. But don't drift too far away–it might be harder than you think to come back."

With those words, Emma thrust the hammer back into Ruthie's hand and walked away into the gathering darkness just as Michael came up behind.

"Who was that you were talking to? It looked serious. And what's this?" he asked. Ruthie stuffed the pamphlet into her tote bag.

"Oh, nothing," she said. "She's an old friend from my college days. Just happened to be in Cambridge and came by to see the demo. Can you believe that? What a coincidence!"

Ruthie took up her hammer and began to pound again, not wanting to answer any more of the questions she saw in Michael's eyes.

One blow for freedom in South Africa….one blow for finding Sasha.

Dear Stan

I'm writing to ask if you've had any contact with Carl in the last few months. You might know by now that he left the Rainbow Ranch with Sasha and didn't show up for our arranged meeting when I got back from Cuba. No one at the Ranch knows where he is or has heard from him. I know you guys haven't been close lately, but I'm desperate to know where Sasha is and why Carl disappeared with her. Please, Stan, if you know anything or have any ideas about where he might have gone, please let me know. I'm working and living in Cambridge, Mass., until I save enough money to keep looking for them. Any news or ideas would be so appreciated.

Warmly, Ruthie

PS: Send any info to:

Ruthie Moreinis

℅ Claudia Morris

64 Harvard St. Apt. 2B Cambridge, Mass.

PPS: Hope things are going well for you. Do you still have a pet goat?

Someone Who Understands

Violeta found Ruthie slouching in front of the weekly shift schedule in the diner's grimy back hallway. The ever-present smell of bacon grease clung to the yellowing pages haphazardly pinned to the bulletin board. Sal's voice thundered from the kitchen pass-through, and the bell signaling another order was ready dinged emphatically. Violeta smiled, and Ruthie winked in reply. Neither rushed to pick up the steaming plates. A few more minutes wouldn't hurt. It was Saturday night, and Violeta was tired. Her back was sore, and her knees ached.

"Ruthie, mira, we are both off tomorrow," she said. "Cookie must have made a mistake. She never gives us the same day off."

Violeta squinted at the calendar again just to be sure. Sure enough. A Sunday off for both.

Violeta turned to Ruthie.

"My church is having a special service tomorrow," she said. "To pray for the desaparecidos—the disappeared—in my country. I will pray for Javi." Violeta paused. "¿Podrías venir, Ruthie? Could you come to my church with me?"

Violeta waited for her answer, worried that she was imposing on her new friend. She knew how much Ruthie liked to stay in bed late on her days off, drinking a cup of coffee on the small balcony of her apartment. Ruthie had described how she did her chores, dancing around the apartment to music blaring on Claudia's stereo. She had even played one of her favorite albums— the husky voice of a Black woman, full of pain, singing the blues. Violeta couldn't really catch all the words, but she understood the feelings in the music. "Sure, claro que sí, I would love to come," Ruthie said, sweeping away Violeta's doubts. How lucky she was to have found such a special friend at Cookie's Diner—una hermana, a sister really, someone she could confide in.

Someone she could talk to about Javi's disappearance. Someone who wouldn't judge her. Someone who understood.

Violeta still found it hard to believe that young men, even boys had been rounded up by the brutal generals who had taken over her homeland. And then they had just disappeared into thin air. Los desaparecidos. She remembered the photo Ruthie had found of thousands of them in the Estadio Nacional. How can this be happening in my peaceful country, she wondered?

But then she had not set foot in Chile, in her village of Portales, since she had left 12 years earlier.

Just a few years earlier, in 1970, she had celebrated, along with the small community of her Chilean compatriotas in Boston, when Salvador Allende had been elected presidente with the promise of a government that would finally pay attention to the workers—simple people like her parents. But the derechistas, the right-wing generals who defended the rich, called him a comunista and did everything they could to force him out of office. Her monthly calls to her mother were filled with reports of las ricas, wives of prosperous businessmen, marching in the streets banging pots and pans calling on Allende to resign and the truck drivers blocking the roads so no goods could get through to the capital. And then came the golpe, the coup, and Allende didn't resign. He stayed in his office in the Presidential Palace, facing the troops who stormed in, defending democracy to his last breath, and then taking his own life before he could be captured.

Ruthie's voice cut through her memories. "Buenas noches, Vi. Hasta mañana. See you tomorrow. Can you write down your address on my pad? Can I walk there, or do I have to take the bus?"

"I live in The Port," Violeta said, scribbling her address with one of the stubby pencils they used to take the food orders. "It's a pretty far walk, but you can take the bus. It's the M22—the one you catch in the Square that goes all the way along the avenida. Hasta mañana, amiga."

Violeta decided to walk home. The night breeze was refreshing after the steamy stale air of the diner. She walked on Mass Ave, a broad, busy street that cut through the heart of Cambridge. When she had first arrived and heard people talking about Mass Ave., her Chilean brain had translated it to Avenida de las Masas—Avenue of the Masses—and then she had felt foolish when she learned it was Mass for Massachusetts—a name from the American indigenas that she still struggled to pronounce. Of course, there would not be an Avenida de las Masas in this city, filled with important universities, banks and mansions. She turned off the avenue to the small, crowded streets of her neighborhood, lined with 3-story wooden houses, triple-deckers they were called, like the BLT sandwiches they sold at Cookie's. She had ended up in The Port because her cousin had found her a room in her building—a house much like the others but divided up into single rooms with a bathroom on each floor and a refrigerator in the basement where the immigrant women who occupied the rooms could keep food. It wasn't much—not nearly as nice as Ruthie's apartment on a street with big houses and brick sidewalks, but it had been home since she arrived in this country. And Violeta wasn't used to much—sharing two rooms in a small yellow hut with her parents and Javi—the kitchen just a covered shed jutting off the back of the house, the bathroom another shed a few steps away. Violeta chuckled to herself as she trudged up the worn wooden stairs to her third-floor room— "The Port" with not a ship in sight. Not like her neighborhood in the hills of Valpo where she could see the brightly colored boats of the fisherman bobbing in the choppy waters. Her father had a boat there and left their home early each morning to wind his way down to the sea, cast the nets that brought the fish and hopefully enough money to take care of their family. It wasn't much, but it would always be home, and she missed it.

Violeta hung her light jacket on a hook on the door and closed it behind her. She looked around the room, trying to see it as Ruthie might. A green carpet that felt soft under her feet covered the floor—and against one wall, a tan couch covered with a nubby fabric that scratched her bare legs in the summer. At night she pulled a special bar underneath the couch, and it made a bed. She had been so surprised when her cousin first showed her. A small table next to the couch held her radio and alarm clock and in the corner was a shelf with a hot plate and a toaster where she could make coffee and heat a little food. Next to that, a sink where she could wash up and brush her teeth.

The shower was down the hall in the bathroom shared by the 4 rooms on the third floor. She kept milk and butter and a few other things in the refrigerator downstairs but ate most of her meals at Cookie's which saved money, so she didn't have to cook.

Violeta had done her best with the few things she had been able to carry with her to make the room look like a home. She had draped a shawl over the back of the couch—the shawl her abuela had woven on the strap loom on the dirt patio of the house and wrapped around her as she began her long journey to El Norte. A couple of embroidered squares depicting daily life in her fishing community hung on the otherwise blank walls. Neighborhood women gathered around tables in their huts and created these pictures from thread and scraps of fabric cut from clothing that could no longer be worn. A straw basket sold by Mapuche women in the market held a few apples and bananas on the cooking shelf.

Ruthie will like my home, Violeta thought, pulling on the bar to open her bed. She will not judge. She knows what it is like to struggle.

Liberation Church

Late September 1973

Ruthie arrived early the next morning, and Violeta clambered down the three flights of stairs to open the door for her friend, who had dressed in a long denim skirt and a Mexican peasant blouse for the occasion.

"Bienvenida, amiga," Violeta said, as they arrived a little breathless from the climb in front of her door. "Bienvenida a mi casa."

"I love it!" Ruthie said, moving around the room, her skirt swirling around her legs. "You brought Chile with you to warm up the cold north." They both laughed.

Ruthie stopped in front of Violeta's favorite wall hanging—an embroidered picture of fishing boats lined up in the bay and small blue, yellow, and orange houses marching up the hill. Her tia, the one who gave her the shawl, had pressed the rolled-up fabric into her hands and insisted she take it—a piece of home, she had said, so you won't forget us.

"It's an arpillera," Violeta said. "Poor women in Chile make them to tell a story and decorate their homes—and sometimes to sell in the market when money is tight. Arpillera means burlap—they use burlap rice and flour sacks to make them."

"I want to visit this place. It's so beautiful, Vi."

Violeta glanced at the clock next to the couch.

"We should be going to the church, Ruthie, if that's OK. I don't want to be late for the service. And there will be more arpilleras to see there."

The church was just around the corner from Violeta's apartment—a large red-brick structure with a bell tower and an imposing triple set of carved wooden doors at the top of a shallow cement stairway. Small stained-glass windows pierced the façade, and a sign in English and Spanish welcomed all to worship at Our Lady of Good Voyage Church. A hand-lettered sign taped below the official one announced that today's mass would be in honor of those suffering under the military dictatorship in Chile.

There were many churches in the neighborhood, but Violeta had wandered into this one because its name reminded her of the fishermen's churches in Valpo. The priest was a gringo but had lived in Peru for many years where he was introduced to la iglesia de liberacion, liberation theology. His Spanish was almost perfect, and the early morning service was conducted entirely in Spanish and the mass was almost like a conversation about God, with lots of singing. Violeta felt at home in this church.

Violeta stopped to greet the two ladies who set up a market in front of the church every Sunday, selling used clothes and heavy workman's boots, children's toys, and jewelry. For some reason, they called it a "flea" market, though Violeta hoped there were no fleas. She and Ruthie continued up the stairs and through the open doors to take their seats in a worn wooden pew near the altar just as Father Thomas was making his way down the aisle, followed by the altar boys swinging brass baskets, leaving a trail of smoke that soon filled the church with the pungent smell of burning incense.

"There are many more people here than usual," Violeta whispered to Ruthie as the opening notes of the organ resonated against the thick walls of the church. "If you're not sure what to do, just follow me," she added, nudging Ruthie to stand, and opening her hymnal to the right page.

Bendito, Bendito sea Dios

Los ángeles cantan y alaban a Dios Los ángeles cantan y alaban a Dios They sang, and she was glad to hear Ruthie join softly on the chorus... After the hymn, Violeta turned to Ruthie, grasped her hand, and said, "La Paz Sea Con Vos," as handshakes were exchanged around the room and "Peace be with you" echoed in the large chamber.

Father Thomas stood at an ornately carved dais in front of the altar and cleared his throat.

"Bienvenidos a todos," he began, "welcome to all who come here today in peace. Today will be a special service to remember and honor those who are suffering in Chile, our neighbor to the south and the homeland of some of our beloved parishioners."

Violeta was glad that Father Thomas spoke in Spanish slowly and clearly enough that Ruthie could follow every word without translation. He explained that the Catholic Church in Chile was supporting those protesting the dictatorship and helping tell the world about the disappearances, torture, and suffering of the Chilean people. He then introduced two women who rose to join him at the dais—nuns, monjas queridas, he called them, from a church in Santiago de Chile, the Chilean capital. Sor Gloria and Sor Aurora wore simple white blouses and blue skirts, with a matching blue scarf covering their heads—so different from the nuns in their imposing black-and-white habits that Violeta was used to seeing at the Catholic school around the corner from Cookie's. Sor Gloria began speaking in a soft but firm voice, telling a story of upheaval and confusion, of people being dragged from their homes in the night and students being rounded up on the university campus. She ended with a plea for help—your brothers and sisters in the Church in Chile need your support—and the altar boys began passing the straw collection baskets on long poles across the pews. Violeta dug in her purse and placed a wrinkled $5 bill in the basket, noticing Ruthie add a $20.

Father Thomas stood tall before the murmuring congregation of about 150 members and spoke in a clear, deep voice. "Today, at this special Mass," he began, "we will again follow the tradition of what our Latin American neighbors call La Iglesia de Liberación—the liberated church. I participated in these traditions in Peru, and I believe they tap into the deepest meaning of our Christian faith, grounded in welcoming the stranger and fighting for justice for those who are poor and oppressed." There were rustles and whispered comments in the congregation as he went on to explain that, in keeping with these traditions, he would extend an invitation to all present, whether Catholic or not, whatever faith they profess, or even if they have no faith at all, to participate in the ceremony of communion. She glanced at Ruthie, who was listening intently, her hands twisting in her lap, her shoulders hunched. And then the organist began to play Pan de Vida, bread of life, and the congregants filed into the center aisle of the church, row by row, to receive the bread and wine.

"¿Entendiste la invitación?" Violeta asked, and Ruthie nodded. "¿Quiere recibir el pan de vida hoy? Do you want to receive the bread of life?" Ruthie nodded again and followed Violeta to take her place in the line. ¿Estas segura? Violeta asked as the line shuffled slowly toward the front of the church. She didn't want her friend to feel any pressure, to do something she was uncomfortable with.

When they reached the small table at the front, Violeta went first so that Ruthie could see what to do. She lifted the small piece of crusty bread from the cloth that Sor Gloria held in front of her, placed it in her mouth, and then drank a sip of dark red wine from the goblet that Father Thomas wiped and offered. He spoke these words as Violeta moved away from the altar and stood waiting for her friend to accept communion.

We share the bread of life with all who are hungry. We lift the cup of compassion for a broken world.

Violeta guided Ruthie back to their pew and opened the hymnal to the back, where a page had been inserted. As the rest of the congregation took their places in the pews, the organ's notes swelled, and the voices of the congregation rose in unison. Nosotros Venceremos. Nosotros venceremos, they sang, and Violeta heard Ruthie's voice in her ear, quavering with emotion. Violeta clasped her friend's hand, and their voices blended as they sang No tenemos miedo, "we are not afraid," and sent up a silent prayer for Javi and Sasha.

Las Arpilleras

After the last notes of the organ had died away, Father Thomas invited the congregation to gather in the church basement where a potluck meal had been set up and the arpilleras were on display.

"You know the song 'Nosotros Venceremos'?" Violeta asked as they walked down the scuffed linoleum steps.

"Oh yes, yes I do," Ruthie replied. "In English, 'We Shall Overcome.' It's like the main hymn of the civil rights movement. We used to sing it in the group I joined in my hometown when I was just 15, and then thousands of us sang it together at the March on Washington in 1963. You were here then. Do you know about that, Vi?"

"A little," Violeta said, pausing and turning to her friend at the bottom of the stairs. "I had only been here a short time, and I didn't really understand why los negros were protesting so much. Now I do."

When they reached the large, open room where tables and chairs were being set up, Violeta parted ways with her friend.

"I'll just help them with the food in the kitchen," she said. "Will you be OK on your own?"

Ruthie nodded, touched that her friend was taking such good care of her. The notes of the stirring song still played in her mind, bringing one more memory with them. "Venceremos" had been the response of the brigadistas in Cuba when they were invited to sing their national anthem. Their Cuban hosts didn't understand why they didn't want to sing the 'Star-Spangled Banner' with its 'rocket's red glare, the bombs bursting in air,' or why they didn't want to display and salute the U.S. flag, which to them represented war and domination.

You must love your country to change it, the Cuban leaders had admonished them, quoting the famous words of one of their heroes, Che Guevara— 'At the risk of seeming ridiculous, let me say that the true revolutionary is guided by a great feeling of love.'"

Ruthie moved toward the wall where the arpilleras were displayed—the bright reds, greens, and yellows of their design bringing warmth to the dimly lit room with dingy linoleum floors and metal folding tables and chairs set up in rows. There was certainly a lot of love captured in these simple fabric collages.

She stopped in front of one square and read the placard posted next to it. "Women Demand Justice!" She studied the patchwork picture composed of appliquéd fabric and embroidered edges. A group of women huddled around a banner that demanded "Justicia," moving down a narrow street alongside colorful square houses in bright sky blue, pink, orange, and lemon yellow. In the background, the sun hovered above brown mountain peaks. A lively, warm scene except for the hulking form of the black and white military van that followed them—its barred windows advertising the potential consequences of their action.

Another arpillera, called "The Coup," pictured fighter jets and helicopters attacking a large rectangular building. Flames were shooting out of every window. In front of the building a line of men in simple peasant clothing defended it with long sticks, while lurking just below them, the shadowy figures of helmeted men in olive drab uniforms with long rifles waited to make an entrance. A small ambulance marked with a red cross was perched like a toy between the two opposing factions. It was not hard to imagine the outcome of this encounter.

Ruthie moved slowly around the room, while behind her the noisy bustle of a meal being set out on the tables, the clank of utensils and laughter of kids chasing each other around formed an incongruous soundtrack to this somber exhibit. For despite their bright colors and whimsical representations, the arpilleras documented the stories of the women who made them and their communities and bore witness to the cruelty of the dictatorship. They had been smuggled out of Chile by exiles and international church officials and were being sold for $10, $20, and $30 to support the women and their families, sometimes providing their only source of income.

Ruthie felt Violeta's arm slide over her shoulder as she stood transfixed before the final arpillera on the wall. At first, it seemed like a peaceful domestic scene: three women gathered around a small round table in the center of a room. Ruthie was impressed by the details—the fabric and stitching on the chairs that suggested rustic leather, the purple floor and window curtains, and large ceramic vases in the corners holding embroidered pink flowers. In front of each woman—burlap fabric, the foundation of an arpillera, with needles and thread neatly placed in the center of the table. And then she noticed the large black question mark embroidered on the one empty chair—and behind it, on the white plaster wall, the portrait of a young man, his black hair parted down the middle, with the words "¿Dónde está?" embroidered at the top. Where is he? The empty chair at the table. Where is he?

The young man who left for university and never came home. Where is he? The father who left for the fields and was last seen being shoved into a white van. It was the first question Ruthie asked herself every morning and her last thought as she drifted off to sleep. Where is Sasha?

It was not the same, she knew that. She knew that Sasha was safe, and she knew who she was with, if not where they were. Violeta and the other mothers in Chile did not know who had taken their children, where they were being held, if they were alive or dead. She would never pretend that it was anywhere near the same.

Ruthie thought again of Andrés—the quiet, serious, dark-eyed Chilean student she had grown close to on the international brigade in Cuba. He had been so proud of his country—the first in Latin America to democratically elect a socialist president. He had played records of Chilean music for her on the scratchy record player in the small camp library, introducing her to Víctor Jara—the son of tenant farmers who became a musical ambassador to the world and a leader of the Nueva Canción, the new song movement that swept across Latin America. His soaring tenor lifted his words above the everyday sounds of brigadistas going about their Sunday afternoon chores in the camp as he sang of el derecho de vivir en paz—the right to live in peace. Víctor Jara's peace, his life, was destroyed in the National Soccer Stadium when he refused to stop singing, and his fingers were broken one by one by the military torturers. Violeta had wept when she read about what they had done to him.

"El derecho de vivir en paz"—Ruthie could hear it now in her head above the clatter of plates being plunked down on tables in the church basement and the rapid-fire Spanish conversations surrounding her. She had played the record of popular Chilean music Andres had given her when they said goodbye for Violeta. He had signed it "To Ruthie, from your comrade in Chile, Andrés." Manny was convinced he had a crush on her, but Ruthie didn't see it—just a valued friendship. Maybe she would visit him one day, she had said as they parted ways. Maybe, he said, with a large smile lighting his serious face.

Where was he now, she wondered. He was a student, a proud communist, and a staunch supporter of the Allende government. Were his parents sitting at their kitchen table, wondering "¿Dónde está Andrés?" Where was their son? "Ruthie, amiga," Violeta's soft voice broke through the thick nostalgia

of her thoughts which she had wrapped around her like a blanket as she faced the harsh truth the arpilleras told. "Why don't you come and eat," Vi went on, gesturing at the tables which were set with colorful woven tablecloths. At a long table outside the kitchen, the women Violeta had greeted when they entered the church, waited behind large aluminum trays suspended over Sterno cans, ladles in hand, ready to serve. The aroma of stewed tomatoes, onions, and garlic wafted through the room.

"Smells good, no? All the favorite traditional foods of my country." Violeta bounced on her heels with excitement as she listed the culinary delights awaiting them—ajiaco, a stew made with vegetables, corn, and pumpkin; crusty empanadas de piño, even better than Argentinean ones—bigger and filled with ground meat, onions, and garlic; humitas, Chile's version of tamales made with ground corn, green chile, and basil, wrapped in corn husks; and for dessert—alfajores—sweet cookies made into a sandwich with dulce de leche in the middle—ay, qué deliciosas. Violeta relayed all this as they walked toward the table where the food was laid out. By the time Ruthie picked up a plastic plate and aluminum fork, she was starving. Violeta led them to the table where the nuns were sitting, and they scraped their metal chairs across the linoleum, careful not to spill their food-laden plates as they sat.

"Bendiciones, hermanas," the older nun, Sor Gloria, Violeta thought, bent her head towards them in a gesture of blessing.

"Bendiciones," Violeta returned the blessing and thanked the nuns for their presence with them today.

"Disculpe, excuse me," said the other nun, Sor María, as they took their first bites of the steaming stew in the center of their plates. "But it seems from your accent that you may be from Chile, no? From Valpo or nearby, I think? I grew up in a small fishing community in the hills."

"Ay, sí, sí, sí—mi familia, my parents and my son Javi are still there—in Portales. Well, but I haven't been able to find out how they are doing since the golpe. My son is, was a student at the university and…" Violeta's voice trailed off, her fork froze in the air above her plate, conversation stopped around the table.

"It is very, very hard, mi hija, to not be in touch with your loved ones. We are doing all we can to help our people survive this terrible blow. That is why we came here to let people know what is going on—and your government, well the U.S. government…" Sor Gloria paused and looked at Ruthie. "Well, the

U.S. government has been trying to overthrow Allende since he nationalized the copper industry."

Ruthie nodded. "I know," she said. "I've seen the reports about the CIA plots and the money that has gone to the opposition. I recently traveled to Cuba with a solidarity brigade. I'm totally against what my government is doing there and in Chile."

Ruthie surprised herself by the vehemence of her response. It felt like a long time since she had engaged in a political discussion or voiced a strong opinion. She was glad she still had them, that she still cared about what was happening in the world, despite her withdrawal and isolation. She wanted to believe that she could be a good mother to Sasha and still be an activist. She sighed. For that to happen, of course, she first had to find her daughter.

"Will you help us spread the word about Chile among your countrymen?" Sor Gloria asked, turning to face Ruthie who put her fork down and wiped her mouth with her paper napkin.

"I don't know if I can," Ruthie started to say…and then thought about the mothers risking their lives to sew arpilleras, knowing that their children might be suffering in detention camps or worse. "Yes, yes, I will," she said, with more determination than she had felt in weeks. "I have friends at the university, and I'll ask them to help."

Violeta squeezed her hand under the table. "¿Estás segura, amiga?" she said, searching her friend's face for doubt or fear. "Con todo lo que…" Then she stopped, seeing the light that had come into Ruthie's eyes, the way she held her body straight and tall as she continued her meal. Ruthie looked strong. Ruthie looked brave and sure.

When they finally stood up after the serving trays were empty and their plates were clean, Ruthie patted her belly. "Wow, qué deliciosa. I don't have room for another bite." She doubled back to the arpillera display, hoping the one that had caught her attention would still be there. She would buy it and a few others and show them to Michael and his group. Ruthie found the arpillera with the empty chair at the table and then walked to the volunteer table with her purchases folded carefully in her hands.

Maybe they could sponsor a fundraiser or hold a demonstration to let students know that young people like them were being tortured with training and money supplied by the U.S. government. That should be something worth speaking out about. And to make it more urgent and closer to home, maybe Violeta would be willing to share her story with them. She could feel the ideas beginning to grow in her head, the energy beginning to tingle in her limbs. It felt good to be organizing something, to be imagining the future, to be thinking about ways to make a difference.

For the first time since Sasha's disappearance, Ruthie felt free of the guilt and shame that had crippled her. This is who I am, she thought. I am an activist fighting for a better world for my daughter, for Violeta's son, for everyone. I am a good mother. I have done nothing wrong.

"I'm going to buy two, Vi," Ruthie said. "Can I buy one for you too? I want to help in whatever way I can."

"Ay, sí, hermana. I would like to have this one," pointing at the women seated at the table getting ready to sew. "This boy, he reminds me of my Javi. Gracias, Ruthie." Working together, they carefully removed the thumbtacks holding their chosen arpilleras to the wall, folded them and brought them to the information table to pay. Ruthie placed some flyers and a couple of posters in the paper bag with the patchwork wall hangings. She would ask Cookie if they could put some information in the window, maybe take up a collection among their regular customers. She would do something.

"Do you want to hear my idea?" Violeta asked as they made their way back through the late afternoon sunshine to her apartment. "I am thinking we could make an arpillera—or maybe two—one for Javi and one for Sasha. I am a pretty good sewer, and I know where we can get some fabric, and…" Violeta's words were tumbling all over each other. Ruthie had never seen her so excited. Finally, she took a breath.

"What do you think?"

"I think it's a wonderful idea. When can we start?"

Violeta took her hand, and they walked, almost skipped over the ancient sidewalks, through the narrow streets, to the cozy room on the fourth floor that Violeta called home.

Organize!

Early October 1973

Violeta was nervous but determined. Her brightly colored woven bag was stuffed with the flyers that she and Ruthie had Xeroxed in Michael's office at the university—after hours so no one would see. Michael had shown up to help them for a while, but they would be on their own now

.Come and Learn What U.S. Tax Dollars are doing in Chile
Hear From the mother of one of the students who has disappeared

After a short paragraph describing the military takeover of the government, the U.S. role in the coup and Allende's death they had pasted a picture of Javi next to a picture of Chilean students marching in the street.

The final slogan: Support Chilean Students and Workers. No U.S. Money to Dictators!!! was printed in bold capital letters across the bottom of the flier, along with a name they had made up—Cambridge Committee in Solidarity with the Chilean People.

Father Paul had enthusiastically agreed to host their first meeting which would be held after the Mass on Sunday. A Spanish flier announcing the meeting was posted on the church bulletin board. It was Violeta and Ruthie's job to try to get some students to attend. After work they would go to Harvard Square and pass out flyers.

"I'm nervous," Violeta admitted as they stepped out of Cookie's into the bright sunlight of an autumn afternoon. "What do I say? What if they don't take the flyer?"

"I usually just stick out my hand with the flyer in it, smile and say something like 'please come to our meeting to find out what's happening after the coup in Chile.' They either take it, or they don't—but a lot of the students will be interested, I think," Ruthie responded, remembering her days at Ft.

Carson. Every Friday afternoon they had driven to the base in Ken's van—the Blue Bomb—to hand out copies of the Home Front newspaper and invite GIs to their Saturday night film showings at the R & R. Many guys just rushed right by, eager to get off base, heading to the honky tonk bars on the main drag in town. Ruthie had learned not to take it personally. But there were a few who took the paper, riffled through the pages and asked a few questions. And out of those few, one or two actually showed up. That was so exciting! It made the long nights of debate over what to put in the paper, the grinding out of the articles and cranking the old mimeograph machine in the basement feel worth it.

"If even one student shows up because they got our flyer that's a start," Ruthie said as they reached the Square, realizing how much she believed that and how she had missed the slow, patient work of outreach and education.

They stayed together at first, Violeta observing carefully as Ruthie approached the students passing through the Square. Many were rushing to class or the library and didn't even stop to see what they were handing out; some took the flyer and then dropped it on the bricks as they walked away. But just like Ruthie said, a few students stopped to look, to ask a question.

"That is my son, Javi. He is a student like you," Ruthie heard Violeta say to one boy, arms filled with books, who stopped to talk. "When the military took over, they took him away. I don't know where he is."

"Wow. Sorry. I didn't know about this. That's pretty scary," the boy said, shifting his books to his other arm to take hold of the flyer.

"Can you come—on Sunday? Can you bring some friends?" Violeta said. "Here is the address—right here. My name is Violeta and I'll be speaking. Como tu te llamas? What's your name?"

"Oh, um…yo me llamo Andrew," the boy said, laughing. "I'm taking Spanish this semester. I'm gonna try, really I'll try…and I'll tell my dorm-mates. This seems important." And with that, he shifted the books again, slipped the flyer on top of the pile, and headed off in the direction of the library.

"

You're a natural, Vi," Ruthie said, sidling up to her friend. "Really that was great."

"Do you think he will come?" Violeta asked. "Maybe?"

"Maybe," Ruthie said. "We'll see on Sunday."

They spent another hour in the Square until all the flyers were gone except for a handful they planned to put up in store windows the next day. It was dark, and the crowd in the Square had thinned to a few commuters passing through on their way home from work when they decided to stop for the day. "What do you think, Violeta? Did you enjoy passing out the flyers?"

Ruthie asked, as they walked back toward Mass Ave, where Violeta would catch her bus home.

"Do you really think I'm good at it, Ruthie? I liked talking to the students. I've worked right here in the Square for so many years and I've never talked to any of them, except to take their orders in the Diner."

"That's what organizing is really all about, mi amiga. Just talking to people, finding out what they think, what they care about–and giving them information. And you're really good at it. You have so much experience to share."

She leaned over and hugged Violeta as they parted at the bus stop. "Hasta mañana, hermana," Violeta said, waving as she boarded the bus.

Ruthie walked through the familiar streets feeling satisfied in a way she hadn't in a long time. It felt good to be active again, to be doing something that counted. And she could feel the fear that had kept her awake at night—that her past would be discovered, that Carl would use her activism against her, that she would lose Sasha–receding with every step toward home,.

Now or Never

The words were on the tip of her tongue. She clamped her lips shut tight to keep them from escaping. It would not be a good idea to tell him. Not here. Not now. Maybe not ever.

Ruthie and Michael were seated in one of the big booths at the back of the Diner with windows looking out on the Square. It was Ruthie's day off, and they had been walking by the river, stopping in at the Diner for a cup of hot chocolate on the way home. Michael had added a slice of the 7-layer cake that was on display at the front. Ruthie blew on her hot chocolate and smiled up at him. She was excited to tell him all about Sunday's meeting which had brought a handful of students to the church to talk about the coup in Chile, but something else was on her mind. They had become good friends in a way that made Ruthie feel safe, and she wanted to share more about herself with him. But where to begin?

It felt strange to be sitting in one of the booths instead of standing by with a pad and pencil in hand waiting to take orders. Violeta, who hadn't given up on Michael as a "real" boyfriend for Ruthie, waited on them, winking at Ruthie when Michael wasn't looking.

He paused with a fork full of moist chocolate cake halfway to his mouth. "What were you going to say?" he asked.

"Me, no nothing. Just thinking that's all."

Not for the first time, she thought Michael had some kind of mind-reading powers. He always seemed tuned into her thoughts. Or maybe—she took a sip of her chocolate and burned her tongue—still too hot. Maybe he knew more about her than she had told him. You're being paranoid—the small voice of reason in her head spoke up. Maybe, maybe not. But she still shouldn't tell him. Or maybe she should. Maybe it was time.

"Earth to Ruthie. Penny for your thoughts."

She reached for a forkful of Michael's cake, and he playfully swatted her hand away.

"Are you up for a movie tonight? That new Fellini is playing at the Art Forum?"

"Um. Sure. That sounds good. Michael?"

"Yeah." Oh god he was sitting across from her like an eager puppy, ears cocked.

Ruthie looked out the window. Cookie had put up Halloween decorations the day before—dancing skeletons framed the windows, and those clingy plastic stencils of pumpkins and witches blocked her view of the students hurrying through the square on their way to midterm exams.

She would be leaving soon. It was now or never. She took a deep breath. "Violeta and I would like to organize a speak-out on campus about the coup in Chile? Can you help us?"

"Um…yeah, sure. We should do it soon, though, before everyone gets jammed up with the end of the semester and Thanksgiving break. I've seen your flyers around the Square. It's a great idea, Ruthie. Yeah, sure, I'll help."

The voice of blame scolded her. You're such a coward. What are you afraid of ?

He's so supportive.

She took another deep breath.

"Hey Michael, have you ever done something you really regretted, something you were really ashamed of?"

"Who, me?" Michael said, laughing. "Not me. I'm perfect. Remember?"

"Oh yeah, I almost forgot—perfect man." Ruthie laughed too and reached across the table for another bite of cake.

Now what? She thought. How do I start this conversation?

"Well, I'm not the perfect woman," she said, swallowing hard. "I have done some things I regret. One big thing I regret–a lot."

The cake was forgotten. Michael's eyes were on her. He took her hand across the table.

"Tell me," he said. "You can tell me anything, Ruthie. Don't you know that?"

<hr>

We'll see, she thought, slipping her hand out of his and into her pocket. She put the photo of Sasha, the one she carried everywhere, on the table between them.

"What a cutie," Michael said. "Who is she?"

"Sasha. My daughter," Ruthie said, looking down at the table. "Your… your what? I don't understand."

"My daughter. She's 5 years old. My ex has her."

"Ruthie, I don't understand—all this time. You have a daughter? You were married? How can you just be telling me this now? I thought we were close." His eyes were pleading for a different story, but she only had this one. And it was time to tell him everything.

"Get me a cup of coffee and I'll tell you the whole story, Michael, please?" They sat for an hour, one cup of cold coffee between them, while Ruthie explained her life to Michael. He kept his gaze on her and said little. "Wow," "But why?" and "How could you?" Sometimes he looked angry or disappointed, but mostly he just looked sad. Ruthie told the story as if she were talking about someone else. She felt the distance grow between them. And then she was done. She had told him everything, even the part about her leaving soon. There was nothing more to say. She waited.

Michael sat with his hands in his lap. Violeta, who had greeted them warmly and refilled their coffee cups a couple of times, shot Ruthie a glance full of questions. Michael cleared his throat, rubbed his hands across his face, and took a deep breath.

"I-I don't know what to say. It's a lot, Ruthie. A lot. I'm angry that you're just now telling me all this. You sleep in my bed. We're supposed to be…at least friends. Do you not trust me? Is that it? You don't trust me?"

He raised his voice on the last question, and Violeta started toward their table until Ruthie waved her away.

"I don't trust anyone, Michael. I don't trust…I just was afraid you wouldn't understand. I'm sorry I didn't tell you sooner."

"Well maybe I don't understand. Maybe I don't. This Carl person sounds like a jerk. How could you just leave your little girl like that and think it would be OK? What was so important about going to Cuba? Did you really think you're going there would change the world?"

He stopped. Slammed his fist on the table.

"How could you not tell me, Ruthie? That I don't think I will ever understand."

And with that, Michael dropped a five-dollar bill on the table, grabbed his jacket from the seat, and walked quickly to the door without looking back. The bells tinkled loudly as he slammed the door shut behind him.

Dear Ruthie

I'm sorry that I stormed out of Cookie's last week. I was very upset that you had kept such an important part of your life from me for so long. Well, I guess I am still very upset. I have tried to understand but I can't seem to wrap my head around it or get past my sense of disappointment in you.

I felt happy that we were getting to know each other better and I really like you, but you have a very complicated life right now and I don't see where I fit in. And obviously you don't want to fit into my life because you haven't made much effort.

I think it's best if we don't continue to see each other. It's been hard for me to pretend that a friendship is all I want. You will probably be leaving soon, I'm guessing, and I need to focus on my studies, so…

I wish you all the best and will remember you with affection.

Michael

Common Threads

"¿Escuchaste algo de Michael? Did you hear anything from Michael?" Violeta whispered to Ruthie as she brushed past her to change into her uniform.

She had been asking every day since Ruthie and Michael had argued at Cookie's, in full view of the staff. And every day, Ruthie had answered no. Violeta seemed more upset about the rift between them than Ruthie was. She couldn't tell whether her friend was sad or relieved. But that was Ruthie–it was not easy for her to share her feelings.

But today, Ruthie nodded yes and passed her friend the note she had received from Michael in the mail. She watched as Violeta bit her lip and frowned as she read it.

"El va a repentir," she said, giving Ruthie's shoulder a squeeze. "You'll see. He will regret it. Oh, buenas noticias, Encontre la tela. I got the burlap for the arpilleras. I'll show you later, after we close."

Ruthie smiled as she passed, both arms laden with steaming bowls of New England clam chowder, one of Cookie's specialties. It had been a few weeks since she and Violeta had decided to create aripilleras for their own children, inspired by the exhibit at Violeta's church, and she had almost forgotten about it, but not Violeta. How could she forget when her son Javi was among the missing in Chile? She had finally gotten a phone call through to her tia in the capital, only to learn that no one had any news or information about Javi—and so many other young men who had disappeared in the first days after the coup. A few of his friends at the university had made it home after a week or two—with stories of interrogations and beatings that terrified Violeta's family—but no one knew what had happened to Javi.

The lull before the dinner rush finally gave Ruthie the chance to sit for a few minutes, folding napkins and filling salt and pepper shakers at the back table, and Violeta soon joined her with a large brown paper sack.

"Mira, amiga—perfecta, no?" she said, pulling a long rectangle of rough burlap fabric out of the bag. "And look!" She opened the bag to reveal spools of brightly colored thread and fabric squares in assorted patterns and colors. "Todo lo que necesitamos. Everything we need," she said with a lilt of pride in her voice. Can you come over on Monday night to get started? I am off on Tuesday next week."

Ruthie checked the work schedule as she got ready to wait on her first dinner customers. She had to work on Tuesday, but she was off on Monday, so that would work. "Monday's good," she said to Vi, as they both reached for plates at the kitchen pass through. Violeta grinned and bounced on her heels, almost spilling her meatloaf, mashed and gravy on the grimy linoleum. Her excitement was infectious, and Ruthie spent the next couple of evenings after work sketching out ideas for the fabric picture she would create. By the time Monday rolled around she had some pretty good ideas.

Ruthie took the bus to Violeta's house, walking past Our Lady of Good Voyage on the way, remembering the promise she had made to Sor Gloria, the Chilean nun, who had asked her to help spread the word about the terrible situation in her country. She had asked Michael to put her on the agenda for the next meeting of his student activist organization, and she would bring the aripilleras she had bought to see if they would be willing to organize a fundraiser. After all, it would take more than banners and shouted slogans to change the world. Now she would have to find a different way to connect with the group.

Violeta opened the door, and Ruthie was greeted by a wave of high-pitched voices and laughter, mingled with an earthy smell that reminded her of the eucalyptus groves in San Francisco.

"Bienvenida, Ruthie. You are just in time to share some yerba mate with us. Entra."

Ruthie stepped into the small room and handed Violeta a brown paper bag stained with browned butter and sugar from the pastries she had bought at the Latin American bakery on the avenue.

"Alaforjes" she said, which brought a ripple of laughter from the 3 women seated around the card table under the single window in Violeta's room. They were passing around what looked like a gourd with a metal straw.

"Alfajores" one of the women said, accompanied by another peal of laughter. Ruthie recognized her from Violeta's church. She had been at the special service they had attended for the Desaparacidos in Chile. "Deliciosas, gracias," the woman went on. "Soy Doña Emilia—de la iglesia. Sientate y toma maté con nosotras."

Ruthie drew a folding chair up to the table and took the gourd in both hands, unsure what she was supposed to do next.

"Yerba mate," Doña Emilia said, "a special tea that reminds us of home—well, for me, that is Argentina."

Violeta placed a plate of the special pastries in the middle of the table and sat in the empty chair next to Ruthie.

"This is a tea we share in friendship and health, to give us energy to face whatever life brings," Doña Emilia said, taking the gourd from Ruthie and turning the metal straw to face her.

"This is the bombilla we all share because between us there are no walls."

"Try it, hermana," she said, filling the gourd with hot water from the metal tea pot and passing it back to Ruthie.

The women watched as Ruthie took a sip from the straw and then gasped and sputtered.

"Oh, wow-- it's so…so bitter. Los siento. Sorry."

"You see, Carmen. You're not the only one," Violeta said, turning toward an older woman with a crown of curly white hair. Small almond-shaped eyes twinkled with light in her dark brown face.

"Azucar. Ponle azucar. Give the woman some sugar, por Dios," Carmen laughed and passed a terracotta sugar bowl in Ruthie's direction. "Maté is an acquired taste."

When the maté and pastries had been consumed, Violeta cleared the table and laid out the burlap squares in the center.

"Why don't we introduce ourselves and say why we came today?" she suggested. "Since it's my house, I'll start, OK?

"Pues, les invite a mi casa…I invited you here to my house to share in the making of a very special artesania—a folk art from my country that we call an arpillera." Violeta unfolded one of the arpilleras from the church and held it up for the women to see.

"Women in the towns and campos of Chile make these to show a picture of everyday life … but now, since the junta, the coup, they have been making them to show the terror and brutality of their lives under the military dictatorship." Violeta unfolded the arpillera depicting a group of women marching with a banner demanding Justicia—with a military van following close behind. "And also," she went on, "to remind everyone of the desaparacidos, the disappeared." With those words, Violeta unfurled the arpillera with the portrait of a young man and the words "Dónde Esta?" embroidered in the frame and held it over her heart. The women clucked their tongues and murmured around the table. "Ay qué triste," Carmen said. "How horrible."

"Como ustedes saben…Violeta went on, "my son Javi is one of the disappeared. He was marching with the students from the university, and no one has seen or heard from him for weeks."

And with that, she lifted one of the burlap squares from the table. "Ruthie and I got the idea to make our own arpilleras, and that's what we will do together today. And if you want, we invite you to join us. But please first, introduce yourself to the group. Carmen, por favor?" Violeta turned to the older woman.

"Why do I have to go first?" Carmen asked, laughing. "With my Spanglish and my Boricua ways. OK, OK. I'll go."

She pulled her chair closer to the table and rested her chin on her hands. "Soy Carmen. I was born in Puerto Rico—in the mountains—una jíbara from the countryside—and I was hoping to raise my family in that beautiful place— but in the 50's everything changed when the big plantations closed, and everyone moved to the cities or to the U.S. looking for work. My husband, Victor, he couldn't find a job and so we came to Boston—me and my two kids and Victor. The bad news is Puerto Rico belongs to the U.S., so we don't have much say over what happens on the island. The good news is we were already citizens, so it was easy to come. There were a lot of jobs at first, but then it got harder. As much as we worked, we never could really get ahead, and Victor felt like a failure. My daughter, Lourdes, and I went back to visit our family on the island a lot, but Victor died a few years ago without ever returning. He was ashamed that he couldn't bring expensive gifts for everyone to show them how good he was doing, so he never ever went back. So here I am—a Puertorriqueña stuck in the cold and snow. But I refuse to die here. I will die on my beautiful isla."

"Que suerte…how lucky you are." A soft voice broke into Carmen's story. Ruthie turned to her right. A short, plump woman with large dark eyes and shining black braids circling her head pulled back into her chair like a turtle into its shell after speaking.

"Sigue, Itzy," Violeta said, gesturing to the woman to go on. "It's your turn now. Tell us your story." The woman shrugged and Ruthie wondered how old she was. She looked like a young girl—her brown skin smooth across features that reminded Ruthie of the small statues she had seen in the Anthropology Museum in Ciudad Mexico.

"Bueno," the woman spoke, and then cleared her throat and spoke a bit louder.

"Soy Itzy—well Itzayana really. In my Mayan language it means gift from God, but everyone here calls me Itzy. I am from Guatemala—a small village in the mountains called Chacula. Mi Tía, my auntie brought me here when I was a small girl. When I was old enough to understand, mi tía explained that a little while after we left our country, the army came to the mountains looking for comunistas who they said were trying to overthrow the government. They got money and training from the U.S. government she said, and the whole village was wiped out, but when I asked what did that mean, she wouldn't tell me anymore—just that my parents and my brother, Tadeus, were hiding. I am glad we escaped, I guess, but I miss my family and my village. And we never found out what happened to them. My aunt says we must forget and make our home here now. We can never return."

The only sound in the small room was the rustling movement of bodies shifting in chairs as the women absorbed Itzy's story.

"Malditos Gringos," Carmen said. "Thinking they can rule the world." "Malditos Gringos is right," Doña Emilia chimed in. "When I was a student, I used to think America was the most civilized country in the world— not like Argentina where the government changed every six months, and they closed the university when we had the smallest protest."

"Why don't you go next, Doña Emilia? I'm realizing in all the time I have known you I don't know much about your story. And our countries are neighbors, after all," Violeta said.

Doña Emilia rearranged a woven shawl over her shoulders and tapped a long crimson painted fingernail on the table. "When I came to this country in the early 1960's," she began, "I was already a professional woman—una doctora pediatra—a pediatrician, and my husband was an architect. We had two young children, and we wanted more for them than our country could offer in that moment—a chance to go to university, to become professionals, to have a stable life. Things were not so bad, like you are describing in Guatemala, Itzy, but they were heading in a bad direction. The military kept rebelling against any elected government, and no one could stay in power for long. And now, with Peron back in the country, who knows what will happen?"

Doña Emilia paused, lifted the shawl from her shoulders and placed it on the back of her chair, leaning forward and sighing as she went on with her story. "But oh, how I miss Buenos Aires—my beautiful city—the wide boulevards, the cafes, the plazas alive with music and families strolling after dinner. Cambridge is so cold is it not? How have we managed to make our lives here?

"But at least I still have my maté," she said, lifting the gourd and laughing. Violeta patted the burlap in the middle of the table.

"Bueno amigas," she said, smiling in Ruthie's direction, "our arpilleras are waiting, but before we start, I want to give our amiga Ruthie a chance to say why she is here with us today."

Ruthie felt suddenly shy and embarrassed, surrounded by women who had left their countries and all that was familiar behind—who had been forced to flee, who lived with so much uncertainty. All she had in common with them was Sasha, her own missing child, but how could she make them understand the choice she had made, not out of necessity, but out of her restless desire for adventure? She heard the self-blame in that thought. She had been struggling to understand her motivation for all these long months. Her own story still felt small and unimportant. But it would be rude not to share, to hide behind her privilege as an American. She lifted her hair off her neck, stretched her shoulders, and began.

"Hola," she said, "and gracias for inviting me here today to share with you. My troubles seem small and insignificant compared to yours..."

"No, no mi amiga," Violeta interrupted. "Estamos contigo. Tell them your story, Ruthie. Please. Somos todas madres…we are all mothers here."

Ruthie began, hesitantly at first and then in a rush of words, to tell them her story. And when she had finished the women around the table were enveloped in a deep silence—and one by one they reached out to take her hand, to pat her shoulder, to stroke her hair—and Ruthie felt their love and solidarity and knew she had found a new source of strength and support.

It was hard to settle into the sewing after their deep conversation, but Violeta encouraged them to select from the heap of colorful fabric and threads in the middle of the table and begin to construct an arpillera. Ruthie had a simple idea for hers—and she had to keep it simple because she wasn't very good at drawing or sewing. She chuckled when she thought of the mandatory pleated skirt she had to make in 9th grade Home Economics that almost earned her first failing grade. She chose several pieces of felt in different colors—red, yellow, blue and brown—and began to draw and cut paper doll-like figures of varied sizes from the brightly colored squares until she had a chain that stretched across the length of the burlap rectangle that Violeta had provided. Somehow, she wanted to represent the way that Sasha was still connected to her even though they were separated—and the unbroken chain of love that would bring them together again. In the background she would sew fabric in a swirling blue and green pattern to represent the ocean that circled the earth. And then she would try the best she could to embroider on the roughly woven burlap the words from the nursery rhyme that Sasha loved: "Thursday's Child has far to go." No matter how far, my Sasha, Ruthie whispered under her breath, I know we will get there.

Doña Emilia was the first to break the concentrated silence that accompanied their sewing.

"Bueno, mis hermanas. I have to go fix dinner now, but I'm so glad I came. I'm going to work on my arpillera at home—maybe we can meet again soon and show what we have created. And maybe we can figure out how to help our sisters in Chile."

Excited chatter around the table greeted Emilia's suggestion as, one by one, the women said their goodbyes, leaving Violeta and Ruthie alone together. Ruthie held up her fabric for Violeta to see—her half-sewn felt dolls stretched their arms out to each other from one end to the other and the wavy ocean encircled them all.

"Que linda, Ruthie!" Violeta said, holding up her own burlap square. Her skilled hands had already appliqued two simple beds, one in each corner, with a large crescent moon in the middle. In each bed, a sleeping figure faced the moon. Behind this shadowy scene, Violeta had embroidered the words "Bajo la misma luna, nosotros buscamos Justicia!"

"Under the same moon, we seek justice" Ruthie read aloud. "This is so beautiful, Vi. It says so much about the connection between you and Javi that can never be broken."

The two friends embraced, tears tracing a path down their cheeks, and then busied themselves with clearing the table and folding away the materials.

"I'd like to come over again to work on my arpillera with you if that's OK," Ruthie said. "I might need some help with the sewing."

"Claro que sí!" Violeta said. "Let's look at our schedules tomorrow at work and plan another day."

Ruthie walked toward home with anticipation quickening her steps, as she had every day that week. She had written to Stan, Carl's brother, and so far the letter had not been returned "addressee unknown." Maybe he would write back. Maybe he would provide some news, anything, of Carl and Sasha. Maybe he would help her find them.

She walked quickly but carefully over the uneven bricks on Harvard St. She had already taken a couple of bad spills on the slippery sidewalks. Her breath puffed out in smoky bursts. The smell of early winter—sharp, acrid, slightly rusty—was starting to infiltrate the air, though it had not yet snowed. She was tired of this frosty air, of this icy landscape, of the cool reserve of its inhabitants. She yearned to move on. But this time, unlike so many other moments in her nomadic life, she had to stay put, no matter how much she longed for something new. She had to keep saving her money and wait for a clue. Maybe it would come today. Maybe Stan would write.

A Clue Arrives

October 1973

Ruthie approached the plain, rectangular building that held her life. She pushed against the cold metal door handle that opened into a tiled entrance, the floor dotted with small pools of melted slush. She fitted her small key into the lock of one of the gray slotted mailboxes lining one wall. A thick advertising folio from the Boston Pops was stuffed into the cramped mailbox, but nothing else.

Ruthie sighed and headed toward the elevator. Had she really expected Stan to write back? He had always been affectionate and kind to her, perhaps understanding, from a sibling's perspective, the challenges of living with Carl. But would he take her side against his brother? That might be too much to expect.

A thin, white envelope fell from the pages and fluttered to the dirty floor. Ruthie picked it up and turned it over. It was from Stan. Could this be her clue? She would wait till she got upstairs to open it. She would take off her coat and her boots and make herself a cup of hot chamomile tea and sit on the futon and open the letter. She held her breath as the elevator doors closed, pushed "4" and watched the elevator rise, one slow floor at a time.

Ruthie closed the door behind her and leaned against it, unable to take even the few steps to the couch. She let her backpack slide to the floor and held the envelope in front of her. The writing on the front was familiar— her mother's slanted scrawl—and she could feel the stiffness of the contents through the thin white paper. So it was not from Stan. What could it be? A photo? Or maybe her parents had sent her a plane ticket back to California to continue her search.

She opened the envelope slowly, careful not to tear whatever it held, and drew out a picture postcard, wrinkled around the edges as if its journey to her had not been smooth. She saw the back first. Her breath caught in her chest and her hand shook.

Don't worry. We're fine. Carl's writing. She was sure of it. In one corner, the smiley face Sasha had used to sign her childish drawings before she learned to write her name. Her parent's address was neatly printed in the address space. They must have forwarded it to her.

She moved to the couch and lowered her body slowly, putting her head between her knees to stop the sudden sensation that the earth had opened up and she was falling through. When the spinning in her head had slowed, she turned the card over.

An empty beach, fringed by coconut palms, azure waters, the waves leaving a frothy white border where the sand met the sea. Ruthie's heart sank. It could be any beach, anywhere. She searched the photo for the scrap of a clue—a rock formation, a fisherman's hut—anything that would bring it out of the jumbled memories of all the beaches in all the places that Ruthie and Carl had visited in the before—before Sasha was born, before Sasha was gone.

Suddenly, she was tumbling in those waves, under the warm, salty waters— tiny pebbles and shells brushing her body, seaweed tangling in her legs—she was turning over and over underwater, eyes open—and she knew. She knew where Carl had taken Sasha.

PART THREE
Leave Taking

Leave Taking

October 1973

Ruthie took the worn leather backpack down from the top shelf of Claudia's closet where she had stashed it when she arrived at her cousin's apartment months earlier. It had been summer then, flowers everywhere, the ivy covering the old brick walls thick and shining green. Now she could already feel the windows leaking cold air into the cozy rooms that could never be home. She would not be unhappy to leave this place.

The backpack was a deep tan, soft and wrinkled, just big enough for two weeks' worth of clothes. She pressed her cheek to the cool, buttery leather—it had been her father's, and it reminded her of him—the soft side of him she hadn't seen much of since she told him that Sasha was gone. He had helped her then, but her mother had flung harsh words at her, and, as usual, he had said nothing. Stupid. Irresponsible. You'll never change. Those words still echoed in her mind, though she hadn't spoken to her mother in months.

She would travel light. She had to be ready to move quickly, to follow whatever clues might lead her to her little girl.

The postcard had been like a flashing neon sign on a dark highway. She hoped she was right about what it meant. But after the initial revelation, doubt had begun to trouble her. Could she really be sure, after all this time, that she was remembering the beach. They had camped on so many beaches. Even if she was guessing right, why would she think they would still be there? Maybe they were traveling down the coast, stopping at a different beach every night. But that wasn't Carl. When he fell in love with a place he wanted to stay, put down roots. And besides, what else did she have to go on? It was that beach, she was sure. She had to find it now.

She took the postcard from her pocket, the empty backpack yawning on the bed waiting for her to fill it. It was crinkled and worn; the postmark hopelessly smudged. But the picture was an address—a sparkling beach, vast and empty, emerald green water and at the end of the sand, a limestone cliff dotted with dwarf pine trees all lined up and bent in the same direction, the way the wind had shaped them as they grew. Her doubt vanished. She knew that place—she and Carl had spent a week there, pre-Sasha, camping on the beach, piling dry sun-bleached driftwood to make a campfire, bobbing in the warm ocean—their naked bodies white in the moonlight. Baja California. She didn't remember the name of the beach, or if it even had a name, but she would know it when she saw it. Carl and Sasha were there—she was sure of it. And she would find them.

Ruthie began to empty the drawers of her cousin's dresser. She was ready. Just 3 things she needed to do before she left: figure out how to get to California, return to Cookie's to say goodbye to Violeta, and talk to Manny. She would begin all that tomorrow.

Good mother/bad mother

"Ruthie? Are you up? It's Dad."

"What? What? Yes, what time is it? What's wrong?"

Ruthie sat up on the bed and tried to assemble her thoughts. She was in Cambridge, in her cousin Claudia's apartment, in her twin bed. She turned on the lamp on the nightstand and looked at the clock---it was 4 AM. Something was wrong.

"Dad, I'm here. What is it? What's happened? Are you all right?"

"I'm fine, Ruthie. I waited as long as I could to call. Can you come home, honey? It's your mother."

Ruthie stood, wrapping the long-coiled phone cord around her hand, pacing as she fired questions at her father.

"Is she…? What happened? Is she in the hospital? Is she sick?"

"She's OK, Ruthie. Just a bit bruised up is all. Just shaken up. But I can't do this alone. There's been an accident. Can you come? Please."

Ruthie's mind was racing. Her mother, an accident? One sharp ugly thought intruded—so like her mother to have an accident just when Ruthie was about to embark on what she hoped would be the end of her search for Sasha. The drama queen. Never a dull moment.

"I'll buy you a ticket. When can you come?"

This was her father—her sweet, gentle, clueless father. Could she really say no? It would be the first time she did. He was always so helpless in the face of the passionate force that was her mother.

Was it Ruthie's fault that her mother chose to ignore whatever fucking pain she was in by drinking herself into oblivion? She knew what would happen when she got to the house with the purple door. A purple door on a New England street full of center hall colonials with brick fronts and black shutters. Yet another flamboyant expression of her mother's pathetic need to be noticed.

Her father had said "come home" but that house was not her home—not anymore, maybe never. It was a house of slammed doors and secrets, of her mother's muttered harangues that filled every corner with venom. Of sobbing confessions, pleas for forgiveness—bullshit! I am not doing this, Ruthie thought. I don't have to do this. Not again. Let Marty do it—it was probably his turn anyway.

"I…I'm not sure I can come right now, Dad. I'm really sorry, but I have to find Sasha. I'm getting ready to leave for California. I can't come home. What happened anyway?"

Her father's voice was high and tight with tension.

"Yeah. It's O.K. I understand. She was drinking with the girls after work. Shouldn't have driven. Should have called me. Thank God she didn't kill someone."

"O.K. Dad. Let me take a little while to figure this out. I'll call you back, OK?"

Ruthie untangled the cord and placed the receiver back on the cradle. She sat on the bed, breathing deeply, fighting the images that were clamoring for a place in her mind.

A little girl in the back seat of a car. Frightened. "Momma, momma. What's wrong?"

The car veering to the side of the road. The darkness of woods and the sound of tires on gravel. The car going too fast.

"Momma, you're scaring me."

The car stopping just short of a tree trunk that loomed, wide and so close she could see the lines in the bark. Her mother's laugh. Why was she laughing? This wasn't funny.

"It's okay, Ruthie. We're fine, aren't we?" Her mother's voice sounding funny—like she had ice in her mouth.

"But we mustn't tell Daddy." That laugh again. Ruthie hated her mother's laugh. Too loud, demanding attention.

"This will be our little secret, Ruthie. O.K? No. Telling. Daddy. You understand?"

Her mother pulling the car back on the road, headlights off, then flicking on when someone honked. Ruthie clutching the leather strap above the window and whispering to herself for the rest of the drive home.

"It will be OK. It will be OK. It will be OK."

So many close calls over the years. And now, an accident, and her father once again asking for her help.

Ruthie looked around the room, the early light beginning to creep into the dark corners.

Her clothes for California were already laid out on the small folding table waiting to be packed. She had a plan—a couple of days to say her good-byes and then she would be off on a Greyhound Bus to San Francisco.

After her visit to her parents with Manny, Ruthie had been keeping her distance. Her mother could only be counted on for pointing out all her flaws, and she had argued with her father about her decision not to involve the police or the FBI. When she tried to explain that she didn't think the authorities would look kindly on her illegal trip to Cuba, he dismissed her concerns—told her this was no time to act like a "clueless hippy" and went even further—refusing to help her anymore unless she followed his advice. So she had picked up the phone when he called but hadn't gone out of her way to stay in touch.

And now she had almost said no to her father's plea for help for the first time. But how could she? Marty was just a kid—and her father…well her father just melted, gave in, until it was all "yes dear" and "sorry dear" and "of course not dear."

But what if this time was different? What if this was the tipping point? The moment when her mother finally faced the toll her years of drinking were taking. Maybe her father had finally tired of rescuing her from any consequences, of making excuses, of looking the other way.

Maybe she could support her father and finally make peace with her mother.

That would be one less worry on her mind as she set off on her trip to find Sasha.

Ruthie brewed herself a strong cup of coffee and sat at the kitchen counter to call her father.

"Hi Dad, So I figured it out and I can come this afternoon. But I'll just stay one night. I've got to get on my way to California as soon as possible. Will that work for you?

She could hear the relief in her father's voice as she relayed the bus schedule, and they said their goodbyes. At least she had a few hours at home to make a few phone calls.

Ruthie packed a nightgown and her toiletries, a sandwich, and an apple for the road…and at the last minute, the California Road Atlas she had been studying nonstop, and a stale Hershey bar she had found at the back of one of Claudia's kitchen drawers.

The bus terminal was empty in mid-afternoon and Ruthie only had to wait about 15 minutes for the next bus to Hartford. She took a much-needed nap and woke just as the bus made the turn off the highway and pulled onto the familiar curve of Albany Road that had always signified "home" on the many bus trips that had carried her here.

Her father was standing at the open door of their Ford Country Squire wagon as the bus pulled into its stall. His face had the pinched look it always got when he was worried about something but lit with a smile when he saw her making her way to the car. As he pulled her into a bear hug and pinched her shoulder just a bit too hard, she was glad she came, glad she was there for her father when he needed her. And then she remembered what awaited her in the bedroom at the top of the narrow stairs.

They didn't talk much on the way home. Just how was the trip and when are you leaving for California.

When Ruthie asked about her mom, and what had happened this time, it was oh you know, the usual, nothing terrible but…a long pause.

"I'm scared, Ruthie, I really am. She doesn't think she has a problem. She just can't admit it at all. But it's getting worse. And one of these days, well…who knows what will happen."

After that, they were quiet until they pulled up the steep driveway and Ruthie pushed open the back door, dropped her stuff in the den, and moved quietly up the carpeted stairs to her mother's bedroom.

The door was part way open, so she pushed her way into the room. Her mother was propped on one side of the King size bed, covers pulled up to her waist. Her mother's left eye was purple and swollen and left exposed, but the rest of her mother's face was in place—foundation, blush, signature red lipstick—and her hair, growing whiter each day, was sprayed into its characteristic brushed back look. Under her semi-sheer nightgown, Ruthie could see a deep red welt where the seat belt had left its mark. Otherwise, it was her mother, turning her face with the usual look of disappointment to see her daughter standing there.

"Oh, Ruthie. You came."

"Yup. Here I am. Just wanted to be sure you are O.K. Sounds like a pretty scary accident."

"Oh, really, it was nothing to get so worked up about. I told your father not to call you. And would you believe that stupid doctor wanted me to go to a rehab. Hah, I told him a thing or two. All I needed was a little valium to relax and sleep and I'd be good as new."

Just then, her father came into the room with a snack tray ---Ritz crackers, a bowl of chopped chicken liver, some olives and the familiar sound of ice cubes clinking in a scotch glass.

"Happy hour," he said, placing the tray on the side of the bed. "Ruthie, can I get you something to drink?'

"Nope Dad. I'm good. I think I'll just wash up and change into something more comfortable."

She fumed behind the closed door of her old bedroom, turned guest room. Fooled again. Tipping point—hah! And the doctor went right along with it. Sent the nice middle class white lady home with her Valium. Ruthie remembered all the stories her black friends from the civil rights group had told about being arrested when they got stopped with an open can of beer in the car.

And her father—fixing her happy hour drink as usual. Nothing had changed. Nothing would ever change.

She didn't need this now—she needed to focus on her trip to find Sasha. But she would have it out with her mother before she left. What did she have to lose?

Marty breezed in about 8 PM with a pizza and some garlic knots from the Oasis and the 3 of them sat around the small table in the breakfast nook and talked between bites.

"I can see that you're just going right back to things as usual, Dad, but I can't do it anymore. I'm going to have an honest talk with her in the morning and it's going to include some hard truths, like it or not. I just can't pretend everything is alright anymore, because it's really, really not."

"Yeah, but," Marty said, talking through a mouthful of pizza. "you'll stir things up as usual and then you'll leave like you always do—and we'll be left picking up the pieces, as usual. Right, Dad?"

Her father sighed, picked up a garlic knot and then put it back on the plate.

"You do what you need to do, Ruth Ann. God knows, something needs to change around here, and I can't seem to figure out how."

"But Dad…" Marty broke in. "She'll just make things worse. She always does."

"Something needs to change, Martin. Your mother is not all right. And the next time might be…well, it might be worse."

And with that, her father stood up from the table, tossed his paper plate in the garbage and made his way upstairs. They heard the bedroom door close, the creak of the bed as he lay down next to their mother, and the clunk of his shoes as he kicked them off, one by one.

Marty sighed.

"You don't know what it's like living here with them, Ruthie. You can drop a few bombs and then leave, but I'm stuck behind with nowhere to go."

"I know, Marty. Believe me, I do know. Maybe when I get Sasha and we find a place to live, you can come stay with us. We would love that."

"Yeah, maybe. Sounds good. If you find her, you know, and things work out. Well, I hope so. Really, I do. Wake me up before you leave tomorrow to say goodbye."

Marty squeezed past Ruthie, gave her a quick peck on the cheek and settled in the den with the TV on. End of conversation.

Ruthie cleaned up the remains of their pizza dinner and made her way upstairs to her room. She stood in front of the needlework poem for a minute before sinking onto the bed.

"Thursday's Child Has Far to Go"—she did have a long and uncertain journey in front of her, but first she would get honest with her mother once and for all.

Ruthie had forgotten to pull the shades the night before and woke early as the sunlight poured in through the sheer curtains. She padded down the carpeted stairs and made her way to the kitchen where her father was preparing bagels and lox, whitefish salad and orange juice on a tray for her mom.

"Wow, quite a breakfast. Can I help with anything?"

"No Ruthie. Thanks. I'm almost finished. Would you like some breakfast now too?"

'No thanks, Pop. But maybe you could fix me a bagel to take on the bus with me. I'm planning to talk to Mom and then catch an early afternoon bus."

Her father arranged the plates on the snack tray, stopping to pour a shot glass full of vodka into her mother's orange juice.

"Really, Pop—isn't it a bit early to start her drinking? Sending the wrong message maybe?"

"It's a mimosa. Hardly any alcohol. I don't have the energy to fight these battles, Ruthie. I just don't." And with that, he made his way up the stairs. Ruthie followed close behind, lost in her own thoughts. Her hope that her mother might be on the verge of realizing that she needed to stop drinking had been shattered the night before—and now it was clear that her father was giving in to her as usual. But Ruthie was determined to break her own pattern. She would not let her mother get to her.

Rose fluffed her hair against the pillow and turned with a smile as her husband and daughter came through the door into the bedroom.

"Oh, Max. What a beautiful breakfast! You shouldn't have, really." Rose reached for the orange juice right away, swallowing her first Valium of the day with a swig of spiked OJ.

"And Ruthie, thanks so much for coming all this way to see your dear old mother. I know you have other things on your mind these days. Any news about Sasha? Well, I guess you would have told us if you had."

Ruthie sat with her lips pressed closed at the side of the bed, trying to find the right words to begin—but there were no right words.

"Mom, we really need to talk. This last incident really scared us. We can't keep pretending you don't have a problem."

Her father was slumped against the desk in the corner and Ruthie realized she was on her own.

"I'm scared for you, Mom. I love you and I don't want you driving off the road into trees because you've been drinking too much. I want you to get help."

Her mother's shrill voice cut through the silence in the room.

"You love me, do you? You're worried about me? I'm the one with problems? What about you, Ruthie? What about the fact that you just up and left your daughter, my granddaughter, and now you don't have the slightest idea where she is? Do you call that being responsible? Do you call that being a good mother? I warned you about that Carl you insisted on marrying from the beginning. But oh no—nobody listens to me because I've got a problem."

Ruthie sighed and plopped into the armchair in the corner. Here we go, she thought.

"Poor Ruthie, whose mother has a drinking problem. Poor Max whose wife drinks too much. You've got a lot of nerve sitting on your high horses and judging me. If you knew what I went through as a child—being born after the beloved baby that died, being named after her for God's sake, but never good enough to take her place."

Ruthie stood and took a few steps toward her mother. This was a new story; one she had never heard.

"Oh, you didn't know that did you?

"Now Rose, that's enough," Ruthie's father finally spoke up from his corner, but her mother dismissed him with a wave of one hand.

"No, Max. Don't do your usual thing of trying to make peace. I'm tired of being the bad mother. Ruthie needs to understand that other people have gone through things, had to deal with them, and done the best they could. I've done the best I could, and I'm sorry if it's never been good enough."

Ruthie watched as her mother began the lead-up to what would inevitably become a full-blown meltdown. It always started this way—with her turning things around, making herself the victim. Soon came the collapse into sobbing self-recrimination, the I'm sorrys that weren't really apologies—and Ruthie would be drawn, despite her rage, into the role of comforter—the tissues offered, the gentle backrubs, the soothing. It was all a lie, and it was exhausting.

Ruthie thought, not this time, not now. She pulled herself away from the bed as if it was a powerful magnet she had to kick free of.

"I'm sorry you're feeling this way, Mom. But I didn't come here to be judged by you…or to cooperate with your denial and I won't stick around for this. I've got a bus to catch and a daughter to find. I love you but I need you to know that if you aren't willing to deal with your drinking problem, I won't be back. I am a good mother. Yeah, I've made some mistakes, but I will find Sasha, and I will not be bringing her around here."

And with that, Ruthie left the room without looking back. She didn't want to watch her father try to soothe her mother's ruffled feelings for the umpteenth time. She didn't want to hear her mother's words echo in her mind one more time. Do you call that being a good mother? She fled to the safety of her room, finished packing her bag, and shuffled down the stairs to the den to wait for her father. She would get back to Cambridge as fast as she could, finish her good-byes there and get on the road.

At the beginning of her trip back to Cambridge, Ruthie still heard her mother's voice in her head—in the sound of the bus wheels on the highway, in the rustling of other passengers shifting in their seats, over and over. Not a good mother, not a good mother, not a good mother. In the stormy days of her adolescence, a different litany of her failures had followed her around the house—selfish, ungrateful, lazy. She had left home at 18 and never looked back, but her mother's voice had followed her, as if she had swallowed it and could never get far enough away. Her insecurity and lack of confidence had been partially responsible for her too-young marriage to Carl, and her escape act had led her to California, then Colorado. Was Cuba part of that act? Was her whole life just one big rebellion against her mother? What a cliché she was.

Ruthie dozed a bit as the bus made its way north on I-84 toward Boston. When she woke, she tried to drown out her mother's voice with positive self-talk she had learned in her women's group. "I will not be paralyzed by my fears but led by my dreams," she whispered to herself, glancing around to see if anyone noticed. "I have made mistakes, but I will not let them define me," she repeated. It was hard to push away all the negative thinking—she had let it rule her for so long—but she had to be strong and believe in herself to embark on this journey—and she would. She was no longer the Ruthie who hid in her room or tried to make herself invisible. She had changed.

A Dose of Manny

"Bueno," the sleepy rasp of Manny's voice let Ruthie know she had awakened him. It was Saturday and he had to be up early anyway to distribute Claridad, the weekly newspaper of the Puerto Rican Socialist Party. Manny was one of the Party leaders in NJ and he never missed a Saturday walking the streets of Hoboken.

"Hey Manny. It's Ruthie. Sorry to wake you." "Ruthie, what's going on? What's wrong?"

Ruthie took a deep breath. How had she come to this point in her life that one of her closest friends assumed that a phone call from her meant that something was wrong?

"No, Manny. Some good news for a change. I heard from Carl—well just a postcard with no real information. But I think I know where they might be—and I'm heading back to California."

"Wow, negra. Finally! I've got some vacation days saved up—let me come and help you, see you off. I miss you girl!"

"No," was on the tip of Ruthie's tongue, but she paused. She was always pushing people away. Why not let Manny come? She could use his moral support. And as much as she wanted to leave right away, today, it would take her a few days to get ready for this journey.

"Okay, Manny. Yes, that would be great. Yes, come! I miss you too."

They talked for a few more minutes, making a plan for Manny to take the bus up to Cambridge in two days. Ruthie would leave a day or two after that.

"Hey, I've got a great idea," Ruthie said after they had worked out the logistics. "How about I invite my friend Violeta to an early Thanksgiving dinner? We can cook up a storm. I want my two best friends to meet each other before I leave."

There was a long pause on the other end of the line.

"You know I love a reason to eat, Ruthie—though I have to admit I'm not too fond of that dried up turkey you Yankees like to serve—but Thanksgiving? Dontcha remember a couple of years ago when they wouldn't let that Native American chief speak the truth about what Thanksgiving really means at Plymouth Rock and the tribes declared it a National Day of Mourning—the start of wiping out their people?"

Ruthie sighed. Leave it to Manny. Couldn't anything just be what it was— just a holiday—without dragging politics into it. She started to talk, to beg him really, to leave Thanksgiving, her favorite holiday, alone—and then fell silent. He was right, of course he was. Whatever her fears and anxieties were about losing Sasha because of her politics were nothing compared to what Native Americans had experienced—the trail of tears, Wounded Knee, their children being ripped from their families and sent to boarding schools that stripped them of their culture and identity.

"Sorry, amiga, it's just…I…"

"No apology needed, Manny. You're right. I wasn't thinking. How about if we turn it into a feast of learning—find some good readings, maybe that speech from Plymouth Rock, and reflect on the day? Would that work?"

"That sounds great. We'll decolonize Thanksgiving and Puerto Rico will be next." Manny laughed the deep rumbling laugh that Ruthie loved so much. "But that doesn't mean we can't eat. You can make us a turkey, Ruthie, but I'm gonna fix us a juicy pernil, a pork roast with some rice and beans and fried platanos."

"That will be so good. And I'll ask Violeta to bring some of her delicious Chilean pastries for dessert. You're gonna love her, Manny. I know you will."

"Okay Negra. Can't wait. Gotta hit the streets with Claridad now. See you soon."

Ruthie hung up the pink princess phone, thinking for a minute that she would miss this place and the life she had made in it—but no, she shook her head to get rid of those thoughts and began writing a shopping list in her notebook.

She was ready to move on, she had to be, and this dinner would be a nice way to say good-bye.

Violeta was excited when Ruthie called to invite her to Thanksgiving dinner. She confided in Ruthie that in all her time here she had never been invited to this special dinner—always worked at Cookie's that day, serving up plate after plate of dry turkey and gravy with mashed potatoes and stuffing to solo diners who, like her, had no place else to be. She would ask for the day off—no, she would demand it. Cookie owed her after all these years.

Manny arrived in all his Manny glory—enveloping Ruthie in the crush of his big bear hug—raring to go shopping as soon as they dropped off his stuff at the apartment.

It was fun to shop with someone else for a change and Ruthie let herself relax and enjoy it. Her neighborhood market was always full of young couples, families with kids and students and she usually felt like an outlier. A single woman, a little old to be a student, moving around the aisles with her handheld basket, picking out 3 apples, one avocado, one chicken breast and a loaf of bread that she would keep in the fridge so it wouldn't go moldy before she could finish it. Shopping trips with Sasha had not always been fun—at the end of a long day she whined and wheedled when she couldn't get the Fruit Loops cereal she saw on TV—but still Ruthie longed for her presence.

"Wow, look at these tomatoes. In Hoboken you can only find pale anemic looking ones in a cellophane package. Just look at these red, juicy beauties!" Manny was exuberant as they wandered through the market—extolling the beauty of each item before lowering it into the cart—the plumpness of the pork roast, the gorgeous green color of the cabbage, and look—perfectly ripe platanos in Cambridge! Ruthie added a few more traditional items for their Thanksgiving dinner—whole cranberry sauce in a can, Pepperidge Farm stuffing mix and the smallest turkey she could find. Wrinkled leaves crunched underfoot as they walked the few blocks back to the apartment.

"I love what you've done with the place," Manny said, sinking into the soft cushions of the futon with a hot mug of café con leche when they had finished unloading their bags. "It has more color, more character…but what are these," he asked, pointing to the embroidered wall hangings Ruthie had hung above the couch.

"They're called arpilleras—made after the coup by women in Chile as a way to express their resistance to the military junta." Manny stood to examine them more closely.

"Remember that Chilean guy from the International Brigade—what was his name? He really had a crush on you, Ruthie. I wonder what has become of him in all this. Scary to think about."

He flopped back on the couch while Ruthie flipped through the record albums she had stacked on the bottom shelf of Claudia's bookcase

"Andres," Ruthie said. "He gave me this to remember him by," she said, displaying the cover—an album by Los Angeles Negros, a popular Chilean group, with the song that she had danced to with Manny at every Saturday night fiesta. "Amor adios, ya no puedo continuar, ya la magia se acabo, y yo tengo que marchar." Ruthie sang a few bars of the song while Manny covered his ears.

"He was a student at the university," Manny said, "Remember…a real hard-core leftist dude. He would've been in the streets. He would've…" His voice trailed off and they both sat in silence for a moment, thinking of their friend, of how full of life and hope he had been, of the photos they had seen of soldiers marching through Santiago, rounding up students.

"Andres, presente!" Manny said, raising a fist in salute.

"To Andres," Ruthie echoed and raised her hand to cover his.

Gratitude

TThey spent all the next day cooking.

"You'd think we were feeding the whole neighborhood," Ruthie said, as she slathered the turkey with a paste made of paprika, salt, pepper and garlic powder—one of the few cooking tricks she'd learned at her mother's side.

"Hey, that's a good idea!" Manny said. "Who else can we invite to this Decolonization Feast of Gratitude and Attitude?" He was puncturing the pork roast with a knife and sticking slivers of garlic into the slits he made. He had already made the softrito and the small apartment was fragrant with the aroma of cilantro, peppers, garlic and achiote. Violeta would arrive at 4 PM, bringing dessert. Not sure when she would see her parents again, or when she would be reunited with Sasha, Ruthie looked forward to their small gathering more than ever.

"Family is who you choose, don't you think?" Manny said, rinsing his garlic flavored hands under the faucet. "And I choose you, Ruthie." With the pernil, the turkey and the stuffing sharing the oven, a salad ready in the fridge and the platanos ready to go into the frying pan, Ruthie sat on the couch and closed her eyes, imagining Sasha skipping down the hall and plopping down next to her.

Manny placed a Cuba Libre, a glass of rum and coke, in her hands and sat beside her.

"Soon, negra. Soon," he said, reading her mind as usual. He squeezed her hand, and they sat quietly together till the buzz of the intercom interrupted the silence.

"That'll be Violeta," Ruthie said. "Can you check the oven while I get the door?"

A couple of hours later, they pushed their chairs back from the card table which was overflowing with the remains of their feast—the turkey carcass nearly picked clean, a few stray pieces of pork left from the small roast, one lonely fried plantain waiting to be scooped up.

"We can clean up later. Let's get comfortable and have some coffee and dessert in the living room.," Ruthie said.

"Cafe no, I have brought maté," Violeta said, winking at Ruthie—and then in Manny's direction. "It's a delicious tea that we drink in Chile, Manny. To have with the alfajores, our dessert."

Ruthie laughed. Her two dear friends had warmed to each other immediately—chattering away in Spanish, trading Puerto Rican and Chilean slang words, laughing together at Ruthie's famous foibles in their native language.

"One time she told one of our Cuban jefes she was "muy, muy embarassada" and they were very surprised to hear that," Manny recounted. "When she found out her mistake, she was even more embarrassed."

"Ay dios, Ruthie—it's avergonzada, embarrassed. You told him you were very very pregnant." Violeta giggled into her hand.

"Well, I know that now, but…" Ruthie sighed. "What about the time I told the waiter in that little Mexican restaurant in Central Square that I wanted "tortillas de arena.""

"Sand tortillas. Oh, that's a good one. I hope he brought you the "tortillas de harina" instead.

They laughed together like siblings retelling old family jokes, and then suddenly the conversation took a serious turn.

"Ruthie told me about your son, Javi is it, Violeta. And I've been following news of the coup—or as much as they cover it in newspapers here. I am so sorry you are going through this. Any news about him?"

Violeta stood and walked to the door that opened onto the small balcony, then turned to face them.

"They found a house—on the outskirts of Valparaiso—where people were saying they had been holding the students they rounded up. One escaped and took them there. But there was nothing, nobody. Disappeared. My son has disappeared."

Violeta's shoulders shook with silent tears. Manny stood and went to her—put his arm around her shoulders, drew her into his broad chest.

No one said anything for a long minute. What was there to say?

Then Manny broke the silence.

"Abajo los generales, down with the generals," he said. "Javi Presente!

"Javi presente," Ruthie echoed, wrapping her arms around Violeta. She and Manny held their friend until she stopped crying, lifted her head and joined in their chant.

"Javi presente!" they shouted in unison.

Violeta left soon after and Manny was leaving on the bus the next morning. Her friends had to be at work on Monday and Ruthie would finally board a bus to go in search of her daughter. She was dreading the long trip, but she hadn't wanted to ask her father to pay for a plane ticket and he hadn't offered. She needed to spend as little as possible now so that she would have money to get settled when she found Sasha. The three-day bus trip was just another hurdle she had to get over.

There was one more stop she needed to make before leaving Cambridge and she invited Manny along to meet the staff at Cookie's. On the way, she described her first day of work–how Cookie had hired her over the phone and put her straight to work, how Violeta had come to be such a good friend. They arrived at the door, covered with a cardboard turkey cutout and a decorative bunch of dried corn. Manny swung it open, the bell tinkled, the familiar sound that had greeted Ruthie on her first day which felt like years ago, and Cookie lifted her frizzy red head from the register to see who was arriving.

"Ruthie!" she said. "I thought you had left without saying good-bye," she hollered in her husky smoker's voice. "Ruthie's here everyone."

Ruthie and Manny moved into the diner, drawing a few weary glances from the regulars at the counter. When Ruthie worked the counter, she imagined their bottoms glued to the old-fashioned red leather stools as she refilled their stained coffee cups and fended off the occasional old flirt. Today there was pumpkin pie with vanilla ice cream to go along with the coffee.

"And who's this guy?" Sol called out from the pass through. "Got a new boyfriend, Ruthie?"

"Well, I'm a boy and I'm a friend, but not a boyfriend I'm afraid," Manny said, striding over to Sol and sticking out his hand. "Not that I'd mind."

Sol laughed and shook his hand.

"I like this one, Ruthie. You ought to keep him around."

Ruthie laughed and motioned to Manny, waved good-bye to Sol and headed for the door. Cookie interrupted her movement toward the exit and extended a hand holding a large envelope.

"We wanted you to have a little something to remember us by, Ruthie. And to wish you good luck in getting your little girl back. Violeta told us why you are leaving. Please open it now."

Ruthie tore the envelope open to find an ornate Hallmark card with an embossed message in curvy red script. "Goodbye and Goodluck from the Whole Gang!" it read, and she opened it to find signatures scrawled all over the two pages inside–Cookie, Sol, ornery Nate who always complained about his coffee not being hot enough, Joe who stopped by every day on his way home from the shipyard, even a few of the students who mostly ignored her–and of course Violeta who wrote "A mi compañera del alma. Que tenemos suerte encontrando nuestros queridos hijos." Several folded twenty-dollar bills were tucked into the card.

Ruthie sighed. Violeta had become a soul sister for her. She put them in the same boat, mothers looking for their children, but Ruthie knew Violeta's situation was far more serious. Her son, her Javi, could be tortured, disappeared, murdered and she could do nothing but sew arpilleras and pray. Ruthie would see Sasha again; she knew she would.

Manny and Ruthie spent a quiet evening at home, reminiscing a bit about Cuba and the Brigade, listening to some oldies on the stereo, and going to bed early.

The next day they said good-bye at the door.

"Sasha presente," Manny said, hugging her close.

"Sasha presente," Ruthie echoed, shutting the door as Manny bounded down the stairs.

She spoke the words quietly into the air of the small apartment that had sheltered her these last few months.

"Sasha is here."

One Way Ticket

Ruthie laid out the few things she would take with her on the striped mattress of the bed, stripped of its white cotton sheets and Indian bedspread, and looked around at the small room that had sheltered her often-sleepless nights for the last couple of months. She would not miss it—though she had felt safe here—as safe as she felt anywhere these days. She had called her cousin last night to tell her she would be leaving.

"Just slip the key under the door, cuz," Claudia had said. "And good luck."

Ruthie slowly placed her things in the backpack—an extra pair of jeans, her khaki shorts with lots of pockets, 3 T-shirts, including the one with a rooster with a plastic comb on its head that Sasha loved, 2 pairs of grey wool socks, her rain parka, a small notebook in which she had written everything she had been able to remember or find out about the beach in the postcard.

On top of all that, she carefully laid the doll she had brought from Cuba—a black woman made of cloth—red dress, white apron and white bandanna tied around her head, holding a long stick with a tiny painted gourd on the end that rattled when it shook. Oya, the Santeria goddess of the wind. "Protect me and guide me to Sasha," Ruthie whispered as she closed the backpack, though she wasn't sure what or who she believed in these days. "Send your powerful wind to push me in the right direction, Oya." And then she added, "Please."

Feeling foolish and looking around as if someone might be listening, she slipped the postcard into the back pocket of her jeans. It was even more wrinkled now from her hours of studying it for clues. She had enveloped it in plastic wrap to keep it from getting wet or torn.

Ruthie looked at her watch. 8 PM. Her bus was at 11. Time to go.

She hoisted her backpack over her shoulder, tied the red Harvard sweatshirt that Michael had given her around her waist, took one last look around and closed the door behind her, slipping the key underneath as Claudia had instructed.

"Oya, let's go. Let's go find Sasha."

Ruthie's footsteps echoed on the metal stairs as she set off on this pilgrimage—the most important journey of her life.

Ruthie snuggled down into her pea coat and wrapped her red woolen scarf around her ears. It was chilly in the bus station and the benches were hard, even with the cushion of her heavy coat. She looked around at the assortment of passengers waiting, like she was, for buses to take them somewhere. The round, gray-haired woman on the bench across from her opened a brown paper bag stained with grease, releasing the fragrance of fried chicken, and two young kids rushed over, reaching their hands inside. The woman swatted them away—wait, now just wait till I clean your hands. Don't be so greedy. On the bench next to her a young woman with stringy brown hair peeking out from beneath a blue wool cap lay sleeping, her head resting on an army green backpack, a red plaid blanket pulled over her body. Ruthie liked to make up stories about people she observed to help pass the time, and she began weaving a tale about the young woman. A runaway maybe? On the road for a long time and coming into the station for a rest.

She wondered if anyone was making up a story about her—with her one backpack, only a box of raisins and an apple she had thrown in at the last minute for the journey. Oh, and a tin of her favorite cookies for Sasha. She had been too anxious to get started to think about food for herself, but now she was hungry.

"You just don't think ahead, never have." Was her mother's voice still hanging around after everything they had been through. "Just go away," Ruthie thought. She almost spoke the words out loud but caught herself. That's all she needed—her fellow passengers thinking they would be traveling with a crazy woman.

She had bought a one-way ticket for San Francisco, deciding on a late-night bus because she might be able to sleep through the night to make the trip seem shorter.

She would check in with Carl's family and hitchhike down the coast from there. She didn't know what she would find but it would be better than endless waiting.

The bus was late. She reached for the box of raisins, pulled off her mittens and let their sweetness melt on her tongue, one by one, as the minutes ticked by.

On the Move

October 1973

The bus moved through the darkness. The steady hum of the engine was interrupted only by the whimper of a waking child, the loud flush of the toilet in the small, smelly bathroom at the back. Neon lights flashed their come-ons when they passed through small settlements but mostly just the dark two-lane highway stretched ahead. She had no idea where they were—just a long way from home. She didn't even know where home was anymore—not Cambridge, that was behind her for good, not San Francisco anymore.

When she found Sasha, she would make a new home for the two of them and it wouldn't matter where it was. She would rent a little house in a small town and paint all the rooms in Sasha's favorite colors—bright yellow in the kitchen, orange in the living room, and Sasha's room a pale, robin's egg blue. She would walk Sasha to school every day. In the fall, they would kick through crunchy piles of dried red and gold leaves. In winter they would slip and slide over icy patches, laughing when they fell together in a heap, Sasha's schoolbooks scattered over the snow. In summer Ruthie would sit on the small front porch watching Sasha play with the neighbor's children in a plastic inflatable pool on the lawn. She would never take her eyes off her. She would never leave her alone.

Ruthie stared out the window. It was very dark on this stretch of highway. Occasionally, a small cluster of twinkling lights appeared out of the dark but vanished again in a flash. All she could really see was the road whizzing by. All she could hear was the occasional grunt or cough of a sleeping passenger.

Her thoughts trailed off and she closed her eyes. One of the little kids across the aisle began bouncing on his seat. I want Mama. I want Mama. He was building up to a full-blown wail

"Hush, child, hush," a whispered murmur from his grandmother who pulled him to her chest.

"You'll see Mama soon. Soon soon. I promise. Now hush, hush."

Was Sasha somewhere crying for her? Were there children everywhere in this world who were missing their Mamas?

Ruthie resumed her position at the window, eyes wide open now, as the road spooled by in the night. The almost full moon was visible, and she watched the play of light and darkness above the dark hills in the distance. There were only a few cars on the road. Three days had not sounded so long when she bought her ticket, but she already felt like she had been on this bus forever.

Ruthie unfolded the map she had bought at the Coop before she left. It was wrinkled and coffee stained from the hours she had studied it at the folding table in Claudia's apartment—zeroing in on her destination—that beach in Baja where she hoped Carl and Sasha would be—planning her route across the country. She spread it across her lap, careful not to tear it. She could barely make out the route she had traced in the dim glow from the light above her seat, but it one thing was clear—she had a long way to go. Chicago was next, maybe, and then the flat empty plains of Iowa and Nebraska. It would take her through Salt Lake City and then on to Reno. She had been to Reno once before, with Carl on one of their cross-country adventures, and remembered her surprise at finding a slot machine in the Ladies Room.

From Reno it would be around 6 hours to San Francisco and then she would have to figure out what to do next. She would stop and see Carl's parents, look for his brother, check in with old friends to see if anyone had any new information—and then she would head down the coast—probably hitchhike part of the way to Baja. Just reciting the steps in her mind made her feel closer to Sasha.

Louise

Ruthie was glad she had left her peacoat on her seat as she returned from a quick rest stop in the heat of the Salt Lake City late morning sun. She sighed as the stale air on the bus enveloped her yet again. A young woman was sitting in her seat.

"I hope you don't mind," the woman said, looking up at Ruthie from beneath lowered lids. "I really need to sit by the window. I'm Louise." She was twisting a small white handkerchief nervously in her lap. Her reddish-brown hair was carefully arranged and flipped up at the ends. She wore a light blue collared shirt under a navy-blue cardigan and black polyester slacks. She kept glancing out the window as if she was looking for someone.

"Um, no, it's okay, I guess. I can sit here. I'm Ruthie," she said, sticking out her hand which Louise ignored. Ruthie sat down in the aisle seat, moving her coat aside and settling the bag with her food on her lap. Her stomach growled and she laughed apologetically but the woman didn't notice. She was dividing her attention between the bus platform and her wristwatch as if waiting for someone to arrive.

"Where are you headed?" Ruthie asked.

The woman turned to her and bit her lip. "California," she said.

"Oh, me too," Ruthie said. "I've been traveling from Boston. I'm getting pretty tired of being on this bus."

"I wish we would get underway," the woman said, and Ruthie was struck by her formal language.

As the bus pulled away from the station, Ruthie shifted in her seat to find a new comfortable position now that she had someone beside her and unwrapped the turkey sandwich she had bought at the café in the bus station. Louise barely took up any space at all and her breath was a barely audible sigh.

During the many hours of travel from Boston to Salt Lake, Ruthie had endured several more obtrusive seat-mates—a bald man in a rumpled suit smelling of cigarettes, who spread his legs so wide she had to shrink against the window, had been the most unpleasant. Thankfully he had gotten off the bus somewhere in Ohio.

Ruthie finished her sandwich, opened a book on her lap, and snuck a glance at Louise. The young woman had her eyes closed. Her thin, colorless lips were sewn together, her hands folded in her lap with just the whisper of her fingers brushing against each other in nervous motion. She must be a Mormon, Ruthie thought—something about her demeanor placing her in that sect that Ruthie knew little about except for polygamy and lots of rules. Where was Louise traveling—alone and on a bus full of strangers? And what was she leaving behind? Her small overnight bag couldn't hold more than a couple of days' worth of clothing.

Ruthie sat gazing at the glimpses of passing landscape she could see through the bus window as Louise dozed. She was fascinated by the vast stretches of nothing but beige flat earth dotted with scruffy pines. Occasionally a tall cactus appeared—arms outstretched as if guarding this desert terrain. And when they passed through a tiny settlement she sat up and peered around Louise to get a closer look, intrigued by the few people she saw going about their daily lives in the middle of the day in the middle of nowhere. What would life be like in a place like this?

Ruthie twisted the silver ring on her finger. It was a plain flat silver band with a fire opal set in the middle and had been a gift from her mother for her 21st birthday—one of the few really thoughtful gifts she had ever received from her. Usually, it was a sweater she would never wear, or a $20 bill tucked into her pocket and barely acknowledged. But this ring was special, though the opal had grown less fiery over time—scuffed and cracked in places—and it was a bit too small now. Ruthie had treasured it, and when she was busy moving on and giving things away, she had never wanted to part with it. It was the glint of fire in the stone she loved. When it caught the light it sparked orange and red and even a hint of blue. Maybe her mother had been able to see Ruthie's fire after all—though she rarely showed any understanding of her only daughter's struggles. Even now, the worst having happened, Ruthie could not turn to her for sympathy or support.

She leaned back in her seat, shifted her left leg, which had fallen asleep, careful not to jostle Louise. Ruthie's curiosity about this quiet young woman was growing. When she awoke, Ruthie would ask her where in California she was travelling to. That was a normal thing to ask on a bus.

She pulled her shawl around her shoulders against the chill of the air-conditioning, which was cranked up as the bus moved through the hot desert. Her ring caught the rays of the afternoon sun and sparkled on her hand. She closed her eyes and dreamed of a fire on a beach in the setting sun and her little girl's face lit by its orange glow.

Ruthie woke sore and hungry again. She pulled the tin of cookies from the backpack at her feet and opened it. The smell of cinnamon wafted from beneath the wax paper she had carefully wrapped around them.

Rug cookies, Sasha called them, not able to pronounce their Yiddish name—rugelach—Ruthie didn't make them often—they required more precision and attention than she liked in her cooking—but the night before she left her cousin's apartment, she had pulled down the rarely used cookie trays from a high cabinet and enlisted Manny to help her prepare the dough,

She would try just one—her stomach was grumbling, and she had nothing else to eat. The bus would stop soon. Maybe the next stop was Denver. And she would get a real meal. She bit into the flaky, buttery crust of the cookie to the sweet cinnamon and nut filling that lay beneath. The cookies were shaped like a snail and had to be carefully rolled from a triangle of chilled dough. The recipe was her mother's, written on an index card stained with fingerprints of dough and sugar, but she didn't remember her mother ever making rugelach—only her Granma Gertie whose kitchen always smelled like fresh baked babkas and rugelach whenever they visited.

Ruthie wiped crumbs from her mouth and chin. She had to be careful not to eat the whole tin before she got to California.

Louise stirred in the seat beside her and opened her eyes.

"Would you like a cookie?" Ruthie asked. "They're homemade. I'm bringing them to my little girl." The words left her mouth before she realized. She hadn't meant to say them.

"You have a little girl?" Louise asked.

"Yes, yes, I do. I'm going to see her." That was all she would say for now. "How about you? Do you have any kids?"

Louise looked at her, her eyes wide with an emotion Ruthie couldn't decipher, and burst into tears.

Louise cried quietly beside her—only the movement of her shoulders and occasional sniffles betraying her deep emotion. Ruthie didn't know what to do, whether to offer comfort or leave her alone. Louise was like a bottle washed up on the shore with a message inside—unexpected, a complete mystery—and Ruthie wasn't sure she wanted to know what the message might bring.

She sat quietly, trying to offer Louise some small amount of privacy on the crowded bus—where everyone was visible in the light of the early afternoon sun that streamed through dusty windows. That's what she would have wanted.

But then Louise grabbed Ruthie's hand in both of hers. Ruthie turned to her. Louise's eyes were squeezed shut, her face red from crying.

"I've left my children. I've left them and I'll never see them again," she whispered through clenched teeth and began crying again—this time loud gasping sobs that rocked the seat and drew the attention of the black grandmother across the aisle who sat with a large picnic basket in her lap and stared at them.

"Shh, Louise. It's okay. It'll be okay. Shh…Shhh. You'll be okay." Ruthie put her arm around Louise's thin shoulders and held her hand. Slowly Louise's sobbing quieted and she began to take deep breaths, "Shh, Louise. It's okay. It'll be okay. Shh…Shhh. You'll be okay." Ruthie put her arm around Louise's thin shoulders and held her hand. Slowly Louise's sobbing quieted and she began to take deep breaths, drawing in the stale air of the bus as if she was drowning. The grandmother turned back to distributing drumsticks to the two small children crowded into one seat beside her.

"Do you want to tell me about it, Louise?" Ruthie said quietly. "You can if you want. I'll listen."

Was this some kind of karma, Ruthie thought as she lifted her arm from Louise's shoulder and turned to face her. Some kind of strange trick of the universe that had chosen her for this moment? Well, nothing to be done. The message was out of the bottle now and she would just have to read it.

Ruthie made herself as small as possible on the seat and turned her head away. She wanted Louise to feel that it was her choice to share her story or not, just as she wanted to be able to make the same choice for herself.

The terrain outside the window was changing from the dry flat brown earth around Salt Lake to the rocky hills leading up to the mountains, and the bus was beginning to climb. Louise blew her nose loudly and cleared her throat. When she spoke, her voice was thin and high as if compressed by the weight of her emotions.

"I have a husband and three children in Salt Lake," she began, and then paused for a long moment. Ruthie turned toward her and sat quietly. She hoped her face conveyed her openness to receive whatever Louise might offer, without judgment.

Let he who is without sin cast the first stone—the phrase from the Bible popped into her mind from somewhere in her earliest memories of Saturday mornings, wriggling to get comfortable on a hard wooden pew in Temple Beth Israel. She would certainly not be throwing any stones.

"I married young, at 19. My husband is an important man—a Deacon in the Church, the Mormon Church. I was lucky he chose me. Louise began to cry again, spreading a tissue over her face, her chest heaving with the effort to contain her sobs.

"I was young when I got married too," Ruthie said, placing her hand gently over Louise's. "Just 20. Too young I think." Ruthie sighed with her own memories of the simple ceremony she and Carl had created in the small rustic Quaker chapel on campus. They had walked down the aisle to the Jefferson Airplane—"C'mon people now. Smile on your brother. Everybody get together and love one another right now." She had been pregnant with Sasha and full of hope.

Ruthie lost herself in the memory of that happy hopeful moment in the wood-paneled chapel—just a few of their closest friends and family—her mother frowning her displeasure, Carl's father dozing in the hard-backed pew. Ruthie, ever the rebel even in this rule-bound tradition, had worn a mod blue and purple geometric patterned mini dress. Her hair, ironed straight that morning, was held back with a rhinestone headband. In the few pictures they took she looks about 16—Carl beside her with his thick dark hair falling over his earnest face, didn't look much older.

She hadn't been showing yet—just three months pregnant—but she could feel Sasha's presence already in the slight swell of her tummy under the satiny fabric. After the ceremony—after they had exited the chapel to the Beatles All You Need Is Love and held a small party in the common room of the dorm across the street—her mother's long laugh drifting over her wine glass, Carl's father asleep on the couch—Ruthie had a moment of trepidation.

What had she, what had they, done. The plan was to drop out of their small liberal arts college in Ohio and move to California where Carl's family lived. Carl would open his long dreamed of "People's Garage" and Ruthie would teach in an alternative school until the baby came. Then what?

It was the summer of 1967—the Summer of Love—and they were joining the great hippie migration to San Francisco. Ruthie had shaken off her worry that day and many days after—wanting to believe their love would carry them forward. But now? Look where she had landed.

Louise cleared her throat and Ruthie's attention was drawn back to the bus, to her seat mate, to the present.

"I never should have married him. I was too young," Louise said, going on with her story.

Ruthie had not been in touch with her father since her visit and decided to call from the next rest stop. He didn't even know she was on the road—and what if something happened to her. It was late, but it was Friday and Friday was poker night so she knew they would still be up. When the bus pulled up to a large truck stop, she stumbled out into the harsh light and found her way to a bank of payphones against the dirty tiled wall outside the rest rooms. Not much privacy but it would have to do. She dropped a handful of quarters one by one into the slots and dialed the familiar number.

"Hello." Tears welled in Ruthie's eyes when she heard her father's voice. In the background she could hear the sounds of the poker party in full swing—chips clinking on the wooden table in the narrow dining room, voices, laughter—her mother's unique laugh, starting low and rising like an inhaled breath floated above the rest.

"Ruth Anne!" Her father liked to call her by her given name. "Honey, it's Ruthie. Pick up the other phone."

She would have preferred a quiet chat with her father, but now she would have to contend with both parents.

"Ruthie. Where are you? We've been so worried."

No Mom, you haven't, Ruthie thought. In fact, you told me not to call you or ask you for any help the last time we spoke.

"I'm fine," Ruthie said. "I'm on the bus to California. Just thought I'd call and say hello."

"What? Where are you?"

"Ruthie, can you hold for a minute. Everyone's leaving."

"Coming," she heard her mother say. "Oh, don't go yet. Have another drink." And then the laugh.

She hung up the phone. She knew this scene well. The long good-byes at the door. The dining table filled with half-empty wine glasses, highball glasses, stacks of colorful poker chips, crumbs from her mother's sour cream coffee cake. After the last guests had left on Friday nights, Ruthie and her brother had sat on the top step of the carpeted stairs listening…waiting.

On a good night they heard murmuring voices, soft laughter, water running, the clank of dishes being placed in the sink. But the good nights were rare.

On the other nights, the bad nights, they heard voices raised in anger, a plate or a glass shattering against a wall, the sound of the back door slamming, the car starting in the driveway.

I'm better off without all that, Ruthie thought, washing her hands at the sink in the bathroom. She studied her face in the mirror—the bright fluorescent lights revealing her red-rimmed eyes, her tangled brown hair and splotchy face. She sighed and walked slowly back to the bus—welcoming the darkness, the quiet, the motion of the wheels that would carry her forward.

Ruthie stood in the aisle, trying to put off sitting back down on the uncomfortable seat for as long as she could. Her seatmate had fallen into what looked like a deep sleep after sharing her story and the bus, half empty now after the stop in Salt Lake, was full of sleeping shapes. Ruthie stared out the window.

She felt completely alone. Louise's story had unsettled her. In some ways it paralleled her own, but in other ways that seemed important it diverged completely from Ruthie's. She turned it around in her mind—the youthful marriage, the kids coming one right after the other, the strict religious boundaries of the Mormon church. Ruthie had felt the walls closing in around her as Louise's story revealed more about her life, and Louise had clearly felt trapped, caged in. She had left—seemingly without warning or plan. She had just thrown some things in an overnight bag and walked out the door.

That's NOT what I did, Ruthie thought, needing to distance her own actions from Louise's. I thought about it. I planned for it. I made a book for Sasha so she would understand. And I was going to do something important, something of value. I wasn't just running away. And it was only for three months. I came back. Her thoughts trailed off into the darkness. Ruthie sat with her eyes wide open, as the road spooled by in the night and Louise stirred uneasily beside her.

A faint pink line was forming at the horizon, hinting at a sunny day, when Louise awakened, stretching her arms and rolling her shoulders in the seat next to Ruthie.

"Have you ever been in love?" she asked Ruthie in a small voice. "I mean really in love?"

Where is this coming from, Ruthie thought, not really wanting to get pulled into a conversation about love. Do NOT fall in love had been her mantra ever since she returned from Cuba to find Sasha gone. Do NOT fall in love.

Michael had threatened her resove and that's why she had pushed him away in the end.

"I don't think I have," Louise said. "I know I never loved my husband." And she began to cry again, softly at first and then big gulping sobs that shook her seat and demanded Ruthie's attention.

Here we go again, Ruthie thought. She had listened for what felt like hours as the bus rumbled through Colorado to Louise's tale of woe. Her sobs were growing louder, attracting the attention of other passengers. Even the bus driver glanced in the rearview mirror to locate the disturbance.

"What have I done? What have I done? Oh God…Oh no…" Louise was wailing now and rocking back and forth in the seat. The toddler across the aisle joined her with his own muffled cries until his grandmother soothed him back to sleep. How could Ruthie soothe Louise? She had no idea what to do or say.

"I want to die. Oh God, I don't deserve to live. Please stop the bus." Louise was half out of her seat. "Please stop. I need to get off the bus now. Please."

"Can you do something with your friend, lady. She can't be standing in the aisle like that," the bus driver called back.

Is he talking to me, Ruthie thought. She's not my friend. Her mind raced around the possibilities. Find an empty seat and ignore Louise. No, it would just get worse. Get off the bus with her and make sure she didn't hurt herself.

She looked out the window. They were in the middle of nowhere. "Louise," she said in as firm a voice as she could muster. "C'mon. Sit back down. Let's talk about it."

Two Mothers

Louise slowly lowered herself into her seat. Ruthie handed her a tissue pulled from a crumpled pack at the bottom of her backpack. Her fingers brushed the envelope she had tucked there for safekeeping, and she drew it out and smoothed it on her lap.

Louise blew her nose loudly, but her sobs had subsided, and the bus was quiet.

"You might think no one could understand how you feel," Ruthie said. "But I do."

Louise mumbled back, the tissue muffling her words.

"How could you?" she said. "You're going home to be with your daughter. I'm running away from mine. How could you?"

Ruthie took a small photo from the envelope and held it in front of Louise.

"This is my little girl, Sasha," she said. "I left her with her father to go on a trip—for 3 months—and I haven't seen her since. I don't know where she is. I'm going to find her. I should never have left her. It was selfish. So I do know how you feel."

Louise took the picture in her hands. She studied Sasha's face, her freckled nose, her hair billowing out behind her, brown with flecks of red, brightened by the sun. Sasha was caught mid-jump on a large boulder in the middle of a rushing stream. Ruthie remembered that day at the water, as she remembered every day since the hour and minute of Sasha's birth.

"So you see, I do understand." Ruthie began to cry. When was the last time she had allowed herself to do that in these shut-down months of waiting—and it was Louise's turn to try and comfort her.

"You'll find her. You will. I'm sure of it. You're a good mother. Oh god, what have I done. I want to die. Please let me die." Louise began to cry again, softly this time, wringing her hands in her lap, crinkling the photo of Sasha in the process.

Ruthie snatched it back. She was tired of this. The crying, the guilt, the laments. At the next stop she would take another seat. She needed to think, to prepare herself for whatever lay ahead.

"You have to help me. I need to get to a hospital, or I'll do something, something bad. Ruthie, I need you to take me to a hospital."

Louise's words made Ruthie tremble with fear and uncertainty. How could she respond to this desperate request for help? How could she not? From the moment she decided to get on the bus and go in search of Carl and Sasha her focus had been laser sharp. Everything else in her life had dropped away— her time in Cambridge, Violeta, Michael, any attachments she had had been left behind.

And now this stranger was pleading for help, asking Ruthie to deviate from the plan she had set in motion.

"Please, Ruthie." Louise had turned in her seat and was facing Ruthie. She grabbed one of Ruthie's hands in her own—the skin unexpectedly rough and chapped.

"I don't know what I'll do if you don't help me."

Ruthie sighed. Her mother was a proponent of the school of tough love and Ruthie felt that same sentiment bubbling up in her. Hadn't Louise made a choice when she walked away from her children? Why was she now expecting a total stranger to save her?

But Ruthie didn't really want to be her mother, her self-protective narcissistic mother who had turned away from her when Ruthie's heart was breaking in two.

"I'll help you, Louise. I will. We'll get off at the next big town and find a hospital. Don't worry. It'll be okay. Try to rest a bit."

Louise closed her eyes and breathed deeply beside her, but Ruthie was wide awake. She unfolded her map on her lap. Where could she find help for Louise? She would have to take her chances at the next decent-sized town and hope there was a hospital close by and someone who could help Louise. She traced the highway with her finger. She didn't recognize the names of any of the towns until she got to Reno, Nevada. They must be close. They'd been traveling for hours since Salt Lake. She'd take a chance on Reno, she thought, and then laughed to herself at the irony of that. It would have to be Reno.

Ruthie folded the map, careful not to tear it. She was afraid to detour from her plan, but there was no other way that she could think of.

She couldn't, she wouldn't, abandon Louise.

Now that she had decided that she would get off the bus with Louise in Reno and try to find some help for her, Ruthie relaxed a bit. From the map it looked like they had another couple of hours on the road. From Reno it would be 5 or 6 hours to San Francisco and then she would have to figure out what to do next. She would stop and see Carl's parents, look for his brother, check in with old friends to see if anyone had any new information—and then she would head down the coast—probably hitchhike part of the way to Baja. Just reciting the steps in her mind made her feel closer to Sasha.

The stop with Louise shouldn't take more than a few hours. She would just take her to the nearest emergency room, explain what was happening, leave her in good hands, and catch the next bus out.

She fought against the memories that came bubbling up when she thought about Reno. She didn't want to soften toward Carl—she would need a kind of firm resolve that was not natural for her to wrest Sasha away from him. But what was meant to be remembered couldn't be ignored, and soon she was lost in images of that summer—the summer before Sasha—the Summer of Love.

Next Stop Reno

The voice of the bus driver crackling over the speaker pulled Ruthie back to the present.

Next stop Reno. Reno, Nevada next stop. If you're continuing on to Frisco, you have exactly 45 minutes to stretch your legs. Reno, next stop.

Louise opened her eyes and began rummaging through the big purse that sat open on her lap. It was one of those embroidered cloth ones with big wooden handles that most women use for knitting or sewing but it was all Louise seemed to have with her, with whatever she had taken from her home. She pulled out a crinkled paper rectangle.

"I bought a one-way ticket," she said to Ruthie. "I can't go back."

Ruthie thought of her own one-way ticket carefully tucked in an envelope at the bottom of her backpack.

"I'm not going back either," she said, patting Louise's hand. "Don't worry. We'll figure it out."

But Ruthie was worried. She would never be able to find a hospital and get Louise the help she needed in 45 minutes.

It was 2 AM. It might be hours before she was ready to continue her travels. Would there be a bus at that time? What would she do? Well, she'd have to figure it out. She had promised to help Louise and there was no turning back from that either.

Flashing red and yellow neon lights announced their arrival in Reno. Slots. Craps. Topless. All on offer on both sides of the road. She watched Louise take it all in.

"I can't. I can't. I can't." Louise began chanting softly, rocking in her seat, and then her chant grew louder till she was almost shouting.

"Lady, keep your friend quiet." The bus driver called back to her. "I'm not gonna ask again. I'll have to put you off the bus if this keeps up."

"Louise, please stop. It'll be OK. We'll go straight to the hospital. There'll be doctors. They'll help you. Please be quiet." Ruthie imagined the bus pulling to a stop right there on the outskirts of town and spitting them out like bitter coffee. Then what would she do? At least she wanted to get to the bus station. Louise quieted down, continuing her chant in a low voice. "I can't. I can't.

I can't."

Can't what, Louise, Ruthie thought? Can't go on…can't go back…can't live. Then it hit her.

Yes, she had left her child. Yes, she had wanted to die. But she was not Louise.

Because she could. And she would.

This was just a detour.

Reno, Reno Nevada. Next stop. Make sure you take all your belongings when you leave.

Reno Nevada. 5 minutes.

"This is us, Louise. We're getting off here." Ruthie gently nudged Louise who had fallen asleep again. She woke with a start as if coming back from very far away.

"Huh, where are we? Reno? Oh god, what will I do?" Ruthie sighed. What had she gotten herself into?

"We're gonna get you some help, Louise. Some help to figure it all out."

The bus pulled to a stop alongside dozens of buses that were disgorging sleepy looking passengers. This was the biggest station they'd stopped at for a while. "Make sure you have everything," Ruthie told Louise, checking her own backpack to be sure her wallet and ticket were there in the outside zippered pocket.

"Okay? Let's go then." They stepped off the bus into the glare of fluorescent lights so bright it looked like the middle of the day. Ruthie blinked against the brightness and checked her watch. 2:30 AM. Hopefully she could find a cab quickly and get to the nearest hospital. Hopefully there's be someone there who could help Louise or at least take her off Ruthie's hands.

They joined a line at the taxi stand. Where were all these people going at this hour Ruthie wondered and then remembered the casinos. You could lose your money 24/7 in Reno.

Ruthie slid into the cracked leather seat of the cab. Louise hesitated for a moment and joined her.

"Can you take us to the nearest emergency room, please, she asked the driver?

"That would be Reno General, miss. You're not gonna be sick in my cab, are ya?"

"No, no, we're fine," Ruthie said. Louise had begun to rock and whimper beside her. She hoped it would be a short trip.

Ruthie put one hand over Louise's and the other in her coat pocket, feeling for the postcard that had become like a talisman leading her to Sasha. She had kept it in her pocket the whole trip and developed the habit of feeling for it whenever she felt doubtful or afraid. Wait. Where was it? Ruthie felt around her pocket and withdrew her hand—a balled up tissue and a few pennies clutched in her fingers.

She reached in again—no postcard.

It was gone. She had lost it somehow. But where? Ruthie dug her nails into the palm of her hand so hard she almost cried out. How could she have lost it? The picture on the postcard was engraved in her mind, the crescent beach, the crayoned smiley face. She couldn't go back and look for it. The only way to go now was forward.

The cab driver let them off in the circular driveway of a large tan brick building in front of a sliding glass door entrance. The word "Emergency" in large red neon letters hung over the doorway. A light snow was beginning to fall, and the flakes danced and swirled around in the light.

"Looks like this is the place," Ruthie said, looping her arm through Louise's to keep her close. She could feel the trembling of Louise's body as she pulled her forward to the entrance. The doors slid open to a scene of frenzied movement and hunched waiting that could have been any emergency room anywhere. But they were here in Reno, Nevada and Ruthie desperately needed to find help for Louise. She needed to be on her way again as soon as possible.

Ruthie felt in her pocket for the postcard, the promise of sand and ocean where she was sure she would find her little girl, before she remembered that it was gone. Lost somehow in the shuffle of leaving the bus.

She looked around for the front desk. There it was—a blond faux wood counter sitting high above the chaos. A tall woman with faded red hair mixed with grey looked down at them through tortoise shell glasses perched on her nose and said, "Name and why you're here."

Oh God, Ruthie thought. What do I say? I don't even know Louise's last name. How do I say why we're here?"

Louise spoke up beside her in a surprisingly strong voice.

"My name is Louise, Louise Wessells. There is a sound in my head, a buzzing sound, like the sound of a thousand secrets and I can't make it stop."

The desk clerk stopped writing and looked long and hard at Louise. Then she pressed a button on the phone in front of her and her voice came through a speaker, "Psych Consult. ER Room One. Psych to ER. Room One."

Ruthie imagined a slot machine spinning to a halt on the word "Psych." 3 in a row, but what was the prize? A thousand secrets spilling out of the chute, clinking like nickels into a bucket.

"You can go wait in Room One," the clerk said—pointing to a cubicle across the waiting area. They wove their way around orange plastic chairs filled with people in varying states of misery—a woman holding a large gauze pad over one eye, a baby wailing in its mother's arms, an older man hunched over holding his stomach, a toddler coughing and coughing.

Room One had two grey metal chairs and an exam table covered in paper. They sat down and waited.

ER Room One had a curtain rather than a door and Ruthie watched the feet passing by—white nurse's shoes moving fast, the small dirty sneakers of a child shuffling slowly. When she tired of that she studied the cracks in the linoleum floor trying to keep her own thoughts at bay.

Louise was quiet for a while, looking at her hands folded in her lap almost as if in prayer. Then she began rocking and chanting again—softly at first, then gathering steam.

"Gracie, Lucy, James, Peter. Gracie, Lucy, James, Peter." After a few rounds, as Louise began to cry through her rhythmic naming, Ruthie realized these must be the names of her children.

"What have I done? Oh God, what have I done? I don't deserve to live. I want to die. Please let me die."

Louise was wailing now, keening and rocking, raw pain reflected in every movement, in the changing expressions on her face. Ruthie went to her side. She laid a limp hand on Louise's shoulder. She felt helpless, angry. Just as she started to speak—what could she possibly say that would make it better—the curtain was pulled aside and a tall man carrying a clipboard walked into the cubicle. He looked young, too young—and tired, dark shadows circling his eyes behind large square black glasses. But his tone was kind.

"I'm Doctor Evans, Lucas Evans, and I'd like to ask you some questions. See how we can help you feel better."

"I don't want to feel better. I want to die." Louise moaned and began rocking again.

Dr. Evans looked at Ruthie for the first time.

"How are you related to the patient?" he asked.

Already Louise had become a patient, and Ruthie felt a welcome distance growing between them.

"Oh, I'm not related. I just met her, on a bus. Just trying to help."

Dr. Evans looked up from his clipboard where he had been filling in a form. His eyes were green behind his glasses, green flecked with amber Ruthie saw and wondered why she was noticing that now. They were kind eyes, like his kind voice, and now they were surprised, one eyebrow lifted in a question mark above the thick frame of his glasses.

"Really?" he said. "You just met her on a bus and brought her here? So, I guess you don't know anything about her history?"

"Hey, I'm here." Louise stopped rocking. Her voice was shrill, on the verge of a shriek. "Don't talk about me like I'm not here. Just don't. That's what he does." She resumed her rocking, arms hugging her body, back and forth, back and forth.

"I'm sorry but I'm going to have to ask you to step outside while I examine the patient." There it was again. Not Louise, but the patient. "Since you're not related." He shrugged his shoulders in apology.

Ruthie was relieved to be asked to step away. The cubicle was hot, and the walls were closing in. Louise's rocking was making her feel slightly queasy. She gathered her coat and backpack and pushed the curtain aside.

"I'll be in the waiting room, Louise. I'll wait for you." Louise didn't look up.

Ruthie had one last thought. She moved closer to the doctor.

"Ask her about her children," she said. He turned his green eyes on her. Ruthie wished for a moment that she was the patient, that she could put herself in the hands of this kind, young doctor.

"Ask her about her kids," she said and stepped into the hallway, almost colliding with an orderly pushing a stretcher with a frightened looking old woman on it. She looked at Ruthie—her silver hair sticking out in all directions around her brown, wrinkled face.

"Help me," she mouthed, no sound coming from her collapsed toothless mouth. "Please help me."

Ruthie sat down hard on one of the orange plastic chairs and dropped her backpack on the grimy floor. What is it about me, she wondered. Am I a magnet for human suffering or something? Don't I have enough on my plate?

The ER waiting room was quiet now. Ruthie looked around. The mother and toddler were gone and so was the crying baby. The old man had been replaced by a teenager with spiky midnight black hair and a bad case of acne, who was holding an ice pack to one eye. In the corner a tired looking black woman in green scrubs stretched tight across her ample body was pushing a mop back and forth and staring into space.

Into the silence entered a memory of another emergency room—another time of waiting when Sasha was just a couple of months old—right after they had come back from the annual school family camping trip that Carl had cajoled her into. They had slept in an old canvas tent in a constant cold drizzle. The tent leaked from every accidental brush with the canvas, and Ruthie spent the week wet, cold and miserable, silently cursing Carl's pursuit of nature that had gotten them there. Wasn't she nature too? Didn't she deserve to stay home with her baby warm and dry in their attic nest?

When they finally got home Ruthie had noticed a discharge from the nipple of her right breast. It was red and cracked and she couldn't nurse Sasha without excruciating pain. When it got so bad she couldn't stand it, and she developed a fever and chills they had gone to the ER—Sasha sucking desperately on Carl's knuckle and withdrawing periodically to wail on his shoulder, Ruthie shivering on the chair beside them too sick to even hold her baby. Mastitis the doctor had said and given her giant antibiotic pills and a shield for her breast when she nursed. It was weeks before she could do so without pain.

I should have said no, Ruthie thought, remembering all the other times she'd wanted to say no to Carl and hadn't. Up until the time she had shouted it at the door closing behind her.

She realized with a start that she hadn't thought about Sasha for hours—she had been so wrapped up in Louise, in getting them to the place where she might find help. Keeping Sasha constantly in her thoughts was Ruthie's way of keeping her safe and she felt a pang of guilt. She shook her head to clear it.

"Miss? Miss? I'm sorry I don't know your name." It was Dr. Evans standing in front of her with his kind eyes and voice that brought her back to the waiting room, empty now but for her and the doctor. Had the teenage boy gone home? She imagined his mother yelling at his back as he trudged up the stairs and slammed the door to his room. Had the woman with the mop finished her shift or gone to push her mop in another room?

"Ruthie," she said. "I'm Ruthie. How is Louise doing?"

"She's agreed to be admitted to the hospital so we can watch her and keep her safe. She'd like to say goodbye to you."

Ruthie followed Dr. Evans to the cubicle stepping around the yellow triangles that warned of a wet floor. Everything in her world right now felt slippery, dangerous. She had failed to keep Sasha safe, failed miserably, and now she was moving through this world with no idea about where to put her feet. "Ruthie, oh Ruthie. They will help me here. I know they will. Thank you for taking me here. You are my guardian angel. God will keep you safe. I know He will."

Ruthie sighed and held out her hand to Louise. She didn't want to get any closer. Not now.

"Goodbye Louise. I'm glad to have helped. Please take good care of yourself."

She hoisted her backpack over one shoulder, pulled the curtain aside and stepped back into the antiseptic air of the waiting room and her own life.

Ruthie walked past the front desk. The red-haired woman had been replaced by a frizzy blonde who was bent over some paperwork. A couple of toddlers played on the floor with a broken red truck at the feet of a young woman who sat with her head thrown back, eyes closed. An older girl, maybe Sasha's age, played Ring Around the Rosy all by herself. Ashes, Ashes we all fall down. And she fell in a heap next to her brothers.

The waiting room was still empty. There was no one to watch her go. Ruthie stepped through the sliding glass doors, squinting into the bright sun of a desert morning. She was surprised to see that the hospital was just a block from the Strip that was lit up and beckoning—slots, blackjack, poker, girls— even at this early hour.

She thought about Louise, wondering where she would end up. Would she go back to her family? Would they take her back? She would never see her again, of that Ruthie was sure. Louise didn't even know her last name. Ruthie hadn't given her an address. She didn't really have one to give. This had been a strange, intense interlude, and now it was over, like so many things in her life these days. She couldn't afford to look back. She had to keep moving forward.

Ready To Get Lucky

Ruthie wanted a cup of real coffee—not from a vending machine—before she got back on the bus. She walked toward the nearest casino. They must have an all-night restaurant or something.

Ruthie stopped at the Lone Star Casino. The doors slid open to a mirror-lined lobby with a grey-tinged floral carpet and the lingering smell of tobacco. She caught a glimpse of herself in the wall of mirrors—her hair tangled around her face, her eyes ringed with purplish shadows—and turned away.

"Good morning!" The way too perky voice of a young, auburn-haired woman in a short black and white uniform accosted her. "How are you doing today? Ready to get lucky!"

Oh boy, am I ever, Ruthie thought.

"Actually, I was hoping to get a cup of hot coffee, some breakfast maybe. Is there a restaurant here?"

"Just keep going straight. It's at the end of the hall. You can't miss it. Have a great day!"

Ruthie moved away down the long hallway—glad to leave Miss False Cheer behind. Slot machines lined the walls. A couple of blue haired older women sat side by side feeding nickels into matching machines, cigarettes dangling from their lips, their buckets held in trembling hands, waiting for the jackpot. They didn't look up as she passed.

At the end of the hall was the promised restaurant and Ruthie sat at a chipped formica table in a corner. A paper placemat with a map of Nevada was the only adornment. This place reeked of cigarette smoke and burnt cooking oil but maybe the coffee would be tolerable, and she needed to put something in her stomach.

"What can I getcha, hon?" A tired-looking waitress with flyaway dirty blonde hair pulled back in a ponytail stood at her table ready to take her order.

Ruthie glanced at the menu.

"Just coffee, black," she said. "And some toast." The waitress turned to leave.

"Hey excuse me. Can I change my order? The breakfast special with eggs over easy and bacon?" Ruthie had suddenly realized she was famished. The waitress sighed and took her pen and pad from her uniform pocket. Ruthie understood her annoyance. She hated it when customers at Cookie's changed their orders.

Ruthie looked around the restaurant. Only a few other solitary diners were scattered around the dimly lit room. Dusty artificial cactuses with spiny leaves were placed here and there with no real attention to décor. The white walls were stained yellow with nicotine and the only pictures on the walls were advertisements for the various gambling options that were available at the Lone Star.

It was depressing, really depressing, but Ruthie observed it from a distance, like a reporter or a doctor, examining but not a part of the scene.

She noticed an aluminum door propped open near her table. Maybe she could get a breath of fresh air before her breakfast arrived.

The door opened onto a small courtyard; a cracked concrete floor surrounded by cement block walls. Real cactuses with big pink bulbous flowers that looked like sex organs lined one wall.

In the center of the courtyard, a young girl was playing a clapping game by herself—Miss Mary Mac Mac Mac, all dressed in black, black, black. She turned to look at Ruthie and grinned.

"Oh hi. Would you play with me?" Ruthie glanced back through the door. Her breakfast had not yet arrived.

"Sure. I'm Ruthie. What's your name?"

"Rita. Rita Jean—ma'am," she added as if suddenly remembering her manners.

"And how old are you, Rita Jean?"

"I'm six, ma'am." Her brown curls bounced as she shook her head with pride and conviction.

"Oh, my little girl is six too," Ruthie said, holding up her hands to start the game.

"Where is she? Does she want to play with me?"

"I'm sure she would, sweetie, but she's far away—with her Daddy." Ruthie's voice caught on the last words.

"Rita—Rita Jean Walker—just what do you think you're doing? Haven't I told you not to bother the customers, not to talk to strangers?" The waitress had appeared in the doorway, and Ruthie noticed how weary she looked beneath her scowl.

"Oh, she wasn't bothering me. I have a little girl just her age," Ruthie said.

"Your eggs are getting cold," the waitress replied.

"And you, miss smarty-pants, need to come back inside and do your schoolwork like I told you." "But Mama…"

"No but Mamas. Just do as you're told.

Ruthie sat back down at her table and moved the runny eggs around on her plate. They were cold and she had lost her appetite. She stole a glance at the table where the little girl sat copying something in a composition book with a fat yellow pencil.

Ruthie breathed out a silent sob. What was Sasha doing right this minute, she wondered? Did she play all by herself and talk to strangers? Did she go to school? Sasha was back in Ruthie's thoughts—deep in the grey wrinkled cushion of her brain and she would keep her there, safe and sound, until she could throw her arms around her and take her home.

Rita Jean looked up from her writing and flashed a smile, as if they had shared a secret. Ruthie smiled back and gave a little wave. She spread margarine on her cold, slightly burnt toast and took a bite. She would eat something and then make her way back to the station.

Ruthie ate a last bite of egg and signaled the waitress who walked slowly to the table and tore off the check from her pad. She looks so tired, Ruthie thought. I know that feeling alright.

"So where are you headed?" the waitress asked, as if she somehow knew that Ruthie was headed for somewhere other than the beckoning slot machines. Rita was sitting quietly nearby filling blank white pages with colorful scribbles.

"I'm going to California. My little girl is there," Rita said, thinking if I say it out loud it will be true.

<hr>

"Well, good luck then."

Ruthie slid a few dollars under her coffee cup—she was always generous in diners—gathered her backpack and moved toward the door. Rita Jean looked up from her coloring and waved. Ruthie waved back, fighting an impulse to run to the table and gather the little girl in her arms. Her Mama would not like that. The early morning street was quiet—the sound of silence, Ruthie thought, hearing the deep harmony of words and music as she walked.

Hello darkness, my old friend…I've come to talk with you again

She passed a man on the corner—solitary, collar turned up against the chill in the air.

"Cigarette?" he asked, holding out nicotine-stained fingers.

"No sorry," Ruthie said and kept on walking. The bus station was not that far and there were no cabs in sight. She needed to stretch her muscles before the last leg of her journey. She would be glad to be away from this sad town. Every mile brought her closer to Sasha.

Back on a bus by mid-morning, Ruthie was relieved to have a seat all to herself. The bus was half empty, clean and free of crying children and unpleasant odors. She dozed for a while, and then woke to a breathtaking vista through the open windows of the bus.

Fields of wildflowers, orange and yellow, peeking through tall grasses stretched their way to low brown foothills which gave way to jagged snow-capped peaks. They were crossing the Rockies and somehow to Ruthie in that moment it felt like the last big obstacle before she would find Sasha.

One more river to cross…she heard Bob Marley's sweet voice in her head…till I find my way over.

Ruthie had crossed many rivers throughout this ordeal—her determination, her hope and even her guilt had driven her forward.

The Rockies receded as the bus rolled on. Ruthie fingered the picture of Sasha in her pocket. She reviewed her plan for the final leg of this search. Contact Carl's parents—maybe they had heard something from him though she doubted it. And Stan, his brother—on the chance he had contact with him.

Ruthie balled her jacket up to use as a pillow and leaned into the window. She would sleep—maybe all the way to San Francisco—and her only dreams would be of holding her child in her arms, smelling the sweet perfume of her soft curls, and feeling her heartbeat next to her own, its regular rhythm giving breath and life. She closed her eyes and let darkness descend.

PART FOUR
Searching for Sasha

California Dreaming

October 1973

Most of the time, during her exile and her long cross-country trek, Ruthie thought only of the moment—getting through the day at work, the town she was passing through on the bus. It kept her from dwelling on her fears, from thinking the worst.

But this night, tucked into clean sheets and covered with a handmade patchwork quilt in one of the guest rooms at the Family Place, she let her mind drift, let herself imagine the face of a happier tomorrow.

It had been almost six months since she had last seen Sasha. She would be taller now. Ruthie imagined Sasha's curls brushing her hip as she stood next to her. And maybe her face would have lost some of its baby roundness, her chin more sculpted perhaps, but her dimples intact. Her brown almond shaped eyes, so like Ruthie's own eyes-- would they still twinkle with mischief and open wide with a gazillion questions? Yes, Ruthie decided. Nothing, not even missing her Mama, could chase those away.

She hugged the soft pillow and pulled the quilt up around her neck. She had forgotten how chilly the San Francisco nights could be and had pulled a skimpy cotton nightgown from her bag to sleep in. The house was quiet. Annie and Will were early risers and asleep by now. It felt both strange and comforting to be here once more—in the first home that Sasha had known, in the place where she and Carl had loved each other and then not.

She could almost feel herself sinking into Annie's strong, warm presence—like a quicksand of love and safety.

But she couldn't, wouldn't, stay here long. She had to keep moving toward her tomorrow, toward Sasha—wherever and whatever it might bring.

"Mama, come see." Sasha said, grabbing Ruthie's hand and tugging her down the path. "Come see the ocean. It's amazing!" Ruthie followed her barefoot daughter who was stepping lightly over the sandy path. Sharp little pieces of iridescent shells dotted the sand and pricked Ruthie's feet, which were also bare. Sasha tugged and Ruthie followed the seductive voice. "Mama, Mama. Come see."

"Ruthie, Ruthie. Wake up. Please wake up."

Ruthie opened her eyes to find herself in an unfamiliar dark room. Where was she? And who was this little girl beside the bed? Where was Sasha?

And then she remembered. She sat up on the bed.

"Ruthie, please take me to the bathroom, please."

It was Sage—Annie and Will's little girl—standing by her bed in her panties, her flowered nightgown wet and crumpled in a heap at the foot of the bed.

"I wet the bed and I'm not 'sposed to cause I'm a big girl now," Sage said, whimpering a little. Ruthie recognized the buildup to a full out meltdown.

"Oh, Sagie. It's okay." She drew the girl to her, pulling a sheet off the bed and wrapping her in it against the cool night air.

"We'll get you fixed up good as new. Don't worry."

She took Sage by the hand and moved through the darkened house to the little girl's room, the dim rays of a Minnie Mouse nightlight revealing her soggy bed.

"First let's get you some clean p.j.'s. Can you show me where they are?"

Sage opened the second drawer of her old wooden dresser and pulled out a pair of flannel pajamas with glittery Tinkerbells flittering around from head to toe.

"These are my favorites," Sage said. "I won't get them wet; I promise."

"I know you won't sweetie. Let's get you cleaned up and dry now, O.K.?"

Ruthie led Sage to the small bathroom at the top of the stairs—the one she had sometimes used when Carl was taking too long in the shower. She grabbed a washcloth and towel from the linen closet in the hall. She heard the squeal of bedsprings as someone turned over in a nearby bedroom.

Ruthie gently wiped Sage down with the warm washcloth and bundled her up in the towel.

"Let's go into my room and I'll get you into your p.j.'s, okay?"

"Please don't tell my mama, Ruthie. She will be disappointed in me."

Ruthie chuckled at the thought of Annie, with her gentle ways, letting her little girl know she was disappointed in her for wetting the bed. Not all that different from a little spank on the tush, she thought. She occasionally spanked Sasha as she herself had been spanked when she did something really naughty. "I won't tell. I promise. It's our secret," Ruthie said as she pulled Sage's pajama top over her bed-tousled curls. The little girl rubbed her eyes with her two little fists.

"You're sleepy, Sagie. Why don't you climb up beside me? You can sleep in my bed where it's nice and warm and dry. I'll go fix up your bed and no one will ever know."

Ruthie took some clean sheets from the closet and made-up Sage's bed, throwing the wet sheets into the hamper in the bathroom. She made her way down the hall. In her room, Sage was already asleep—her curls fanning out over Ruthie's pillow, her long eyelashes brushing her downy cheeks, her thumb in her mouth.

Ruthie climbed in beside her and snuggled close to the warm, sleeping child. If she closed her eyes, she could pretend it was Sasha—just for a minute.

Ruthie and Sage sat across from each other at the long wooden table at breakfast. Will had already headed out to work so it was just the four of them—Ruthie, Sage, Annie and Sage's older brother, Oliver.

Annie had laid the table as she did for every meal—with woven red and yellow Guatemalan place mats and a mason jar of fresh flowers from the garden—purple pansies and a multi-colored assortment of long-stemmed snapdragons. A terracotta clay bowl of apples and pears dotted with glistening figs from their own tree sat in the middle of the table. Annie ladled chunky oatmeal into Ruthie's deep blue ceramic bowl. Everything on the table was made or grown by someone's loving hands. Ruthie had always loved that about the Family Place.

Ruthie plucked a fig from the bowl, biting into its tender flesh, feeling the thin skin give way to juicy sweetness as her teeth pulled away a bit of tender flesh. She caught Sage looking at her across the table and winked, feeling the bond of their shared secret in the night. Sage smiled then popped her spoon in her mouth, sticky maple syrup dribbling down her chin.

"I think I'll go to the library today," Ruthie said, spooning maple syrup into her oatmeal. "I want to look at some books about the Baja peninsula. See what I can figure out." Ruthie had described the lost postcard and her plan to go in search of Carl and Sasha to Annie as soon as she arrived. Annie was worried about her setting out for Baja on her own but understanding about her need to do this.

"You can take my bike if you want," Annie said. "It's the blue one—you should recognize it from when you lived here, I think."

"Oh sure, that would be great." The library was about a mile away and Ruthie had often ridden there in the past. When Sasha was big enough, she had bundled her into a baby backpack and ridden there with her—putting Sasha on a blanket on the floor with brightly colored picture books surrounding her while Ruthie stole a little adult time to read.

It was then she had discovered the poetry of Pablo Neruda and lost herself in its rhythms and images while Sasha played at her feet.

Today she would study maps and try to find the beach. Would it be like finding a needle in a haystack? One small beach, sand, sea, palms—among so many? No matter, it was her next step. She was sure of that.

Ruthie carried the heavy bike out to the porch. Annie met her there with a brown paper bag.

"I packed you some lunch," she said, "a little fruit and a peanut butter and jelly sandwich." Ruthie burst into tears—remembering the last time she had packed just such a lunch for Sasha. When was the last time anyone had packed her lunch?

Sage had come up behind Annie and was peering at Ruthie from behind her mother's long Indian print skirt. Ruthie's face was scrunched up in an anxious frown, and she caught herself and smiled at her. She didn't want to worry Sage or burden Annie with her troubles.

"Thanks, Annie, for the lunch. Well, I'm off. See you later, Sage. Maybe I'll bring you a book back from the library. Would you like that?" The little girl gave her a shy smile and Ruthie bumped the bike down the stairs, hoisted one leg over the bar, settled herself on the seat and pedaled away. It was time to get moving again.

At dinner that night, Ruthie studied her dear friends while Will opened and poured the wine. They were such an odd couple—Annie, tall, lean, blonde close-cropped hair, icy blue eyes in a tan weathered face, decisive, quick in her movements. Will—taller, muscular, shining ebony skin, languid with a deep easy laugh. Sage and Oliver were a perfect combination of their parents— golden skin, red-brown curls, their father's laugh.

Ruthie sipped her wine, letting the mellow fruity taste slide down her throat. She felt herself letting go, slowly, of the tension of her constant state of vigilance, of the need to be on guard, alert for possible clues—watchful, always watchful.

"So," Will boomed, breaking through the comfortable silence that had descended on the table, the drowsy warmth that Ruthie had relaxed into. "What's next for you, Ruthie? Annie tells me you're headed to some beach in Baja. How will you get there?"

"I don't know yet. Still trying to figure it all out." Ruthie said, slipping back into her vigilant skin.

"Not the safest place to travel alone," Will said. "We'd be worried about you."

Will had put words to one of Ruthie's fears—how could she do this alone? But somehow, she would. She had to.

People Get Ready

Ruthie shook her head as if she could shake out her fears and worries like a rock in her shoe. Will's question—a simple question really—made her feel dizzy, nauseous—like she was fighting to stay afloat in rough waters but sinking— slowly and steadily sinking.

How would she get to Baja?

She had studied the maps in the library. It would not be like buying a ticket at the Greyhound ticket counter and riding in a comfortable bus. There were whole sections of the peninsula that barely had roads, let alone buses. She would have to hitchhike. A woman alone. In the middle of nowhere.

She and Carl had borrowed his brother's camper van to make the trip, sleeping on beaches or a mattress in the back of the van by the side of a deserted road. Once they had awakened on the beach to find scorpions scurrying around them, crawling out of their shoes and the pile of their rumpled clothing. And they had had the dogs with them—their rambunctious shepherd-husky pups who barked and yipped at their own shadows. Ruthie sighed, then noticed Will, still at the table spooning honey into his tea, waiting for her answer.

"Well, I guess I'll take the bus as far as it will take me and then—well maybe I can hire a driver to take me the rest of the way. I saved some money while I was in Cambridge. I guess I have enough for that."

Annie came back to the dining room. She and Will exchanged a long look across the table. Something seemed to be decided between them.

"We'll take you," Will said. It was not a question. Annie nodded in agreement.

"I haven't had a vacation in two years and Children's Place can get a long without us for a bit. We can borrow Evan's camper and head down there. It's a Chevy van he's got all tricked out with a fridge and a little portable toilet thing. And it's got 4-wheel drive so I know it can handle the roads. It'll be fun." Will said and then caught the look on Ruthie's face.

"Well, not fun—but the kids will see something new. They'll enjoy it.

Annie came around to Ruthie's side of the table and put her arms on her shoulders, massaging gently with her strong hands.

"We won't let you do this alone, Ruthie. It's no use arguing."

Ruthie felt herself coming up for air. She took a deep, cleansing breath like Annie had taught her when she was preparing for Sasha's birth.

She wouldn't argue. She would begin to plan their route. And she would let herself be protected and cared for by these dear beloved friends.

"Okay, that's settled," Will said. "We'll tell the kids in the morning.

They'll be excited. And we'll leave in a week. We've got a lot to do to get ready."

Annie placed a flowered Mexican bowl with a baked apple rich with cream in front of Ruthie. She inhaled the familiar smell of cinnamon and brown sugar and let a spoonful of the soft, sweet apple slide down her throat. She smiled, then nodded at her friends. This would be all right.

Now that it was settled—that Annie and Will and the kids would accompany her to Baja—Ruthie began writing letters to the people she wanted to be in the loop about the trip.

She wrote a long letter to Violeta. As far as Ruthie knew, Violeta was still waiting for news of Javi. The coup in Chile had disappeared from the news just as so many had disappeared off the streets during that violent upheaval. Ruthie felt an unbreakable thread of shared sorrow connecting her to her friend.

She wrote to her parents, unable to face a phone call—the disappointment in her father's voice, the judgment in her mother's.

One night, sitting at the dining table late in the night after the house was quiet, everyone asleep, she started a letter to Michael. She got as far as "Dear Michael, I am writing to tell you…" then stopped and crossed the words out with a back and forth of her pen—tearing the paper with the force of her marks.

To tell you what, she thought. What do I want to tell you, Michael? That I think of you more than I thought I would? That I am off to find my daughter— the secret I kept from you for so long? That I will probably never see you again?

She crumpled the paper and threw it in the trash. She was not ready to write that letter.

Once they had a plan and had picked a date a week away to begin the trip to Baja, Ruthie's time was filled with making lists of what they would need and figuring out how far the money she had would take them. She threw herself into the planning with an energy she hadn't felt in a long time—as if every item on the list, every box checked on her checklist was bringing her closer to Sasha. And as Will carefully extended the red line on the map of the route they would follow, she could picture the beach, the joyful reunion that would occur.

"Ruthie," Will's voice broke into her reverie, and she sat up on the edge of the bed. "I think we've figured out the route we'll take. Come and see."

"Coming," she called back and pulled the door to her room closed behind her.

Ruthie stopped in the doorway to the dining room which was bathed in the soft light of the candles Annie always lit after dinner.

Annie and Will—one blonde head and one dark—were huddled over the map on the table. Sage and Oliver's curly tops—golden in the candlelight— kept popping up between them with barely contained excitement.

Watching them, this complete happy family, Ruthie felt a sudden surge of anger—unexpected—boiling up from her belly and leaving an acid taste in her mouth. For them this is just one more family vacation, she thought. They're having fun. They're looking forward to it. But for me—she tried to put the brake on her careening thoughts. She knew Annie and Will were dear friends just trying to help.

"For me this is life and death."

"What?" Annie asked, coming to her and taking her hand. "What, Ruthie?"

"Oh nothing. Just scared I guess." Ruthie took her hand back and joined them at the table.

"Don't be scared, Ruthie. I'll protect you from anything." Oliver proclaimed. "Even sharks."

"And I'll go in the water with you. I'm not even scared of the waves anymore cause I'm a big girl." Sage chimed in, climbing in her lap and throwing her arms around Ruthie's neck.

"I know you are Sagie." Ruthie said, giving Sage a hug. She could feel her ribs through her T-shirt. She was a skinny little thing.

"And I know how to swim, Ruthie." It was Oliver's turn to boast.

How sweet they are, though Ruthie, and innocent. They think I'm scared of the ocean. If only that was what was scaring me.

But the kids were not completely off-base, for Ruthie did have a fear of the ocean that she had to conquer each time she picked her way over shells and stones, seaweed brushing her legs, salt-spray tickling her nose.

Only once, but once was enough wasn't it, jumping the waves at Stinson Beach where she and Carl often went to picnic, she had been pulled away from shore by a rip tide—its force taking her breath away and leaving her powerless. In her panic she'd forgotten all she knew—the warning instructions on a sign posted at the entrance to the beach—and had tried to swim against the tide— her arms cutting through the water, her legs kicking until she could kick no more. Then she relaxed and let the water take her where it wanted to, and just like that she was in calm water and could swim again—and eventually reached the shore, spent but safe.

"I'm so glad you guys will be there to protect me." Ruthie said, pulling the kids into her body and kissing each tousled head.

"Here I come to save the day." Ollie sang, pulling away from her and flying around the table.

"Me too. Me too." cried Sage, trailing behind her big brother.

"Okay you two, settle down." Will said. "Go on and get into your PJs now. Almost time for bed."

And to Ruthie— "I'm just gonna get them ready for bed. Why don't you take a look at the map? I'll be back in a jif."

Ruthie pulled her chair closer to the table and traced the red line that would bring her to Baja, to Sasha, with one finger, noticing the torn edge of a fingernail, the skin cracked and dry. She would have to start taking better care of herself.

She traced the line all along the long, jagged coast, imagining the thundering of the waves, the spray against rocks, the gulls soaring and calling and the tides moving in and out each day, unchanging.

Unknown dangers lay in wait there, but she would try to be brave. She would follow the children into these uncertain waters and let hope wrap itself around her and keep her safe.

Buenas Noticias

"¿Tía… tía… ¿eres tú?"

Violeta could barely hear Tía Marta's voice over the crackle and hiss of the bad telephone connection. It was the middle of the night in Valparaíso, only an hour behind in Boston. There must be news.

Violeta sat on the edge of the bed and pulled her shawl around her. "¿Tienes noticias, tía? ¿Algo nuevo de Javi?" She was almost afraid to ask the question, afraid of what the answer might be. Six weeks after the military coup, and still no news of Javi. A few of his friends who had been detained had been released. Many others were still missing.

She heard sniffling through the static on the phone line. Was her tía crying? Was her worst fear about to be confirmed? Was Javi…? No, she shook her head violently, as if Tía Marta could see her. No! She would not believe it.

"Espérate, Violeta. Wait one minute. Someone wants to talk with you." "Marta, no… just tell me what you have to say. Just tell me. ¡Dímelo!" "¿Mami?" His voice was deeper than she remembered it. "¿Mami? Te quiero tanto. I'm home, Mami. Estoy en casa. ¡Estoy vivo!"

Violeta heard the sounds of her family in the background…crying, laughing. She imagined the celebration…music, dancing, all the neighbors crowding into their little cottage to see her boy—returned from the missing, returned from the dead.

"¿Estás bien, Javi? Are you alright? What did they do to you? Are you hurt?" "Mami, mami, cálmate. I'm ok. I'm free. Padre Luis found me and brought me home. And he's going to help me leave… to France, or Canada—to a safe place. My bones will heal. I'm OK. Maybe we will be able to see each other… soon."

Now it was Violeta's turn to cry all the tears she had been holding in for weeks. For all the weeks of praying and putting up flyers and raising money. For all the weeks of searching the newspapers for a scrap of information. Of going with Ruthie to give talks to the students about the coup. She sobbed and gulped and then took a deep breath. She didn't want to upset Javi. And Ruthie…she needed to tell Ruthie.

"Mamá… I have to go now before they cut the call. I will try to call again soon or to get word to you by letter. I am safe, Mami. I love you."

And with those words hanging in the air, the click and the dial tone signaled the end of the call. Violeta drew in a deep breath and held it as long as she could, filling her lungs. Letting them expand with the joy of finally knowing her boy was home.

"France, Canada?" she thought. Can they really get him there? If it's Canada, I can go too. It's not far. Only a bus ride away. Why would I want to stay in este puto país anyway? I don't want to stay in this country that helped the soldiers take over and hurt my boy.

Violeta was not about to try to go back to sleep and busied herself in her small kitchenette brewing a cup of mate tea. As she drank the rich, slightly bitter brew and inhaled the familiar earthy smell of the leaves, she imagined her family passing the gourd around the table and Javi, her Javi home at last, drinking from the straw the elixir of home.

If Ruthie were home, Violeta would have called her…maybe even asked her to come over to share in her happiness. But Ruthie was on a bus somewhere in the middle of this big cruel land traveling to find her daughter. She couldn't call her. She didn't even have a phone number for her.

Violeta rustled through the drawer where she kept all her important papers for the card Ruthie had given her with the address in California. She would write a letter right now and mail it on her way to work.

Violeta sat with the blank page torn from a yellow legal pad she had bought at the Coop in front of her, her pen poised in mid-air. How could she capture in simple words the singing in her heart? How could she give her friend hope that she too would find her child?

Querida amiga,

Javi está en casa. Javi is home safe! I heard his beautiful voice tonight on the phone saying Mami, te quiero mucho. Do you believe it?

She took another sip of her mate and smoothed the paper on the small wooden table.

You will find Sasha, mi amiga. This is a sign. I know you will find her.

Call me when you get this letter. Por favor, llámame. I really need to talk with you.

Abrazos y besos,

Tu hermana, Violeta

Choice

"Mama," A high voice calling for her from down the hall, woke Ruthie from a deep dreaming sleep. "Sasha," she answered, sitting up and sliding her feet into the fuzzy slippers waiting at the edge of the bed. "Coming, Sasha."

A small figure in pink, topped by a tousled mop of brown curls, flung herself across the room and into her arms.

"Shasha's not here, silly Ruthie. It's me, Sage. I need my Mommy to help me find my clothes for school."

"Ruthie? You up? Everything O.K.?" Annie's footsteps stopped outside the door to her room. "Sagie, leave Ruthie alone and let her wake up," she said, tapping Sage's tushie and shooing her out of the room. "I'll be there to help you get dressed in a minute. Ruthie, hot coffee and oatmeal's in the kitchen when you're ready."

Ruthie lay back down and closed her eyes, but the dream was just out of reach. Was Sasha calling out for her somewhere, needing her help? What had Carl told her? What must she be thinking after all this time? Did she think her mother had deserted her?

She imagined a vast, empty desert with windblown sand shifting on the surface and a small dot that could be Sasha way off in the distance. English was such a funny language. Once she had been reading to Sasha from one of her books about children who lived in different places around the world and the picture of a little boy on a camel in the desert had popped up.

"No Mama," Sasha had protested. "Not desert, dessert. He lives in an ice cream sundae."

They had both dissolved into laughter and a tickling match, rolling around together on the bed till the book slipped to the floor and was forgotten.

"No coffee for me today, Annie," Ruthie said as she stepped into the warm kitchen. "My stomach has been a little off, and I decided to see Dr. Bennett before we head out to Baja. Make sure everything's OK." What she didn't say, what she could barely stand to even imagine, was that she was worried she might be pregnant—and needed to be sure before they embarked on their journey.

When she had first started feeling queasy a few days earlier, she had dismissed it as nerves—the stress of preparing, the departure date growing closer. But then she tried to remember when her last period had been and realized she was a couple of weeks late. Again, maybe stress. She and Michael had been careful, hadn't they? And they had broken up. But then she looked at the calendar and realized it was possible. Not likely, but possible. Shit! Was she ever going to catch a break. They were set to leave for Baja in a week.

Dr. Bennett was a holistic doctor, not much older than her, a bit of a hippie with long dirty blond hair pulled back in a ponytail, sporting a turtleneck and beads under his white coat. His daughter Skye and Sasha had been best friends at school. She would often find them curled up together in the reading nook, foreheads creased and thumbs in their little mouths as they pored over their word boxes—small wooden boxes with multicolored cards containing words each child picked out—one a day—to learn how to read and spell. On the back of each card was a picture of the word. Ruthie had read about this in an article by a Brazilian educator, Paolo Freire, who taught farmworkers to read and write using this method and, with no real experience, was promoted to "reading teacher" at the alternative school. The idea was that they would pick words that came from their world and put them together to make their own books. Sasha's first word was "drum," and when Ruthie asked why she hopped on one foot and said, "because I like the sound it makes, Mama," moving her hands on an invisible drum.

"Here's a little something in case you get hungry later," Annie interrupted her daydream —thrusting a brown paper bag into Ruthie's hands. "I'll be home all day so call me from Bennett's office if you need me."

"Sure, don't worry. I'll be fine. See ya later," Ruthie said, pulling the creaky old door open to the grey mist lifting off a San Francisco morning.

It had been a long time since Ruthie had taken the streetcar and she fumbled for change and almost missed the coin slot on her anxious entry. She took a seat toward the back and nestled her backpack in her lap. The car was half-empty at mid-morning—a few older folks with canes held tight between their knees taking up the seats near the driver and a couple of teenagers horsing around in the seat in front of her. She settled into the familiar clackety-clack rhythm of the wheels on the track and kept an eye out for her stop.

"Market Street," the driver called out as they approached the busy intersection and Ruthie scrambled to her feet and slipped out the doors, which closed with a sucking sound behind her. She had to switch for the Sunset Line to Dr. Bennett's and she could see the streetcar approaching. She hurried to get to the stop ahead of the green and yellow car and boarded with a large group of passengers. No seats on this car, which was full of weekday shoppers, mostly women, with large bags over their shoulders heading back to the suburban streets of the Sunset District. Out to beat the Christmas rush at the Emporium, I bet, Ruthie thought, remembering Sasha's delight the year she turned 3 and they took her to see Santa and ride the carousel on the roof of the big downtown department store. Carl had objected—some revolutionary, he had scoffed, lining up to see Santa, but Ruthie wanted Sasha to know the magic she had felt as a little girl dressed in a matching wool coat and hat sitting on Santa's lap with a serious look on her face. Why had her Jewish parents taken her to G. Fox and Co. all those years ago? Probably for the same reason.

Ruthie sighed. Everything in this damn city reminded her of Sasha.

She couldn't wait till they hit the road to Baja. At least she would be doing something to find her.

Dr. Bennett's office was on the ground floor of a stucco house with a bay window and a small lawn bordering a cement walkway. The Sunset was one of the few neighborhoods in San Francisco where the sun could be counted on once the fog lifted and, as far as Ruthie was concerned, that was its only charm. Rows of identical houses, set apart only by the choice of paint color or lawn decorations marched on straight streets to the bay. Ruthie was reminded of the song "Little Boxes"—and they're all made out of ticky-tacky, and they all look just the same.

The office was a blast from her doctor's not-too-distant past—brightly colored Indian fabric draped the comfortable couches, Jimi Hendrix and Janis Joplin jammed in wall-sized posters and a speaker was playing the Jefferson Airplane softly in the background. Dr. Bennett—Dr. Dan as he preferred to be known to his patients—still spent one day a week at the Free Clinic in the Haight.

"Ruthie—such a long time. How are you?" He greeted her with a bear hug and a big smile.

"Oh-okay I guess."

"And Sasha? How is my favorite girl? Well, besides Skye of course. She must be so big by now."

"Yes, she is. She turned six this year." Despite her efforts to hold them back, tears welled up in Ruthie's eyes. She should have known Dr. Dan would ask about Sasha.

"Oh, man. I didn't mean to upset you. I heard you and Carl split up. So sorry. Why don't you take this cup to the bathroom, and we'll get a urine sample. Then come back and tell me why you're here."

Ruthie followed him down a narrow hall to the bathroom and got ready to pee in the cup. As soon as she pulled down her panties her worries were over. Sure enough, her period had come down—late but heavy as usual. She'd need a Kotex and a new pair of panties, but she wasn't pregnant. She breathed a sigh of relief, cleaned up as best as she could, slipped into a cloth gown and found her way to the exam room. An older woman with glasses dangling from a beaded chain over a long-tie-dyed tunic entered with Dr. Dan when Ruthie was ready. He introduced her as Connie, a volunteer who was helping him set up a women's clinic as part of his practice.

"Do you mind if Connie observes?" he asked, and Ruthie smiled her agreement.

"So, what brings you here today, Ruthie?" Dr. Dan said. Ruthie pulled the skimpy gown tight around her legs and sighed, explaining in a soft voice that it had been a while since she had seen a doctor and she just had not been feeling right—queasy in the mornings, bloated, tired for no reason.

"I thought I might be pregnant," she said, saying a silent thank you to the Santeria goddess of the wind, Oya, for blowing that trouble away . "But I just got my period. I'll need a sanitary napkin and some paper panties if you've got them."

"Hop up here and let's see what's going on," Dr. Dan said, patting the cushioned table. For all his eccentricities, the exam room was all doctorly apart from the colorful batik wall hangings and strains of soft rock playing through a boombox on the counter.

"C'mon people now, smile on your brother. Everybody get together try to love one another right now." The Jefferson Airplane's version of the song she and Carl had walked down the aisle to in their small homemade wedding just seven years earlier.

Ruthie pulled herself onto the table, slid her heels into the cold metal stirrups and took a deep breath. She felt gloved hands probing her soft belly, felt the cool gel slide into her vagina and the push of the speculum opening her up to his examination. Connie stood over Dr. Dan's shoulder.

"Hope this is not too uncomfortable, Ruthie. I don't see any signs of pregnancy. And the fact that you just got your period confirms what I'm seeing. You may have a stomach bug that's causing your symptoms. We'll do a test to confirm that and get you some medicine if you need it."

" Oh God, thank you, I'm so relieved. I know things have changed but I was remembering the bad old days and I didn't want to have to—well, I just can't have a baby right now."

"It shouldn't be such a burden for a woman in my opinion," Dr. Dan said, "but at least now there are choices. At least we don't have to come up with something to justify terminating a pregnancy in the first trimester. It doesn't have to be a life and death situation anymore. We've been running our women's clinic on Saturdays since February, and…oh sorry, you don't need to hear all this. Why don't you get cleaned up and dressed and I'll get you that prescription."

An abortion, Ruthie thought, shivering as she wiped gel from her vaginaand slipped on a pair of paper panties and a Kotex under her clothes. Well, one less thing to worry about. Finally, women had won the right to go to a clinic in broad daylight to terminate a pregnancy, but Ruthie was relieved she wouldn't have to take advantage of this victory that had been decades in the making. She remembered the days of "The List" passed around among high school friends and in college dorms—doctors who set up clandestine abortion sites in sleazy midtown hotels in NYC or Chicago. She remembered helping friends scrape together the cash for the procedure, carrying posters with bent wire coat hangers taped on to them to street demonstrations. And she remembered Julie, her best friend in high school, whose strict Catholic mother sent her away to a home for unwed mothers and forced her to give her baby up for adoption. Julie had a nervous breakdown and ended up in an institution. Ruthie visited only once—it was too painful to see her friend, devastated by the electric shock treatments they gave her, barely able to have a conversation.

She thought of her long late-night conversations with Angela, one of the young Cuban jefes on her Brigade. How impressed she had been with

Angela's clarity about her life, her commitment to the revolution. Ruthie wanted that kind of life for her and Sasha—a life of clear intentions, part of something bigger, dedicated to building a new and better world. She was tired of letting the currents carry her from place to place, from experience to experience.

Annie had come with Will to pick her up, but Ruthie didn't join in the chatter from the front seat as she watched the neighborhoods change. They passed through the Sunset, along the edge of Golden Gate Park to the Haight. Haight-Ashbury, not that long ago a mecca for young hippies and wannabe revolutionaries like her, felt sad to her now. The Diggers Free Store where they distributed hearty stews and bread at 4 PM every day was still open, and the Free Clinic had a straggly line in front of it, but the streets had lost the freewheeling energy she remembered from her early days in the neighborhood. Drugs had taken over and every block was home to one or two street dwellers perched on slabs of cardboard with crudely written signs asking for spare change or food.

"Sad, isn't it?" Will said, echoing Ruthie's thoughts, as the Park gave way to the long narrow Panhandle and then to the sunny streets of the Mission District and the green expanse of Mission Dolores Park rising above the grey granite walls of Mission High School—and then right across the street—the Family Place—and home.

"It looks like we have a visitor," Ruthie said, as Will maneuvered the van into a parking spot.

"And he looks familiar," she went on. "Did you guys tell him to come?" "We couldn't have kept him away with an army," Will said. "That man

was bound and determined to see you before we leave, Ruthie. Seems like he really cares about you, girl."

"Yeah, I guess he does," Ruthie sighed. "I just wish…" She let her thoughts trail off, not sure what she wished, and took a deep breath.

"Sorry guys. I guess you have one more mouth to feed. And believe me Manny can eat."

"We're glad he's here, sweetie," Annie said as Will pulled the camper into a parking spot a couple of doors up from the house. "He can help with the last-minute preparations for Baja—and it'll be nice to have someone see us off on this adventure."

Ruthie stepped down from the van and got ready to deal with Manny— the dear, loving, infuriating bear of a man who had risen from the swing and was coming to meet her.

A Long Way to Go

Ruthie had barely put one foot on the porch when she was hugged tight to Manny's broad chest and lifted off her feet.

"Manny, take it easy. You'll break her!" Annie called out from the sidewalk. "Yeah, Manny. Take it easy. I'm fragile!" Ruthie echoed, squirming down till she felt the wooden planks of the porch under her feet.

"Sorry, sorry—are you OK, Ruthie? Did I hurt you for real? I'm just so damn glad to see you, negrita."

Ruthie laughed. "I'm OK, but let's go inside and sit down."

They settled in the front room and Ruthie put her feet up on the old ottoman that she had used to take a rest when she was pregnant with Sasha. She sighed. This house held so many memories of Sasha. It would be good to get on the road and head towards where the real Sasha might be waiting.

"Penny for your thoughts, Ruthie." Manny said softly. "Though I'm pretty sure they are worth more than that. With inflation and all."

"Just thinking about Sasha, as usual. The closer we get to leaving on this trip, the more sure I get that we are going to find her, Manny. But what will I do if we don't?"

"You'll do what you always do, Ruthie. Pick yourself and keep going. You are a lot stronger than you think, compañera. A lot stronger than you think."

The rattling sound of teacups on a tray announced Annie's entry into the room, and Will followed close behind.

"I figured a cup of hot tea would be just the thing right now—chamomile OK, Manny? I know Ruthie could use something soothing right now. And a few homemade oatmeal raisin cookies won't hurt. I'm going to rustle us up some dinner in a bit, and Will has to go grab the kids from school. They're going to be glad to meet you, Manny—probably climbing all over you and asking you a million questions in the first five minutes."

"No worries," Manny said. "I got a gazillion little cousins and nieces and nephews that do the same. Truth is, I love it. But don't tell them."

Ruthie lifted her cup off the tray and sipped the steaming liquid slowly. She could feel her shoulders and neck beginning to throw off the tension of the day. Annie was right. It was good that Manny was here. He always made her feel so safe, even when he was so annoying.

"Glad you came, Manny—even though you should have asked," she said. "And argue with you about it when you were going through so much.

Nah, nah. When in doubt, try it out—that's my motto. And here I am. Do you want to go lie down for a bit before dinner? I can see if Annie needs help in the kitchen."

"Yeah, that would be good. Annie will tell you no but just try out your motto on her."

Ruthie lifted her feet from the ottoman and pushed herself up out of the chair. It would be good to lie down for a bit.

Ruthie closed her eyes as soon as her head hit the pillow. \She drifted off to sleep with the distant sounds of pots and pans clanking in the kitchen. The next few days would go by quickly, and soon they would be on the road to Sasha. Her last waking thought was…Sasha.

After a short nap, Ruthie stumbled down the stairs to the sound of the dinner bell. As they all sat around the table in the sunny dining room, Manny announced his intention to see them off on their journey.

"Really, I wish I could go with you, but that van will be stuffed to the gills, and I have a job to get back to. But I'd like the last thing you see before you hit the road to be me waving good-bye. Does that work?"

Will and Annie looked at Ruthie. Annie nodded and Will winked his approval.

"That would be great, Manny. You can help me get my shit together these last couple of days. And I would love to see you in the rearview mirror…well, I mean, that didn't come out exactly how I meant it–I would love for you to see us off."

Manny ran around town with Ruthie as she did her last-minute errands and calmed her down when her nerves got the best of her

The night before their departure they sat together in the small room at the Family Place she had been calling home for the past few weeks. As usual, she had settled in fast. The house was familiar, which helped, but wherever she went, even for short visits, Ruthie added personal touches—a few family photos, a colorful postcard. She wondered if hermit crabs traveled from shell to shell with a few relics from their distant past as she did. She laughed out loud at the idea—imagining a naked crab, scurrying for shelter with a special piece of dried seaweed tucked under her armpit—did they have armpits? —then laying it out just so in her new home—a seaweed rug or wall hanging perhaps.

Manny surveyed her relics, laid out neatly across the top of the dresser. "What's this?" he asked, holding up a roll of paper tied with a pale blue ribbon.

"Oh god, don't open that," she said, trying to grab it. But Manny held it above her head, then uncurled it with a flourish.

Summer is here It makes me glad
When winter comes It makes me sad

"C'mon, Manny. It was 2nd grade. I was 8. And you know what, I still feel that way about winter."

Ruthie continued taking inventory. A small mason jar of shells she had collected sat on the nightstand—one from each beach she visited—not just any one but a unique shell discovered on a long walk over the cool wet sand near the water's edge. The jar was almost full, but she would add shells from Baja as they traveled. A purple ribbon that had been tied around the neck of Sasha's Lambie—her favorite stuffed animal friend, a small grey lamb actually made of Persian lamb wool, fraying at the seams, dingy and bedraggled. The ribbon had been left behind when Ruthie packed Sasha up for her stay with

Carl and had come to represent, in her mind, their inevitable reunion. A small cobalt blue glass bird—how she had come to have it was long forgotten— that caught the sunlight when she placed it on the windowsill of whatever room she was inhabiting.

And her favorite picture of Sasha in a tarnished silver frame—the one she had showed Louise—caught mid jump on the rocks in a creek—sunlight glinting off the water and her long reddish curls lifted by the wind to form a curtain of gold behind her face. The picture was full of delight and energy. Ruthie took it from the dresser and wrapped it carefully in a pillowcase to tuck in her backpack. She wrapped the jar of shells in a worn dishcloth and tied the purple ribbon around it. The bird she wrapped in another dishcloth, securing it with a rubber band, and the poem she carefully enveloped in a thick tube sock for safekeeping.

These reminders of her past would have to remain in her backpack while they traveled—no room in the van to decorate—but she would know they were there waiting for her to find a new home—a home with Sasha.

"Let's call Violeta!" Ruthie said to Manny who was dozing on the bed while she packed. "I need to hear her voice before I leave. What time is it in Boston?"

Manny yawned and stretched, then looked at his watch.

"It's, let's see, 3 hours later there, so…10 PM. Will she be home? She just has that phone in the hall, right?"

"Yeah, but let's try. Here's the number—can you dial while I put this stuff in my bag?"

"Hola, Violeta, it's me Manny. I'm with Ruthie in California. Can you hear me OK?"

Ruthie heard an ear-piercing scream through the receiver that stopped her breath. Had something terrible happened? She grabbed the phone from Manny.

"Vi, ¿qué pasó? Is everything OK?"

"Ay, mi amiga. ¿Recibiste mi carta? Did you get my letter?" Violeta asked, but didn't wait for Ruthie to answer before plunging into a rapid-fire burst of conversation.

"Ruthie, it's Javi, you won't believe it. He's home. He's safe. He's alive!"

"Oh my God," Ruthie let out a long, relieved breath. "¿Cómo, cuándo?—how, tell me. Oh, I'm so happy I'm crying with joy for you!"

Ruthie sat on the bed as she listened to Violeta recount the story of Javi's homecoming—the priest who had found him and was working to get him out of the country, his friends who had not been so lucky, the things Javi had not yet told her about his imprisonment, that she could only imagine. Ruthie's heart lifted with each sentence and by the time Violeta told her that she might be able to reunite with her son in Canada, Ruthie felt like she was floating in midair. Manny just looked at her with a broad grin and shining eyes. He knew it was good news and that was all that was important.

"Ruthie, I have to go. Someone wants to use the phone. But you will find Sasha, I know you will. We will all get together someday, and it will be maravilloso! ¡Dios te bendiga, my friend! Travel safely and bring your little girl home."

The click on the other end of the line ended the call. Manny took the phone from Ruthie who was crying and laughing at the same time.

"You see, amiga," he said, sitting down next to her on the bed and taking her hand, "sometimes things just turn out all right—and they will for you, too. Now get some rest, Thursday's child. You still have a long way to go.

Just Get on Board!

They had decided to leave at dawn and had packed a few things into the van after dinner. The kids had already staked out their spots in the back—blankets, pillows, and one stuffed animal each piled up for the journey.

Ruthie lay with her eyes open, hoping sleep would come eventually. She tried the relaxation exercise she had learned in her childbirth classes during her pregnancy with Sasha—tightening her muscles one by one, then releasing them. How Sasha used to laugh when she scrunched up her face to relax it.

Her body settled into a familiar sleeping position—curled on her side, one arm under her pillow, the other stretched across her chest, one knee bent over her other leg. Usually she could feel her bones settle, her mind clear, sleep falling over her like a soft cotton sheet. But not this night. Her bones seemed to be talking to her, rustling and creaking, shifting into uncomfortable positions, heavy and in the way. Finally, she must have dozed, because she woke with a start to the simultaneous clanging of her alarm clock and Will's knock on her door.

"Up and at 'em," he said. "Breakfast is on the table."

She glanced at the clock and the still-dark window—5 AM. Will hadn't been kidding when he said they would get an early start. Ruthie stretched and groaned, feeling the tightness in her muscles from a night of restless movement. "Up and at 'em," she said to her rebellious body that was sinking back onto the bed.

In the dining room, Annie was ladling steaming oatmeal into their bowls, and Ruthie's purple cup was already filled with her morning coffee. The kids were spilling oatmeal on the table and down the front of their shirts as they hurried to get to the van and start this much-anticipated trip. And Manny was standing in a corner of the room, eyes half-closed, sipping from a mug of hot coffee.

"All right you two. Slow down. Go wash up and come back to the table. We're gonna have a little ceremony to bless our journey," Annie said, clearing their bowls from the table.

"A ceremony. A ceremony. We're gonna have a ceremony." Sage bounced and sang her way to the bathroom, with Oliver racing ahead to get there first.

When they had all finished their breakfast and the dishes had been cleared and washed, Annie invited them to form a circle in the living room where the first pink light of morning was visible under the shades.

"Let's join hands," she said, and Ruthie felt Sage's warm little hand curl into hers. Manny's soft smile beamed across the circle.

"Let's say one wish we have for this trip we are about to take. Who would like to start?"

"I'll go," Will said. He was not a big fan of this circle thing, but he knew better than to undermine Annie's need for ritual.

"My wish is that the van runs well and gets us where we need to go," he said, always the practical one.

It was Oliver's turn next. He looked down at his shoes and mumbled, "I wish to see the biggest wave I've ever seen," and glared at Sage, daring her to make fun of his wish.

Annie took a deep breath and began her wish. "I wish we all learn something new and open our hearts to the universe in a new way." Oliver rolled his eyes.

Sage hopped up and down, tugging on Ruthie's hand. "I'm next. I wanna go next," she said, then looked at Ruthie. "I wish we could find Sasha so Ruthie can be happy again," she added.

Manny gazed at Ruthie as he spoke in an uncharacteristically soft voice. "I wish that Ruthie is reunited with her little girl, because she is a good mother, and she deserves everything good in this world."

Ruthie was on the verge of tears by the time it was her turn, and her voice trembled with emotion.

"I wish that Sasha is reunited with this wonderful family and feels all the love and warmth that I feel in this circle right now."

Manny lifted his eyes to her and spoke his final words into the circle in his usual loud, enthusiastic tone.

"La Tierra Nos Bendiga," he said. "Let the earth bless us and this journey

Vamos a buscar a Sasha. Let's go find Sasha."

Will pulled the camper up in front of the house and nestled the back wheels snugly against the curb on the steep incline of the street.

They had organized their belongings on the street. The plan was to camp along the way wherever possible, so they were bringing a lot of camping gear—a large canvas tent that Ruthie remembered from Children's Place camping trips, a set of well-seasoned cast iron pots and pans, boxes of staple foods—all organized with her usual care by Annie.

The kids were hopping with excitement despite the heavy backpacks they wore that were almost as big as they were.

"We're going on a trip. We're going on a trip," Sage sang, circling around her brother.

"Stop. You're so annoying," he said, reaching out to swat her backpack. "Ma, make her stop."

"C'mon you two. Help me get this stuff in the camper. Time to hit the road." Will, in his customary denim jacket and blue jean overalls, was all business. Ruthie lifted her duffel into the back of the camper, but Will placed it back on the curb.

"Not yet, Ruthie. I'm gonna pack the boxes first."

Ruthie moved to the steps leading up to the house and sat for a minute as Will and Manny methodically packed the camper. The scene blurred and faded as she thought about Sasha and the search that was finally taking shape. This was it—after all the months of waiting, working, saving, hoping and planning. This was it.

They would drive down the 101 to LA and then move to the coast on route to Baja, camping along the way. Luckily, a two-lane paved road was nearing completion, but it would still be a challenging trip, 3 or 4 days depending on road conditions

Ruthie had narrowed the possibilities from the unnamed beach on the postcard to several options, and they would try to find each one. Sasha had to be waiting on one of them—waiting for her Mama to come. If not, Ruthie had no clue what would come next. She was out of ideas.

"Will, did you pack the clothesline? I can't find it." Annie came to the door, her hands full of a few last-minute items.

"Yup. It's in the box with the laundry soap and rain gear," Will said, motioning for Ruthie to bring her duffel. She watched him squeeze it into a secure spot against the back seat, his hands strong and sure.

"I'm in good hands," she said aloud. "I'm so grateful to you guys. I can't imagine making this trip on my own. Thank you, thank you, thank you."

Will snatched her up in a bear hug, and the kids moved closer and threw their arms around both of them.

"What's this?" Annie said, unloading her arms into the back of the camper.

"Group hug without me? I don't think so." Manny leaped in and the circle was complete.

Ruthie felt the warmth of Annie's body envelop her, the cinnamon scent of her hands, and the faint odor of patchouli oil carried in her clothes.

"I'm so lucky to have you. All of you," she said, her voice muffled against Will's chest.

"Lucky Ruthie. Lucky Ruthie. Lucky Ruthie," Sage sang, and they broke their group hold on each other, laughing.

"OK. Let's get this show on the road. Baja or bust," Will boomed, hoisting the kids one by one up onto their seats. Annie climbed into the front passenger seat and Ruthie moved onto the seat opposite the kids in the back. She opened the curtains on the small windows and took a last look at the house, the street fill with high school kids smoking one last cigarette before class.

"Off we go," Will said, gunning the engine of the old trusty van and pulling away from the curb.

"Off we go," they all shouted in unison. Manny's wave was the last thing Ruthie saw as they turned the corner.

On the Road Again

Ruthie always threw herself into travel, no matter how close or far, how familiar or exotic the destination. The past, the future, and the everyday of her life fell away when she traveled, and she suddenly became a different person—unanchored, open to the world in a new way.

But this trip was different. While Sage and Oliver chattered in what they called the "way back" of the van and Will and Annie murmured in the front, Ruthie couldn't tear her mind away from the destination, the end point on the map they had drawn and worries about what they might or might not find there.

Highway 101 hugged the rocky coast as they moved south from San Francisco. The exit for Half Moon Bay triggered a memory of that sleepy little fishing town she and Carl had loved visiting, both before and after Sasha, famous for its Portuguese fish stews and artichokes. They had stayed in a bed and breakfast near the crescent-shaped bay, hiked through fragrant onion fields and along cliffside paths during the day, and settled into the warm leather booth at their favorite restaurant for a bowl of hearty stew as dusk approached.

Scenery whizzed by. Will pushed the old van to the max to meet their daily distance goal, but Ruthie stopped looking. Her gaze drifted around the van. Her mind wandered between images of Sasha. She tried to stop the endless wandering by focusing on one image—Sasha today, tomorrow, next week, when they would surely find her on that beach.

Her little girl emerged from the fog in her mind like a Polaroid taking on shape and color. The Sasha she saw was tanned by days in the sun, long limbed and tangle haired. She saw her from the back at first as they approached—on the beach, alone, kneeling in the sand, digging and forming a mound of wet brown sand—a lopsided tower for a castle. Sasha lifted a red plastic bucket and stood to face the ocean—her back still to Ruthie. Then she ran toward the waves, curls flying, small brown feet kicking up sand and bits of shell. Still, she did not turn toward Ruthie. She did not see her or feel her presence.

"Ruthie. Ruthie." Sage's tug on her sleeve pulled Ruthie out of her daydream.

"Oliver's singing it. He's singing that song you said we couldn't. Make him stop," Sage said with her hands over her ears.

"87 bottles of beer on the wall. 87 bottles of beer. You take one down and …"

"Oliver, please remember my wish," Ruthie said, laughing with the relief of not having to watch Sasha in her mind, to watch her until…until what?

Till her little girl turned and looked right through her. Till she turned and Ruthie saw it was not Sasha at all.

Till Carl came and took Sasha's hand and led her away down the beach. Things could go so many ways.

"How's everybody doing back there?" Will asked. "Ready for a pit stop for lunch?"

"Yes, yes. We want lunch. We want lunch. We want lunch." The kids chanted, bouncing in their seats. Ruthie chanted with them, forgetting her worries for the moment in anticipation

After lunch, Annie took over the driving, her back ramrod straight and her hands clenched on the steering wheel. The night before, the first night of the trip, they'd stayed in the only organized campground on the route—a state park near San Diego with bathrooms and running water, probably the last they would encounter for a while. It was about 600 miles from San Francisco to Ensenada, their first destination on the Baja peninsula. Their goal was to cover a few hundred miles each day. They had crossed the border into Mexico at San Ysidro a couple of hours earlier, the kids serious and quiet in the back while the men in uniforms checked their papers. Now they were back to playing I-spy, sleeping and squabbling on the fold-out double bed in the way back.

"How ya doin, Annie?" Ruthie asked, touching her friend's shoulder lightly.

"Oh hi, you're up. I'm fine. I just need to concentrate pretty hard. It's really foggy, and I can't see anything but the road in front of me," Annie said, tightening her grip on the steering wheel.

"If you want me to drive, just say the word," Will said. He was so finely attuned to Annie's voice that he probably heard it in his sleep.

"Just go back to sleep, Will. I'm fine," Annie said firmly, with a hint of annoyance.

"What's wrong? Where are we?" Oliver piped up from the back seat, untangling his lanky limbs from Sage's plump body and poking his head over the back of Ruthie's seat.

"Just let me drive you all. I'm doing fine. We'll pull over soon for dinner and the night. We've picked a beach to camp at about 30 miles ahead."

"Okay, Mom. Whatever you say," Oliver said, flopping back down on his quilt.

Ruthie pressed her cheek to the cool window, watching the piney woods along the side of the highway go by as the van moved forward. The ocean was a dark presence below the cliffs, and the silence was broken only by the occasional honk of a horn as a truck passed them on the narrow road.

Ruthie sat alone in the middle seat watching the scenery fly by in a blurry daydreaming state, occasionally brought back to the present by an uncomfortable crick in her neck or a foot that went to sleep.

"Hey Annie," she called across the seat. "Rest stop soon? I have to pee, and I don't think I can wait till we get to the beach."

"Again," Sage and Oliver piped up from the back in unison. "Ruthie, you have to pee even more than me," Sage said.

Annie turned to smile at her, that wise woman smile she had, as if to say Don't worry girl, we got this.

But did they, did she?

Cruising down Highway 1-D, the Pacific always on their right, forested hills giving way to sandy desert expanses on their left, in a battered old Chevy camper van in search of a beach that was no more than the barest indentation on the map, in search of a girl and her father who might not be there, did not seem like the smartest thing Ruthie had ever done. But here they were—and she had to pee. Again.

They finally arrived at the beach campground as the late afternoon sun was glinting across the azure water. Waves crashed hard against the rocky cliffs surrounding the beach. A few other families were already settled around fires along the beach, and they looked for their own spot of flat, dry sand to set up camp, deciding to forgo the tent and sleep under the stars. Annie and Ruthie got busy warming up dinner, while Will and the kids laid out their sleeping bags in a circle and rustled up driftwood for a fire.

"Help…I can't eat one more," Ruthie whined, as Sage shoved a golden-brown toasted marshmallow in her face. "Please, Sagie…time to wash up for bed."

The kids conked out as soon as their heads hit their pillows, tucked into their cozy flannel bags around the dying embers of the campfire.

Ruthie closed her eyes to the sound of Will and Annie murmuring quietly beside her and to the far-off call of a bird she could not name.

All the months of imagining where Sasha might be, what she might be doing, how much she had grown, how she would feel when she saw Ruthie again, were drawing to a close. They would either find her on the small crescent no-name beach that Ruthie remembered so well, or they wouldn't. And then?

That thought brought the fear. And then, what?

Ruthie shook her head to clear her thoughts, imagining an old woman stooped over a straw broom, sweeping them out of her head. The night's sounds faded, and she drifted off to sleep.

Día de los Muertos

November 2, 1973

One more day. One more night. If all went well.

They got an early start and had been driving the curvy road for about 4 hours when Will's voice broke the silence in the van.

"Hey guys, I'm just about ready for a taco stop, and there's a little town just off the road ahead. What do you say?"

"Sounds good to me," Annie said, unfolding the map on her lap to find the turnoff.

"Tacos. Tacos. Yay for Tacos." Sage and Ollie piped up from the way back seat. They could turn anything into a high-pitched chant, which was starting to get on Ruthie's nerves.

The closer they got to "Ruthie's beach," as the kids had named it, the more nervous she grew. The thought of a plate of warm tacos, stuffed with beans, grilled pork, and gooey cheese made her stomach quiver, but maybe she could eat some white rice.

Will steered the camper onto a packed dirt road that climbed into the hills and away from the coast.

"I hear music," Ollie said. "Where's it coming from? Can we go see?"

They didn't have to go far. The road narrowed and was lined with small adobe houses, like Monopoly pieces painted in bright shades of cobalt, yellow, and orange. The source of the music came into view. In front of each house, a family stood in their best attire. Ruthie noticed that the women balanced large straw baskets bursting with flowers on their heads—gold and orange marigolds, white chrysanthemums, and long-stemmed purple and red gladiolas.

In their arms, they held large clay pots, and some carried what looked like family photos in antique frames.

"A parade. Stop!" Sage commanded. "I wanna get out."

Tacos were forgotten as mariachis decked out in gold-fringed white suits led the parade down the dusty street. The trumpets blared in the front, followed by a lone accordion player, and a violin and guitar brought up the rear. The music was lively, and the kids began clapping to the beat as they ran to get a better look. "Is this a holiday, or a party?" Ruthie wondered aloud as she joined the kids, with Will and Annie not far behind.

"What day is today?" Annie asked. Just then Sage raced up and grabbed her hand.

"It's Halloween, Mama. And there's skeletons. I don't like them. I'm scared."

"Not Halloween, Sagie. In Mexico, they call it Día de los Muertos, the Day of the Dead. We're so lucky we found this parade. Let's watch for a while and see what comes next."

The kids settled in, cross-legged at their feet, as the little parade straggled down the road. As the parade reached each house, the families joined in, threading themselves among the musicians and skeletons until the whole town seemed to be marching.

"C'mon, kids, let's go," Will said, lifting Sage onto his shoulders and pulling Ollie along beside him.

Annie and Ruthie scuffed along behind. One of the skeletons, a tall female figure with a skull painted on her face, a large garland of flowers on her head, and a flowing skirt, approached and smiled, taking their hands and leading them into a dance.

"She's called a "Catrina Calavera." Annie raised her voice above the trumpeting mariachis as the skeleton moved on. "In Mexican tradition, death is a natural part of life, not something to be feared, so they welcome their dead loved ones back to be with them on this day. Kinda cool, huh? You OK, Ruthie?"

A welcome breeze blew Ruthie's hair off her neck, and she nodded. "Worried about tomorrow?"

Ruthie nodded again and Annie squeezed her hand just as the parade turned into a small cemetery. The bare dry earth was dotted with gravestones, some grey and weathered, others well-tended and painted in bright colors like the houses. Some were crowned by large, sculpted crosses or Jesus figures, others surrounded by low picket fences.

The parade broke up into family groups, then they gathered around the gravestones and began cleaning them, adorning them with flowers and the photos they had brought, and setting out small plates of food in front of them—corn, roasted brown in the husk, tamales, and small jars of sauces were laid carefully on oilcloth to form small altars. Candles were lit, and the cemetery was transformed into a twinkling, magical kingdom. Even the kids were in awe. "Who is going to eat the food?" Ollie whispered. "And what about our tacos?"

"Let's just stay a bit longer," Annie said, "and then we'll go look for some tacos. The families are going to spend the night here. They believe that the people they love who have died will come and be with them in spirit, and they'll eat the food together."

"Dead people can't eat food," Sage's voice got louder, as it always did when she was excited. "They're dead, silly."

"Sagie, hush sweetie. We can talk more about it later. Shall we go get some food?"

Even Ruthie felt a bit hungry as they wound their way back to the road and the van, leaving behind the sounds of music and murmuring voices, the flickering candles.

"That was a special surprise," Will reflected, folding his long legs into the passenger side of the van as Annie took the wheel. "Everybody ready for some grub? I know I am."

They found a taco stand with picnic tables at the junction where the road from town met the coastal route. A small outhouse with real toilet paper brought a smile to Ruthie's face. The contented silence was broken only by chewing and gulping, and an occasional burp as dusk settled around them, until Will hustled them back into the van.

When they reached the beachfront campground where they would camp for the night, Ruthie spread her blanket on the sand in front of the fire Annie had built. Sparks crackled and leapt into the night sky as if straining to reach their sisters, twinkling far away.

Annie leaned against Will's knees, eyes closed, asleep or lost in one of her vision dreams, and the kids traced the trails of the hermit crabs in the wet sand along the frothy rim of the water.

All along the beach, campfires glowed, and small groups huddled around them. At the far end of the shore, where the sand met the tangled jungle, a group of boys set off firecrackers that pierced the quiet like gunshots. Rockets wobbled skyward before fizzling out and falling into the waves.

Tomorrow they would finally reach the no-name beach if all went according to plan.

Ruthie felt a whisper of hope settle over her shoulders like the soft wool of the multicolored ruana Violeta had pressed into her hands before she set out on this journey.

It was her grandmother's shawl that had traveled with her from Chile and Ruthie had refused the gift at first.

"No, no, mi amiga. You must take it." Violeta had insisted. "It will bring you luck."

Ruthie brought the shawl to her nose and breathed deeply. It carried so many scents in its tightly woven threads—the earthy smell of the mountain and a piney scent from the forest, mixed with a whiff of the strong mate tea that Violeta steeped each night, carrying the odor of twigs and dark red clay. A hint of lavender from the calming lotion Annie rubbed into Ruthie's shoulders when she gave her a back massage.

"To keep you warm, amiga," she had said. "And safe."

A new day…and the possibility of holding her daughter close.

She shivered, not from cold—she was sweating under the warmth of the fire and her shawl—but from anticipation.

Oliver stirred under his sleeping bag.

"Doesn't it feel like New Year's Eve?" he said, throwing a twig into the fire and watching it spark.

"Happy New Year!" Sage cried out, standing up in her bag and hopping over to where Ruthie sat.

Just before dawn, Ruthie awoke to the sight of a few small wooden fishing boats heading out to sea. The sun sent silvery ribbons across the waves, which broke over a sandbar in the distance.

Will stirred the still-glowing coals of last night's campfire and added some dry driftwood to get the fire going. Soon, the smell of freshly brewing coffee and bacon filled the air. Were there any better smells in the morning? Ruthie thought—shaking the sand out of her sleeping bag and rolling it into its stuff sack.

They would hit the road early this morning, right after breakfast, to go in search of the crescent beach.

Ruthie's Beach

The sun was already beating down on their heads by the time they got the van loaded. Sage had to be persuaded to leave a bucketful of wriggling hermit crabs on the sand.

"Look, Ruthie," she squealed, upending the bucket. "They're going to find new homes." How easy it is for them, Ruthie thought. Any shell will do for a while. She watched one burly fellow scurry to an empty snail shell and disappear inside.

"C'mon, Sagie. Wash that bucket out and get in the van. Time to hit the road," Will said, climbing into the driver's seat. Ruthie gathered the multicolored rainbow of her skirt between her legs and hoisted herself onto the middle seat as the kids clambered into the back, shedding sand on the carpeted space carved out for them among their belongings. Annie rinsed the old tin coffee pot in the small creek that wound its way down to the ocean and nestled it under her legs as she took her place beside Will.

"Ready, guys?" she asked, sending a big smile in Ruthie's direction. "Let's go find Ruthie's beach."

"Ruthie's beach…Ruthie's beach…Ruthie's beach." Oliver began another sing-song chant, and Sage joined in.

"Pipe down back there. I'm trying to drive," Will shouted back at them, and they dissolved into giggles.

Ruthie didn't know what she was feeling. A mix of hope and fear simmered inside her. Images of Sasha running toward her on the beach flashed into her mind's eye.

About an hour into the drive, the landscape changed from the flat tropical forest to rocky, rolling cliffs that climbed over and away from the sea. Was this what Ruthie remembered? Was the crescent beach down there, below one of these cliffs?

Will slowed and pulled the van onto the shoulder, gravel crunching under the tires, then took the well-worn map from its plastic cover.

"Just want to take a quick look," he said. "Make sure we're heading in the right direction. I think we're here." His leathery hand covered the map, and he pointed a finger at one of the curvy points along the coast. Ruthie noticed the dirt under his fingernails and how close they were to the red circle she had drawn around their destination many weeks earlier, when this trip had been just a wish.

"I think this is the road," Will said, pointing to a deeply rutted dirt road that forked right and descended steeply to the beach below. Ruthie looked at the outline where the sand met the water. It was the same crescent shape she remembered, with a fringe of coconut palms marking the edge of the tangled growth surrounding the beach.

"Are you sure," she asked, her voice sounding thin and light in her ears. A lone woman walked the beach with a basket on her head, her long gauzy skirt trailing in the water.

"As sure as I'll ever be without driving down there," Will said. Annie turned to look at her, and the kids started their chant again.

Ruthie's beach Ruthie's beach Ruthie's beach

"Can the van make it down that road?" she asked. "It looks pretty bad." "I've driven this thing down worse roads than that one, Ruthie," Will said.

Now he was looking at her, too.

She knew she was acting strangely. After all the waiting, the preparation, and the time on the road to reach this destination, Ruthie's determination suddenly stalled. What if Sasha wasn't here? What then? Or what if she was here and Carl didn't want Ruthie to take her—or, she almost couldn't bear to think the next thought that popped into her mind.

What if Sasha didn't want to come?

She took a deep breath. There was only one way to find out.

"Okay, let's do it," she said, and they began to bump down the road toward the beach.

Will guided the van slowly and carefully. Shells and branches crackled under the tires, but inside the van a hushed silence fell around them. Even the kids stopped giggling and squirming, noses pressed to the dusty windows, peering at the beach.

As they grew closer, Ruthie noticed a couple of thatched shelters set up near the coconut palms. A man emerged from the hut closest to the water and waded out to a boat bobbing in the waves. A raggedy hat made of palm fronds shaded his face. He turned at the sound of the van's rattling progress down the road and lifted his hand to his eyes, watching.

At the other end of the beach, where the land came to a point and disappeared into a rocky outcropping pounded by the incoming tide, Ruthie saw the woman with the basket on her head stop and set it on the sand beside her. She stood, hands on hips, talking to someone, but Ruthie could make out only a small shadowy shape against the blinding noonday sun.

Will eased the van onto a gravel-covered parking area next to a battered green pickup, careful not to dig in the wheels. The engine clicked and then went quiet, and Ruthie heard the man's voice carried high on the stiff ocean breeze.

The woman at the other end of the beach lifted her basket onto her head and began a slow rolling walk back to where the man was taking something from the boat.

The small figure on the sand stood up, and Ruthie gasped and squinted into the sun. She opened the door and lunged from the van, tripping over the hem of her skirt. Shells cut into the bottoms of her bare, tender city feet, but she didn't notice.

"Ruthie?" Annie called after her, stepping down from the van, but didn't follow.

The kids watched from their nest in the back.

Ruthie moved slowly but purposefully across the small parking lot, down the rocky path, and onto the sand. It was silky and warm underfoot. The person at the end of the beach turned back to whatever she was doing. Ruthie could now see that it was a girl or a small woman in a brightly colored 2-piece swimsuit, with long brown legs and brown curls glinting red in the sun.

Ruthie's walk became a dance.

Her hips swayed, her legs bent and straightened, her toes curled into the sand. She felt the presence of other dancers beside her—other mothers walking with her.

Violeta put her arm around her waist and whispered in her ear. "Soon, mi amiga, very soon."

At her other side, the arpilleristas of Chile walked in silence, holding brightly embroidered portraits of the disappeared before them. And she felt Manny's presence, his feet leaving big footprints in the sand.

She was not alone.

Ruthie stopped her dancing walk halfway down the beach. She turned toward the van—Annie, Will, Sage, and Oliver, her loving family of choice for this journey, formed a tableau of anxious waiting on the small gravel precipice that hung over the beach. As she watched, they spread apart and began a flurry of nervous activity. Will opened the hood and fiddled with something in the engine. Annie gathered an armful of driftwood—did she think they would spend the night here? The kids were piling rocks and shells into some kind of castle.

Ruthie's eyes swept the end of the beach where she had first seen the man and the boat. He had returned to the sand and was standing in front of one of the huts. The woman stood beside him, the basket tucked at her feet. They seemed to be watching Ruthie's progress.

She turned back to the girl. She could see now that it was a long-legged girl, not a small woman, who had pulled a blue T-shirt on over her bathing suit. Ruthie could barely make out the outline of a large, colorful bird on the back of the T-shirt. Was it a rooster? Was that a plastic hair comb on its head? She remembered Sasha's favorite T-shirt—how she had refused to put it in theBgiveaway pile, insisting on wearing it long after it was too small, pulling it down over the belly that protruded over her pants in a vain attempt to make it fit. That shirt had finally gone to one of the smaller kids at school.

Ruthie shook her head to clear the image. A ball of fur shot across the sand from the huts, ruffling Ruthie's skirt as it passed, and came to rest beside the girl, who squealed in delight and bent to throw her arms around what Ruthie could see was a gray-and-white husky, or maybe a shepherd. Sasha had loved

Ken's dog Loki—their mascot at the house in Colorado Springs—and had begged for a puppy.

"My very own, Mama. My own puppy."

But Ruthie couldn't take on any more responsibility at the time. She had said no.

Now the girl threw something toward the edge of the water, and the dog bounded after it and returned to lay it at the girl's feet, shaking water from its coat so vigorously that the girl was wet from head to toe. She laughed, a tinkle of a laugh with music in it, and Ruthie held her breath. Did she know that laugh, or was she imagining it was familiar?

She began to walk again—slowly, so slowly, almost in slow motion. As soon as she took one step forward on the sand, she felt Violeta at her side, Manny trailing a little behind.

She turned toward a familiar sound on her right and, to her surprise, there was her mother, clearing her throat and lifting her hand in greeting. Ruthie smiled in return.

She thought of the women in Chile, crafting arpilleras to bear witness to their opposition to the military coup. She thought of the photos Violeta had showed her from the newspapers in Chile—mothers with kerchiefs tied over their unruly hair searching makeshift bulletin boards, scanning scraps of paper that might bring news of the missing. She took the arpillera she had made with Violeta out from under her arm and held it aloft like a kite, blowing in the wind. And she continued her slow dance-walk forward, feeling Manny's warm hand curled around her shoulder. The mother figure at one end, cut out of colorful batik material in swirls of purple and yellow, joined hands with a chain of felt women that stretched all the way to a childlike figure at the other end. She had appliqued the figures onto the burlap and cross-stitched a sky of blue above them. A small plane drifted through the clouds trailing a banner that read Where are our children?

I promise I will join you soon and help you get justice for your children. Ruthie whispered to the women of Chile, the arpilleristas, whose support she felt as she walked.

The girl was busy playing with the dog, throwing a gnarled and twisted stick, laughing, and bending to caress the dog.

Had she noticed a strange woman coming closer down the beach? Ruthie couldn't tell.

When she looked up, the girl had stopped her playful twirling and was running with the dog to the water's edge.

"Spotty, c'mon girl. C'mon Spot. Let's go. Good girl."

Ruthie heard the girl's voice for the first time, confident and boisterous, as she called the dog to the water.

She'd named the dog Spot, but it was gray with white paws and a white blaze between its ears. Not a spot in sight. Ruthie drew in a breath. Could it be?

'Please, Mama, please tell about Spot again. Tell about when you were a little girl like me. Please.'

One of Sasha's favorite stories, told as a fairy tale, began to spin itself in her mind.

Once upon a time, there was a little girl… 'Like me, Mama?'

'Just like you, Sasha-bear.'

She had many nice things—a room painted her favorite blue with white curtains at the windows, a bookshelf with lots of good books to read, dolls and toys, and a stuffed bear she cuddled with every night.

'Like Lambie, Mama?'

' Yes, like Lambie. Let me finish the story, sweet girl, so you can get to sleep.'

But the one thing she wanted…

'More than anything in the world?' Sasha piped up from under Ruthie's

More than anything in the world, was a puppy, a real live puppy of her very own.

One day, her mother brought home a box tied with a big red bow.

'Come see what I found,' she said to the girl. The box was moving, and they heard little cries coming from inside. Something was scratching at the sides. Something was trying to get out.

'What could it be?' Sasha said, cupping her hand over her mouth. She knew the story by heart. Ruthie smiled and tickled her neck.

'Stop, Mama. Finish the story,' she said.

What could it be, the little girl wondered? Then her mother untied the ribbon, opened the box, and out jumped the roundest, furriest, cutest puppy the little girl had ever seen. Right in the middle of his forehead, between his two bright eyes, was a perfect black spot.

'Can we keep him? Can we? Can we? Is he mine to keep?' The little girl jumped up and down around the puppy, curled into a ball on the kitchen floor.

'All yours,' her mother said. 'Let's give him a name.'

The little girl studied the puppy—his white paws, white-and-black fur, and sticky-up ears.

'Spot,' she proclaimed. 'His name is Spot.' Sasha yawned and snuggled under the covers.

'And when I have a puppy of my very own,' she said in a sleepy voice. 'You will name him Spot. Now get to sleep. Tomorrow is playgroup, and we have to get up early.'

But Sasha was already asleep, thumb in her mouth, dreaming of a puppy named Spot.

The girl's voice drifted across the sand again. She was clapping her hands and calling the dog to the water.

"Spot. Spotty. C'mon, girl."

Ruthie stood very still. She was about halfway down the beach, halfway from where Annie and Will and the kids stood watching, where the man with the palm hat stood looking out to sea, where the woman with the basket was bent over a small fire, where the girl had sunk to the sand with the dog beside her drawing with a stick in the sand. Her back was to Ruthie. For a moment, Ruthie felt frozen on the spot where she stood. She felt her heels sink into the wet, warm sand; her body too heavy to move.

"Sasha," she called out across the distance. The wind and waves muffled her voice. It sounded like a whisper in her ears. "Sasha." She called more loudly this time.

The girl stopped her drawing and dropped her stick. Ruthie felt Violeta's hand brush hers, then move away. She took a breath, then a step forward.

"Sasha!"

The girl turned her head toward the sound of Ruthie's voice. A whisper of a smile crossed her face.

Ruthie lifted her foot from the sand, shook it free, and took one step forward. Suddenly she was running, her skirt like a sail behind her, her feet flying across the sand, her eyes fixed on the girl who watched her draw closer. She was aware of the kids cheering from the cliff above the beach, the dog yipping as it circled the girl, and the flapping of the arpillera she had been holding like a flag, now dropped on the sand. Her breath came in gulps, her mouth was dry, and her arms lifted in anticipation of an embrace. When she reached the girl, she stopped. She didn't want to scare her. Or maybe Ruthie was scared. She closed her eyes and put out her hand. She felt a small hand, gritty and wet, slip into hers. She heard the whisper of a question. Mama?

And then they were both running toward the blue-green ocean that touched every corner of the world, letting the waves tickle their feet and stepping together into the rest of their lives—w

Epilogue

July 1991

Sasha pulled the hood of her sweatshirt up over her messy bun and shivered in the air-conditioned deep freeze of the Miami airport.

"Told you to keep your shawl out," her mother, Ruthie, said, shifting their carry-on bags as they moved forward in line.

"Quit nagging," Sasha responded. "I'm 24 years old already." Then her attention was drawn to the woman in front of them, and she couldn't help giggling.

Ruthie shushed her and stifled her own laugh behind her hand, opening her eyes wide to take in the spectacle of the woman wearing layers upon layers of clothing, several hats piled on her head, gold bangle bracelets lining her arms, and a pair of sneakers that looked like clown shoes and had to be covering at least one other pair of shoes. She had read about Cubans going home to visit their families during this time of economic hardship trying to get around the weight limits on their luggage in inventive ways, but she had never seen anything like this. Off to the side was a machine that wrapped their fellow travelers' large black duffel bags in plastic—a way to ensure the hard-won treasures they were bringing would not be rifled through by Cuban customs officials, whom they were convinced would steal from them. The duffels were called "gusanos," the Spanish word for worms, as were their owners—the traitorous "worms" who slinked away to the U.S. after the 1959 revolution. Ruthie had heard stories from her Cuban friends on the Brigade about being encouraged to go to the port to throw eggs at those who were leaving. Now the joke was that the "gusanos" arrived for a visit with their family with the gift of a dozen eggs, which were hard to come by on the cash-strapped island.

"Hey, chicas, let me in on the joke. What's so funny?"

Manny came up behind them, late and rushing as usual, and then burst into laughter as he caught sight of the woman they were eyeing, who turned to give him a sharp glance of disapproval.

"Tio Manny, stop," Sasha hissed, embarrassed as she frequently was, by the exuberance of her Uncle Manny—the man who had been like a father to her for most of her life and who she loved dearly, but why did he always have to talk so loud?

Manny threw his arms around her, drew her close, and whispered, "Is this better, Negra.

I promise I won't embarrass you too much in Cuba."

Cuba… Sasha's thoughts drifted away on the frigid air as Manny and her mother bickered over how to repack their carry-ons, which were too heavy. This trip to Cuba was their graduation gift to Sasha, and it had been her idea. She wanted to visit the place that had brought her family together. She wanted to see for herself the island in the shape of a crocodile that her real father, Carl, was convinced had taken her away from him. She wanted to understand how the spirit of this small island had moved through her life.

For the past year, even in the crush of her last year in law school, Sasha had begun to keep a journal—trying to piece together the puzzle of her life. And the missing piece always seemed to be Cuba. A turning point in her mother's life, for sure, but for Sasha, a kaleidoscope of memories, shadowy and indistinct, that she tried to bring into focus as she paged through the photo albums that had recorded that time: the photo of her jumping in a creek, her hair billowing out behind her, or wriggling on her Mama's lap during one of the endless meetings that peppered her childhood. Or the one, creased beyond repair, that her mother had carried with her to Cuba, where she stood waving the Cuban flag from the steps of her father's trailer with a faraway look on her face, And the soundtrack—the rum-kissed laughter of Manny's stories, the hum of serious voices, the thump of a fist on the old oak table. She had let the images and sounds float through her mind—trying to bring that young girl into focus. Sasha reached into her tote bag and fingered the journal, full of scribbled reflections. Maybe actually being there would help.

Manny beckoned Sasha over to the small table where he and Ruthie had settled, surrounded by an array of backpacks and tote bags filled with items that could be useful to the Cubans they would visit—pens and pencils, notebooks, shampoo, deodorant. Sasha had thrown in some lollipops at the last minute. All kids deserved a sweet treat every once in a while.

"Hey Sash, can you sit here and watch this for a few? I gotta call Camila to let her know we're through with all the bureaucracy, and your Mama wants to touch base with Dragon Lady Rose one more time."

"Sure. Take your time, Tio. From that line it doesn't look like we'll be leaving anytime soon. Give Camila my love and tell the boys not to give her a hard time."

She watched as Manny walked away. She was so lucky to have him in her life. Not that she remembered much of her life before him. When her mom first took her to visit Annie and Will and the kids at the house in San Francisco, she had only fleeting memories of their room on the top floor and of the park across the street, where her father had pushed her on the swings and she had cried out, "Too high, daddy. Too high!" The time when her mom was in Cuba—those 3 months when she didn't really understand where Ruthie had gone or when she would come back—was just a blur. The trip with her dad and his girlfriend, well, now his wife, Cindy, had been fun—they got her a dog, they lived in a shack on the beach, and she didn't have to take showers—but she had been so relieved to finally see her Mama. For a while, she had worried she might never see her again.

But the aftermath—that was still engraved in her memory. The arguments and accusations, the constant changes to adjust to. After Claudia came back from England and reclaimed her apartment, they moved three times in one year. He and Cindy stayed together, had two sons, and built a house on a piece of land not far from the Rainbow Ranch in Sonoma County. Ruthie went to court to change their visitation agreement after she found Sasha on the beach in Baja—requiring supervised visits, which Carl mostly chose not to go along with—so he was pretty much a voice on the phone for ten years. When she was 18, she had sought him out on her own. Their relationship now was warm but not close. He just never seemed to take responsibility for anything in his life—it was like stuff just happened to him. At least her mom would talk things through with her.

Sasha shook her head. It's amazing, she thought, that after all these years of talking about it, years in therapy—there's still a part of me that feels like I did something wrong. Like it was my fault somehow.

Then Manny had come—just packed up his stuff in New Jersey and moved to Cambridge to help Ruthie raise Sasha after she got her back, and things just seemed to fall into place. He and Ruthie eventually bought a big old triple-decker with a wide front porch in The Port. A few years later, Manny and Camila (a Chilean friend of her Tia Violeta's) married, and soon Sasha became like a big sister to Victor and Gabriel, their twin boys. Manny found a steady job on the docks and became a shop steward in his union, while Camila worked as a counselor for immigrant women at the nearby church. Just in the past year, they received a grant from the church to set up a welcome center and were busy fixing up the first floor of their house. Their lives would change a lot now that she was leaving and Ruthie too, at least for a while.

Sasha wondered whether her mom knew how proud she was of her. After years of supporting their small family as a health educator at the Cambridge Women's Health Center, Ruthie was finally pursuing a long-time dream. In the fall, when Sasha moved to Washington, D.C., to begin her first job as a lawyer with a global human rights firm, Ruthie would head to Kentucky to study midwifery at age 43! Her mom had not had it easy—and Sasha knew that, despite the impact some of her choices had had on her own life. Now she was finally getting to choose something just for herself.

Sasha could see her mom at the wall of payphones, her frustrated look visible all the way from the table. Her Granma Rose had never been easy, but since Grandpa Max had died of lung cancer before his 70th birthday—"too young," everyone said—she had been impossible: she no longer waited for happy hour to drink and had alienated friends and family with her argumentative ways.

Sasha stayed clear of Granma Rose as much as possible, but she missed her Granpa who would have gotten a kick out of the fact that she was following in his footsteps by becoming a lawyer. She didn't get to see her Uncle Marty very often—he had moved to Vermont—but maybe she would visit before she started her job. She loved being around his big ideas and crazy energy. She watched as the phone settled heavily on the receiver and gave her mom a knowing shrug as she walked slowly back to the table.

"Well, that was fun, but at least I can check it off the list," Ruthie said, rearranging the bags around her chair. "I hope they don't give us a hard time about all this stuff we're bringing. On the Brigade, everything was taken care of for us. I hope this trip is well organized."

It was still illegal for U.S. citizens to travel to Cuba through regular channels, so they decided to join a tour with an organization called Global Exchange—the theme was public health and the law in Cuba, so it seemed perfect. Sasha hoped to learn more about how human rights were protected (or not) in Cuba, and Ruthie was looking forward to visiting a maternity home where high-risk pregnant women could live close to the hospital as their due dates approached. She didn't think they encouraged home births by midwives, since the Cuban medical system had trained thousands of primary care doctors and nurses—but she would poke around to see what she could find out. And Manny—well, Manny would just be his usual friendly, open self and start conversations with anyone within an arm's reach.

"Anyone else we should call?" Manny said almost tipping over the small plastic chair as he plopped down. A certain special someone to say goodbye to maybe?

Sasha sent him a knowing grin. He meant Saul, her mom's longtime boyfriend—patient, supportive Saul, who would be waiting when they got back—and still waiting when Ruthie returned from Kentucky. They were both fiercely independent, but Sasha was glad he was there for her mom, no matter what.

"Oh shit, I promised to call Sage. She's due any day, and I won't be able to reach her from Cuba, will I?" Sasha remembered how long she had waited for her mother to call her from her "venture" trip to Cuba all those years ago.

And how the call had never come.

Sasha sashayed across the floor, knowing her mother's eyes were following her every step and glad they were about to embark on this journey together. She chuckled to herself, thinking how surprising it was that she, Annie, Will's daughter Sage, and Sasha had become such good friends. On the surface, they seemed nothing alike. Sage had absorbed Annie's love of nature and had moved north to Oregon with her parents when they finally said goodbye to The Family Place. They had bought a few acres of land where Annie's garden could grow and Will could work on a book about his evolution from Vietnam veteran to "warrior for peace". Sage was studying for her master's degree in education and writing her thesis about The Children's Place, which survived for 10 more years as the neighborhood changed around it and finally succumbed to gentrification and high rents. And she was about to have her first baby as a single mom. Sasha felt light years away from all that.

Pasajeros y pasajeras del vuelo número 1470 con destino a La Habana, Cuba, deben presentarse en la puerta 12. Su vuelo abordará pronto.

"Sasha, where are you? What's all that noise?" Sage sounded breathless, like she had run to answer the phone.

"Hey Sagie, take it easy. I don't want you to have your baby while you're on the phone with me. We're leaving in a couple of minutes. When I get back, you'll be a Mama. I can't believe it!"

"Me neither, Sash. Bring me a simpático compañero from Cuba, huh?"

Sasha hung up the phone and grabbed a couple of bags from her Mama's overloaded arms.

This was it. They were doing it. No FBI taking their pictures, as her mom had told her about from her first trip to Cuba. No machetes in their suitcases. Just 3 people, one family, who had come through a lot together, heading off to the "First Liberated Territory of the Americas" on their very own 'venture'.

Acknowledgements

I have been lucky in my life— as a social justice activist, as a writer and as a mother— to find communities that offer strength and support and inspire me to grow. Like Ruthie, my life has been shaped by seeking to build a better world —over many decades, taking many different forms, and now, with the publication of Thursday's Child, expressed in my writing. I am grateful to all who have accompanied me on this journey—listening to this story when it was just a string of ideas and encouraging me to take it off the shelf when I thought I couldn't finish. And now, at long last, I have.

I would like to extend a million warm thanks to: my long-distance writing partner of many years, Darlene Goetzman, who was the first to meet Ruthie on the page and offered deep insight and editorial support along the way; Karen Winkler who read early pages and helped me find an ending, the women of my Activist Fiction Writer's Circle—Juliana Barnet, Maritza Arrastia and Rain Zohav— as we create a collective home for our writing; the NY Writer's Coalition whose workshops provided a nurturing home for a writer and workshop leader in formation, and Project Write Now where a 6 month revision workshop allowed me to say I'm writing a novel and mean it. And finally, to my family—my husband Paul Stein, the most loving cheerleader and proofreader a self-doubting writer could have, my children Jonah Gensler and Angelica Velazquez whose love has been steadfast and true around every curve, my brother Rick Schwolsky, egging me on as always –even though he sold his van before we could go on a research road trip to Baja—and all the mamas, aunties, sister-friends and compañeras who lift me up each day in this weary, troubled world.

As Ram Dass so eloquently put it, "We are all just walking each other home."

EXPLORE THE HISTORY…

EXPLORE THE HISTORY…

If reading Ruthie's story has made you curious about the 1970's and the struggles that Ruthie was a part of (and I hope it has), here are a few books and films you may want to check out.

Civil Rights Movement

Ruthie (and this author) was inspired by her involvement in the Civil Rights movement in her hometown of Hartford, Connecticut. My involvement with the Northern Student Movement (the northern version of the Southern Nonviolent Coordinating Committee (SNCC or "Snick")) in high school was the beginning of a transformation that eventually led to Cuba.

Parting the Waters: America in the King Years 1954-63 by Taylor Branch

Eyes on the Prize: America's Civil Rights Years, 1954-1965 by Juan Williams March (Book One, Two, Three) by John Lewis

Anti-Vietnam War Movement and GI Coffeehouses

Ruthie, like the author, is recruited to participate in the Venceremos Brigade trip to Cuba from a GI coffeehouse project. Here are some resources that explore the role of active-duty GIs and Vietnam veterans in the anti-war movement.

Dangerous Grounds: Antiwar Coffeehouses and Military Dissent in the Vietnam Era by David L. Parsons

Peace Warrior by Greg Payton, 2025

Another Brother (film by Tami Gold, 1998, Third World Newsreel)

Disobeying Orders: GI Resistance to the Vietnam War (film by Pam Sporn, 1990)

The Venceremos Brigade and Cuba

Like Ruthie, the author spent 3 months in Cuba building houses for workers, and it changed her life. Consequences for her and other brigadistas included having their name read into the Congressional Record with the lie that they were learning to make bombs in Cuba! But she did not have to go in search of her son who was 18 months old and who she did, in fact, leave with his father on a hippie commune.

Venceremos Brigade: Young Americans Sharing the Life and Work of Revolutionary Cuba, edited by Sandra Levinson and Carl Brightman, Simon and schuster, 1971

Conversations with Cuba, C.Peter Ripley, Univ. of Georgia Press, 1999

The Coup in Chile

On September 11, 1973 (often called the "other" 9/11 by Latin Americans) there was a military coup in Chile to overthrow the democratically elected president. The role of the U.S. CIA was eventually disclosed. The author met a young Chilean man on the Brigade and wonders about him still.

Chile, Pinochet and the Caravan of Death by Patricia Verdugo:
House of the Spirits, a novel by Isabel Allende
Battle of Chile, film by Patricio Guzman

The Fight for Legal Abortion: Roe v. Wade

I am Roe: My Life, Roe v. Wade and Freedom of Choice by Norma McCorvey Pro: Reclaiming Abortion Rights by Katha Pollit

Killing the Black Body: Race, Reproduction and the Meaning of Liberty by Dorothy Roberts